Lost in Prosperity

Judy Hannigan

"I'm behind you, but don't turn around."

Before she could respond, he added, "The ravine plunges at least another fifty feet from where you're sitting. Do you understand the danger?"

Sensing the alarm beneath the calmly spoken words, she nodded—but only once because of the pain. She was aware there wasn't any solid ground beneath her dangling feet but hadn't realized the drop was deadly.

Boots scraped against rock as the man knelt behind her. Strong arms encircled her waist, while his chest supported her head and back as he dragged her slowly from the precipice. Shivering, her body molded to his, seeking his latent heat. After settling her head in the crook of his shoulder, he turned her hips and legs to the side.

With his torso wrapped around hers, his hand found her chin and tilted her head up before he lowered his mouth to cover hers. Surprised, she held very still—but only until his lips moved against hers in a tender, undemanding kiss. She responded with no hesitancy, giving back—right up to the moment she realized she shouldn't. Emitting a faint sound of protest, she pushed weakly against his chest.

Concerned, he withdrew immediately. "I'm sorry, darlin'. I didn't mean to hurt you," he apologized, his tone soothing. The backs of his curled fingers grazed her cheek before sliding into her hair to explore the bump on the crown of her head.

Reflexively, she clutched a handful of his vest and shirt. Though his touch was gentle, she couldn't muffle the gasp that escaped her lips.

"I know it's painful," he murmured near her ear. "It's a wonder you're conscious."

His warm breath against her neck sent a tremor through her, making her forget the pain and remember the kiss.

LOST IN PROSPERITY

Book 1—Prosperity Series

ISBN: 979-8-9909624-0-8 (Print)

ISBN: 979-8-9909624-1-5 (eBook - EPUB)

Library of Congress Control Number
2024915677

Cover Design: Judy Hannigan/Cheryl Perez

Copy & Line Editor: Maggie Fenton: *www.maggiefenton.com*

Author Photo: Waters Photography LLC:
www.waters-photos.com

Interior Design: Cheryl Perez:
https://yourepublished.wixsite.com/youre-published

Dedication

To MaryAnn Hayden, who listened to a million "what ifs" and "buts" with as much joy and excitement as I felt posing them. She took this journey with me, sharing the highs and lows of plot and character development and propped me up when I was uncertain.

Because she knew I could do it—I did. And when book one was finished, I wrote book two.

Coming Soon

Book 2—Prosperity Series

Everything in Prosperity

ACKNOWLEDGMENTS

Thank you to my Beta readers for your enthusiasm, encouragement, and feedback: Sue Bevard, Mark Drager, Teryn Fischer, Cindy Horsman, Beth Kuhn, Debby Kearney, Donna Masche, Michelle Moser, April Pickering, Shiela Pitcher, Tonya Pressley, and Sara Stevenson.

A special thank you to David Frost, who had no experience with a book in this genre before I asked him to read this one. He ended up enjoying it so much, he wrote 17 pages of feedback.

He'll never be the same, and I'll always be grateful.

Chapter 1

August 1875, Wyoming Territory

The stagecoach should have already arrived in Prosperity. Because the driver took extra time at each stop to check the left rear axle, it was more than an hour late.

A man and woman, the stage's only passengers, were returning from business in Laramie. At the start of their journey, the male passenger had been both amused and disappointed when his traveling companion made a point of saying he was a "distraction" and chose not to sit next to him. He was amused because he knew she was strongly attracted to him and found it difficult to concentrate when he was nearby. He was disappointed because he'd hoped to "distract" her all the way home. So here they were, on opposite sides and corners of the coach, riding in silence, while the only distraction he dared was studying her when he thought she wouldn't notice.

Bored, he crossed his arms over his chest and stretched his long legs in the space between the seats. From under the brim of his black Stetson, he surreptitiously watched his companion.

He liked looking at her. Almost any man would. She had a graceful neck, slender shoulders, and a long-legged frame blessed with curves that fit against him in all the right places. He admired how easily those curves swayed with the motion of the coach. The symmetry of her face was pleasing but upstaged by the arresting boldness of her slate blue, widely spaced, and oh-so-very expressive eyes. He'd seen them clouded with suspicion, sparking with anger, and darkened with passion. Men caught in her unblinking gaze, depending on insecurities and confidence, would either lose their conviction and courage or become trapped in the mesmerizing power of her allure.

Shifting in his seat, the man lifted a corner of the heavy leather flap that served as a window curtain. The sky's purple and gold autumn colors were fading, anticipating the surrender of day to sunset.

Inside the coach, the dim light revealed that his companion continued her reflection. Seeing her drop her gaze to the jagged lightning bolt scar near the curve of her thumb on the back of her right hand, he recalled the pleasure of feeling its imprint pressed against his lips. Outwardly, she appeared composed, but he wasn't fooled. He knew she was disappointed with how she'd handled the unwelcome, crass advances from the owner of the Bar W Ranch the day before.

When she leaned back in her seat, she tucked an escaped, honey-tinged curl behind her ear before raising her hand to examine the bruise on her left cheek.

He hadn't been present when the rancher had backhanded her. But when he'd arrived soon after, he'd enjoyed watching her make the sonofabitch pay for touching her. He would have pummeled the bastard to within an inch of his sorry life, except for having learned from experience she wouldn't welcome his interference. Had he dared to step in, his reward almost certainly would have been to sleep alone until her anger dissipated enough to forgive him.

She often accused him of being hot-tempered. He couldn't deny it, especially where she was concerned. He did, however, find it ironic she tended to ignore the trait in herself, which, in his opinion, made it a clear case of *it takes one to know one*, whether she cared to admit it or not.

Less than a minute later, her slate blue eyes turned to him, and a delicate brow arched in an unspoken question. The corners of her mouth curved in an inviting smile, signaling she'd set reflection aside and was ready to engage in a little "distracting" behavior.

God, he loved this woman.

Straightening, he leaned toward her, offering his assistance to help her change seats. She scooted forward and was reaching for his outstretched hand when the left rear axle separated from its hub, sending the wheel careening and the coach bed slamming into the road, stripping the door next to him from its frame.

Caught off balance, he pitched sideways out of the coach, sailing several feet above the ground down a steep incline until his shoulder plowed into loose gravel and rocks. He tumbled once before falling to his side and rolling. Fighting momentum, he grabbed onto a cone-shaped boulder halfway down the slope. The coach had already flown beyond his resting place, and he could hear it colliding with the ravine walls as it hurtled to the distant bottom.

***

The woman's back hit the coach wall with so much force she couldn't draw air into her lungs. Then the floor beneath her feet fell away, and she was propelled out of the gaping chasm created by the missing door.

When she woke, she didn't recall sailing through the air or striking the ground. Those memories were interred in the void of unconsciousness and the torture of sharp spears piercing her head, back, and shoulders. The pain was debilitating, offering but two choices: fight it or surrender to it. She elected to fight.

Willing her senses to assess her surroundings, she heard the high-pitched screams of a horse rising from somewhere down the steep incline. In her peripheral vision, she recognized the dark shape of the stagecoach's severed luggage rack. Careful not to move her head, she slowly fanned her arms, examining the granite beneath her.

She rolled to her side and swallowed the agony it triggered. Because she hadn't anticipated the waves of nausea and vertigo that accompanied it, she was forced to rest. Minutes later, she struggled to a sitting position by pushing against an outcropping of stone. With her legs dangling over the boulder's edge, she placed her palms on its surface, steadying herself. Then she waited motionless with her eyes closed while concentrating on breathing.

As the dizziness receded, her mind began to clear. She remembered the fading light and a few brief moments before the coach collapsed. Now, the stars and the moon were evidence dusk had come and gone. A man's strong hand had brushed against hers before he'd been pitched from the coach, but she couldn't recall his face or whether she knew him.

"Is anyone there?" she called into the night, concerned for the man's safety. "Can you hear me?"

She held her breath while listening for a response. But there was no answer. Even the horse she'd heard earlier was quiet. Then the faint scuff of boots scraping stone reached her ears, followed by footsteps and the clattering of dislodged gravel bouncing off boulders as it rolled down the incline toward her. Her eyes searched the embankment. A male silhouette separated from the night shadows and a voice answered.

"Is that you, Sam?"

He sounded anxious. The name Sam puzzled her until she realized he must have been searching for the stage driver. She raised her chin to answer, hoping her voice was strong enough to project up the slope.

"Be careful. We're not at the bottom of this hellhole," she warned.

Though she could hear him working his way down to her, he didn't reply. Perhaps he was hurt.

"Are you all right?" she asked.

"My shoulder's bruised, but nothing's busted," he replied. "Sam, I still can't see you. Say something else so I can find you. Are *you* hurt?"

Although relieved he'd answered, she wondered why he called her "Sam." Following his instructions, she admitted, "I hit my head. I caught a glimpse of you earlier, but I don't see you now." Each word was an effort, and she recognized her voice was weaker. "You sound close," she added, wanting to encourage him.

Seconds later, he quietly announced his arrival. "I'm behind you, but don't turn around."

Before she could respond, he added, "The ravine plunges at least another fifty feet from where you're sitting. Do you understand the danger?"

Sensing the alarm beneath the calmly spoken words, she nodded—but only once because of the pain. She was aware there wasn't any solid ground beneath her dangling feet but hadn't realized the drop was deadly.

Boots scraped against rock as the man knelt behind her. Strong arms encircled her waist, while his chest supported her back and head as he dragged her slowly back from the precipice. Shivering, her body molded to his, seeking his latent heat. After settling her head in the crook of his shoulder, he turned her hips and legs to the side.

With his torso wrapped around hers, his hand found her chin and tilted her head up before he lowered his mouth to cover hers. Surprised, she held very still—but only until his lips moved against hers in a tender, undemanding kiss. She responded with no hesitancy, giving back—right up to the moment she realized she shouldn't. Emitting a faint sound of protest, she pushed weakly against his chest.

Concerned, he withdrew immediately. "I'm sorry, darlin'. I didn't mean to hurt you," he apologized, his tone soothing. The backs of his curled fingers grazed her cheek before sliding into her hair to explore the bump on the crown of her head.

Reflexively, she clutched a handful of his vest and shirt. Though his touch was gentle, she couldn't muffle the gasp that escaped her lips.

"I know it's painful," he murmured near her ear. "It's a wonder you're conscious."

His warm breath against her neck sent a tremor through her, making her forget the pain and remember the kiss.

"I recall reaching for your hand, but I can't remember your face. Please, let me see you." She'd endure the pain for the reward of seeing the face that went with the voice and the kiss.

Supporting her head and upper body, he shifted, dipping his head so the moonlight illuminated his features. Unaware a muscle worked in his jaw, he watched her examine his face.

Uncommonly handsome, his eyes, filled with kindness, were almost as dark as his black hair, which was so thick it begged a woman to run her hands through it. The strong planes of his face were ruggedly, pleasingly male. His mouth was firm, pleasantly curved, and sinfully compelling. His square chin completed the composition of masculine good looks and sensuality.

When her eyes lowered, he drew her back against him.

"It's beginning to cloud up," she murmured, frowning her displeasure at losing the light.

"It's all right," he replied, gently stroking her arm. "I can see well enough to get us home. Your pain is what's stealing the moonlight. Soon, you won't be able to see anything at all."

Her eyelids drifted shut, and she whispered one last random thought before consciousness left her. "I bet you're kind to horses, too."

Chapter 2

She opened her eyes when she heard the man who'd kissed her ask about "Sam." He was standing at the foot of the bed. She'd been right about his being handsome. He looked like the description of a hero who had stepped from the pages of a dime novel, except the stereotypical words "tall, dark, and handsome" understated his appeal. A few seconds passed before she thought to look at anything or anyone else. When she did, she saw five people were in the room.

To the handsome man's left was a pretty, young woman holding the arm of a distinguished, older man. Next to the older man was a tall, athletically built man about the same age as her rescuer but an inch or so taller. He had tousled straw-colored hair and nervously worked his fingers around the wide brim of a gray hat.

Her eyes moved back to her rescuer, appreciating his handsome features and the unexpected flash of green flecks sparkling in the depths of chocolate-brown eyes.

When she forced her gaze to the person sitting on the edge of the bed, she took in the salt-and-pepper mix of gray in his hair and mustache and the three deep lines in his forehead. She guessed his age close to fifty and surmised he hadn't shaved recently. He gently grasped her wrist and asked her to tell him what hurt.

"My head and my back," she murmured. She didn't see any sense in explaining *how much* they hurt. To redirect his attention, she gestured toward the black-haired man. "What about him? He told me he hit his shoulder."

The doctor placed his hand on her forehead to position her head to see into her eyes. "Jackson was luckier than you, Sam. He only bruised his shoulder."

Although puzzled by the name Sam, she was glad to learn *Jackson* was all right. Before she could ask about the name, the young woman moved closer to the bed. "We've been worried about you. This is the first time you've opened your eyes since Jackson carried you into the house last night."

The yellow-haired man with the hat nodded in agreement before chiming in. "I wasn't worried, Sam. You're tougher than anyone I ever met, so I figured you were taking advantage of the situation to work in a little extra shuteye." He smiled broadly and winked, clearly pleased with his cleverness and confident she'd understand he was glad she was all right. She managed a weak smile of appreciation although he, too, had called her Sam.

The older man cleared his throat. "We *were* worried, Sam, but now that we see you're better, we should leave you. You need rest." He put his hand under the young woman's elbow as if to escort her from the room. But they didn't move toward the door.

Because she was preoccupied with them calling her Sam, she didn't notice that no one made a move to leave. When Jackson crossed to the side of the bed across from the doctor, she realized they were waiting for her to say something.

"Thank you—all." Except for Jackson, she didn't know their names. "You're kind to take me into your home and care for me. I don't have the words to say how grateful I am." Exhausted, her eyelids were drifting closed when Jackson took her hand in his.

"Sam, I don't understand why you said that."

Confused by Jackson's bewilderment, she turned to the doctor. "Why doesn't he understand?" Not waiting for an answer, she turned her head to look at Jackson and the others. "I'm sorry if I said the wrong thing. I only meant to express my gratitude for your kindness." Then, before she realized she would voice it, she asked, "Why do you call me *Sam*?"

No one moved. No one spoke. Something was wrong. Trusting Jackson, her eyes sought his. Though he still held her hand, his grip had tightened, and he looked as shocked as if someone had slapped him.

"Why—why do you look like that?" she asked, her voice trembling.

The doctor intervened. "Your question surprised us. Would you tell us your name?"

She tore her eyes from Jackson's stricken face to look at the doctor. Searching her mind, she lowered her gaze to the bed cover, as if she could discover her name written there. Unfortunately, she saw only a delicate pink and gray flower pattern. She closed her eyes to concentrate. *Where was her memory?* There weren't any names, places, or dates.

When she opened her eyes, she found it easier to stare at a spot on the wall than the faces of the people in the room. "I can't seem to recall my name," she admitted, her tone defensive. "Sam doesn't sound familiar, that's why I asked about it. Last night when he—I mean, when Jackson called me Sam, I thought he'd confused my name with the stagecoach driver's name. I wasn't thinking clearly, though. Now, I realize he couldn't have thought I was the driver because he kissed me." She could feel tears form in her eyes. "I sound like a crazy woman."

The man with the hat bit back a smile. The young woman stared shyly at the floor. The older man looked at

Jackson as if he'd just heard a funny story. She didn't move her head to see the doctor's reaction.

Ignoring the others, Jackson reached out to stroke her hair gently. "It doesn't matter about your name. You hit your head, so it's only natural it's difficult to think clearly. I knew you when I kissed you. I was so relieved to pull you back from the edge of that drop-off that I forgot my manners," he explained, his tone soothing. "Your name *is* Sam. For now, all you need to know is that you're safe. After you've rested, you'll remember."

She felt like a wild mustang penned in a stall being gentled with soothing words and reassuring pats. His hand continued to stroke her hair. The corners of her mouth turned up in a tremulous smile. He did make her feel safe.

"Last night when I saw your face, I decided to trust you. I didn't mind that you kissed me because you were gentle. Remember? I said I bet you were kind to horses. I was right, wasn't I?" She'd directed the question to the older man, who appeared to be considering his answer carefully.

"You sized him up correctly. Jackson is a man you can trust." Then with an amused half smile, he added, "He's *always* kind to horses and children—and, *occasionally*, to damsels in distress."

Thankful to have her judgment affirmed, she ignored the humor. She saw Jackson dart a quick, sideways glance at the older man.

"I appreciate the testimonial, Parker," Jackson drawled, amusement glinting in his eyes.

Sam's energy drained and a filmy veil began to cloud her vision. "I'm very tired," she whispered. Settling her head deeper into the pillow, she didn't notice Jackson lift his hand from her hair. Before sleep claimed her, she murmured, "I'm sorry about my name."

***

Jackson glanced at the doctor before moving from Sam's side to sit in a chair near the bed. Should she wake, he'd be there to reassure her. "*Will* she remember when she wakes?"

"I don't know, Jackson," Doc murmured, passing his hand over his forehead. "This might be temporary. On the other hand, she could have amnesia. It sometimes happens with a severe head injury." Wanting to offer some hope, he added, "Try not to worry before we know the facts. Even if it's some degree of amnesia, most people recover after a few weeks or months, especially in cases where there are people who can help them recall things. What puzzles me is why she *thinks* her name isn't Sam. I haven't seen that manifestation before." He rolled his shirtsleeves down and buttoned the cuffs while Jackson's gaze stayed on Sam.

"I think you should stay with her. You did the right thing stepping in to reassure her. She responded to you and Parker." Doc's integrity prodded his sense of responsibility not to sugarcoat things. "We're friends and we've always spoken plainly. The same is true of my friendship with Sam. She may have amnesia, so you need to prepare yourself to deal with it."

"I understand, Doc," Jackson replied, though he wanted to deny the possibility. It wasn't possible to prepare to live in a world without Sam's love. He couldn't wrap his mind around the thought of her treating him as if he were a stranger. If her memory didn't return, *would she still love him?*

"I'll be back tomorrow to check on her," Doc promised while hefting his bag and starting for the door. "I'll see myself out."

Jackson nodded, acknowledging the doctor's departure. For now, he would hope and take comfort from being near Sam while watching her sleep. In her slumber, she looked peaceful. It was easy to believe she was unchanged and still loved him as deeply as he loved her.

Chapter 3

When she woke, Sam tried to remember something, anything, that happened before the crash. Nothing came to mind—nothing at all.

Jackson slept in the chair next to the bed with arms folded across his chest and his long legs stretched out in front of him, his boots crossed at the ankles. He looked uncomfortable. Grateful he'd stayed, she found his presence reassuring. Remembering his kiss, she wondered about their relationship.

Though she was on her side, her back felt like one big, aching bruise. She tried to shift her position and failed. Her movement woke Jackson. Straightening in the chair, he drew up his legs while studying her face.

Her gaze met his, slate blue eyes holding steady to dark brown ones. "Is my name Samantha? Is that why you call me Sam?"

"No, your name is Sam—Sam Hilliard Stone," Jackson answered, a hint of disappointment sounding in his tone. "Your father believed women should be as respected as men are. That's why he gave you a man's name."

"Is the older man who was here earlier my father?"

"No. He's my...I mean, *our* business partner, Parker Evans. He owns this ranch, and this is his house. Your father died when you were six. Your mother died when you were born." He hesitated before adding, "I'm sorry. I didn't think it would be right not to tell you."

Odd, she didn't feel sad. She felt as if he were telling her about someone else. The fact she felt no emotion disturbed her more than learning her parents were dead. She didn't know what to say.

Jackson looked upset, making her wonder whether he regretted telling her the truth. "It's all right that you told me. I don't remember anything about them. I wonder if it's normal not to feel emotion when you lose the memories of the people you love."

Jackson's expression changed, and she couldn't guess what it meant. For an instant, he resembled a child reaching for a gift who instead received a sharp rap on the back of his hand. That impression evolved to another—a professional gambler, skilled in hiding his thoughts about the cards he held. Instinctively, she knew he didn't want her reading his thoughts or his feelings.

"Have I upset you?" she asked.

Parker Evans spoke from the doorway. "Don't worry about Jackson, Sam. Nothing but rotgut whiskey and bad business bother him."

"That's right," Jackson affirmed.

Searching Jackson's face, Sam saw something different. If she were to guess, she'd wager he kept his feelings to himself; however, that didn't mean he didn't have them. If asked for her opinion, she would've said his feelings ran stronger and deeper than most men's. She'd noticed nothing superficial about him. Without thinking, she said, "I don't believe you."

Sam saw surprise flit through Jackson's expression. Concerned he thought she was challenging him, she added, "I didn't mean anything by saying that, Jackson. A man who helps others couldn't be as unfeeling as you claim to be. Although I can't remember anything before the crash, I remember what's happened since, at least during the times I've been awake." Her last statement was a gentle attempt at humor, sending a message not to take her too seriously.

"Parker assured me you're kind to horses, children, and damsels in distress. A man as tough as old leather wouldn't give a whit about those things." Her voice dropped to a silken whisper. "Nor would he sleep in a bedside chair to watch over someone. You shouldn't pretend to be heartless when it isn't true." Pausing, she laughed self-consciously, embarrassed she'd spoken so boldly.

Looking up at him through her lashes, she added, "I shouldn't repay your kindness with contrariness. That blow to my head must have scrambled my brains, too."

Parker broke the silence that followed her words. "Although it's difficult for you to remember things because of your injury, nothing is wrong with your intellect."

"True," Jackson agreed.

Sam raised her hand to her head, wishing it weren't so difficult to focus. Jackson had been telling her about their being Parker's partners. *What did that mean?* A partner would have assets invested. Of course, she knew an asset could be defined in a multitude of ways, depending on one's perspective. She wondered what she brought to the partnership: Money? Property? Contacts?

It occurred to her "partner" could be a euphemism for companion—meaning the sort of woman a rich man could buy for company and pleasure. She didn't think she fit the latter definition but couldn't dismiss the possibility. Turning from those disconcerting thoughts, she asked about her memory.

"Did the doctor say my memory would return?"

"He suggested you might remember when you woke and that he'd be back this afternoon," Jackson hedged.

"I wish I did remember, but I don't." Determined not to court sympathy, she made a joke. "My head is as empty as a cowhand's pockets on the morning after payday."

Parker smiled. Conversely, Jackson frowned, as if he believed she was submissively accepting her condition. Watching him, Sam was certain he'd judged her a quitter.

"Doc mentioned memory loss isn't necessarily permanent," Jackson explained. "It could return in a few weeks or months, especially if things are familiar and people are willing to help you."

Though Sam didn't question Jackson's sincerity, she believed his optimism was inflated. However, had she been in his place, she would have used the same assurances. The man had a heart.

"Do I live here?" she asked, turning to Parker. "Jackson said this is your house."

"You live on this ranch, but not in this house. You built your house opposite this one, closer to the ranch gate. Your brother, Morgan Garner, lives there with you when he isn't in Chicago or New York overseeing your business affairs."

Surprised, Sam glanced at her empty ring finger. "I have a brother? Why is his last name Garner? Am I married?"

Again, glancing at Jackson first, Parker replied, "Morgan is your stepbrother. You introduce him as your older brother. You aren't married."

Sam wondered why Parker needed to look at Jackson before answering. She also wondered why she would build a house on someone else's land. She decided to pursue those answers later.

"Parker, who's the young woman I saw here earlier? She was standing between you and Jackson. Another man was here. He made a joke about my being tough."

"My daughter, Becky, was here, and the man is our friend, Jim Ryder. We call him Ryder because he rides a horse like a bat out of hell. You and Jackson say he makes a pony express rider look like an old geezer riding a stick broom. Ryder is foreman on the ranch, and he would do just about anything for us. That makes him much more than a friend. He's part of our family.

"You and Becky are close. She looks to you as her older sister and stand-in mother. My wife passed away a few years after Becky was born. Five and a half years ago, we bought this ranch. A year later, Jackson drifted in. A year after that, you came to Prosperity. We form a close family, maybe because we chose one another."

Parker took Sam's hand. "I've been grateful for that. Becky has too. She loves Jackson, Ryder, and you, and for good reason." The corners of Parker's mouth turned up. "But I should warn you that I suspect she has marriage designs on your brother, Morgan."

"Thank you for telling me," Sam murmured, touched by his sincerity and humor. Parker had spoken with such warmth, she didn't doubt his affection. Although she had no idea what had brought her to this place, why she'd decided to stay, or why they wanted her, she knew the answers couldn't give her more comfort or reassurance than the acceptance and love she felt at this moment offered by this man.

"Could you eat something?" Parker asked. "You haven't had anything for more than two days. And Doc said to encourage you to drink lots of water and tea."

"I'll try," she replied, though she wasn't hungry.

"Even if you can't manage much, it will comfort Becky to see you try," Parker remarked. "I'll go and help her bring a tray."

Turning her head toward Jackson after Parker left the room, Sam said, "I'll need help sitting up. I can't manage it myself."

"I can prop you against some pillows, or you can lean against me. What do you think?"

Sam hesitated. "Maybe lean against you. The buttons on the back of this nightdress feel like a line of arrow points on my back. If you hold me like you did when we were on the boulder, you won't put pressure on them. Would that be all right?"

"I don't want to hurt you, and I'm worried about your dizziness. The other night after I moved you, you passed out."

"I'm lightheaded but not like then. The worst that can happen is I'll faint. If I do, at least you won't have to carry me up a ravine." Sam smiled conspiratorially. "We'll ask Parker to watch for falling teacups." Then remembering Jackson's injury, she added, "I forgot about your shoulder, though. Maybe pillows would be better."

Instead of answering, Jackson folded back the bed covers and slid his arms under her. She instinctively wrapped her arms around his neck and rested her head against his chest. When he straightened, lifting her from the bed, the dizziness did get worse, but it wasn't as bad as when she tried moving on her own.

Jackson carried her to the other side of the bed and sat down with her still in his arms. Leaning against the headboard, he swung his legs up and scooted to the center, making a place for her near the bed's edge while letting his chest and shoulder support her upper body. Once eased into place, she relaxed against him with her eyes closed, hoping to quell the vertigo. A few moments later, though, she opened her eyes when Jackson reached out to gather the bed covers in a hand that was a little unsteady and pull them up to waist height.

Believing Jackson's sore shoulder was the reason for the unsteadiness, Sam raised her head to ask if it was causing him pain but stopped when she saw he was leaning nearer to kiss her. She didn't move away. Instead, she tilted her head and moved closer to him. At first, his kiss was tentative, as if he were questioning whether she'd allow it—or maybe it was the other way around—maybe he was unsure whether he'd enjoy it. For her part, the answer was favorable. She enjoyed it very much and was disappointed when he abruptly ended it.

Hearing Parker and Becky entering the room explained the abrupt ending. When Sam pulled her gaze from Jackson's, she saw Becky was fussing with a tray on the nightstand.

As Becky passed her a teacup, Sam felt Jackson exhale slowly before softly muttering something that sounded suspiciously like an expletive. Though she was mildly discomfited over Parker seeing them kiss, he showed no sign of being upset about it, so she relaxed against Jackson and accepted the proffered tea. She surmised Jackson kissing her must not be all that surprising of an event.

"This is the first time I made you tea," Becky announced, sounding proud of her accomplishment. Sam nodded her thanks and lifted the cup to take a sip.

"Mr. Harper, who owns the mercantile, told one of his clerks to pack your tea with the ranch supplies," Becky commented. "He said Mr. Bainbridge had it sent there from the freight office because you ordered it almost two months ago. I thought it was considerate of Mr. Harper to think of sending it with the rest of Trinity's supplies, but Ryder said he only did it because he's sweet on you."

Unexpectedly, Becky turned to Jackson, "Sorry, I shouldn't have said that. I was only making conversation. It's odd talking to Sam when I know she doesn't remember things."

Sam realized Jackson didn't like hearing about Mr. Harper's interest. She'd felt his body tense at the mention of the shopkeeper's name and sensed his face must look as stiff and disapproving as his body felt. No wonder poor Becky apologized.

"Don't mind Jackson, Becky," Sam soothed. "I agree with you. Mr. Harper was thoughtful to send the tea. I must remember to thank him when I'm well."

Becky looked relieved. "Did I brew the tea strong enough, Sam? I've only made coffee before now because that's what we drink. JB, our cook, prepares your tea." She hesitated before tossing an impish smile in Jackson's direction. "Jackson says it smells like dirty socks steeped in orange blossoms."

Sam laughed. "He probably thinks roses smell like pigs."

Becky giggled.

Endeavoring to please Becky, Sam managed to drink a full cup of tea and eat a slice of toasted bread. The effort exhausted her. Before Parker and Becky left the room, she settled deeper into the crook of Jackson's shoulder and let sleep claim her.

***

Alone with Sam sleeping in his arms, Jackson absently brushed a lock of hair away from her temple and placed a light kiss on her forehead. Though she slept soundly, her breaths slow and deep, she responded by snuggling closer and drawing her knee up and over his thigh.

Earlier, when he carried her to where they rested now, it hadn't been easy pretending he didn't notice the swell of her breasts pressed against his chest or the fullness of her bottom draped over his arm, especially when he couldn't forget the intimacies of loving every tantalizing inch of her.

A shadow of a smile touched Jackson's lips as he reflected on the kiss Parker and Becky interrupted. When she'd looked up at him just before his mouth dropped to hers, the gray color in her blue eyes had lightened, making them look soft and inviting.

He'd been relieved she'd accepted his kiss and pleasantly pleased she'd returned it. He'd planned to deepen it, but Becky and Parker's arrival nixed his plan.

Jackson found patience difficult to exercise in relation to Sam. No woman affected him as she did. He admitted losing her would come close to breaking him. He'd be able to function on a basic level, but without her, his world would be empty. His father had called it "soldiering on." Soldiering on wasn't enough anymore.

Sam was her own person, and impatience would gain him nothing. Jackson leaned the back of his head against the headboard. If he weren't careful, Sam would sense his feelings and ask questions that would elicit answers she wasn't ready to hear.

Jackson needed some sleep before Doc Baxter arrived. He pressed his lips to Sam's temple again and closed his eyes. Consciously clearing his thoughts, he relaxed against her softness. He slept best with Sam in his arms.

Chapter 4

Deep lines etched Doctor Roy Baxter's forehead. Though Jackson had told him Sam had followed his orders to rest and had finished a cup of tea and some toast a few hours earlier, she wasn't much improved from the previous day.

By now, he'd expected her to be experiencing less vertigo and nausea. However, when he'd questioned her, she'd admitted the dizziness was coming in waves whenever she moved her head. She'd also told him she was tired—the sort of tiredness that made every part of her body feel too heavy to move. Doc could see the effort was wearing her out, and he'd only been with her a little more than five minutes. At the moment, though, her slate blue eyes were watching his every expression.

Doc felt as if she were reading his thoughts before he finished forming them. Jackson often teased she was a witch and had clairvoyant powers. While it was true Sam bewitched Jackson, she didn't cast spells. Her power came from her independent spirit, intelligence, and compassion. Those traits in a woman who looked more like an angel than a white witch could ensnare a man's senses. A man in love with her would love her with all his heart.

Knowing she'd expect honesty, Doc sighed. Sometimes varnishing the truth was too tempting. "Frankly, I'm concerned about your dizziness. You should be improving, but you're not."

Addressing Parker, Doc said, "I think we should move Sam downstairs to the study. It has that chaise daybed with arms that can be raised and lowered. Changing position and sitting up is almost impossible in a regular bed because of her back injuries. She'll mend faster if she can rest comfortably. Up here, she's too far from the rest of you."

"That's a good idea, Doc," Parker replied, nodding. "It will be easier for Becky and JB's wife to help her when Jackson's not here."

Including Jackson in his instructions, Doc replied, "I'm holding you and Parker responsible for making sure she doesn't move around on her own. She'll fall, and mending broken bones on top of her other injuries isn't something any of us want to see her suffer."

He wagged a finger in Sam's face. "I mean it. Don't even think about getting up on your own." Then his stern expression softened, and he covered one of her hands with one of his. "The truth is I'm afraid for you, so please humor me for once and follow orders. If you fall and hit your head again, you'll do permanent damage."

Sam squeezed his hand, reassuring him before she agreed. "I promise, Doc." Darting a mischievous smile at Becky, she added, "I'll wait until you say I'm completely recovered before I raise hell. Surmising from the way you bark orders at me, I must be pretty good at it."

Doc flashed a wry smile. "I'd go so far as to say you have a God-given talent for it, and Jackson's not much better. With you two around, a doctor doesn't need other patients to make a good living."

Abruptly, he turned to Becky. "Honey, you aren't strong enough to escort Sam. I'll count on you to call your father, Jackson, Ryder, or one of the men if she needs to get up."

***

Because Doc intended to oversee Sam's move to the study before returning to town, Parker and Becky went downstairs to prepare the room. The study connected to Parker's office through a set of paneled library doors. However, each room had its separate entrance from the main hallway. Sam and Jackson used the study when working in the main house because it gave them privacy and afforded ready access to business papers, files, books, and maps kept in Parker's office.

Running his hand over the scrollwork carved in the beautiful tiger oak frame of the daybed, Parker thought of his wife. In the early stages of her illness, she would sit with a blanket draped over her legs as she leaned against a raised arm, pretending to read a book while waiting for him to glance up from his work and notice her. Her loving eyes and smile had made his breath catch in his throat. Odd how memories were both a comfort and a torture. Returning to his task, he lowered one of the daybed's arms.

While he moved a small round table and straight-backed chair next to the daybed, Becky smoothed fresh linens over the surface and placed a couple of folded quilts on the floor near the lion's paw feet at the lowered end. When they were done, he waited at the foot of the stairs while Becky went to tell the others things were ready.

*****

With Becky and Doc watching, Jackson lifted Sam from the bed. Though she knew he was trying to be gentle, pain sliced through her head and back, and she couldn't contain the involuntary gasp that resulted.

Resting with her forehead on his chest, several seconds passed before she realized Jackson had recognized her distress. His lips grazed her neck in a soft caress as he whispered, "I'm sorry, darlin'." Sam shivered, but not from pain.

Before maneuvering her through the bedroom doorway, Sam saw Jackson wink at Becky. "Since you probably won't follow Doc's orders, I should save myself the burden of carrying you downstairs." Certain he was trying to distract her, she raised her head and smiled. "Maybe I should just toss you over the railing for Parker to catch," he teased.

As they approached the railing, Jackson redistributed her weight in his arms. Not expecting the movement, Sam cried out in fear and pressed herself against him as if clinging for her life. Thankfully, he recognized her panic and immediately backed from the stairs to the wall behind them. Then, cradling her, he began murmuring reassuring words, swearing there was no need to be frightened and that he would never do anything to hurt her.

***

Though Sam was doing her best to assure Jackson she'd overreacted and was all right, she was having difficulty orienting herself. His unexpected movement had triggered something she couldn't explain. Amazingly, her mind had shifted in time, dropping her into a memory in which she was both participant and observer.

As an observer, she watched herself and Jackson in a house she didn't recognize. Jackson was carrying her. They wore formal clothing, although her emerald silk gown was too revealing to be in good taste. Its heart-shaped décolletage showed so much cleavage, it was a wonder she didn't fall out of it.

As a participant, she was vaguely aware something was wrong with her right leg and that was the reason Jackson carried her. The house they were in had two flights of stairs. They'd almost reached the first landing, where the stairs turned.

Someone was watching them, but Sam couldn't see the person. She smiled at Jackson, doing her best to look as though nothing improper passed between them. It was important the watcher not see the liberties he took. When his left hand began exploring the contours of her bottom and his right hand cupped her breast, she started in surprise and pushed his hand away.

It wasn't that she found his touch unpleasant. Had no one been watching, she'd have encouraged him. But Jackson was playing a dangerous game, and, if seen, his behavior would enrage the observer.

When Jackson repositioned his arms before starting up the second flight of stairs, the curve of her hip pressed against the front of his trousers, the ridge of his arousal unmistakable. Momentarily forgetting the watcher, Sam tightened her arms around Jackson's neck, bringing him closer. He responded with a deep kiss, while his fingers stroked the mounded flesh overflowing her bodice.

After breaking the kiss, his voice gruff from desire, Jackson said, "Darlin', if you aren't careful, I'll lose control. Do you want me to put you down on the top landing and continue my attention where anyone might see us?"

Deeply aroused, Sam drew in a ragged breath and made herself go limp in his arms. "I haven't intentionally done anything to encourage you. If we don't stop this, we'll infuriate—" She didn't finish. Instead, she moved her mouth close to his ear and whispered, "Look, my room is there. You can be patient that long. The truth is we're both past the point of return."

Jackson pressed his lips to the place on the curve of her neck he knew would make her tremble. Then with heightened purpose, he climbed the last of the stairs, strode to her door, and reached for the doorknob.

*****

When the memory vanished, it took Sam a few seconds to recognize she was in the upstairs hallway of Parker's house.

Becky and Doc were watching, and Parker was observing everything from the foot of the staircase. The memory had been so vivid her body's response to Jackson's caresses in the past left her desirous in the present.

Later, when contemplating the experience, she identified three actions that might have triggered the memory. In the present, Jackson had been about to descend the stairs rather than ascend them as he'd done in her memory. In both present and past, he'd playfully teased her—although his past threats were sexual—very different from his threat of tossing her. The third was that someone watched them—in the past, the person wasn't revealed—while in the present, Parker had watched from the downstairs hallway.

As Jackson slowly carried her down the staircase, she was acutely aware of his nearness and the placement of his hands on her body. She tried to think of other things, but the memory of the two kisses they'd shared since the crash popped into her head. God, if she didn't stop thinking about them and the way he'd touched her in the memory she'd just experienced, she'd need a cold bath.

While placing her on the daybed, Jackson's stubbled jaw accidentally brushed her lips, and with no effort on her part, an image of a waterfall rushing over rocks into a small blue lake materialized in her mind. Startled, Sam asked, "Is there a waterfall somewhere nearby? It cascades into a picturesque lake."

"You remembered something!" Becky exclaimed. "It's one of your favorite places. We walk there sometimes. I'll show you when you're better."

***

When Sam asked about the waterfall, Jackson had almost replied that the lake was *their* favorite place—where they went on warm evenings to be together.

While Becky responded to Sam's question, Jackson recalled a memory of Sam gazing at him with love shining in her eyes by the shallow pool where the falls cascaded gently to the first of the three-tiered steps to the lake. Her breasts were plumped alluringly against the wet, clinging fabric of the almost transparent undergarment she wore.

Consciously putting the erotic picture of her aside, Jackson reminded himself to exercise patience. Impulsively sharing intimate memories, especially when they had an audience, wouldn't gain Sam's trust or win her love. Besides, if he kept thinking about her physical charms, he'd need to dive into that lake and stay there.

When Jackson brought his mind back to the conversation, Doc was explaining it was a good sign Sam had remembered something. "It supports my diagnosis that your memory loss may not be permanent. Your best chance for recovery is exposure to familiar places and people. Have you any idea what made you think of the lake?"

Jackson noticed Sam didn't look at him or any of the others when she said she didn't know.

Chapter 5

"**S**am, it's two in the morning, and neither of us has slept a wink. If you don't stop being stubborn and drink this medicine Doc left for you, you'll leave me no choice but to force you."

"You wouldn't!" Sam retorted. "I told you I don't like to take opiates, and that medicine is laudanum. I don't want it."

Jackson slid an arm under her shoulders, careful not to hurt her, and raised her to a sitting position. "Let's do this the easy way, Sam. Please, just drink it."

"You're mean!" she huffed, overwhelmed. He was so big and so close, yet gentle.

"*I'm* mean?" Jackson replied, repeating her accusation. "Will you take a good look at me? I'm dead on my feet. Three nights ago, I climbed down that ravine. Then I struggled back up it with your dead weight in my arms. Before Ryder returned from town where he'd waited to pick us up, I'd carried you more than a mile. Then I sat up with you the rest of the night and the whole next day. The next night and day were a repeat of the first, except I didn't have to lug you all over creation. Today, I strained my injured shoulder carrying you down the stairs. Tonight, I've spent five hours trying to sleep—with no success. Every time I get close to dropping off, you make some pitiable whimper that makes me sorry for you. So, tell me again, Sam. *Who* is it that's being mean?"

Sam opened her mouth to answer but shut it abruptly because she couldn't think of anything that would leave her any dignity.

Jackson softened his tone and offered a bribe. "Drink it and I'll bring you a glass of Parker's brandy to chase it with."

"You don't need to bribe me," she replied, her tone softer.

"Don't I?" Jackson chuckled. "Parker's brandy is top-shelf."

Sam averted her head but accepted the glass he put in her hand. Then she quickly drained its contents in two gulps. The shock of its bitterness showed in her expression, and her body shuddered.

"Good girl!"

Sam suppressed the urge to throw something at him. "Would you just get the brandy? That medicine is vile."

After handing her the brandy, he muttered, "Sweet dreams," before guzzling half the golden liquor in his glass.

"You're supposed to sip it," Sam criticized.

"The man who made that rule didn't spend three days caring for you," Jackson snapped back.

"I *am* sorry," Sam admitted after taking a moment to study him. "I know you're only trying to help me, and I'm making it difficult. Will you forgive me?"

"Yes, if you'll let me cut the buttons from the back of your nightdress and rub some liniment on your bruises."

Shocked, Sam almost choked on a second sip of brandy.

Holding up a pair of embroidery scissors, Jackson reminded her, "You said the buttons were hurting you. If I remove all but the top one, it will solve the problem. The liniment will help heal your back. It's done wonders for my shoulder."

Her face hot from imagining Jackson's hands on her bare skin, Sam resisted. "What you say may be true, but it's not proper."

"Since when did you start caring about what's proper?"

"How would I know?" she countered. Thinking coherently while staring into his dark gaze was impossible. "I lost my memory, remember?"

"It was a rhetorical question," Jackson replied. "Though to be truthful, if propriety affects someone you care for, you'll pretend to stay within its bounds."

Sam wondered if he was feeling the desire she was.

"I'll save the buttons so you and Becky can sew them back on. I promise I won't look at anything a gentleman shouldn't see."

That last comment caught her off guard. "A gentleman wouldn't do what you're proposing."

"Gentlemanly behavior won't get the job done," he retorted. A moment later, Sam sighed and nodded her permission.

One by one, Sam felt the buttons come off, her gown gaping wider with each snip of the scissors. She felt her cheeks heat as she pictured how much "scenery" Jackson was "not seeing." When he picked up the bottle of liniment, she started to move away, but he stopped her by resting one of his hands lightly on her shoulder.

"Becky can do the liniment in the morning," Sam protested, certain his touch would stir desire. She was in no shape to explore their relationship—physically or emotionally.

"Waiting until morning won't help you sleep tonight," Jackson replied calmly. He lifted his hands, though, signaling he wouldn't use force. "I only want to help you," he murmured in a soft, tender voice, his breath warm on her neck. "Trust me, darlin'."

He was downright dangerous. "I guess I *don't* care if it's proper," Sam mumbled, giving in against her better judgment.

Jackson unfastened the top button of her nightdress while Sam concentrated on the pungent odor of the liniment, willing her body not to betray how disconcerting she found his touch. The heat in her cheeks was mild when compared to that in her breasts and—other places.

***

Applying the liniment in a light, circular motion, Jackson tried to keep his touch impersonal. To slow his libido, he examined the angry midnight blue, yellow, and purple bruises mottling her skin. They looked wickedly painful. As he skimmed the darkest bruises between her shoulder blades, he felt her wince. Her pain eliminated the ache in his groin.

"There, I've finished," he announced, relieved his voice didn't betray his thoughts. Nor did his hands falter refastening the top button. Then he helped her turn onto her side.

"I shouldn't have refused the help of a knight-errant," Sam teased, her words expelled in a rush. Jackson realized the laudanum was affecting her—jumbling the thoughts in her head.

Grateful she wasn't angry, he smiled. "You must be thinking of Parker joking about my being kind to distressed damsels."

"Mmm-hmm," Sam sighed. "Rescued damsels fall in love with knights."

Jackson would have bet a fortune she wasn't aware she'd said that last comment out loud.

"Will you fall in love with your knight?" he asked, unable to keep the laughter from his tone.

"Perhaps I will. Your surname is Knight," she murmured. "It's nice being here with you like this. I wish I wasn't so sleepy." Her eyes fluttered shut but opened when he gently shook her arm.

"How do you know my last name is Knight?" Jackson asked. Several breathless moments passed while he waited for Sam's answer.

"I—I guess Parker told me," she finally managed. "No. That's not true." After pausing, she admitted, "I don't know, and I've forgotten why it's important."

"I'll tell you in the morning," Jackson responded as he rescued her empty brandy glass from her limp hold.

After watching Sam slip into sleep with a breathy sigh, Jackson tucked the bedcovers around her. Then he dimmed the lamp and returned to his makeshift bed in Parker's office.

Sam *remembered* his last name.

Chapter 6

"What time is it?" Sam mumbled, waking to find Becky sitting next to the daybed embroidering the edge of a pillow covering.

"It's early afternoon. Jackson and Daddy asked me to sit with you in case you need anything. Jackson said you'd sleep a long time because he gave you laudanum last night."

"Where are your father and Jackson?"

"Daddy is working in his office, and Jackson left midmorning. I heard him tell Daddy he was going with the sheriff and some men from the stage company to where the coach crashed. They'll retrieve the mail pouch and what's salvageable of your and Jackson's luggage. Jackson wants to find your Colts. You packed them in your valise because you were wearing your shoulder holster."

Sam tried to digest the information that she owned three guns and that two of them were important enough to her that Jackson would go looking for them. God, she hoped he wouldn't climb to the bottom of that hellhole!

Becky barely took a breath, giving Sam no chance to ask about the weapons or Jackson's plans. "Jackson brought some things for you from your house before I came downstairs this morning. He thought you might feel up to eating with us in the dining room tonight. He said if you stayed close to the chaise and used it for support only when necessary to dress, I could help you. He brought one of your nightdresses too."

Becky's eyes darted to the pile of buttons Jackson had left on the table. "Daddy explained Jackson cut those off because they were pressing into your back. I'm sorry I didn't think about that when I pulled the gown from my bureau. I saw your bruises the night Jackson brought you home. I should have realized the buttons would be painful."

"I wouldn't have thought of it either. Thank you for understanding about Jackson removing the buttons." Sam smiled warmly at Becky, impressed she exhibited more tact and maturity than many grown women. Sam saw no sign of shock or disapproval on the girl's face.

"When I'm well, we'll go to the dressmaker. Judging by the length of this nightdress on me, I imagine it's too short for you."

"Oh, it is, Sam," Becky confirmed, excited. "Daddy hasn't noticed how much I've grown this year, and I haven't said anything. You said you would talk to him about it, but, of course, that was before you went to Laramie. It's good of you to think of it again, especially with your being unwell."

"I plan to get better as fast as I can, so shopping will give me incentive to try harder. I'm hoping my memory returns. Right now, I'm feeling like a student who's fallen behind because I don't remember my letters and numbers. I'm concerned I may not be able to learn them again."

"You'll see it's easy once you get started."

"You're a darling, Becky. I'm wondering how old you are."

"Fifteen. My birthday was last month. You bought me a lovely, blue silk dress. When I wore it to the spring social, Daddy stopped at the bottom of the stairs and stared at me. He said I looked like my mother, who was beautiful.

Jackson whistled and told me, with you standing right behind me, that soon you'll look like an old witch next to me. Of course, I knew he was teasing, because, even while he said it, he couldn't take his eyes off you. He thinks you're the most beautiful woman in the world. Morgan danced with me twice at the social and said how grown-up I was. I think he made John Monroe, a boy from my class, a little jealous."

While Becky paused for breath, Sam smiled, thinking she sounded wistful about Morgan making the boy jealous.

"I'll bring you some tea and a tray of food from the kitchen, then we'd better start getting you dressed. It'll take some time. I expect we'll have to stop every so often so you can rest."

Becky was right; making her presentable enough to sit in a dining room took most of the afternoon. She'd had to rest several times. She'd only been able to drink half the tea. Jackson's opinion about the taste wasn't far off the mark. And though she'd been hungry, the oatmeal and toast sat uncomfortably in her stomach.

Standing was difficult because her balance was so out of kilter. Once or twice, the walls and straight lines of the furniture curved in her vision, distorting distance. When it happened, she'd feel nauseous and dizzy, and her hands and knees trembled. Her upper body tended to sway from side to side, like a faulty compass needle bouncing between two points.

Working carefully because of her head injury, Becky tackled the tangles in Sam's waist-length hair. Using a few pins and a hair ribbon, she left most of it loose and draped over her left shoulder. "Arranged this way, it almost hides the bruise on your left cheek," Becky commented, after passing Sam the hand mirror.

Curiously, up until that moment, Sam hadn't wondered about her looks. The woman in the mirror didn't look familiar. She had gray-blue eyes, high cheekbones, a narrow chin, and thick, wavy, honey-colored hair. She judged herself handsome rather than beautiful. In her opinion, her lips were a little too full and her jawline too firm. She noticed the dark smudges beneath her eyes that she rarely blinked. The bruise on her cheek was lighter than she expected, considering how sore it felt when she touched it.

Sam didn't need the mirror to know she was tall. Judging by her height next to Jackson, she was about five-foot-seven to his six-foot-two. Handing the mirror back to Becky, she shrugged. She refused to let herself get caught up in her looks when the most important part of her, the part that people couldn't see, was missing.

She heard Parker call from his office, asking whether she and Becky were ready for supper. Becky met her father at the door and invited him in. "Sam's going to join us, Daddy. She looks stronger, don't you think?"

Parker looked up from his daughter's smiling face to inspect Sam. "Yes, sweetheart, she does look stronger. I'm a lucky man to have two such lovely dining companions." After patting his daughter's shoulder affectionately, he crossed the room to offer Sam his assistance.

Sam held Parker's arm tightly, fearing her knees would buckle. She thought it odd she felt worse than when she first awoke.

Parker put a steadying hand on her waist. "Jackson said he expected to be home for supper but not to wait for him." Sam felt herself sway and tightened her grip on Parker's arm. "Steady, Sam," he crooned. "We'll take it slow. I won't let you fall."

She took a breath and a tentative step. "You're more confident than I am, Parker. It's only fair to tell you the walls of the room are moving, and my legs feel as if they belong to someone else."

As Sam and Parker made their way past the front door, it unexpectedly opened, and Jackson almost collided with them. Surprised, Sam took a quick step back. The room tilted, and she felt her legs giving way. Parker's arm tightened around her waist, and he supported her full weight, preventing her from collapsing to the floor.

Trying to help, Jackson caught her other arm. Sam overcorrected and fell against him. Parker released her, and Jackson lifted her in his arms.

"Jackson, what're you doing? Parker had me! I'm not a rag doll to be tossed between the two of you!" she scolded, until the dizziness threatened to engulf her, dimming the light. She leaned her head against Jackson's chest.

Evidently, Parker sensed her distress because he asked, "Sam, do you want Jackson to carry you back to the study?"

"I just need a minute to be still. My balance, what little I've left of it, goes to hell when I move too fast. My stomach isn't doing flips, so I think I can eat."

"I'm sorry this happened. You were doing very well."

"Parker, please don't apologize. It's not your fault. Jackson can't help playing knight-errant and scooping up damsels whenever he gets the chance."

Becky stifled a giggle.

Sam raised her eyes to look at Jackson. "See, I remember," she teased. While watching Jackson's face, she addressed Parker. "I'm beginning to question how Jackson manages to be present every time a calamity befalls me. I suspect he's playing a dual role. First, as Divine Providence, he creates a heroic opportunity. Then he switches to the role of valiant knight so he can rush in to rescue the fair damsel."

Jackson's amused smile disappeared, and he raised his eyes to cast a questioning look in Parker's direction.

Sam saw the look they exchanged. "What did I say this time?"

Parker chuckled. "Nothing to worry about, Sam. I suggest we continue this in the dining room."

Jackson placed Sam in the nearest chair, with her back to the archway. Before seating himself directly across from her, he held a chair for Becky. Parker took a seat at the head of the table.

"Do you know my first name?" Jackson asked, directing the question to her.

While considering her answer, Sam wondered why he asked it. Certain he was setting her up, she replied, "It's Jackson. That's what everyone calls you, and I haven't heard you correct anyone."

"Jackson is my *middle* name."

In her peripheral vision, Sam saw Parker and Becky watching, following every word.

"My first name is Providence."

Sam's hand drifted to her mouth to conceal the smile she hadn't been quick enough to hide. She repeated the unusual name—putting a questioning inflection at the end. "*Providence*? Your full name is *Providence* Jackson Knight?"

Looking uncomfortable, Jackson nodded, while Becky and Parker openly chuckled. Then, on Jackson's behalf, Becky volunteered, "It's true, and he *hates* it!"

Jackson's eyes didn't waver from Sam's. "I abhor the name."

"I'm sorry," Sam offered.

"Why should you be sorry?" Jackson countered. "You weren't responsible for my being christened with it. I'm trying to make a more important point, Sam."

"Let me see if I can guess. You're suggesting I subconsciously remember your first name is Providence. You think that's the reason I made that joke about Divine Providence earlier."

"Yes," Jackson replied, nodding. "Do you remember last night that you asked me why using my last name was important?"

"Vaguely. The laudanum made me sleepy."

"I told you I'd tell you in the morning, but you were still sleeping when I left the ranch."

"And—" Sam prompted, encouraging him to continue.

"It's important because *you're beginning to remember. Yesterday you remembered the waterfall and lake. Last night you remembered my last name is Knight. Today, you've made more than a coincidental reference to my first name, Providence.*"

Sam's eyes dropped from Jackson's gaze while her mind raced. *I wonder what he'd say if he knew my first memory was of his caresses while carrying me up a staircase. Would he find it interesting to learn three of the four things I've recalled, were about him? Was the waterfall and lake memory also related to Jackson?* She wouldn't be surprised to learn it was.

Jackson's voice interrupted her thoughts. "Is the shocked expression I see on your face because your memory is returning or astonishment from learning an adoring parent would name a child Providence?"

When Sam didn't answer, Jackson commented, "I doubt another woman in this world has the name of *Sam Hilliard.* It's not *normal* for a woman to have a man's name."

Sam shrugged. "I'm beginning to believe there's very little *normal* about either of us."

***

"How long have you been here?" Parker inquired when he looked up and noticed Morgan, Sam's brother, leaning in the archway behind Sam.

"Long enough to hear Jackson announce Sam remembered his name and hear her tell him he's not normal."

Jackson scowled. "That's not what she said."

"Close enough," Morgan replied dismissively.

Jackson's gaze abruptly shifted to Sam. "That's your brother, Morgan, standing there behind you."

Sam forgot not to turn quickly, and the inevitable wave of dizziness swept over her. Although she tried to regain her equilibrium by gripping the edge of the table, it was too little too late. If not for Morgan's quick reflexes, she would have fallen.

After centering her in the chair, he let his hand rest on her shoulder while he exchanged questioning looks with Jackson and Parker.

Both men shrugged in response.

"Thank you for catching me," Sam murmured, drawing his gaze to hers. His dark eyes raked over her, and she saw concern register in them.

"You'll get used to it, Morgan," Becky said, interrupting his candid assessment. "Sam can't seem to do much of anything without falling. It's like when you and Jackson drank too much after you came home from the cattle drive to Canada." After pausing for a quick breath, she added, "Doc Baxter ordered Jackson and Daddy to escort her so she doesn't fall."

Grateful for the interruption, Sam leaned toward Becky and whispered affectionately, "Tattletale."

Becky grinned, apparently proud of mentioning Jackson and Morgan's drinking escapade.

Sam rather enjoyed it too.

As Morgan scooted Sam's chair closer to Becky so he could pull out the chair beside her and seat himself, Sam surmised he must have decided the best approach for the time being was to treat her and the others with casual interest while gathering facts. "Is what Becky said about falling true, Sis?" Morgan asked. "I wondered if you were just going through an awkward phase."

At a loss how best to respond to his teasing, Sam gazed at his roguish features: a finely chiseled nose, dark, arching eyebrows, high cheekbones, and intelligent eyes that seemed to see everything.

"Come on, Sis," Morgan prodded, with mocking charm. "You must admit it's surprising. I haven't seen you eat gravel since you were seven!"

After noting the faint laugh lines crinkling the corners of his eyes and mouth, Sam found her voice. "I can't argue with you, Morgan, because I don't recall a horse throwing me. I'll have to take your word for it."

Morgan pretended surprise. "Take my word for it? Since when? They told me you lost your memory. No one mentioned you lost your backbone, too. From what I heard when I was listening, you were holding your own with Jackson. In fact, I rather enjoyed that."

Sam sighed. She was tiring and, for the first time in several days, feeling hungry. "Morgan, do you think we could eat supper now and resume this conversation later?"

"Sure, Sis. What did JB make for supper? I didn't rush home just because I was worried about you or anything like that."

Sam looked at Parker for help. "JB is short for 'Jerky and Biscuits.' That's the nickname the hands gave Mr. Donovan because he served tons of it on cattle drives," Parker explained. "He's our family cook now."

Parker turned toward the kitchen door and called out, "JB, you might as well come in and answer Morgan. No sense pretending you didn't hear."

A gray-bearded, rotund man wearing a once-white apron tied around his belly waddled into the room and scowled at Morgan. Then he turned and smiled benevolently at Sam. "It's nice to see you up and about, Miss Samantha. You haven't been eating half enough to keep a bird alive. I made you some of those mashed taters with the green onions sprinkled in 'em that you like. If I were you, I'd eat the whole bowl myself and not share a lick with that no-account brother of yours." Turning back to Morgan, he barked, "You'll eat whatever I put in front of you. You know better than to ask." With that pronouncement, he sniffed and retreated into the kitchen.

Sam blinked, and Becky winked at her. "This is the most fun we've had at supper since the time Daddy and Jackson forbade you to name your stallion Hooker."

"I named my stallion *Hooker*?" Information was coming at her too fast to process.

"Yes," Becky replied. "May I tell her why, Daddy?"

Parker flushed. "You most certainly may not explain why. Young ladies aren't supposed to know about such things."

Just then, JB carried in a platter of steaks, and conversation ceased until he placed all the serving dishes on the table. There were two bowls of "mashed taters." He deliberately placed the smaller bowl near Sam and a second, larger bowl between Parker and Jackson, after which he carried in a basket of freshly baked bread and a tray of braised carrots and string beans. The final thing he brought was Sam's tea.

Sam wanted to groan when she saw the tea, but she made herself take a few sips because she didn't want to hurt

JB's feelings. The flavor of oranges and a hot, biting bitterness coated her tongue.

While she ate, she tried to puzzle out the mystery of the name Hooker. This "name game" was getting tiresome. Next to her, Morgan nudged her foot and mumbled into his napkin, "General Joseph Hooker."

What the devil?

Then she recalled a rather risqué story from an unorthodox history textbook. Curious she could remember something she had read but not her name. She would ask Doc about that. As she pieced together the details, her eyes widened.

Union General Joseph Hooker had the infamous reputation of being a ladies' man and for having a weakness for a particular variety of "camp follower" of the female variety. He facilitated arrangements to ensure the ladies moved with his troops from camp to camp. Over time, the "followers" were called "Hooker's Division" until eventually the label was shortened to "hookers." Sam surmised the name alluded to a breeding mare's behavior around a stallion. After spooning mashed potatoes on her plate, she looked up to find all three men watching her.

"Your father's right," Sam commented, turning to Becky. "It's not a proper topic for supper conversation. Besides, it's not good manners to remind your father and Jackson that I won the argument."

Darting a quick look at her father and Jackson, Becky's eyes were sparkling with mischief. In a voice intended to include everyone at the table, she administered the *coup de grâce*. "I don't know why Jackson and Daddy bother arguing with you. They never win."

Sam wanted to hug her. Instead, she flashed Becky a dazzling smile.

Chapter 7

"What I said earlier is true," Morgan commented conversationally. "You haven't been thrown from a horse since you were seven." After supper, he and Sam had stayed in the dining room when Jackson, Parker, and Becky excused themselves, saying they were going to the barn to check on a new foal.

"Do you know I'm six years older than you?"

"That's the point, Morgan. I don't know."

Morgan shrugged. "I get it, Sis. Anyway, we were out riding on the ranch you inherited from your father, and you were showing off, riding hell-bent for leather, when your horse reared because of a rattler. You held on at first, but when your mount's hindquarters backed into the fence, he went wild, thought the snake got behind him. You were pitched backward and caught your hand on a raised nail. That's where you got that lightning bolt scar near the curve of your thumb," Morgan said, taking her hand in his and brushing his fingers over it. "I expected I'd need to scrape you off the ground and carry you home to Grace, but by the time I dismounted, you'd scrambled to your feet, picked up a rock, and crushed the snake's head."

Still holding Sam's hand, he continued the story. "You had dead aim even back then. After killing the snake, you rolled the hem of your shirt around your bleeding hand and started limping back to the ranch house. Not once did you glance back over your shoulder at me." Hoping to see some glimmer of memory in his sister's face, he paused. What he saw was rapt attention. Hiding his disappointment, he resumed his narrative.

"You wouldn't stop to let me check you over, and you refused to ride with me. Whenever I asked, you'd shake your head and take another step, so I dropped back to trail behind, thinking you'd get over being mad and let me carry you home. Eventually, you stumbled and fell. I wanted to pick you up, dust you off, and tell you it was all right, but the set of your shoulders told me you'd brook no help or sympathy. You were only a little girl, Sam, but already prouder than the Queen of England." Sam's face still showed no sign anything he'd said stirred a memory.

"I waited while you tried to get up. You failed four times. That's when I realized you broke your foot. Your eyes were blazing when you finally looked up at me. Then politely, as if nothing were wrong, you said, 'Brother, my foot is broken. Will you please help me?' A tear rolled down your cheek and you bowed your head because you didn't want me to see you cry. You about melted my heart, so I dismounted, scooped you up, and put you on my horse. I took you straight to Grace at the Golden Crown because I knew she'd want me to bring you to her instead of to Mac at the ranch."

Eyes wide and questioning, Sam listened intently.

"Someone must have told Grace we were riding in because she was waiting for us in front of the Golden Crown. She held out her arms, and I lifted you down to her. I thought you might be too heavy, but she refused to let me take you from her. She carried you through the gaming salon, past all the 'gentlemen,' straight up to her suite. When the doctor came, he couldn't believe you could stand, let alone walk. You broke your foot in a couple of places. You must have caught it in the stirrup. You didn't whimper or cry while the doctor worked on you. Grace did, though."

Morgan smiled at the remembrance. "Grace is a tough businesswoman but tenderhearted when it comes to her children. Later, Grace told me to sit with you while she went downstairs to the salon. You were sleeping but woke before she returned. When you realized I was sitting with you, you said, as solemnly as reciting a speech in Sunday school, 'Thank you, Morgan, for helping me. You're a good brother, and I'm sorry I cried.'"

Morgan interrupted the story to comment, "Jesus, Sam, one tear wasn't crying, but you said it like you were responsible for starting the flood that floated Noah's ark."

Sam smiled at the thought of a child being able to cry enough tears to float an ark.

Seeing Sam's smile, Morgan flashed her a grin. "Then you said, 'You don't need to worry about having to rescue me again.' I was touched and amused. When I asked you why, with no hesitation, like a drunk swearing to his maker he'd never take another drink, you replied, 'Because there ain't no horse in this world gonna be able to make me eat gravel again, Brother.' You were that serious! I didn't know what to say, so I just patted your hand."

"Did you tell Grace what I said?"

Morgan nodded. "When Grace returned, I told her the whole story, how you fell, killed the snake, everything. She told me I did the right thing watching over you and bringing you home to her. Then she said she had the two best children in the world, kissed me, and went into your room. She sat up with you all night."

Sam was confused. "Grace is my mother too? I don't understand. Jackson said my mother died when I was born."

"Your father married Grace when you were three. He died when you were six. When the Eden Ridge bank was robbed, he got caught in the crossfire."

"Why do you call your mother Grace?"

"You do too, at least most of the time. You'll understand when you see her."

"Where is she, Morgan?"

"At the Golden Crown, of course, in Eden Ridge. She wouldn't sell it and move here, although we asked her to come run Gracelyn Palace. She said she'd miss the Golden Crown and didn't want to live that far from Mac."

"Mac?"

"I'll tell you about Mac some other time. We can't cover twenty-odd years of memories in one evening!"

"Well, at least tell me about the Golden Crown. Is it a saloon?"

Morgan laughed and shook his head. "Don't let Grace hear you call it that. She insists the Golden Crown is a *gaming salon*. Grace is a real lady, from an old Southern family. She'd never run a rough-and-ready establishment. The Golden Crown is elegant—no cheap booze, no crooked games of chance, no fighting, and no 'soiled doves' for entertaining the gentlemen."

"It sounds rather nice."

"You love the Golden Crown, Sam. You always have! You can run a roulette wheel and deal cards with the best of 'em. Didn't Jackson or Parker tell you about our place?"

"Our place? What do you mean?"

"You and I own Gracelyn Palace, but you're the majority investor. It's the reason we came to Prosperity. We wanted our own place. Gracelyn Palace has a ballroom, gaming salon, and bar—it's elegant, legitimate, and profitable. Jackson built a hotel right next door. You were mad as a firecracker at the time, but it was a good business decision. Gracelyn Palace has hostesses who aren't allowed to give—favors—shall we say, or drink too much. Part of their pay, if they need it, is a room at the hotel. Grace sent Miss Jenny to manage it for us. Guess she figured it would give Jenny and Ryder a chance to see if they were as in love as they pretended."

"Miss Jenny and Ryder?" Sam mused, before shrugging and waving her question away. "Never mind. You can tell me about them another time.

"I had no idea about Gracelyn Palace, Morgan. Parker and Jackson didn't mention it, only that I'm their business partner, own a house, and you manage my business holdings—nothing about a gaming salon. Of course, it's only been a few days since the crash, and I haven't been awake much."

"I'm sure they thought it would be better to wait until you were feeling better," Morgan responded. "With you not remembering much of anything, it's difficult to decide what to tell you. Ryder met me at the station this afternoon. He thinks it's odd you haven't asked many questions. Why is that, Sam?"

Morgan was surprised to see a flicker of embarrassment cross her face. He noticed she was rubbing the lightning bolt scar, something she did when she was upset or uncomfortable.

"C'mon, Sis. I thought I'd find you mad at the world and hell-bent on learning about your whole life in one day. You're acting too calm about this. Why?"

***

I'm a saloon owner and professional gambler! When Sam had studied her reflection earlier that day in the mirror, she'd seen no sign that an establishment like Gracelyn Palace was a part of her life.

Overwhelmed by so many of the things Morgan had told her, she put her musings aside to concentrate on how best to answer his last question.

Squaring her shoulders, Sam decided to tell her brother part of the truth. "What Ryder says is true. I haven't asked much because the answers don't sound real to me. If I don't ask, I won't need to decide how I feel about the answers— and not having to think or worry is—well, easy."

Seeing puzzlement in Morgan's eyes, she added, "I'm worried I'll hear things that will make me afraid. I doubt it's logical to feel like this, but the fear reminds me of stories about children afraid to get out of bed in the dark because they believe a monster is hiding, waiting to grab them. Other times, when I hear things like this story about breaking my foot, I can't associate it with—*me*. I don't know who I am or what sort of person I am. Some things I don't understand—"

"What things? Have you remembered something you haven't told us?"

Sam looked at her hands. She wasn't ready to talk about that first flash of memory, partly because of its intimate nature and partly because of the danger she sensed emanating from the unknown observer—that person wanted to hurt her and Jackson. She was sure of that. Dodging Morgan's question, she offered a shocking answer to distract him.

"No, I didn't mean anything specific." Then, gesturing as if she were a shy ingénue hiding behind an ornate fan to disguise her interest in a gentleman, she said, "I suspect I haven't asked because whenever I'm in the same room with Jackson, I think about swooning so he'll catch me in those *manly* arms of his. Satisfied?"

Morgan raised an eyebrow and looked at her quizzically. "What about it? Ryder said that's all that's been happening. You fall, and Jackson picks you up. What's the problem?"

"You don't look shocked. Are you saying you don't think what I said was absurd?"

Morgan shook his head.

Sam tried again. "Well, maybe the real problem is that I can't control when I'll swoon, so I can't, let's say, 'benefit' from being in his arms."

Morgan laughed. "Sam, nothing is shocking about you and Jackson, except that you won't marry him. Even if you don't *know* it, you must *feel* it. It's always been that way between you. Don't think you can dodge me or fool yourself. I'm saying it plain."

"Honestly, Morgan, there are more important things for me to figure out just now than why Jackson kisses me or how I feel about it—he is *not* the most important thing in my life."

Morgan's expression turned dead serious. In a quiet, stern voice, he replied, "You're wrong about that, Sis. Jackson *is* the most important thing in your life."

Staring at the scar on her hand and rubbing her fingers over it, Sam flushed from recalling the memory of Jackson carrying her up the stairs while caressing her. Her body had responded to his every touch. He was fire, and she'd wanted to be consumed. She felt something strong and caring between them. Hadn't her fear for Jackson been greater than her passion? She'd held back because she'd wanted to protect him.

As much as she wanted to deny her feelings and tell Morgan he was wrong about Jackson—that she'd meant what she said, she couldn't do it. Because it wasn't true, her brother would know she'd lied. "That was bravado talking, and I shouldn't have said it. I'm confused about lots of things—one of them is Jackson—and, as I tried to explain, I'm afraid of something. I don't *know* anything, yet, I *feel* everything. How am I supposed to ascertain what's real? I'm sure something is out there waiting to hurt me. Maybe it already has. What if the broken axle on that stage wasn't an accident? The driver was killed. Jackson might have been killed too. It would be easier to deal with it if I could stand on my own, but I'm dependent because of this vertigo. Doc sent a telegram to a colleague in Chicago asking for an opinion. He should get an answer soon."

"To tell you the truth, Sis, I was shocked when I saw you almost fall off that chair."

"Do I have money to get help?"

"Yes. You're wealthy—rich enough to do or buy anything you want."

"Do you mean buy my way out of trouble?"

"In a manner of speaking—I'm not talking about shirking responsibility or anything illegal. I meant you have money to prevent things from happening that shouldn't."

Sam was silent for a few moments. She wanted to return to the conversation about Jackson. "Morgan, from before, what you said about Jackson—I need to ask—*am* I in love with him?"

"Sweetheart, there's no other man in the world for you."

"Is—is Jackson in love with me?"

"I'm surprised you need to ask that," Morgan replied. "Did you lose your eyesight in that crash, too? Even your stallion recognizes there's no other woman for him."

"I'm not blind. I'm confused. Today, I looked in the mirror and didn't recognize the woman I saw. I don't even know how old I am. This not knowing makes me doubt myself. Feelings are only feelings when you don't know facts to sort them out—*nothing seems real*. Damn—I don't want to think about it anymore tonight. My head is traveling in circles."

Compassionately, Morgan touched Sam's shoulder. "We'll sort it out another day." Rising to hold her chair, he added softly, "You're twenty-five." Then placing his hand under her elbow to help her up, he said, "C'mon, Sis, it's time you went to bed. Can you walk that far or should I carry you?" Before she could answer, he flashed her a roguish grin and suggested another alternative. "Would you prefer I find Jackson and ask him to carry you?"

"Stop teasing, Morgan," Sam scolded, working to suppress a smile.

"Maybe I wasn't teasing, Sis. Maybe I was trying to be a good brother and help you get what you want."

"Just for that, Brother, *you* can carry me."

Chapter 8

Jackson went directly to the study instead of the dining room where Morgan and Sam were still talking when he and the others returned from the barn. He mixed laudanum with berry currant and left it on the table for Sam. It was getting late. Parker and Becky had already gone upstairs. He poured a glass of brandy for Sam. Then he poured another for himself.

It had been a long day filled with physical exertion and worry. Despite his sore shoulder, he'd climbed to the bottom of the ravine to examine the broken axle. He hadn't found any obvious sign of tampering. But then, what would "obvious" look like? The debris was so broken apart from bouncing off the rocky walls of the ravine that it was difficult to conceive it had been a stagecoach.

Discouraged, he'd turned from the axle to search for Sam's guns and holster. He hadn't let his eyes linger on the dead horse rotting beneath a section of the coach. It was too easy to envision Sam in its place.

As he scanned the ravine floor, Jackson saw the sun glinting off the metal barrel of one of her Colts that had slipped out of its holster, only a foot from the gun belt. Sam valued the pearl-gripped six-shooters because Mac had given them to her. They were precision weapons crafted for an expert marksman. She was a wicked-fast draw and the most accurate sharpshooter Jackson had ever seen, not that he was a greenhorn.

He smiled, thinking he wouldn't like to test the issue. Soon after Sam came to Prosperity, they'd goaded each other into entering a shooting competition at the town festival. Sam had almost won, but to his utter amazement his last shot, one he'd never made before, hit true. The judges called a tie.

Smiling wider, Jackson remembered how pissed Sam had been. She'd *known* he'd been lucky—she'd wanted to prove she was better than he was. When the judges had made the announcement, she'd shaken his hand with dignity. Then, while the crowd had applauded politely, she'd spoken so the audience could hear every word. "We both know you got lucky. I wonder what deal you made with the devil so you could pull that off." Then she'd given the crowd a big wink, thrown her arms around his neck, and kissed him with a passion that still excited him whenever he thought about it. God gave her the power to do that to a man.

When she'd released him and stepped back, Jackson had seen the glint of satisfied revenge in her eyes. What he hadn't expected to see was the puzzled, disconcerted surprise that fleetingly touched her features. *Had she felt something when she kissed him?* While he'd watched her turn and make her way through the crowd, a slow, rising certainty grew in him. Sam Hilliard Stone had surprised herself. The kiss had ignited a flickering flame of desire, and Jackson suspected the desire diminished the triumph she'd felt from administering her punishment.

Jackson glanced at the clock and decided to join Sam and Morgan. While approaching the dining room, he overheard Sam say, "Honestly, Morgan, there are more important things for me to figure out just now than why Jackson kisses me or how I feel about it—he is *not* the most important thing in my life."

Stunned, Jackson stopped short of the archway and quietly returned to the study, all the while hearing her words repeat in his head. With that statement, she extinguished the ember of hope he'd been nursing. He was realizing his deepest fear. No wonder she didn't ask questions. She'd decided the answers were irrelevant. She'd ended his campaign before he'd been able to mount it.

Patience! He'd lulled himself into inaction because he'd believed there was no reason to rush her. She'd seemed to turn to him on her own, giving every indication she trusted him. She'd returned his kisses. But now, he learned she'd fool him, and his heart turned cold, froze, and cracked into a million splintered shards.

Well, she wouldn't break him. He'd soldier on exactly as his father taught him. His mother had been fond of saying the true role of Divine Providence was to look to the future to provide for others. Jackson decided he'd do that with one slight alteration. He'd look to his own future and provide for his own needs. If Sam changed her mind and decided she wanted him to be important in her life, he wouldn't let himself care. He was determined to make sure the decision would be his, not hers.

Jackson stood with his back to the study door, staring at the glass of brandy he'd placed for Sam on the bedside table next to the liniment bottle and the laudanum mixture. He'd been looking forward to sharing the brandy with her. But he had no claim on her now, and her words made it plain she wasn't interested in staking a claim on him. After all, she'd said she didn't know how she felt about his kisses. Wasn't that evidence enough they didn't mean much?

***

Sam thought it odd Jackson didn't turn when Morgan carried her into the study. *Was he staring at a glass of brandy?*

"Jackson," Morgan said for a second time, "are you going to take Sam? She insisted I carry her in here, and I didn't refuse because she looked weary enough to fall off the chair again."

"Put her on the daybed, Morgan," Jackson replied, without turning. "It makes no sense for me to take her from you. I've been lugging her from place to place for days now. It's your turn."

Morgan stopped short, apparently astounded by Jackson's reply. Before carrying her to the daybed, Sam saw him look at her as if asking what the hell was going on.

Heat flooding her cheeks, Sam recognized she was the target of Jackson's remarks, but she had no explanation to offer.

When Jackson turned toward them, his eyes were dark and angry as he gestured toward the table and spoke to her brother. "I've put what she needs there," he ground out, his jaw set and the line of his mouth hard and unyielding. "I'll sleep at the bunkhouse tonight. You can see to her. She'll tell you what to do."

Morgan nodded. Put that way, he could hardly refuse.

Up until now, Sam hadn't thought Jackson a stranger. But at this moment, he looked and acted like one. Nothing about him resembled the caring man she'd seen so far. Where had his tenderness and compassion gone? *Was this the man Morgan said loved her?*

Jackson turned to go to Parker's office. "I'll clear out my things."

In a trembling voice, Sam called to him, "Jackson, please turn around. Why are you acting like this?"

***

Jackson's steps didn't falter as he trudged away from Sam and Morgan. It was best not to think about why he was doing this. He wouldn't explain. He had to leave because it hurt knowing she didn't care about him. Why did she even bother to ask?

Bitterly, he ran Sam's words through his mind once more. *He is not the most important thing in my life.* Well, he wouldn't let her be the most important thing in his life, either.

***

"Morgan, do you know anything about this?" Sam asked.

Shaking his head in reply, Morgan recognized the bewildered hurt in his sister's tone.

"Brother, please go after him," Sam implored. "Get him to tell you what's wrong. I'd go, but I wouldn't make it to the door. He's not only angry. He's hurt. I'm sure of it. I've done something to hurt him, and he's too proud to explain."

Morgan saw the hurt in his sister's eyes. When she called him "Brother" like that, she said it as if she believed he could rope the moon and give it to her. He wished he could set everything in her world in order, but this wasn't as easy as riding her into town to put her in Grace's care like when she broke her foot. But because she asked, he'd try.

"Don't try to get up on your own while I'm gone. Promise?"

"I promise."

Morgan didn't have to go far. From the porch of the main house, he saw Jackson sitting on the front steps of his and Sam's house, staring at the ground.

Morgan knew Jackson heard his approach and elected to ignore him.

"May I sit?" he asked.

Jackson shrugged. "You shouldn't have left her alone."

Morgan perched on the step above Jackson. "I know, but she looked at me with those gray-blue eyes of hers and said in that voice that makes me think I can perform miracles, 'Brother, please go after him.' You know I can't refuse her anything when she asks me like that—neither can you—besides, if I didn't come, she'd have tried to do it herself. She thinks she hurt you. She said anger is the way you hide your hurt."

"How would she know? Besides, it won't matter how she asks me anything ever again." Jackson rose to his feet and almost growled the next words. "She's pretending she cares. I don't know why she's doing it, but she is. I know the truth, now. Well, I'll tell you this much because you know how it was with us. I can't settle for a life with her pretending to care about me. It would be torture, and I can't do it." He said the last sentence with finality before turning and beginning to stride toward the bunkhouse.

Morgan started to follow.

Jackson turned. With his fists clenched at his side, he growled, "I've said all I'm gonna say. Don't make me hit you."

Morgan would have stood his ground and traded blow for blow with Jackson if he believed it would help. But it wouldn't and now wasn't the time. Jackson was torturing himself over something that wasn't true. Morgan was sure Jackson had overheard some of his conversation with Sam—but when Jackson was like this, the best thing to do was to leave him to cool off.

Morgan raised his hands and took a step back.

Jackson turned on his heel and marched toward the bunkhouse, his fists still clenched at his side.

Morgan watched him go. Then he made his way back to the main ranch house to explain the situation to Sam. He wasn't looking forward to it.

***

The next morning, Jackson argued with Parker in his office, his tone strident. "I don't care what Morgan told you earlier this morning about me and Sam. I'm telling you I don't need to hear it. I'm riding to Cheyenne to talk to Grant Johnson about the lumber deal he wants to make for the timber grove east of the river."

"Please talk to Sam before you go," Parker entreated.

Jackson's face paled at the thought of talking to Sam. What was wrong with Parker that he didn't know that? The man knew him better than he knew himself. He took a calming breath. This wasn't about Parker, and he didn't want to say anything to hurt their relationship.

In a moderate tone, he said, "Listen, Parker, I know you're trying to help. You care about me, and you care about Sam. But you can't fix this, and you're wrong. I do have to go. I need a few days away from here because—" Jackson didn't finish the sentence. Instead, he started a new one. "Morgan's home and Grace will be here in a couple of days. Sam has everyone she needs. She doesn't need me."

"Jackson, I can't believe you mean what you're saying. I've never known you to lie to yourself. You must know you're dead wrong when you say she doesn't need you. By God, man, if Saint Nick were to walk through that door this minute and give her everything she ever wanted, she still wouldn't have what she needs because he couldn't give you to her. *You're what she wants and needs.*"

Jackson swallowed hard, wishing fervently what Parker said was true—he steeled himself against being weak. Reality was reality—he wouldn't believe in something that wasn't true. It made no sense to continue this conversation. But as he turned to go, Sam's voice stopped him.

"Jackson, Parker is telling you the truth. Please let me explain."

Surprised, Jackson spun in Sam's direction. She'd managed to make it to the office door before the vertigo threatened her balance. From the corner of his eye, he saw Parker was similarly surprised. Sam was leaning against the door, clinging to the knob. Her eyelids fluttered, and her grip loosened. She slid down against the door as if she were a silk scarf released from an invisible hook.

Jackson momentarily forgot himself and started toward her, but he halted after taking a few steps and turned. In a dispassionate voice, deliberately modulated to communicate he was unconcerned, he said, "You'd better see to her, Parker."

Then he left the room.

***

Sam and Parker heard the front door close and the sound of Jackson riding out. Their eyes met briefly. Sam rested her forehead wearily on her arm. Gently, Parker helped her to her feet and guided her back to her bed. She turned her head away from him.

Parker had only seen Sam cry twice. The first was when Becky was thrown from a horse and knocked cold. The second was when he and Sam found Jackson, looking more dead than alive, by the stream after searching for him all night. Some rustler had taken a lucky shot, and Jackson hadn't been able to make it back to the ranch on his own. Parker didn't think she was crying now, but she was distressed, and he didn't know how to comfort her.

When Morgan came in, he instantly deduced the reason for the helpless look on Parker's face and the droop in Sam's posture. For an instant, he wished he'd stood his ground with Jackson the night before and knocked some sense into him. He moved to take Parker's place. Sam resisted when he tried to put his arms around her. That was Sam, proud and defiant, even when she was hurting. He waited. Finally, she turned to look at him. Her face was ashen, but her eyes were dry.

Quietly she said, "He left because he hates me."

Morgan's heart wrenched. He tried to stroke her arm, but she pulled away. "No, he doesn't. C'mon, think about it. You're smart—if he hated you, he wouldn't have left because nothing you said or did would matter to him. Jackson left because he loves you and can't trust himself when he's near you."

He put his hands on her shoulders and shook her gently. "Stop being so melodramatic. Grace will be here in a couple of days. She'll be able to make you see what I'm saying is true."

"Grace is coming?" Sam asked, distracted by the news.

"Sure, she is. That's why Ryder met me at the station yesterday. Jackson and Parker sent him to Eden Ridge to fetch Grace and Mac. They'll be here by suppertime, day after next."

Morgan was glad Grace was coming because Sam's face was showing the same fierce determination as when she was a little girl swearing no horse would make her eat gravel again. Morgan feared bigger trouble was on the horizon if Jackson stayed away too long. Sam's stubbornness would take over, and she'd likely raise barriers to protect herself from feeling love and trust again.

Sam's gaze was direct and her voice clear when she replied, "I'll dress and eat something. After that, will you take me for a walk? I need to work harder to get well."

Chapter 9

While walking slowly up the curve of the drive to the main house, Sam and Morgan noticed JB talking to Parker and pointing toward an animal in a pen.

As they approached, they saw a huge pig stumble and fall on its side and heard JB explain he'd been feeding the pig scraps from the last few days' meals, which included Miss Samantha's leftover tea. As JB recollected, the pig began acting oddly almost immediately. At first, it seemed confused and half asleep. Then he noticed it had trouble standing. Now it couldn't get up. Its behavior made him think of how Miss Samantha had been having the same sort of trouble.

The pig made one last attempt to struggle to its feet. In silence, they watched it raise its head and suck in one more agonizing breath before dropping its head heavily into the muck. It died with its eyes rolled back in their sockets.

Sam couldn't tear her eyes from the animal's carcass, evidence the nebulous feelings of fear and danger she'd been experiencing since the crash were real. Someone was trying to hurt her, maybe even murder her.

"I think we should keep this quiet," Sam said, surprised to hear her voice was steady. "Some ranch hands may notice the pig is gone, but they won't be curious enough to ask about it or to mention it in casual conversation. It might be wise not to let on about it until Doc gives us an opinion.

After that, we'll decide whether we need to worry or take action. Agreed?"

When all three men nodded, Sam turned to JB. "Would you please bring that tin of tea to the study? We need to give it to Doc when he comes this afternoon."

JB nodded.

Parker looked at Morgan. "Most of the hands are on the north range and won't be back until dusk. We'll bury the pig after Doc leaves."

***

Later that afternoon, after examining the pig and analyzing the tea, including taking a tiny sip, Doc rubbed his forehead while surveying the small group assembled in the study.

"The tea was soaked in a sedative solution called chloral hydrate. It slows the central nervous system and brain activity. It's commonly used as a sleeping sedative and begins working within a half-hour or less of being ingested. Its side effects include headache, vertigo, nightmares, and confusion."

"I remember reading about it in the Chicago newspapers," Morgan commented. "A group of Irish tavern owners mixed it with whiskey to knock out customers so they could rob them. They called it a Mickey Finn."

"That's right," Doc replied. "Even after it wears off, some people exhibit behavior that mimics drunkenness. In higher dosages, which are often lethal, it causes an uneven heartbeat, shallow breathing, faintness, weakness, vertigo, nausea, and loss of muscle coordination. It shouldn't be mixed with alcohol or laudanum."

The doctor's eyes met Sam's gaze. "It's exaggerated the vertigo and other symptoms you sustained from the crash. You're lucky you didn't like the taste and drink more of it.

Given your concussion and the laudanum, it might have killed you. Where did you get the tea?"

Sam shrugged. "I'm not sure. Becky said something about it coming from the mercantile. I think she said she and Ryder picked it up with Trinity's supplies while Jackson and I were away." Sam looked quizzically at Parker, hoping he could fill in the details. Becky wasn't there because they didn't want to worry her.

Parker responded to Sam's unspoken question. "Becky and Ryder said Wade Harper told one of the clerks at his mercantile to pack the tea with the rest of the ranch supplies. Evidently, Sam ordered it a couple of months ago. No one else cares for it, so she didn't bother keeping any here at the main house. Becky and JB thought Sam would prefer it to coffee."

"So, it was meant only for Sam," concluded the doctor.

Sam considered the doctor's words before saying in a sardonic tone, "Well, thanks to a dead pig, I won't be drinking anymore. No wonder I wasn't getting better. Now, all I need to figure out is who drugged it. Trouble is, when you don't have memories, it's hard to come up with a list of suspects."

"I heard in town Jackson left for Cheyenne this morning to negotiate a timber deal with Grant Johnson," Doc stated. "Was it urgent he go now?"

Instead of answering, Sam's cheeks flamed and she looked away.

Parker cleared his throat and offered a vague reply. "Jackson thought so."

Doc wasn't fooled. He'd glimpsed the telltale color in Sam's cheeks and noticed how Morgan had shifted in his seat. "If we were playing poker, you'd all lose—but, I'll let it go for now." He excused Parker and Morgan, saying he needed to examine Sam to assess how much damage the tea had done.

As the two men walked toward Parker's office, Doc gave them one last instruction. "I suggest you figure out how to send Jackson a telegraph message telling him to come home without alerting every citizen in Prosperity that someone is trying to murder Sam. I also suggest you make it clear that his return isn't optional. Without him, a credible suspect list isn't possible, and I'm not in the mood to go to Cheyenne and drag him back here. Do we understand one another?"

Morgan half-turned and gave a mock salute. "You read my mind, Doc. Parker and I'll take care of it."

Doc began Sam's examination, particularly focusing on her balance and coordination. Finally, he commented, "You're steadier today. Do you still feel nauseous?

"Yes, but it's better than it was."

"How much tea did you drink yesterday?"

"About half a cup in the afternoon when Becky was helping me dress and only about a third of a cup last night at supper."

"Did you take any of the laudanum last night?"

Looking at her hands, Sam answered flatly. "No."

"Why didn't Jackson make you take it?"

Several seconds passed before San answered. "Because Jackson slept at the bunkhouse last night, and Morgan stayed with me."

"I see." Doc heard the hurt in her voice. "Sam, you know you and Jackson love each other, don't you?"

"That's what Morgan told me," she replied, her tone defensive.

Fed up with evasive answers, Doc didn't bother hiding his irritation. "It's not like you to play games, Sam. That wasn't an acceptable answer."

A defiant gleam entered Sam's eyes. "I'm gonna tell you what I told Morgan, Doc. I don't *know* anything." She crossed her arms and looked at him as if they were in a standoff.

Doc Baxter simply waited.

Finally, Sam said, "All right, I know I love him because I *feel* it. I guess remembering why or what's happened in the past isn't half as important as what a person feels."

The doctor approved. "Good thinking."

Sam smiled wryly. "It doesn't matter what I know or what I feel, because Jackson believes I don't love him and has decided he's fine with that. He overheard me say something to Morgan last night that I didn't mean. Unfortunately, he didn't listen long enough to hear me retract it and admit my feelings for him."

Doc sighed wearily. This reminded him of when she first came to Prosperity. How two people who were so right for each other could mess things up, he'd never understand. Maybe their independence held them back. They both acted as though they could depend only on themselves—but everyone needs someone—and they were the best kind of right together.

Practically the whole town breathed easier when they stopped challenging each other. Most people thought they'd marry, but Sam had refused for reasons only a few knew. Doc gave Jackson credit for understanding and not forcing the issue, but now, maybe they needed to rethink that decision. This drugged tea situation and the stagecoach crash proved the past couldn't be forgotten or assuaged. The amnesia made Sam shockingly vulnerable, like a calf staked out to graze innocently at the mouth of a cougar's den. She needed Jackson's knowledge as much as she needed his love. Thank God, Grace and Mac were arriving soon. Together, maybe they could protect Sam.

"Jackson, Morgan, Grace, and Mac will help you figure this out. Don't be too proud to let them help you. Be patient with Jackson, though. When he comes back, he'll keep his distance, telling himself he didn't return because he loves you. He'll convince himself he'd do it for any stranger facing the same danger. Sooner or later, you'll get a chance to show him how you feel about him, and he'll believe you."

The doctor grinned. "You have a way of turning that man's heart near inside-out. Meanwhile, concentrate on getting well and stick close to Parker and Morgan. Don't take any more laudanum unless you really need it. When Mac and Grace arrive, question them mercilessly. They can tell you things to help figure out who's trying to hurt you and why."

As the doctor stooped to collect his bag, Sam spoke up. "Before you go, I need to understand something else. Why have I lost only my personal memories? I remember things I was taught and things I read in textbooks. Morgan mentioned I know how to play cards and run a faro game. When he said that, I realized I do know how to do those things, but I don't remember doing them. Becky said Jackson would look for my guns in the ravine where the crash happened. Last night, while I was waiting for Morgan, I noticed Jackson left my gun belt on the back of the chair. I'm sure I know how to handle those guns, load them, and shoot them. I'm sure I'm good with them, but I don't remember an occasion on which I fired them. Why is my memory working this way?"

Doc put down his bag. "You've lost your episodic memory, Sam. You haven't lost what's called your implicit memory, which is why you've retained your personality, identity, and procedural memory. Your motor skills and physical memories, like shooting a gun and riding a horse, are stored in a different place in your brain than your episodic memories. Perhaps this will help you understand. When I was in medical school, I was introduced to a patient who lost his memory but played the piano as well as a virtuoso. He was, as it turned out, a famous pianist, but he couldn't recall who taught him to play, where he'd learned to play, or whether he'd ever played a recital."

"Did the others tell you I remembered Jackson's surname the night before last and made more than a coincidental reference to his first name?"

Doc shook his head. "Why no, Sam. I guess with the tea discovery, they forgot about it. It's positive news." He patted her shoulder reassuringly. "Remember what I said about being careful and focusing on getting well. I'll visit again in a few days. If you need me before then, ask Parker or one of the others to send for me."

Left alone, Sam felt all the anxiety and confusion from the last few days rise to the surface. Wearily she rubbed her temple. It was hard to believe she was the capable, independent, and strong-willed woman they described. While resting, she began chanting silently, "This too shall pass." Briefly, she wondered where she learned the phrase.

***

Reed Ferguson watched Morgan, Ryder, and JB bury the dead pig. Too bad Bainbridge sent the drugged tea to the mercantile to be delivered with Trinity's supplies. Its discovery would put them on guard.

When he'd heard the news a stagecoach crash had destroyed Sam Stone's memory, he was sure fate had smiled upon him. Her amnesia made her more vulnerable. The town gossips said she didn't know who she was—or even who

Jackson Knight was. Rumors were circulating that Sam didn't want Jackson.

Earlier that morning, Reed had watched Jackson Knight ride through Prosperity starting his journey to Cheyenne. Jackson's absence was the main reason he'd decided to ride to Trinity a few hours later to spy on Sam.

***

The next morning, Morgan and Sam sat on the steps of her house enjoying the fresh air, mild temperature, and gentle breeze. Morgan thought Sam was better today. She swayed less, and her steps were more confident. Her balance was improving.

Earlier at breakfast, she'd eaten a modest helping of scrambled eggs mixed with bits of ham, which JB made specifically to please her. Morgan had noticed her looking speculatively at the empty chair at the head of the table a few times. But she hadn't commented regarding Parker's absence last night at supper or breakfast.

After supper last night, Sam and Becky had adjourned to the study to look through pattern books and talk about the dresses they'd buy when Sam was well enough to take Becky shopping. When Becky had noticed Sam yawning, she'd said good night and retired to her room.

Alone with Sam, Morgan had poured them each a brandy, and while sipping it in companionable silence, he'd thought about Sam's father trying to recall what he knew about Chase Stone's life before he came to Eden Ridge. He'd assumed Sam was quiet because she was trying to make sense of the chaos of the last week's events. She was a person who liked to "walk around things," studying them from every angle. How frustrating it must be for her to have so little knowledge of her life. Morgan had imagined she must feel as if she were trying to solve a puzzle missing most of its pieces. When they'd both drained their glasses, they'd gone to bed.

"Are you going to tell me where Parker went?" Sam asked, interrupting Morgan's thoughts. Unexpectedly, the breeze grew cooler and the sky began to cloud up.

Morgan shrugged. "He told Becky he was riding to Laramie to sign a contract to sell horses and would be back in a couple of days."

Sam waited. When Morgan didn't volunteer more, she retorted, "We both know you sidestepped the question."

Morgan rolled his eyes. "Parker rode out to find Jackson. He left a couple of hours after Doc. Our first plan was to send a telegram to Jackson from Laramie. However, after talking it over, we decided it would be better for Parker to go after Jackson. Sending a telegram from Laramie wouldn't keep the news from traveling back to Prosperity."

When Sam cast him an uncertain look, Morgan went on to explain. "With Jackson being mad and in no real hurry to get to Cheyenne, he won't be traveling hard. At a comfortable pace, it takes three days to ride to Cheyenne. Parker will have caught up with him near dawn this morning—if he was able to keep riding after dark. Parker bringing Jackson home is faster and safer. Whoever drugged that tea won't know we found out about it. Doc's telling people you can't have visitors, except for Grace and Mac, who're rushing here from Eden Ridge."

"And—?" Sam pressed.

Morgan raised an eyebrow and expelled an exasperated huff. "And what? Do you think I'm lying?"

Sam kept her voice level. "No, I think you left something out because you think it will upset me."

"For a woman who doesn't remember me, you know me pretty well, don't you?"

Sam flashed him an affectionate smile before nodding in answer to his question. "From the moment I heard your voice behind me in the dining room two nights ago, I've felt a bond with you. I didn't recognize your face, so in that sense, you are a stranger. But I *feel* you're someone I love and trust. In a way, I feel as if I've always known you, although I have no recollection of anything we ever did together. That must sound strange, but I swear it's true, Morgan. I feel it with Parker, Becky, Ryder, and Doc, too."

"And?" prompted Morgan, using her earlier interrogation technique.

Caught in her own omission, Sam answered, "And—Jackson, of course."

Satisfied with her answer, Morgan replied, "What I didn't say before is Parker and I aren't sure Jackson would come home if we sent a telegram. He's feeling sorry for himself. He's not thinking logically. He wants to believe you're cold-hearted and not worth two seconds of his concern. In other words, he's busy building a wall around his heart. Something he won't be able to do, but it might be a while before he admits it. Once he calms down, he'll realize Parker wouldn't have come if you hadn't been in danger. He'll come home because he won't be able to stop himself."

Sam looked at the door of her house. "Will we stay here when Grace and Mac arrive?"

"I hadn't thought about it, but I'm guessing we won't. There's no one here to do the cooking, and the main house has plenty of bedrooms. Now that we're here, do you want to go inside?"

"Not today," Sam replied.

Morgan wondered what was on her mind.

"Did Jackson stay here with me?" Sam asked in a lowered tone, as if she feared someone was nearby listening.

The question surprised Morgan, but he answered without equivocation. "Yes. You and Jackson are open about your relationship. Even Becky knows."

When she didn't comment in response, Morgan stood. "Will you be all right for a few minutes while I go in and get some papers? We should look through them before Grace and Mac get here. Perhaps we can piece some things together about your father."

"Do you think what's happening is connected to my father?" Sam asked.

"I don't know. He left papers with things you may need to know. Grace gave them to you when you turned twenty-one. Last night I was thinking about your father and some hardships Grace alluded to when he was a young man. Mac knows those things, too. You can look at the papers by yourself, or we can do it together."

"I'll wait for you here while you go inside," Sam replied, glancing around, as if she felt apprehensive about being left on her own.

When Morgan returned, they started back to the main house, and Sam broached another topic. "Why does JB call me 'Miss Samantha'? Jackson told me Samantha isn't my name. He said my father named me Sam Hilliard Stone. I noticed none of you think it odd when JB calls me Miss Samantha."

"The answer is complicated," Morgan replied. "You don't want people, mainly business associates, to know the real Sam Hilliard Stone or that you're a woman. You give the impression you're a reclusive, powerful businessman, who prefers to run your empire from behind the scenes. You don't meet them personally. I'm your front man so they deal with me."

Pausing a moment, Morgan let her consider his response before continuing. "Most people naturally assume your name is 'Samantha Stone.' They see a beautiful, intelligent, and charming woman. Why wouldn't they? They don't associate you with the rich businessman, *Sam Hilliard Stone*. People know you have money, but it doesn't often occur to them that *Samantha* and *Sam Hilliard* are the same person. That gives you the freedom to do as you please. As Samantha, you live here, unmarried. Few people question your relationship with Jackson, even those who judge it sinful. The predominant opinion is you're an unconventional, free spirit. You often dress like a man, ride like a daredevil, handle weapons like a professional gunman, own a gaming salon, and do pretty much anything you please."

God, it *was* complicated! But Sam understood. She remembered Jackson saying that no other woman was named Sam Hilliard. Ironically, she'd replied that she doubted anything about them was normal. Now, she began to grasp just how not normal she was.

She leaned against Morgan more heavily as they entered the main house. Before he deposited her in the chair by the bedside table, she impulsively hugged him.

"I'm grateful to have you by my side. You're a rare man. I bet entrepreneurs everywhere are plumb discombobulated by the time you get done with them."

Morgan hugged her back. Then holding her at arm's length, he chuckled and said, "You learned that word when you were nine. We've pulled off some beauties together, Sis. I can't imagine a different life."

"We need to get past this," Sam murmured, her eyes misted and her tone dead serious.

***

Reed Ferguson had watched Sam while she sat on her porch waiting for her brother. It pleased him to see her nervous and afraid.

He wondered if she was sorry Jackson Knight left her. He hoped not.

Reed wished Sam would move back into her house. It would make watching her so much more pleasurable. In the past, on nights when Jackson Knight wasn't with her, Reed had often stayed in a spare bedroom. It was easy to come and go as he pleased, and he enjoyed watching her.

Sometimes he thought she did certain things because she knew he was there.

Chapter 10

The night air had taken on a damp chill, but there was no rain. Parker raised the collar of his jacket and wished he'd spent less time behind his desk. He was feeling the strain of the ride, not to mention the worry and emotion from the past week. But his concern for Sam wouldn't let him stop.

When he left Trinity, Parker estimated Jackson was ten hours ahead of him. By now, the odds were high he'd stopped to make camp for the night, so Parker planned to keep riding. Because traveling in the dark was dangerous, he was careful to watch the roadway and not push his horse too hard. With luck, he'd catch up with Jackson before dawn. His arrival would ignite Jackson's temper, and he'd blow up like a powder keg. Parker needed to figure out a strategy to make him listen.

Parker had the timing almost perfect. He smelled the faint smoke from a nearly dead campfire and threaded his horse off the road and through the brush, stopping near the camp. He gripped the saddle horn while lowering himself to the ground and felt the ache of his protesting muscles.

Praying this was a friendly camp because he hadn't disguised his approach, Parker called, "Hello, the camp!" Friend or foe, the camp's occupant was sure to have a gun trained on him.

***

Jackson was awakened by the sound of a horse moving through the undergrowth. He heard the scrape of boots on hard ground and the crack of a branch snapped in passing. His Colt was already drawn. His grip on the handle was light, but his finger was poised on the trigger, and the barrel pointed in the direction of the sounds.

Having moved silently away from the fire, Jackson was only about ten feet from his friend when he answered Parker's call to the camp. "Sonofabitch, Parker! Are you trying to get yourself killed?"

Parker shrugged and walked forward to crouch next to the fire, which had burned down to a bed of embers, producing little in the way of light or heat. He pulled a couple of branches from the woodpile stacked next to the shallow fire pit and worked to build up flames. He wanted light *and* heat.

Walking softly, Jackson moved around to the other side of the fire and sat, warily watching Parker.

When a few flames licked at the wood, Parker glanced up while stretching his hands out to feel the warmth. Keeping his tone matter of fact, he said, "I can tell by the look on your face that you rode all day, Jackson, but didn't get very far—and I don't mean in miles. You look as if you could bite off a rattler's head." Then he deliberately locked eyes with his friend before adding, "You and I need to do some straight talking. If you don't listen, we'll have to fight, and we both know I'm older than you and what the outcome will be. If that's the way you want it, though, I warn you, I won't quit until you pound me into the ground. Do you want to do it that way?"

"Goddamn you, Parker," Jackson growled, "why can't you leave this alone?"

"I can't leave it alone because some crazy, cowardly sonofabitch is trying to murder Sam, and I'm afraid his hate will spill over onto the rest of us. I won't let Becky get caught in it or risk losing Sam, Morgan, Ryder, or—*you.*" Parker hit his thigh with his fist. "You damn well better stop being a stubborn cuss and hear me out!"

Stunned, Jackson stared at his friend for a long minute. The anguish in Parker's voice had penetrated and disarmed his anger. His chest felt like the grim reaper's arms were squeezing his life from him. If something happened to the people he loved—yes, he'd admit it, especially to Sam—his life might as well be over because it wouldn't have much appeal. Parker knew about that. He'd lost the love of his life after only five years together.

Jackson shook his head to clear it and ran his hand wearily over his face. "All right, Parker, tell me. I'll listen."

Parker recounted everything.

A shiver went down Jackson's spine when Parker described how the pig died. His mind flashed to the mangled horse crushed beneath the stage at the bottom of the ravine. Both animals had suffered, and it was far too easy for Jackson to envision Sam in their place. His gut felt as though someone had planted a foot in it.

"I almost forced laudanum down Sam's throat the other night. Then I gave her brandy to chase it with," Jackson confessed, his voice ragged with emotion after listening to Parker explaining the drug's side effects and how alcohol shouldn't be mixed with it. Jerking to his feet, he turned away and walked into the brush where there was no light.

Parker gave Jackson a few minutes before he spoke. "Doc doesn't think the drug caused permanent damage. He says Sam will recover. She only drank small amounts of the tea because she didn't like it." His voice sounded amused when he added, "She didn't complain about the taste because she didn't want to admit her opinion was the same as yours."

Jackson came back to the fire as Parker told him Doc ordered them to do whatever it took to bring Jackson home. "Doc believes you, Morgan, Grace, and Mac are critical to solving this. God knows, *Sam* doesn't have any of the puzzle pieces. Christ, Jackson, she's the proverbial innocent lamb!"

When Parker finished, they sat in silence. Jackson felt completely wiped out, so when Parker brought up the issue between him and Sam, Jackson didn't have the energy to protest.

"Jackson, the other night, when you heard Sam say you weren't the most important thing in her life, she didn't mean what she said. Don't look surprised I know about it. She told Morgan, and he told me. Sam also told Doc, who told me. Sam said it to put Morgan off. If you could look past your pride and anger for a minute, you'd know you mean the world to her. She hasn't changed about that. It's only her memory that's gone—not her love."

Jackson ran his hand through his hair and closed his eyes.

"You know I wouldn't lie to you about this, Jackson, don't you?" Parker asked, pushing for a response.

"I know you're sincere, and you believe you're telling me the truth," Jackson conceded.

"Very well, I guess I'll have to accept that," Parker replied, with a tinge of sorrow in his tone. "Are you going to come back with me?"

Jackson nodded. How could he not come back? He had no choice.

Jackson knew it had been an exhausting ride for Parker and that his friend hadn't stopped to eat or rest. "We'll bed down here for a few hours before we start back. I'll fix us some coffee and grub at daybreak so you can sleep a little longer."

Crouching near the fire to shift a log, Jackson said, "When we go back, I'll circle Prosperity to avoid it completely. I know it will add almost two hours to my ride, but it could prevent whoever is behind this from learning we discovered the drug in the tea and give him the opportunity to try something else. What did you tell Becky about where you were going?"

"I told Becky I was going to Laramie to sign a deal for some horses—none of us want her to know about the drugged tea—at least right now. Morgan will tell Sam where I went after Becky leaves for her morning ride. He'll also tell Wilson, who rides with her, to be extra vigilant watching over her."

"Good. I think you should ride through town as though you were returning from Laramie. You'll get home more than an hour before me, but everyone will think you did exactly what you told Becky you were doing."

It was Parker's turn to nod.

***

Sam looked up from the paper she was studying and glanced at the clock. "It's almost noon, and Becky's not back from her ride, Morgan. I thought you said she'd be safe with Wilson. What if whoever is trying to hurt me—" Sam's voice broke.

Morgan had hoped it would take a day or two before Sam realized the rest of them could be in danger. He should have known better. "Don't worry, Sam. She always pushes the rule right to the wire—she'll ride in with only five minutes to spare, especially today because she doesn't expect Parker back before nightfall at the soonest."

Morgan and Sam were seated at the desk reading the papers Morgan took from her house. "This says Highbreeze is mine and that Grace is my guardian until I reach legal age. I own property in Chicago, investments, and cash."

Holding the paper so Morgan could read it, too, she asked, "What's this part about a family estate transferred to my great-uncle, along with funds and income from specific investments for the duration of his life if he abides by an addendum of terms placed in the safekeeping of the law firm that's named here? It goes on to say the estate and assets revert to me when my great-uncle dies."

Before Morgan could answer, they heard hoofbeats outside on the drive. Morgan looked at the clock and smiled. Yup, it was exactly five minutes before the hour. He sensed Sam's relief. "Don't say anything to her, Sis," Morgan cautioned. "She didn't break the rule, and we don't want her to sense our anxiety."

The front door slammed, and Becky raced noisily through the hallway calling, "I'll wash up and be right there."

Brother and sister looked at each other and laughed.

"I bet we were no different, Morgan."

"My manners were better—though I did tend to slam the door a bit harder," he shot back, pretending to be offended.

After eating the noonday meal, Morgan and Sam returned to the study while Becky went to the barn to groom her horse and exercise Sam's stallion. Hooker was a one-woman horse. He obeyed Sam to the letter, but he allowed Becky to see to him when Sam wasn't available. He preferred women to men. Jackson, Ryder, and Morgan were only tolerated when the women were absent.

"From what I can remember," Morgan said, "your father's parents were killed when he was fifteen. I think there was something suspicious about their deaths, but I don't know why I have that impression. Your father mentioned an Uncle Aaron who took guardianship of him and controlled his inheritance. I gathered your father ran away long before he was of age. He came west, drifting here and there, learning how to be a cowboy, working on ranches, and moving on when he thought his uncle was closing in on him. Until we read that part about your great-uncle in your father's will, I didn't know he'd communicated with him, let alone negotiated a settlement. Your father based his decisions on facts. He must have had a good reason to turn over the family estate and fortune to his uncle."

"Did my great-uncle know about my father's marriage and my birth?" Sam asked. "Maybe he thought he could inherit or steal property and money?"

"It's a possibility, Sam. After all, we know when your father married Grace that he ensured she'd be your legal guardian and the executor of your inheritance if anything were to happen to him. Mac was forever warning me to watch over you and be wary of strangers, even for myself. He said he didn't want to make me afraid, only careful, because your father had been concerned about both of us."

Morgan paused while remembering how it had been. "Mac trained me well. When it was time for me to go to school in Chicago, I felt as if I were abandoning you. I was excited to go, but I knew I would miss you. Though I'm older, we spent a great deal of time together. Unlike most older brothers, I enjoyed your company and admired your daring. You didn't hold me back as I saw some sisters do. No matter where we were or what we were doing, you always made it seem like we were on an adventure. You never made a fuss when I went off with my friends."

Morgan's brows drew together. "Boys were starting to notice you the year before I left. I was worried about your being able to handle them. I was afraid one of them would go too far. If I stepped in, though, you got madder than a hornet. You told me you could take care of yourself. When some older boys resented your rejection, you began wearing your gun. They knew you could use it, and they were afraid of Mac, so they mostly left you alone. Grace started keeping you away from men at the Golden Crown, too."

"Is that when Mac gave me the derringer, Morgan?"

Morgan looked away, hoping Sam wouldn't pick up on the fact he didn't like talking about the derringer. "It was somewhere around that time," he said vaguely. "The teacher didn't like you having a gun at school. She'd lock it in a drawer."

"Did the teacher keep it?" Sam asked.

Morgan ran his finger around the inner placket of his shirt collar, reluctant to answer. "Once the teacher left early and forgot to give your gun back. She was the only one with the key to the drawer, so you had to walk home without it. Mac didn't like you being without a gun, so he got you the derringer and taught you to use it. He said what the teacher didn't know wouldn't hurt her."

Morgan was careful to phrase his explanation to give the impression he was uncomfortable saying straight out that Mac told her to break the rules. Thankfully, Sam caught on and dropped the topic.

"Morgan, do you think Jackson really will come back with Parker?"

Morgan's voice turned soft, and he squeezed his sister's arm. "Yes, Sis, he'll come back. I told you this morning. He won't be able to stop himself."

Chapter 11

Though it was close to midnight, Parker and Jackson weren't back. Sam was worried damn near out of her head. She'd gone to bed around nine, telling Morgan she was tired. However, sleep eluded her because her mind wouldn't let her rest. The careless words that caused Jackson to leave could have put both men in as much or more danger than she was in. I'm nothing but trouble, she thought. Maybe I should go, at least for a while.

What if whoever was doing this hurt the people she loved? Parker was aware someone was out there and dangerous, but Jackson left before the discovery. The killer could be stalking him. Hell, maybe all of them. For the hundredth time, she wondered what she could have done to make someone want to kill her. Was the fact that she was rich enough of a reason?

The door between the study and Parker's office was open. Sam could hear Morgan's even breathing. Three hours earlier, he'd fallen asleep after kissing her good night and reassuring her again that Parker and Jackson would be home long before morning. Each passing minute seemed like an hour. The cool breeze from this morning had ushered in a fine drizzle in the afternoon. After supper, the wind increased, and the rain came down steadily. Around eight, the sky opened and pelted the earth with hail. Now, the wind raged and drove the heavy rain sideways.

With the storm's intensity increasing, it was difficult to distinguish other sounds. Sam went to the window next to the front entrance. She could see the porch, the road in front of the house, and the road below that angled off to the barn, bunkhouse, corrals, and outbuildings. She stared into the night, less anxious now that she could watch the road. Ten minutes later, she saw a horse and rider. She held her breath—she saw only one horse—not two—where was the second one?

She swallowed around the lump in her throat. Jackson didn't come back. She saw the single rider stay on the lower road and dismount in front of the barn.

Returning to her bed, she turned her back to the study doors and concentrated on controlling her breathing, pretending to be asleep. Parker would be exhausted, and she wanted to save him the embarrassment of explaining why Jackson wasn't with him. She heard Parker hesitate at the study door before taking two tentative steps toward her and stopping. She assumed he'd convinced himself no good would come from waking her to convey bad news.

She didn't realize he left the room until she heard soft sounds on the stairs. When he reached Becky's door, he stopped. She imagined the smile that would touch his lips while looking at his daughter. He was a loving father and a good friend. How many miles and hardships had he endured trying to bring Jackson home to her?

After Sam was sure Parker was asleep, she got up. To keep Morgan and Parker from worrying, she left a note on the daybed saying she'd gone to her house. Then, not bothering to dress, she strapped her gun belt on over her nightdress. She stopped in the hallway to take a slicker and scoop up a pair of mud boots abandoned next to the coat rack. As she opened the door, she noticed a walking stick propped in the corner and took it, too. It would help her keep her footing.

Once on the porch, she shoved her arms into the slicker and fastened its top buttons. Then she sat in the rocking chair and pulled on the mud boots. She adjusted her holster, making sure she could get to her gun easily beneath the slicker. Finally, she picked up the walking stick and stepped down the stairs into the cold wind and rain.

She wanted to mourn Jackson in a place where they'd been close—a place where they'd loved each other. This morning, when Morgan asked about going into her house, she'd declined because she wasn't ready. She'd sensed she'd feel Jackson's presence there, and it would have made her feel the house was haunted. She'd known his spirit would be there, a ghost intent on punishing her for her hurtful words.

However, those were her feelings earlier—when she still harbored hope he'd come back. Now that she knew he wasn't coming home, she felt different. If she couldn't be with the flesh-and-blood man, she'd settle for his ghostly presence because punishment was better than feeling nothing. *She needed to feel something.*

Slowly, she made her way down the sloping drive. It was slippery and thick with mud that sucked at her boots, making it difficult to move forward. Without the walking stick, she wouldn't have been able to raise her knees high enough to break free. She fell twice onto her side, but the thick layer of mud cushioned her landings. Each time, she used the walking stick to get back on her feet.

As the rain came down harder, Sam couldn't see much more than the outline of her house. Though it wasn't far, it seemed to take forever to get there. When she stepped over the threshold, she left the door open behind her, hoping it would provide a little light to help her locate a lamp. She reasoned one should be near the entrance, so she felt along the wall to her left. Almost immediately, she encountered the cold metal of a drawer pull. Moving her fingers up, she found the top of the furniture piece. Slowly gliding her hand sideways, she found the base of the lamp—now, to find the matches.

After lighting the lamp, she raised it and surveyed her surroundings. The study and office were located similarly to those in the main house, which made sense. They were the most used rooms and needed to be convenient to the entrance. The parlor was to her immediate right and the dining room beyond it. The kitchen was through the door behind the dining table. That meant the bedrooms were at the back of the house. She guessed the main bedroom shared a wall with the office. Stepping to the open office door and scanning the wall behind the desk, she found the door she assumed would open to her bedroom.

Glancing down at her boots, she noticed the water and muddy footprints on the hallway floor. She returned to the front door and sat on the floor to pull off the boots. When she stood, she shrugged off the slicker, letting it fall carelessly next to the boots. The bottom of her nightdress was dripping and caked in mud. After scraping the mud onto the slicker, she stepped to the open door to wring out the water onto the porch. It never occurred to her to shut the door.

Peering into the dim interior of the dining room, the shadows looked ominous, as if an entity lurking in their depths would reach out to wrap bony fingers around her arms and drag her away to its lair. She took a trembling step forward and stopped. Was there someone there? Only light would disperse the shadows and reassure her. She needed to see light everywhere. Scooping up matches from the container next to the lamp by the front door, she went to light a lamp in the dining room, one in the parlor, and another in the kitchen. Then she made her way back to the office. Once there, she paused to light a lamp on a table near the doorway. After studying the room's layout, she crossed to the door she felt certain opened to the bedroom she and Jackson had shared.

She reached for the doorknob but hesitated to turn it because some intuition or premonition crept over her, cautioning her to be wary. She imagined someone on the other side of the door, pressing his ear against the panel, listening and anticipating her entrance. She'd presumed she'd feel Jackson's spirit, not the presence of a flesh-and-blood voyeur.

The sense that someone was there set her hand shaking, and she stepped back from the door. Was it her imagination that stole her courage to enter the room where she was sure Jackson's presence would be strongest, or something else?

It's only that I'm tired—I need to gather my strength before I confront Jackson's ghost.

Her knees trembled. Fearing her legs would give way, she reached out to grip the back of a chair that faced the desk and inched around it until she could sink into its soft cushion and protective shadow. She needed a few minutes to collect herself and rest. Surely, Jackson's ghost could wait a few minutes more.

*****

Reed Ferguson thought Sam must have sensed he was in her house, watching and waiting for her. With Jackson Knight gone, she was coming to him. He'd always known she would.

It pleased him to watch her explore her house, light the lamps, and look longingly at the door to her bedroom. When she sat in the chair in the office, he smiled, certain it was a signal she wanted him to come to her.

Sam was the most beautiful woman he'd ever seen. With Jackson Knight gone, she'd need someone else to warm her bed—a virile man to give her what she needed.

Reed had watched Sam at Gracelyn Palace. Other men had watched her too. While pretending to notice only Jackson Knight, she'd sipped that foul tea to keep her wits about her when dealing twenty-one, running faro games, and playing poker. She'd stirred and aroused men until some were driven to release their pent-up lust in the dark alley behind Gracelyn or in the nearest brothel.

Smiling, Reed reminded himself he was alone in the house with Sam. She needed him—wanted him to come to her and give her pleasure.

Chapter 12

The ride returning to Trinity was cold, wet, and miserable. Jackson was tired and hungry, and the weather made it hard to stay in the saddle. However, as challenging as the physical discomforts were, they were less concerning than his mental ones. He both longed and dreaded to be back at the ranch—no, the truth was he both longed and dreaded to see Sam.

His feelings were warring with his logic. He recalled a story in which the devil and an angel metaphorically sat on the opposite shoulders of a man and took turns tempting him to do their bidding. Jackson felt like that. He was no longer certain his decision to leave Trinity had been the right one. Anger, hurt, worry, loss, and fear were with him. He questioned his resolution to forget Sam and soldier on.

Had she denied her love for him, or had she, honestly, in her ill and drugged state, only expressed her fears and confusion about what she didn't know? Had he run away from a woman who didn't love him or had he let his fears overwhelm him to the point where he decided to retreat rather than stand and fight? Was this his personal war, a war in which he was the only participant?

He'd engaged in personal wars before. After he'd left the graves of his father and mother behind in the South Pass gold region, he'd fought desperately to find a new direction and purpose. The victory finally came in the form of Trinity.

By the time Jackson separated from Parker to circle Prosperity, the drizzle had turned to a cold, pounding rain. He piloted his way through the terrain, unable to use existing paths. He wasn't looking forward to crossing the southeast stream. Normally only a foot wide, the stream's flow was slow and lazy. However, in a storm like this one, its girth could swell to as much as six feet or more, making its speed and power difficult to fight when crossing. The hail hadn't melted completely, so the banks would be muddy and slippery.

When Jackson reached the stream, it looked exactly as he'd anticipated. He spurred his horse to spring from the bank into the middle of the muddy, swift current, which immediately forced them sideways. He was almost to the opposite bank when a large shirred-off branch banged into his upper calf, startling him and his mount. Thankfully, his horse's feet touched bottom, making it possible to climb out of the raging water.

Cold and waterlogged, Jackson crested the hill overlooking Trinity. He was surprised to see light streaming from several of the rooms in his and Sam's house. *What the hell?* Jackson slid to the ground and led his horse as quietly as possible to the barn. The fury of the wind and rain would prevent anyone from hearing his approach, but he was taking no chances. After settling his horse in a stall, he darted out the side door and moved through the shadows to his and Sam's house.

The front door was standing wide open. He saw a pair of boots and a slicker abandoned on the floor. Nothing else looked out of place. He saw no movement; yet, he sensed someone was there. Seconds passed while his eyes scanned the room spaces visible from the doorway. His Colt was drawn and ready.

He moved stealthily into the house. Trusting his instincts, he entered the office and cautiously approached the door to the master bedroom. *Was someone near?* His eyes fell to the wing chair where he saw a woman's hand resting on the armrest. *Sam?* How could she be here? He moved to stand facing the chair. Sam's eyes were closed, and she was wearing her holster over her nightdress.

* * *

Reed Ferguson was considering whether he should go to Sam when he detected movement outside on the porch. Jackson Knight entered the house.

Shocked by Jackson's arrival, Reed quietly eased the door to Sam's bedroom closed and crossed to the door that opened into the back hallway to return to the spare bedroom he used as his main observation post.

As soon as the storm cleared, he'd return to town.

Though disappointed, Reed was careful not to let his need consume him. He knew how to temper and conserve his passion. When the time came, it would be there to pleasure Sam.

* * *

When Sam opened her eyes, she saw Jackson's ghost had materialized before her. She could only surmise it had come to confront her because she hadn't mustered the courage to go to it. It stood tall, shoulders squared, and face inscrutable.

Involuntarily, Sam tried to wipe the vision from her eyes, thinking the ghostly form would dissipate when the remnants of sleep fell away. But it didn't vanish. Leaning toward the apparition, she whispered in a sad and accepting voice, "Jackson, are you so powerful you can conjure your spirit to torture me?" Her eyes moved to the Colt in his hand.

"I knew you'd haunt me here," she said, "but not like this, although perhaps it is what I deserve. I only thought to be near you, in whatever way I could. I have no right to question how it happens. You look so…so real."

Tears spilled out of her eyes and over her cheeks, blurring his form. As if in a trance, she rose from the chair and reached out to touch him, certain her hand would find nothing but air. Shockingly, she encountered cold, wet flesh. Still believing him an apparition, she leaned against the hard, muscular length of the specter, her hand rose to cradle the back of his head and urge his head forward to bring his lips to hers.

Cold, rigid lips moved against hers. Was this the kiss of an apparition? How was it possible she felt the warmth of his tongue pressing against hers? She decided not to care. If this was how death kissed, she welcomed it. At first, the kiss was uncertain, exploring her as if he'd never tasted her before. Then he was hungry, arousing while consuming. The kiss stirred all her nerve endings, overwhelming her, pushing her toward oblivion.

She fainted in the arms of the ghost.

***

Sam eased her way out of the darkness, gradually becoming aware her ghost lover was struggling to put her arm in the sleeve of a nightdress. Fleetingly, she wondered how it was possible a ghost could be comprised of enough matter to feel real—then reason made her doubt her perception, and she tried to push the specter away. "I'm not in my right mind. How can you be here?"

"Stop it, Sam. Be still," Jackson commanded, his words sounding harsher than he intended.

Shocked, Sam obeyed.

After threading her arms through the gown's sleeves, he gently eased her back against the pillow. Then he deftly caught the nightdress hem with his hands and tugged it down past her waist and hips. They both were shivering with cold. He piled blankets on top of her and shook his head in wonder. "You think I'm a ghost, Sam?"

She watched him strip off his wet clothes, put out the lantern flame, and slide under the covers next to her. She didn't answer his question.

"Ghosts don't kiss like I kissed you or shiver from cold like I'm shivering now," he said, gently pulling her closer and molding her arms and legs to fit the haven of his body.

Sam didn't resist, but she wasn't exactly pliant either.

"Don't worry, darlin', I didn't mean to kiss you like I did. I swear it wouldn't have gone any further, and I promise it won't now. I'm only trying to warm you up—and you're doing the same for me—although I admit some of my parts are warming more than others."

Seeing no change in her demeanor or appreciation of his joke, he decided he'd better change the subject. "Does Morgan know where you are?"

"I left him a note. I didn't want him to worry." Sam could hardly believe it was her voice answering.

"Good. I closed the front door and locked it. I also extinguished all the lamps. What in God's name were you doing in here, Sam?"

"Jackson, is it you?" she whispered, still not fully convinced.

Christ! She *had* believed he was a ghost! He pulled her closer and brushed his lips across hers before answering. "Yes, it's me, Sam."

She felt his warm breath on the curve of her neck before he kissed the hollow of her throat. "But I saw Parker come home, and you weren't with him. I knew you—I mean— that's why I came here. At first, I thought I wanted to come because I'd feel your presence and it would bring me comfort. But then I began to imagine someone was here, and I lacked the courage to deal with it. I told myself I'd rest for a few minutes before I went into our room. When I woke and saw you standing there, I thought—I mean—" She couldn't say the words. A sob caught in her throat.

Jackson whispered tenderly, "I understand. It's all right, darlin'. I'm here. Go to sleep now."

Trusting him, she let her softness melt against him, and they fell asleep soon after.

***

Jackson awoke abruptly. Sam was pushing him away and shouting. "No! Stop! Oh, God in heaven, please stop!" A fierce look came upon her face, and she raised her fists.

Jackson deftly captured her wrists in one strong grip and, as gently as possible, pinioned her arms above her head. With his free hand, he lightly shook her shoulder. In response, Sam struggled even more wildly, almost breaking free of his hold.

Jackson was surprised. He'd believed she was over this nightmare. When they were first together, she'd wake from it at least once a week, but, gradually, they'd tapered off. He couldn't recall her having one for six months or more.

Worried she'd injure herself or that his efforts to restrain her could do just as much or more damage, he cautiously allowed more of his weight to settle on her and tightened his hold to immobilize her arms. He shook her shoulder with a little more force than before and called her name. "Sam. Sam, darlin', it's only a nightmare."

Before Sam's eyes flew open, her head moved from side to side as if she were denying something. When her gaze settled on Jackson's face, she stopped struggling, though her breathing remained labored. Weakly she turned from him. "I—I was dreaming—Is it morning?"

"Hell, it was almost morning when we went to bed, Sam," Jackson scoffed. "We've only slept a few hours."

"Then can we go back to sleep, or did you want to watch the sun come up?" she asked playfully. When he saw the faint smile on her lips, he let himself fall back against his pillow and drawled, "There's other scenery I could appreciate more, but I don't think you're up to it, so I vote we sleep."

Sam started to shift away, but he caught her hand and laid it on his bare chest before covering it with his. Silently, he warned himself about his impatience. Sam was uncertain—she felt something for him, but she was a woman who needed to know why she felt things.

"Sam, don't look like that. We're together and that's all that matters for now. Nothing needs to happen between us unless you want it to."

Sam pulled her hand from his grasp so she could rise to study his face. A moment later, she reached for his hand and brought it to her lips. Then she rested against him.

"And while you wait for me, Jackson, will you keep the demons out of my dreams?"

Jackson wrapped one of his arms protectively around her waist. "I may not be able to keep them away, but I promise, should they come, I'll chase them away for you."

She laughed softly and whispered, "Forever my knight-errant."

"Sam?"

"Yes, Jackson?"

"Could I be your knight in shining armor instead?"

Sam yawned and smiled. "You already are."

Chapter 13

Late in the afternoon, Ryder and Mac jumped down from the buggy that had pulled up in front of the main house. Sam leaned against the porch post with one arm extended near her head, while the other was bent at the elbow resting on the butt of her holstered Colt.

Standing inside the open door, Jackson watched Sam. Though she appeared relaxed, he knew she was keyed up, wound tighter than a coiled spring. Just then, Becky dashed past him and down the porch steps to fling herself into the arms of the fine-boned, five-foot-five, slender woman Mac had lifted from the buggy.

In her early fifties, Grace Garner Stone still resembled the angel that Sam mistook her for when she first saw her standing in front of the Golden Crown gambling palace— only Sam didn't remember that. Grace possessed an ethereal beauty that made her appear youthful, delicate, and benevolent. If any gray existed in her hair, her natural pale blonde color hid it.

As Grace's arms wrapped around Becky in a warm hug, Jackson heard Sam make a soft sound of distress. She wrapped an arm around the post as if she needed to put a barrier between herself and the visitors. Parker, Morgan, and Ryder were watching Becky and Grace, so they didn't notice.

Mac's gaze, however, had sought Sam's after helping Grace alight from the buggy. He didn't like what he saw.

Sam's eyes were wide and unfocused, her posture stiff. While he watched, she bowed her head, turned, and stumbled past Jackson into the house.

In the hallway, Sam looked to her left and right before letting her eyes travel up the stairs. Without thinking, she started up, wanting only to reach a place where she could put a door between her and everyone else. She heard Jackson behind her and felt his hand brush her shoulder. "Let me go, Jackson, I need to get away," she implored.

Jackson dropped his hand, but followed her, ready to catch her should she lose her footing. Upon reaching the top, she hurried to the room she'd been in before moving downstairs to the study and quietly closed the door behind her.

Uncertain whether to enter, Jackson stood in the hallway eyeing the closed door. Then he heard the lock click and the glide of Sam's clothing brushing against wood as she slid to the floor.

When Mac saw Sam turn and rush away, he double timed it to the house. After he stepped over the threshold, he heard Sam tell Jackson to let her go. Then he watched her enter the room and close the door. A moment later, he called to Jackson from the foot of the stairs, "Come down, Son. It's the best thing for now. When she comes out, let me tend her—I reckon it will be a while, though."

***

Sam sat on the floor with her eyes closed and her head resting against the door trying to make sense of the memory she'd experienced while watching Grace and Becky embrace. The memory was different from the others she'd experienced, though it was no less vivid.

Sam saw herself as a very young child walking with a man who must have been her father. Suddenly she broke free of his hand and darted across the street to capture the lavender silk folds of a dress worn by what appeared to her to be an angel. With fabric scrunched in her tiny hand, she tilted her head up to gaze into the angel's blue eyes. The angel smiled as if she'd just discovered a wondrous treasure and lifted Sam in her arms and hugged her.

Delighted, Sam's arms circled Grace's neck and she snuggled her head against Grace's breast. "You're the angel Mama sent for me."

Laughing, Grace patted her back and kissed the top of her head. And when Sam looked up, Grace was staring into her papa's eyes like they were the only two people in the world.

After that, the memory dissolved into another. She was a little older, sitting in a parlor, next to a handsome older boy. Morgan—it had to have been Morgan. They were smiling as they watched Sam's father pull Grace into his arms and softly sing, "'Amazing Grace, how sweet the sound, that saved a wretch like me. I once was lost but now I'm found, was blind, but now I see.'" Then her papa kissed Grace.

Now, recalling the memory, Sam whispered what she remembered of the hymn, "''Twas grace that taught my heart to feel. And grace, my fears relieved. How precious did that grace appear, the hour I first believed.'"

Sam cried then—for what, she wasn't certain. Maybe her tears were for the kindness and love emanating from Grace; maybe for her father who was gone from her life; maybe for the sweetness and intensity of the love she and Morgan had witnessed between her father and Grace; or, maybe because she couldn't remember anymore.

Then Sam sat in the quiet peace of the bedroom, grateful for the memories, while she mourned deeply having no others.

***

Over brandy in the study, Parker, Morgan, and Jackson explained to Ryder, Grace, and Mac what had taken place since the crash, including the dead pig, drugged tea, and Parker's ride to bring Jackson home before he reached Cheyenne.

Parker mentioned Sam had been asleep when he came home after midnight. Knowing Jackson would go to her when he arrived, he'd decided not to wake her.

Jackson interrupted, "That's not what happened, Parker. She left a note and went to our house during that storm. She's worried half to death, not about herself, but about endangering us. She's not the self-assured Sam we're used to dealing with. When I crested the hill, about two hours after you arrived home, I saw half the lamps in our house were lit. The front door was wide open.

"I put my horse in the barn before I went to investigate. I found Sam, muddy and soaked to the bone, huddled in the wing chair in the office. She was in some sort of half-dream state. When she saw me standing in front of her, she thought I was a ghost who came to punish her and fainted. It makes me shiver to remember how she looked and acted.

"Early this morning, she had the old nightmare about the man hurting her. She hasn't had that dream for a long time, and this one was intense. She was fighting and begging him to stop. Then today, when she looked at Grace and made her way up those stairs—I just don't know—I think she remembered something, but I don't know what."

***

Supper was over, and Mac and Jackson sat in the dining room listening for signs of Sam coming downstairs. When they heard the bedroom door open, both men stood.

"Don't let her do the stairs by herself, Mac—and get her to eat something if you can. I'll wait in the study."

Mac nodded. A moment later, when he moved to the foot of the stairs, Sam was poised at the top watching Jackson cross to the study. Then her gaze flicked to him before slowly raking over each and every tread of the staircase. Given what Jackson had told him about her vertigo, Mac surmised navigating the steps must seem a formidable challenge. As she stood there, hesitating to start down, Mac half-expected her to retreat to the bedroom from which she'd finally emerged.

Making a quick decision, he began mounting the steps—and Sam surprised him by taking a step back—something totally outside her nature. His girl didn't back away from anyone.

When he reached her, he offered his arm. "May I escort you downstairs, Sam?" he asked, knowing his proud, independent daughter wouldn't ask for help.

Their eyes connected and several seconds passed before she took his arm. "Thank you," she murmured, gripping the banister with her other hand and taking the first step down. "You're Mac."

Mac felt her sway but pretended not to notice. "Yes," he answered simply.

In silence, they traveled down several steps, Mac allowing Sam to set the pace. Sam stopped and looked up at him. "You were my father's friend and helped raise me." It wasn't phrased as a question. "Morgan told me. He said you watched over me and protected me—taught me to ride and shoot."

Mac nodded. He could see she was struggling for words. Her eyes dropped to his hands. Finally, she managed to say, "I don't remember you. Jackson and the others must have told you my memory is gone."

Mac patted her hand. "Yes, sweetheart, I know. They told me, and it's all right."

Sam raised her head and grasped his arm more firmly, ready to resume their descent to the hallway. When they reached the last step, without meeting his eyes, she asked, "Will you tell me about my father?"

"I'll make you a deal, sweetheart. If you'll accompany me to the kitchen and allow me to keep you company while you eat supper, I'll tell you anything you want to know."

Sam gave him a solemn nod and headed for the kitchen. He was surprised she still clung to his arm.

JB wasn't in the kitchen. Mac held a chair for Sam to seat her at the table. Then he removed his jacket and rolled up his shirtsleeves. "We don't need JB, sweetheart. I'll scramble you some eggs the way you like 'em with bits of ham, and you'll have a meal fit for a queen."

Pouring her a glass of milk, he continued, "You just start on this here milk. While I work, you can begin asking away—or would you rather I just tell you as I recollect it?"

Without waiting for an answer, Mac began, "My full name is Matthew Andrew Covington. 'Mac' is from my initials, but most people don't know that. When I met your father, Chase, I'd been traveling from town to town earning my living as a gunman. I wasn't famous, like a lot of 'em— not because I wasn't just as good. I'm not bragging when I say that I was the fastest and most accurate gunman roaming the Arizona, Nevada, and Wyoming Territories in those days, but I was smart enough to downplay my reputation and stay out of the public eye, newspapers, and dime novels." Mac looked up from the skillet he was tending and winked at Sam. She'd finished her milk. Mac nonchalantly refilled her glass as he resumed his narrative.

"Now, a famous gunman, like Ben Thompson, for instance," Mac commented, "who was said to be the fastest shot in the West, partly because he shot the gun out of several opponents' hands, was partial to dressing in tailor-made duds and flaunting his success. When he drank, he'd shoot out lights in saloons and the streets! Not me, though. I'd keep to myself and draw no attention to my skills. I lived modestly, saving my fees and drifting on when a job was done. I didn't figure it was healthy for a gunman to take up residence nor was a gunman encouraged to stay by permanent residents. I never used my skills to earn money illegally, and I always chose my employers and jobs carefully."

Sam lifted the glass and took a swallow of milk, her eyes riveted on Mac.

"While travelin' around the area established as the Arizona Territory, I got a hankering for some downtime indulging one of my few vices, playing poker. During one rare gaming occasion, I met a young man I found favorably dispositioned. Your father was a green kid. In lots of ways, though, he was old beyond his years. In others, I'm here to testify, he didn't know much about anything that would keep him alive. Something about his determination and intelligence struck a chord in me. I could tell he was from the East and running from something. In my line of business, if a man isn't a good judge of men and situations, he doesn't survive long in the profession. My ability to size men up, determine their nerve, and judge their skill kept me employed and alive."

Mac sighed. "The truth was I was sick of the profession. I once had a wife, boy, and ranch of my own, but they were gone. I was about done being mad about it, so I sort of adopted your papa and taught him everything worth knowing about how to use and take care of a gun. Your father was a special man, and I loved him as a son. When Chase and I drifted to Highbreeze, we both reckoned it was the right place for us." Mac smiled at the remembrance.

"Your grandfather was a self-made man. He'd built Highbreeze into one of the wealthiest ranches I'd ever seen. He had no sons. But it didn't concern him, because he'd been blessed with an exceptional daughter, Mary Ann, your mother. She was smart, pretty, and sweeter than any woman has a right to be. Well, your grandfather, ol' Daniel, took to Chase right away and saw a son in him, just as I had. Daniel was good to me, too. He never asked where I was from or what I'd done before I came to Highbreeze with Chase. He sized me up, though. I would've told him anything he wanted to know, but no, the man never asked. I had enormous respect for that man." Mac's head nodded to emphasize his approval of Sam's grandfather.

A half-smile touched Mac's lips. "Well, of course, what man wouldn't fall in love with Mary Ann—but just any man wasn't good enough for her. She said it was Chase she wanted and Chase she'd have. Your papa only pretended to resist a little in the beginning. Truth was, he was smitten the first time he saw her. We had some good years together, living, you might say, like in some of those fairy tales I read you when you were a little girl, *happily ever after*."

He paused before he continued. "The third year of their marriage, our luck changed. Life has a way of doing that to you. The trick is not allowing the lows to overshadow the highs. First, your grandfather died of what must have been a heart ailment. There wasn't any warning. He went to bed one night and didn't wake up in the morning. Your mother and father inherited the ranch. Mostly, they lived modestly, continuing to raise beef cattle and horses. With their wealth, they would've been able to hire overseers and live high on the hog, except that wasn't the way they wanted to live."

Mac directed his gaze at Sam. "You were born soon after, but your mother died in childbirth. Your father was devastated. I was worried he wouldn't come through it, but he found comfort in you. You were easy to love. He would have had to have no heart at all to be able to deny your adoration. Your papa was the sun in your sky. You have his hair color and solemn gray-blue eyes. Like him, you rarely blink. You just look at a man until he loses his nerve or confesses everything he knows. It's the damnedest thing I ever did watch—even worked on me a time or two," he admitted, chuckling.

By this time, Mac was sitting across the table from Sam watching her eat the eggs he'd fixed her. He doubted she tasted what she ate.

"Your father was always worried about an uncle in Chicago—that's who he ran away from. According to Chase, his uncle was twisted 'bout a whole lot of things, including young girls—if you take my meaning. Your father was terribly afraid for you, Sam. He told me he needed me to look after you extra special. When you were grown enough, I was to teach you how to shoot and defend yourself. Later, after he married Grace, he said the same for Morgan. It was you, Sam, that caused Chase to meet Grace."

Tears welled in Sam's eyes. "I remembered that today, Mac—that's why I went upstairs. I needed to—to think about it, I guess."

Mac's hand covered one of Sam's. "I figured as much, sweetheart. You always have been one who needed to study on things. I saw something triggered when you watched Grace hug Becky. From the first time you saw Grace, you loved her. You two have a special bond, maybe because you have similar spirits in a time when women are told what to do and how. You and Grace defy convention. Like you, Grace does what she wants with little regard for what people think of her. Yet, she always conducts herself as a lady. She's not a woman who resorts to flirtatious mannerisms. To this day, few men can resist her wit and charm. Some men make the mistake of underestimating her business acumen. They pay dearly for it."

Mac rubbed his jaw thoughtfully. "After Chase's passing, you and Grace depended on me to manage Highbreeze. Even if you hadn't needed me for Highbreeze, I would've stayed because I couldn't leave you. Besides, I promised your father I would always keep you safe." He gazed past her as if looking into the past.

"I taught you and Morgan everything I knew, just as I did your father. Morgan was a fine boy, and I knew he'd grow up to be a fine man. Although he was older than you were, he treated you special and cared for you. You and Morgan can do any job a ranch hand can, from cowhand, drover, or calf brander. You know how to pull your weight. When it came to shootin', you were the most natural marksman I ever saw—doesn't matter whether you shoot a six-gun, derringer, or rifle. You're fast too. A person can hardly see you draw." Mac chuckled. "Morgan and Jackson have to work some to keep up.

"I made sure you learned survival skills too, like camping in open country, tracking, and hunting for food. You took to riding as if you were a part of the horse. You were fearless and already able to burn the breeze fast enough to threaten the ranch's top hand by the time you were ten."

Mac's forehead wrinkled, and his voice lowered, giving weight to the seriousness of his next words. "I was always careful to hire men known for their loyalty to the brand and its owners. Any one of them would have laid his life down for you, Morgan, or Grace. When you were older, sweetheart, and began to understand the special vulnerabilities of being a woman—especially when you weren't wearing your gun, I got you that pepperbox derringer and shoulder harness and taught you to use it." Mac's voice trailed off and he became lost in some reflection. He shook his head regretfully before looking at Sam with love in his eyes. "I should have done that earlier, Sam. That's a sorrow I'll always have."

"What do you mean, Mac?"

"That's another story for another day. It's late and Grace will be upstairs wanting to know from me what we've been jawing about all this time. She won't go to sleep until I tell her you'll be all right. Besides, Jackson's waiting for you in the study. I'm happy to see you figured out he's as important to you as the air you breathe. You're a matched pair—that's a certainty. Now, run along to him."

Chapter 14

Though the sun wasn't up, Sam was awake, her backside resting against Jackson's big—and naked—body in their four-poster bed, mulling over the things she'd learned from Mac.

"Go back to sleep, darlin'," Jackson murmured, as he pulled her closer.

"I need to talk to Doc Baxter," Sam replied without considering how he would interpret her remark.

Jackson sprang up, tossed back the covers, and began searching for signs of injury. Seeing none, he put his hand to her forehead to check for a fever.

Sam impatiently batted his hand away.

"I said I need to *talk* to Doc Baxter. I'm not hurt, at least not any more than I was when I went to bed last night. I've been thinking about something Mac said—I need to ask Doc some questions before I talk to Grace and Mac."

Sam perched on her elbow. Jackson had stripped down last night before getting into bed, just like the night before. She hadn't watched him, but she'd heard him, and when he'd cuddled with her, she sure as hell heated up over it. He had a lean, muscular body. She especially liked the width of his shoulders and the…

Damn. She brought her eyes up to his face and felt herself blush when she realized he was watching her look at him. She jerked the bed covers up over them. He laughed before lifting her to lie on his chest. "Jackson, seriously, I need to ask you some things—about us." She felt him tense.

"I need you to tell me how it—went—between us—"

Jackson tilted her head up to see her face. "Darlin', do you want to know how it was you came to let me love you?"

Sam nodded. "Yes—but I want to know more than that."

Jackson put her away from him and sat up.

Sam gathered her courage. "Was I—experienced?"

Jackson didn't want to tell her. "How do you know we've gone that far?"

While she wasn't ready to admit her knowledge of her responses to his caresses in her first memory, she saw no reason to pretend she was ignorant of what their physical experience must have been.

"Jackson, my feelings for you are strong. I don't believe there's any way we didn't take it that far. Morgan told me you openly stay here with me—we don't hide it from anyone. Besides, you aren't embarrassed to come to bed as—as you are now. Although, I concede you don't seem to expect me to do the same."

It was Jackson's turn to blush. "To tell you the truth, I didn't think about it the other night—if I had, I wouldn't have done it. Finding you as I did, with you thinking I was a ghost and us both being wet and cold, shut down my sensibilities for judging what's proper and how you'd feel about it. I didn't do it deliberately. Then, last night, I thought it would be better to act natural rather than pretend it hadn't happened once before."

Sam raised an eyebrow and smiled coyly. "Jackson, I only mentioned it as part of my reasoning to explain why I thought we'd taken it to that level. I'm *not complaining about the scenery*. Now will you answer my question?"

"All right. I'd say you weren't experienced."

Something about his phrasing said something different. "Jackson, I wasn't a virgin, was I?" Sam pressed.

Jackson looked as though he'd rather be shot than answer. "Please tell me. I don't want to hear it from Doc. I wasn't a virgin when I came to you, was I?"

Jackson slid his hands up her arms to grasp her elbows. "If you were to ask Doc, he'd tell you some pervert hurt you when you were a young woman, around about thirteen." Then consolingly he added, "I told the truth when I said you weren't experienced. You'd never been with a man willingly. All you knew about it was fear and pain. From what you told me, you didn't even remember everything that happened to you. That's what the nightmares are about."

Sam let Jackson pull her onto his lap. "You were patient with me," she said, working it out—intuitively understanding. "That's why you're patient with me now."

Jackson kissed her neck, but she wouldn't let herself be distracted.

"Is that one of the reasons we're not married?"

Jackson ignored the question, preferring to let his lips travel to her mouth while his hand brushed the curve of her breast. "I'm not feeling very patient right now, Sam."

"I know, Jackson," Sam said, refusing to let him dodge the question. "I'm sitting in your lap. I can feel your— impatience—growing."

Jackson's hand moved to her rib cage before gliding to her bottom and giving it a gentle squeeze. "I can wait some more, Sam, but not if I don't put you aside for now."

Obligingly, Sam wiggled off his lap. Groaning in frustration, Jackson collapsed against his pillow, then tugged her arm to urge her to lie down next to him.

"You didn't answer me. Is it one of the reasons we're not married?"

"You can be heartless, darlin'."

"Jackson, I need to know."

"We're not married because, like a lovesick schoolboy, I haven't pushed you. You asked me to back off, so I did. The truth is I'm too damn soft with you. I thought if I gave you enough space, you'd come around to the idea and say yes. And for the record, this is the kindest way I can explain it without sounding like a riled-up grizzly bear."

Jackson expected a denial of some sort—seconds ticked by—nothing. He turned sideways to look at Sam. She was staring at the ceiling.

"Well, aren't you going to say anything?"

"What am I supposed to say, Jackson? You wouldn't lie about this, and you certainly have a right to express your feelings. I must assume what you say has some validity—at least from your perspective. I'm wondering, though, if you know what my perspective is. Did I give you reasons?"

Jackson managed to get out a long, slow, "Yesss," which he quickly followed with, "But for a person that can be more logical than a lawyer, I gotta say your reasons don't hold much water."

Sam couldn't help but smile. "I see. Would you mind elucidating?"

"You want details?"

"Yes. Would you please explain what my objections are? As you know, I don't remember."

Sam heard him mutter, "Maybe I shouldn't tell you so you won't have them anymore."

Sam laughed. "How old are you, Jackson?"

"Twenty-eight, which is old enough to know better than to have this conversation with you when I can't love on you."

Sam laughed again. "You could kiss me while we're having this conversation."

Jackson growled, "No I can't, because all my logic would move to another place in my body."

Struggling not to let amusement show in her voice, Sam replied, "I see." Then she waited, sensing he needed time to find the words.

"You said you wouldn't marry me because you're bad luck. You said powerful men resent a rich woman who does what she wants and refuses to bow to them. You said you were afraid a few of them would use me to get revenge for your treating them like idiots. You said a couple of others tried to maneuver you into marrying their sons, and you weren't kind turning them down. You said marrying you would put a target on my back—as if I can't take care of myself, Sam. I'm a self-made man with assets, too. How do you know some rich widow that I rejected wouldn't want to do the same to you if we married? You also said—oh, never mind, Sam. This is pointless. Marry me or don't, I'll take you any way you'll love me. Do you have more questions?"

"Will Doc have anything else to tell me?"

"Aw, Sam," Jackson groaned.

Sam's voice lowered to a whispered plea. "Please, Jackson. It will be easier for me to hear it from you."

"You can't have children because of how you were hurt."

Sam let out her breath. "Is Doc sure about that?"

Jackson nodded. "I'm sorry, darlin'," he replied, his voice soft with compassion. "He's sure. Ask Grace. The way I put it together, she took you to specialists in Chicago after it happened."

"Is that one of the reasons I said I wouldn't marry you?"

"Yes, Sam. Sometimes I think it is the only reason—I think you refuse to believe it doesn't matter to me."

"I don't need to talk to Doc now, but I do have a few more questions for Grace and Mac."

Sam was quiet for a time before deciding to broach one more subject. "Jackson?"

"What now, Sam?"

"I just want to say I'm sure you're the only man in this world I could love—and would you please answer one more little question?"

Jackson sighed.

"Do you think you could kiss me now?"

Chapter 15

From the shelter of her front porch, Sam was deep in reverie, studying the hillside where her brother and Parker had buried the pig.

Jackson had left soon after their talk, saying he needed to tend to some things. Sam thought he'd gone because he was finding it increasingly difficult to keep his feelings and need for her in check. With sudden clarity, she understood that her memory loss was perhaps even more difficult for him to accept than for her. Based on feelings and a tantalizing bit of memory, she knew she was in love with Jackson. But Jackson's love wasn't based only on feelings; it was rooted in and strengthened by his memories of their experiences together. Her memory loss must have collapsed his familiar world just as surely as it had voided hers—Jackson knew for a certainty *exactly* what she'd taken from him.

Sam leaned her head against a porch post. He must be feeling hurt and confusion different from hers. She wondered if she had it within her to replace what had vanished. Could he be patient enough to give them a chance to build another world together? She was sure of her love, but not of her ability to show it or to make a world where he wouldn't care about what she took from him.

Blast it, *she* didn't take it from him—*someone* stole it. Anger consumed her. She needed to punish something. Her gaze fell to the porch railing, where a pot full of withered marigolds sat. Snatching it up, she stepped from the porch, raised it over her head, and hurled it to smash against the slate walkway in front of the house. The sound wasn't as satisfying as she'd hoped. She looked around for something else. That's when she saw Grace standing to the side of the porch watching her.

***

While traversing the path between Sam's house and the barn, Grace had been studying her daughter's profile. It told her all she needed to know about the fragile state of Sam's mind.

Grace was certain Sam was nearly overcome with sadness and anger. At times like this, she tended to feel alone in the world because her independence and confidence were undermined by hurt and injustice. Her inability to restore order and control things, for which no person has control, impelled her to castigate herself for not trying harder to prevent the unpreventable. When in that frame of mind, she couldn't accept that sometimes fate was just fate—and there was no such thing as control.

Grace sighed. She understood Sam's sadness, as well as her anger and frustration. She'd experienced things in her life that had caused her to rail at God's door. Had it been possible, she would have pounded her fists on his chest. In the end, God always showed her compassion and gave her something to replace what he'd taken. Grace had to trust he'd do the same for her daughter.

Grace was from an old, established Virginia family that had fallen on hard times because of her grandfather and father's mismanagement. Though neither of them had been interested in managing their family's assets, her father did possess the talent, charm, and considerable knowledge required for running a successful gaming business, thus enabling his family to retain a modicum of social status and enjoy certain essential elements of gracious Southern living, such as a comfortable home, servants, elegant clothes, and education. In short, they "kept up appearances."

At sixteen, Grace had the head, nerve, and skill to partner with her father in his enterprises. He taught her to play cards, run the roulette wheel, and deal faro. She'd a mind for numbers. Without trying, she could at any moment tell you the number of aces, royals, and face cards remaining in a twenty-one or poker deck. She could also recite the pocket number for the last twenty spins on a roulette wheel.

When her father passed away, Grace continued the business on her own, despite ruminations from her impractical mother about the unsuitability of such a profession. Grace paid her mother no attention. The "profession" paid the bills, and Grace enjoyed it. Never had she thought of herself as a traditional woman. When her mother passed away and a successful, professional gambler approached her about buying into the business, Grace considered his offer.

Drake Garner was handsome, charming, educated, and rich. He didn't need a business partner. He needed Grace. Her beauty, talent, and independence fascinated him. Grace knew from the beginning he intended to marry her. At twenty-one, she became Mrs. Drake Garner. When she was twenty-two, Morgan was born.

Drake was a devoted husband, and she loved him. He was also a good father, although he was frequently away on business, promoting and participating in high-stake games on Mississippi riverboats. When Morgan was only five, Drake was killed in a riverboat accident. Widowed, Grace had no family ties except for her young son.

Drake's death was the first time Grace railed at God— and what did God do? He told her to find a decent town in which to open an elegant, quality gaming establishment and raise her son. She had money from her enterprise and money from Drake, so she sold her business, moved to Eden Ridge with Morgan, and opened the Golden Crown. Then God gave her Chase Stone and his daughter, Sam.

Setting her thoughts aside, Grace realized Sam was looking past her to the corral fence by the barn, where Jackson, Ryder, and Mac were perched.

In a detached tone, with her gaze pinned on the men at the corral, Sam asked, "Did Mac tell you I ran upstairs yesterday because I remembered something about you and my father?"

Grace didn't answer. Instead, she waited for Sam to focus on her. When Sam's gaze finally connected with Grace's, Grace held out her arms.

Slowly, Sam moved into them. Mother and daughter stood entwined, drawing strength and comfort from each other.

Grace felt her daughter's body relax as her anger and uncertainty receded. A soothing sense of peace wrapped around them.

As it turned out, Grace did have the ability to ease pain in a person's soul.

***

A short while later, watching Sam rummage through her kitchen pantry for the makings of tea or coffee, Grace asked, "Daughter, have you stopped to consider whether you know how to light the stove? Though you can run a gaming salon, ranch, and business empire, you've never bothered to learn your way around a kitchen."

Just then, Sam found an unopened tin of tea—the same brand someone had drugged. Puzzled, she pried open the lid and sniffed. It smelled less pungent, different from the tea she'd consumed after the crash. Without comment, she put it back on the shelf and went to stand in front of the stove. When she turned to her mother, she was grinning. "You're right, Grace. I don't have a clue!"

Grace laughed and shook her head. "Don't look at me, Daughter. I know nothing about it." Then she took Sam's hand and led her to the office.

While Grace filled two glasses with brandy from a decanter sitting on a sideboard near the double doors leading into the office, Sam sat in the same chair where "Jackson's ghost" had appeared the night he returned. Grace placed the decanter on the desk, took the chair next to Sam's, and passed her a glass.

Sam chuckled. "I haven't even had breakfast yet, Grace."

Unperturbed, Grace responded, "Well, this is the only sort of breakfast your mother knows how to 'rustle up.'"

Sam grinned. "Judging by my ignorance of how to light the stove, I assume you taught me the same culinary skills. I congratulate you on your choice of cuisine, Madame, and thank you from the bottom of my heart for passing on your expertise." The women clinked glasses and took small appreciative sips.

"You always were a quick study, Sam. I must say this is a fine choice in brandy."

"Thank you. After I finish this glass for breakfast, I may enjoy a second for my dinner."

After another sip, Grace ventured, "Would you tell me what you remembered about me and your father?"

"Morgan and I watched Papa put his arms around you and tease you by singing the first lines of 'Amazing Grace.' Then he kissed you."

Grace's expression turned tender with the memory.

"I recalled the second verse and recognized how like the lyrics you are. I sense you can lessen fear and open hearts to feel the wonders of the world. Now that I'm with you, I understand the reason that Morgan and I call you Grace instead of Mother is because you are grace—and you make us all believe."

"Child, you have the soul of a romantic buried in that enigmatic exterior of yours. You remind me of your father."

Sam sobered. "Morgan and I read through the papers you gave me when I came of legal age. Morgan and Mac said my father wanted to protect me from Great-Uncle Aaron. Is that why Father made that deal with him about the family inheritance?"

Grace nodded. "Your great-uncle, Aaron Edward Stone, was a dangerous man."

Sam was surprised. "Was?"

"Yes, he died about six months ago. The family estate and business enterprises are now yours."

"But Morgan doesn't know that. He would've told me while we were looking at the papers."

Grace nodded again. "You're right. I don't believe you've told him."

"Why?"

Grace hesitated. "Let me go further back and end with that. You see, your great-uncle Aaron engineered your father's parents' deaths, but your father couldn't prove it. He was only fifteen when they died, and Aaron became his guardian. Chase knew it was only a matter of time before his uncle would arrange his death. Aaron Stone was a greedy, vile man. His main purpose for living was to satisfy his appetite for young females. Chase told me he took young girls in under the guise of being their ward.

"Chase escaped his uncle when he was seventeen. He thought it better to give up his inheritance rather than die claiming it. Soon after your birth, Chase discovered Aaron knew where he was, of his success, and, even worse, about you. Chase didn't underestimate Aaron's ruthlessness or his debauchery. He knew he needed to protect you should anything happen to him. He was more fearful of his uncle's twisted need to satisfy his appetite for young, innocent woman than he was of his greed. You were your father's most treasured possession, and he wouldn't risk losing you."

Grace sighed before continuing, "You see, Aaron always expected Chase to return. He couldn't conceive anyone would willingly give up a fortune. As your father's guardian, Aaron lived in the family home and enjoyed a comfortable life and income. Fearful of your father's return, Aaron hired detectives to keep track of him. He would've killed Chase if he'd dared return to Chicago. When he learned Chase had married a rich rancher's daughter, inherited the ranch, and had a daughter of his own, Aaron recognized an opportunity to profit. If your father died, Aaron could have become your guardian and stolen your inheritance, Highbreeze, and everything else."

Grace took a sip of brandy. "Your father hired detectives to find and document proof of Aaron's mismanagement of his inheritance and his carnal mistreatment of the young wards put under his protection. Your father told me it wasn't difficult because Aaron hadn't bothered to cover things up. The women didn't have relatives to question or protest Aaron's guardianship, and the lawyers overseeing the estate didn't much care. They did care about their fees, though they did little work to earn them."

Grace laid her hand comfortingly on Sam's arm. "Your father confronted Aaron and offered him a deal he couldn't refuse. Essentially, Chase proposed transferring the estate and the other assets of his inheritance to Aaron, but only if

Aaron didn't interfere with Chase or with you. Your father even guaranteed that, should anything happen to him, Aaron would continue to live in the residence and receive income from certain investments for the rest of his life. Again, the only stipulation was that Aaron must not meet, communicate, or interfere with you, especially not contest or fight for your custody."

Sam felt Grace's hand on her arm tighten.

"Your father gave Aaron copies of the evidence his detectives compiled and told him that he put the two other packets containing the same evidence of his crimes and sexual deviance in the safekeeping of two unnamed trustees. He made it clear should Aaron violate the conditions of the agreement, the estate and income would revert to you. In addition, his lawyer and the two trustees in possession of the envelopes had instructions to use the evidence to expose and prosecute Aaron. Your father also told him Mac would kill him."

Grace's hand slid down to grasp Sam's wrist. Sam doubted she was aware of it.

"Though Aaron died more than six months ago, it took almost three months for the lawyers to go through the papers and inform you. I assume they collected larger fees by taking their time. When you received the news, you weren't without knowledge of this situation, but you hadn't focused on it. Why should you? Aaron didn't bother us. Consequently, we didn't waste much time thinking about the bargain your father made with him. You had mixed feelings about what to do. You visited me in Eden Ridge, and we had a conversation like the one we're having now. Much like your father, your first thought was to let the whole thing go—liquidate it and donate it to charity, feeling anything connected with Aaron was tainted. It was nothing you needed."

Grace released Sam's wrist. "Then you thought better of it, saying your father would have expected you to be responsible and visit the estate, if for no other reason than to preserve a few family keepsakes and learn more about your heritage. You decided to go to Chicago to settle the estate personally, knowing the lawyers would only deal with you, not a third party. Because you didn't know the true situation, you didn't think it necessary to inform Morgan. At the time, he was busy brokering the Jamison distillery deal in New York. Jackson was in San Francisco with Parker, so you traveled to Chicago on your own. That was less than two months ago. You stayed for ten days. Becky told me about the beautiful blue dress you bought her there for her birthday."

"Did I tell you anything about what I learned, Grace? Could anything be connected to what's happening now?"

"No, you didn't, sweetheart. As I said, Aaron was an evil man, but if he's dead, how could he be responsible for the crash or drugged tea?"

"What if he isn't dead? Perhaps news of his death was a way to lure me to Chicago or to lull me into complacency so he could have me killed, except that doesn't make sense. Did he have children?"

"I employed the agency that did the investigation for your father to continue to monitor Aaron's activities after Chase was killed. Mac and I thought it prudent to make sure he wasn't planning anything. According to the reports we received, Aaron never married."

Grace added, "I haven't been with you since you came to Eden Ridge to discuss your inheritance with me, Sam, so I don't know what you discovered in Chicago. I assumed it wasn't anything of real importance. I wasn't curious about it. Since you weren't upset, I was content to let it be. I did see Morgan a few weeks ago and noticed he didn't say anything about it. I thought it a little odd you hadn't mentioned it to him, but then you're all busy. How could you possibly keep up with everything? You have a reason for almost everything you do, Sam. I didn't give it any more thought." Grace shrugged and took another sip of brandy.

At that moment, Becky burst through the front door and headed straight for the office. "Daddy said to come and get you. Dinner is ready."

Grace demurely rose from her chair and waited for Sam to rise. Studying her almost empty glass, Sam realized she'd not only consumed breakfast and dinner but also supper. Three glasses of brandy, little food over the last several days, and the remnants of a concussion—she doubted she could stand, let alone walk.

Grace shrewdly sized up the situation. "Becky, would you please ask Mac and Jackson to come and escort us? Tell them we're feeling a little under the weather."

Becky's eyes were as large as saucers. She backed three steps before comprehending the situation. "Oh, like Morgan and Jackson after the trail drive." Then she spun on her heel and sprinted out the door.

"I'm sorry, Sam. I shouldn't have encouraged you. I forgot about your illness. We'll wait for Mac and Jackson."

"It's not your fault. I should have kept track," Sam admitted, already projecting Jackson's reaction. "I doubt Jackson will let me forget this—drunk on three glasses of brandy before noon."

"We all have our trials in this life, Daughter. I'm sure this too shall pass," Grace responded.

Recognizing the phrase, Sam murmured, "So that's why I chant that—I wondered."

Morgan and Jackson almost collided trying to come through the door at the same time. While Grace looked askance at their manners, Sam laughed.

Mac was only a step or two behind the younger men. Finding Grace calm and in command of her faculties, he declared, "See, I told you. Grace is always a lady."

Sam made an offended tsk-tsk sound. "Mac, are you implying I'm not a lady?"

Enjoying herself, Grace watched Mac pale. He could coolly face down a band of outlaws, but let that girl of his challenge him and he'd fall right to pieces. Grace took pity on him.

"Mac wouldn't say that, Sam. I believe you misunderstood. Morgan and Jackson, though, appear to have doubts."

Accepting Mac's arm, Grace took a step toward the door. Over her shoulder, she saw Morgan and Jackson looking at Sam with dread. Grace took pity on them too.

"For heaven's sake, Jackson, give her one of your dark, forbidding looks and pick her up. If she opens her mouth, kiss her." Then prettily, she cooed, "Morgan, darling, be a dear and hold the door for your sister."

Both men obeyed.

Jackson kissed Sam three times before they made it through the door of the main house.

Chapter 16

Tired after walking back to their house with Jackson's assistance, Sam dropped gratefully onto the divan near the office window overlooking the front porch. Her eyes followed Jackson as he crossed the room to bring her the woolen shawl he'd retrieved from their bedroom. His eyes held hers an instant before draping it around her shoulders.

When he sat next to her, Sam settled close against him and lifted his hand to her lap. "Was the driver of the coach the regular driver?" she inquired, stroking his palm with her thumb.

Sam noticed Jackson heaved a resigned sigh before replying, signaling he preferred concentrating on her soft caresses rather than questions. "The driver who began the trip said he was ill when we made our first stop. The stationmaster told him to stay behind and look after things there. There was no shotgun messenger that could take over, so the stationmaster said he'd finish the run. That was one of the reasons the stage was running behind schedule. The other reason was the stationmaster took time to inspect the rig every time we stopped. As I thought back on it, I wondered if he noticed something in the handling of the coach that made him suspicious something was wrong."

A series of emotions flitted across Jackson's face while he recalled the carnage strewn over the rocky floor of the hellhole. "The day Morgan returned to the ranch, I went with Sheriff Cooley and some men from the stage company to the ravine. I climbed down to the coach, hoping to find your gun and to inspect the axle. Unfortunately, the coach was so broken up, it was impossible to conclude anything."

"Jackson, the first driver may have tampered with the axle and feigned sickness. Did you know him or ever see him before?"

"I didn't know him. I don't think you did either, because he tried to shine up to you and you paid him no attention."

"Did his illness seem real?"

"I didn't notice. You were in one of your 'think-it-through' moods. I was hoping you'd get over what was bothering you so you'd come sit next to me." Jackson smiled roguishly. "We were the only passengers on the stage and I had a few ideas about what we could do to pass the time. You knew I'd try to distract you, though, so you sat on the opposite side and corner of the coach. You'd just begun to rise from your seat and take my hand when the axle broke and the wheel came off. You must have been thrown hard against the back of the coach. I expect that's where most of your bruises came from."

"Why was I in one of my think-it-through moods? Had you done something to upset me?"

"You were upset because you thought you should have resolved a situation from the previous day differently than the one you chose."

"Jackson, you look half amused and half mad as a polecat. What the hell happened?"

"How did we get on this, Sam? It doesn't matter what happened the day before. We should be talking about the original driver of that coach."

"All right. I'll let you off the hook for now."

"I'm not on the hook. I told you true, Sam. You weren't mad at me."

"Jackson, I think we should ask Mac to go to Laramie and find that driver. Maybe someone put him up to sabotaging the stage. I suspect Mac has a way of getting people to talk."

Jackson grinned. "I'm ahead of you on this. I talked to Mac, Morgan, and Parker this morning while you were here with Grace. Mac will leave for Laramie tomorrow. I'd go myself, except I think you'll be safer if I stay with you."

"Can we find out anything about where or how the tea was drugged?"

"Parker will talk to Doc about how long it would take to soak the tea in chloral hydrate and dry it out. We need to know whether it was treated after it arrived in Prosperity or somewhere else. Parker and Hank Bainbridge, who owns the freight office, have been friends for almost six years. Parker says Hank wouldn't press him if he asked Hank to investigate. Hank knows how to keep his mouth shut. Morgan and Ryder will find out from Miss Jenny who at Gracelyn Palace knows you're fond of that tea. You lived at Gracelyn Palace before you moved here to Trinity. You have a suite there for when we stay in town."

"Jackson, there's something else I find puzzling about the tea. I found an unopened tin of it in the kitchen pantry. Why would I order more when I already have a good supply?"

"That is odd. We'll tell Parker so he'll look for the name of who placed the order when he reviews the paperwork. We'll give Parker the tea you found to pass on to Doc, too. Maybe he can figure out what's in it."

"We need to consider one more thing." Sam hesitated because she knew Jackson wouldn't like it.

Jackson was watching her suspiciously. "What's up your sleeve? I can tell by looking at your face it won't sit well with me."

"We need to go to Chicago."

"Go to Chicago! Sonofabitch! You're not going anywhere, Sam. You're barely well enough to walk to the main house, let alone endure the demands of a three-day train trip to Chicago to find Lord knows what. I'm not going to risk your being hurt again—or killed. What put this fool notion in your head?"

"Jackson, calm down and please listen. What's happening could be connected to my Great Uncle Aaron and our family estate. The timing is too coincidental. Grace said I went to Chicago before Becky's birthday, while you were in San Francisco with Parker. Apparently, I haven't said much of anything about it. Aaron was a dangerous man. He could be engineering things."

"Damn it, Sam. He can't engineer anything. The man is dead!"

"Do we know that for sure? Even if he's dead, he was the type to seek revenge even after his death. Please stop cussing long enough to at least consider the possibility, because I'm serious about this."

Jackson looked at her long and hard. She did have a point, but he couldn't let her go. Hell, in Chicago, it would be too easy for someone to hurt her and get away with it.

"Jackson, I admit I'm not well, but I can't ignore this. The estate lawyers will only talk to me. If you don't go, I'll ask Morgan. If Morgan refuses, I swear, I'll go alone. I don't need anyone's permission."

"Sam—"

"You can't stop me. I've been thinking of leaving Trinity anyway. I'm worried I'm endangering you and the others. I'd be gone already if you hadn't come back with Parker. I keep imagining how you might have been killed in that crash. Whoever is trying to get to me doesn't care if he hurts others. I'm putting you in more danger by asking you to go. You should turn me down."

"If I were to let you go alone, I wouldn't be any safer here. Parker, Mac, Morgan, Doc, and Ryder would have my hide. We'd better take Morgan with us, though. He knows your business and Chicago better than I do."

***

Later that afternoon, Jackson went in search of Parker, hoping to catch him before he left for town. He found him in his office, the first place he looked.

"Here's the tin of tea Sam found in our pantry," Jackson said. After you give it to Doc and talk to Hank Bainbridge at the freight office, would you stop in at the bank and check with Thornton McKinley to ascertain whether the draft we deposited for the bull we sold to Martin Webster was transferred to our account? Sam and I deposited the money the day before we left Laramie, but things got dicey when it came time for Webster to pay up. It wouldn't surprise me if Webster used his influence to persuade the Laramie bank manager to cancel or delay the transaction. What with the crash and everything else that's transpired, I forgot all about it."

Parker was surprised this was the first he was hearing of it. "What do you mean things got dicey?" he asked. "It should have been a cut-and-dried deal."

"Do you recall that Webster was adamant Sam close the deal? He didn't like it one bit that I came with her, but he tried to hide it. As we suspected, he had designs on her.

"He invited us to supper and suggested we stay at his ranch. Sam told him we were staying in town at the hotel and would bring Hercules out to the ranch the next day. Then to make plain the situation between us, she smoothed the lapel on my jacket, leaned on my arm, and invited Webster to join *us* for a drink in *our* room at the hotel.

"I thought Webster would pop a blood vessel. The next day when we carted Hercules to Webster's ranch, his foreman came to the office and asked me to help get Hercules settled. He was nervous and vague about why I was needed. I knew it was a ruse so Webster could get Sam alone. I also knew Sam was aware of what Webster planned, so I played along when she said she'd finish the paperwork for the sale."

Remembering his unease with leaving Sam alone with Webster, Jackson added, "I almost changed my mind when I saw the foreman close the door to Webster's office behind us, but you know how Sam is about my butting in. I knew she had her derringer and would put Webster in his place. She can take care of herself, but that polecat, Webster, is ruthless and in deep lust. I believe he wouldn't have hesitated to put a bullet in me to get to Sam."

Jackson kept his tone even so Parker wouldn't detect how angry and fearful he'd been for Sam. "According to what Sam told me later, the door no sooner closed than Webster sidled close, grabbed her around the waist, and tried to kiss her. The varmint even suggested he'd pay double the amount for the bull if she gave him a ride—Sam said he was that crude." Jackson took a steadying breath.

"Mind, it took a bit for me to wheedle some of this out of her after the fact. Anyway, Sam was pissed. She gave him her knee. He managed to hit her, though, when her skirt caught on the corner of the desk. He hit her hard enough to knock her back against the desk where he proceeded to lift her skirt. That's when Sam got serious and pulled her gun." Jackson said the last sentence with satisfaction.

"Meanwhile, I didn't even make it halfway to Hercules's freight wagon before I decided to go back to the office. The foreman tried to stop me. I slugged the bastard and pulled my gun. He backed off, saying his job wasn't worth his life, so I let him go. When I walked in, Sam was smoothing her skirt down with one hand and pointing her derringer at Webster with the other. I wanted to kill the son of a bitch, but because Sam had things under control, I only asked casually if the price of the bull was too steep."

Jackson smiled sardonically. "Sam didn't give the polecat a chance to answer. She said, 'Mr. Webster has offered to double the amount if I'll provide a personal service for him.' She threw a disgusted look in Webster's direction before aiming her gun at his privates. I swear I saw her finger tighten on the trigger, Parker, but I pretended not to notice and walked over to the desk to scoop up the bank draft and bill of sale."

Jackson saw amusement play at the corners of Parker's mouth.

"Webster just couldn't keep his mouth shut. He spit at Sam's feet and said, 'You're nothing but a broodmare in heat to let that stud mount you.' In my side vision, I saw it took all Sam's self-restraint not to shoot him dead then and there. Instead, she looked the pisser cool in the eye and said, 'Why, Mr. Webster, when I'm in the market for stud service, I choose the best stallion in the Territory.' Then she gave me a look that put weight to her words and added, 'Why would a fine *broodmare* like me settle for anything less?'"

Grinning, Parker asked, "Did you keep a straight face? I would've burst out laughing."

Eyes twinkling, Jackson nodded. "Parker, I'm here to tell you, I thought I would pop the buttons on my vest trying to hold back my laughter, but I managed to walk past Sam with all my buttons intact and a pleasant smile on my face. While I waited for her by the door, she nudged Webster at gunpoint over to the closet and told him to get in. Then the hellcat hit him over the head with a vase, checked his pulse, and propped a chair under the doorknob. When we returned to Laramie, we went to the bank. The next morning, we boarded the stage for Prosperity."

"Did you tell Mac that story? He should hear it before he leaves for Laramie. Webster is probably behind that stage wreck."

"I thought so, too, until you all figured out the tea was drugged. That couldn't have been Webster because it was planned too far back. I told Mac and Morgan about Webster, just in case. I dodged telling Sam about him, though. She's already blaming herself for putting us in danger and is worried we'll get hurt. I didn't think it would be wise to add fuel to the fire. She said she would have left Trinity if I hadn't come back with you. You know Sam. I bet she's still planning to do it. The only thing stopping her is this trip to Chicago. She was smart enough to admit she wasn't well enough to travel on her own because she hasn't been able to hide her symptoms from me. Hell, have you watched her when she gets up from a chair? She holds on to the back of it until she feels steady enough to move." Jackson looked a little embarrassed before adding, "It's even more pronounced when she gets out of bed."

"When do you leave for Chicago?"

"Tomorrow, mid-morning," Jackson replied.

"Morgan's agreed to go?"

"Yes. He left to make arrangements. He'll spend the night at Gracelyn Palace and do a little snooping. He wants you to meet him there once you talk to Doc and Bainbridge."

Parker nodded. Jackson's manner suggested he wanted something else. "Spit it out, Jackson. I can see something's on your mind."

"Would you tell Doc what I said about Sam admitting she isn't well enough to go to Chicago by herself? He'll know that's not like her. I also want you to tell him her dreams are back. Doc knows about all that. Mention she's holding on to things when she first stands up. Ask him for the name of the doctor he wrote to about her symptoms. Tell Morgan what Doc says."

"You're that worried? It's only been nine days, Jackson. You can't expect she'd recover so soon."

"I understand that, but if you'd seen her the night I came back and how she looks when I wake her from those nightmares, you'd know she's terrified." Jackson stopped and looked away before continuing. "She wants me with her, understands we've been everything to each other, except married, but she can't bring herself to trust me fully. I can see she wants to. I can also see she doesn't understand why she feels as she does.

"The other night when Mac started up the stairs to help her down, he said she backed away from him. Grace said Sam wouldn't look at her when she first approached her. I'm more than worried for her, Parker. We've seen Sam physically hurt worse than this. Normally, she'd spit in your eye before she'd admit she was in pain or needed help. I need to know what Doc thinks, and I want the name of that doctor in Chicago as a precaution. I'd talk to Doc myself, but I can't put her through the worry of wondering where I've gone. I don't want her to know I'm this troubled."

"I'll tell Morgan everything, Jackson."

***

Grace was helping Sam pack for the trip to Chicago while Jackson was at the main house with Parker. "You won't need to take much, Sam. You have a townhouse with everything you'll need. Jackson and Morgan keep full wardrobes there too. Morgan is making the arrangements, including sending telegrams to your housekeeper and her husband, Mr. and Mrs. Hadley, and Thomas Miles, your lawyer. Morgan's staying in Prosperity tonight at Gracelyn Palace and will meet you and Jackson at the station tomorrow."

"Grace, with Mac going to Laramie, what will you do?"

"I'll stay here with Becky, Parker, and Ryder until you all come back, of course. That way, if you need anything, we'll be here to pass on information and help." Grace patted Sam's cheek. "I'd worry more if I were alone in Eden Ridge."

Grace sat on the bed and patted the spot next to her. "Would you sit by me a minute, Sam? I need to tell you something."

Sam hesitated, not sure she was feeling up to learning much more about herself, at least now. She was doing her damnedest to keep her worry and emotions under control. Most of the time, she felt she was losing the battle. That fact alone intensified her fear.

"All right, Grace."

Grace sensed Sam doubted her strength. "You can do this, Sam. We're here to help you. I know you aren't certain because you have no memories of how we've always supported one another. You need to trust your feelings. When you can do that, your doubt and uncertainty will disappear."

"I tell myself I know that."

"Telling and knowing are very different, Sam. Your logic won't get you what you need this time. You've allowed your feelings to bring you some understanding—I see how you are with Jackson, Morgan, Becky, and the rest of us. You partially believe in us. The time will come when you can open your heart the rest of the way. Your healing and confidence will be fully restored then. Rely on your instincts, sweetheart, and trust in your feelings."

Sam's eyes were shining. "I need to be able to come back to Jackson. Without my memories, will I have enough to give him?"

Grace smiled and smoothed Sam's hair. "Daughter, if that's what worries you most, your answer is already given. Your worry says you care more for Jackson than you do for yourself. Tell me, how could you have more to give him than what's inside you now?"

Sam bent her head, holding back tears. Grace put her arm around Sam's shoulders. "Mac told me you remembered when you were a little girl and clutched at my skirt, thinking I was an angel. You trust in that, don't you?"

Sam nodded.

"Then you'll trust in the rest soon. I want to discuss one more thing. Jackson told me you pressured him into telling you about being hurt when you were a young girl and about not being able to have children. You need to know that it happened a long time ago, through no fault of yours. The man was a neighbor, and no one had any idea he was obsessed with you. He died in an accident the same day he hurt you. We weren't there when it happened, and you didn't remember much about it. I took you to a doctor right away, but you were so young, the damage couldn't be repaired. I even took you to specialists in Chicago to be sure.

"Mac and I were glad you forgot most of it. Over time, you seemed to put it behind you. Mac will never forgive himself for not suspecting the man or better preparing you to defend yourself. It wasn't his fault or anyone else's. The blame was with the man, and he was dead. I was glad of that because, otherwise, Mac would have killed him. Morgan was away at school, or we'd have had that worry with him too."

Sam's head was aching from emotion, and her determination to hold on to her control was slipping. She put a hand to her head. "Don't tell me anymore now, Grace. I thank you for this much, especially for knowing the man is dead. I've been having dreams. Maybe they'll go away now that I know he can't hurt me."

Sam kissed Grace's cheek. "Let's finish packing. Jackson will be back soon. We can enjoy a glass of brandy with him." Then Sam gave Grace an impish smile. "Notice, I said *a glass* of brandy."

Grace smiled fondly at her daughter. "I told you. You've always been a quick study."

Chapter 17

Sitting opposite Morgan at a table in Gracelyn Palace, Parker reported what he'd learned at the freight office. "Hank Bainbridge said he saw the tea tin in the storage room at the freight office and sent it to the mercantile because he knew it was for Sam. He's seen her drink it at supper in the hotel dining room and while dealing faro and twenty-one. Since he knew Sam and Jackson were out of town, he thought it would be a courtesy to send it to be picked up with Trinity's supplies. While Hank was looking for the paperwork, his partner, Reed Ferguson, came in. Since Reed handles the bookkeeping, Hank asked Reed for help."

Morgan frowned and shifted in his chair. He didn't like hearing Reed Ferguson had gotten involved but didn't say so.

"With Reed's assistance, we discovered the tea arrived almost two months ago," Parker said. "They had no idea why it stayed at the freight office so long. Reed did offer that he'd turned over the bulk of the goods distribution to their two clerks. He said it was an oversight, maybe because Sam has been out of town frequently over the last few months. He was smooth about it, Morgan. Not nervous or cagey acting at all."

Morgan looked thoughtful. He'd never warmed up to Reed Ferguson. There was something about him. Though, if Ferguson had something against Sam, he was taking his time getting around to it. Ferguson had arrived in Prosperity seven months ago.

"What do we know about Ferguson, Parker?" Morgan asked.

"Not much. He's pleasing enough. He must come from money because he bought into Bainbridge's freight business, no loan involved. That was why he came to Prosperity. Hank wants to concentrate less on freighting and more on his ranch. No one was surprised when he took on a partner."

"What else?"

"Ferguson lived at the hotel before buying a house near Doc's place. He's young but smart and ambitious. He has an education to go with his money. As I recall he was raised in Chicago. He spends a great deal of time at the gaming salon, although he isn't a heavy gambler."

"Does he see anyone?" Morgan asked.

"Although he's considered a good catch," Parker murmured, "he doesn't see any woman for long."

Just then, Alexa Danforth, Miss Jenny's assistant, brought two glasses and a bottle of bourbon to their table. She smiled fondly at both men, but her eyes lingered on Morgan.

"Miss Jenny said you two look much too serious sitting here, and she's sure this will help you get to the bottom of whatever's on your mind." She had a mischievous twinkle in her blue eyes and her mouth was turned up at the corners.

Morgan nodded. "Miss Jenny has real discernment, Alexa. Please thank her for us."

Alexa stepped closer to Morgan's side of the table and leaned near. "It's been a while, Morgan. I heard about Sam's accident from Miss Jenny and Ryder. I'm sorry she isn't well. She's always been good to me. Would you tell her to send for me if I can help her with anything?"

Morgan nodded, touched by Alexa's offer. "I'll be sure to tell her, Alexa. When she's feeling better, she'll appreciate your help in getting reacquainted with Gracelyn's business." Morgan couldn't help but be aware of her nearness and the light scent of her perfume.

Alexa patted Morgan's shoulder and excused herself, saying she needed to tend to some things for Jenny.

Watching her walk away, Morgan admired the sway of her hips. Alexa Danforth was a pleasing woman, what with those blue eyes and all that honey-colored hair. Once a man got past those, his breath would catch when his eyes took in her hourglass figure and long legs.

At one time, Morgan had been more than interested in Alexa. She was smart, refined, and good at her job. Jenny spoke highly of her, and Morgan had on occasion witnessed her expertise in handling tricky situations at Gracelyn. Sam thought her capable and especially depended on her whenever she stayed in town. But, in those early days, Alexa was said to have had eyes for Jackson, despite his being in love with Sam. Morgan was proud. He told himself he couldn't love a woman who thought he was second best, no matter how strongly he felt about her.

Morgan's body didn't listen to his head, though. He found it impossible to be indifferent to Alexa. When they were in each other's company, he constantly had to remind himself she was a respected employee—nothing more. It was getting harder to pretend, and, lately, he'd begun wondering why he bothered.

With amusement, Parker noticed Alexa's deference to Morgan and how Morgan looked at her when he thought she wouldn't notice. He knew about her supposed former interest in Jackson. Personally, he didn't think a woman as forthright and intelligent as Alexa Danforth would chase a man so obviously in love with another woman. "She's a beautiful and appealing woman," Parker commented.

Morgan realized Parker had been watching him "appreciate" Alexa. Looking faintly embarrassed, he agreed, "That she is."

"Ryder says she concentrates on her job and doesn't socialize much, although she gets plenty of offers," Parker replied. "He's been teaching her to ride, and Sam's been teaching her to shoot. Ryder says she was raised in Chicago in what sounds to be a comfortable style, but not with luxuries like riding lessons." Casually, Parker added, "I don't know as I've seen her paying attention to any man in particular—except you, Morgan." Parker rubbed his chin thoughtfully while waiting for a reaction.

Morgan cleared the memory of Alexa's swaying hips from his mind and looked at Parker suspiciously. *Was Parker goading him?* Morgan leaned back in his chair and ran his finger around the rim of his empty glass before pointedly turning the conversation back to the tea. "Did the paperwork indicate Sam ordered the tea?"

Parker was disappointed Morgan didn't react to his insinuation about Alexa's interest, but he shrugged it off and answered Morgan's question. "The paperwork didn't show who ordered it. He doesn't know whether Sam placed the order or someone from Gracelyn Palace placed the order on her behalf. He said it wasn't unusual for personal items for Sam to be ordered through Gracelyn."

Frustrated, Parker added, "The delay is suspicious. All we know for sure is that it *could have* been treated here. We also identified the employees who had access to it. I'm sorry there isn't more to tell."

Morgan's tone was confident when he replied, "The pieces will come together."

"Well, I'm wondering how this fits," Parker remarked, "Doc says the tea from Sam's pantry isn't drugged."

Morgan considered the information. "I wonder if there's tea in Sam's suite. I'll make it my business to find out later."

"Good thinking," Parker replied while sliding a folded slip of paper across the table. "Here's the name and address of the doctor in Chicago that Doc consulted about Sam. Jackson asked me to ask Doc for it and give it to you."

Morgan nodded. "Jackson mentioned it before I left the ranch. Did Doc say anything when you told him about taking Sam to Chicago?"

It was Parker's turn to nod. "You're not going to like it," he warned.

Morgan swiped a hand over his eyes. He didn't expect he would, because he also thought it was folly, as did Jackson. The problem was Sam was giving them no choice. When she was this hell-bent on something, nothing short of tying her up and standing guard could stop her.

"Let's hear it," Morgan replied.

"Doc said you and Jackson are weak puppies where that girl is concerned, and you should lock her in a room."

Morgan dismissed the advice. "That's easy for Doc to say. Even if we did it, Sam would figure out some way to get away from us. At least if we go with her, she'll cooperate, and we can watch over her."

"Don't get mad at me, Morgan. I'm only relaying the message."

"What else, Parker? Spit it out."

"He said we were right to worry about how well she is. The train will be hell on her. He said to travel in your private rail car because Sam's going to have motion sickness the whole way. He said to bring JB's wife along, stock up on soda crackers and broth, and force Sam to drink lots of water to prevent dehydration." Parker took a small bottle out of his jacket pocket. "Doc said this won't help much, but to follow the instructions he wrote on the paper I already gave you."

Morgan paled. It would be worse than he thought. He'd already arranged the private rail car.

"Dottie, JB's wife, can't make the trip." Parker said.

"Why not? I thought it was all settled."

"JB's youngest daughter, the one with the two little girls, sprained her ankle and needs Dottie's help looking after them."

"That's not good news," Morgan replied.

"I know. You need someone who can help with Sam. And since Jackson can't stand to see her suffer, he'll be a handful, which will make it difficult for you to keep a lid on him."

Morgan groaned and poured each of them a shot. The two men's eyes met as they raised their glasses. The liquor seemed to burn more than usual.

Parker hesitated before offering a suggestion. "I know I needled you a few minutes ago about Alexa, but I'm serious now. I bet she'd help if you could find your way to ask her."

The same thought had occurred to Morgan. He could find his way to ask her. But could he stop himself from asking her for—other favors? With a resigned sigh, Morgan said, "I'll ask."

Parker picked up the bottle and refilled their glasses. "Doc also said Jackson isn't exaggerating about the state of Sam's mind. He says Sam is on the edge. She could have a breakdown. You and Jackson need to watch for signs. Take her to Doctor Friedman if you need anything."

Morgan raised a brow and shifted in his chair.

"One last thing, Doc said you'd better be damn careful because he can't afford to lose good friends. His parting words were, 'May God watch your backs.'"

Morgan took his turn refilling their glasses before offering a simple toast, "Amen!"

***

After Parker left Gracelyn Palace to return to Trinity, Morgan let himself into Sam's suite. He was surprised to find Alexa working at Sam's desk. "Sorry, Alexa, I hope I didn't startle you. I forgot you work on the accounts in here."

Alexa smiled. "Hello, Morgan. I was hoping you'd stop by. Frankly, that's why I decided to go over these accounts tonight. I thought this might be a good opportunity for us to talk."

Morgan noticed her perfume again and the lamplight reflecting in her hair. Casually, he replied, "Do Miss Jenny and you have a problem?"

Alexa assessed the expression on Morgan's face. He was feigning employer interest. Alexa was tired of pretense. "This isn't about Miss Jenny or Gracelyn Palace business. This is about you and me."

Morgan was surprised by her directness but recovered quickly. "I wasn't aware there was such a thing as *you and me*, Alexa."

Unfazed, Alexa challenged him. "Is that why you pretend not to notice me as a woman when you talk to me then watch my hips when I walk away?"

Morgan dropped the pretense. "Was I that obvious?"

Alexa answered with a boldness she didn't feel. "Let's say I notice men looking at me—especially the man I'm interested in." She sought his eyes. "I'm not being coy or playing games, Morgan, so I'd appreciate it if you would

143

knock off the employer routine and listen to me. Downstairs, you said Sam would appreciate my help getting reacquainted with Gracelyn's business. Does that mean she does have amnesia? I asked Miss Jenny and Ryder straight out, but all they said was that she isn't herself."

"Before I answer your question, Alexa, will you tell me why you want to know?"

Alexa considered his request. "That's only fair. Sam's been good to me, and I like her."

"You said that downstairs. That's not an explanation."

Alexa's eyes widened at his tone, but she kept her composure. "There's no need to be aggressive. I feel something for Sam, and it pains me to think about her being ill and losing her memory. I can't imagine how lost and afraid that must make her feel. That was the only reason I asked."

Morgan softened. "All right, Alexa. Except for Jackson's name and a couple of memories about Grace and her father, she doesn't remember anything."

"I'm very sorry, Morgan. Is there any chance her memory could come back?"

"Doc thinks there's some hope."

Alexa took a deep breath. Now that she'd started this conversation, she wouldn't quit. "When I decided to come to Prosperity to work at Gracelyn Palace for you and Sam, I had a chip on my shoulder. I knew this job was a good opportunity, but I believed you and Sam had inflated egos. I told myself I wasn't compromising my principles by accepting the job. I knew I'd give you my best as your employee, even if I didn't like you." Alexa saw she had his serious attention now.

"What do you mean you thought we had inflated egos?" Morgan was exercising a great deal of control to keep the anger building in him from sounding in his voice.

"I'll be blunt. I thought you were superficial, didn't have a serious bone in your body, and were living off your sister. I thought Sam was rich, spoiled, and using you. I didn't think she deserved a quarter of the things she has." Alexa was telling the truth—just not all the truth. She wanted to tell Morgan everything, but she couldn't say more without breaking a promise she'd made to Sam before the crash.

Morgan's eyes bored into Alexa's, and she recognized the unforgiving set of his jaw. His hands wrapped tightly around a glass paperweight sitting conveniently nearby. "You have a right to look at me that way, Morgan. If I were in your place, I'd throw that paperweight at me, tell me to go to hell, and slam the door in my face."

Morgan carefully placed the paperweight on the table before replying coolly, "I won't throw this at you, but telling you to go to hell and storming out isn't a bad idea. Since this is Sam's suite, though, I'm not the one who will be leaving."

Alexa admired his control. He was nothing like the man she had prejudged him to be.

"Your sister said pretty much the same thing when I had this conversation with her a few weeks ago. As I recall, she said, 'You can take those blue eyes and long legs of yours and go straight to the devil's brothel in hell, Alexa Danforth.' Right after that, she laughed and asked me how long it took me to change my mind. I gave her a smart-mouthed answer because I was embarrassed. I told her it took a day and a half—because I didn't meet either of you until the afternoon of the second day." Alexa raised a brow and locked eyes with Morgan. "I gather she didn't mention any of this to you?"

Amazed, Morgan shook his head.

"I didn't think she would—because she told me to work it out with you on my own."

Puzzled, Morgan asked, "What did she mean by that?"

Alexa moved close, put her hands on his shoulders, and kissed him. He started to pull away, but she tasted even better than he had imagined. Hadn't he thought about kissing her and a whole lot more whenever he was near her? Morgan deepened the kiss. It was Alexa who broke it and stepped back.

"I liked that, Morgan. I wondered the first time I met you what it would be like to kiss you—and I've wondered the same thing every time I've seen you since then. I was wrong to judge you before I met you. You aren't anything like I expected, and neither is Sam." She let her words settle before continuing.

"By the end of my second week here, I was so ashamed, I decided that I should leave. I didn't give notice. I was headed for the train station when I ran into Jackson. He noticed me because of a few conversations we'd had at Gracelyn Palace. On one occasion, he mentioned my hair was the same color as Sam's and *almost* as pretty. I was amused because I knew he said it without stopping to think how it wasn't a compliment to me. He blushed and stumbled all over himself trying to explain, but every word got him in deeper. I thought it was kind of him to be concerned about hurting my feelings. That's when our friendship began. I thought it was endearing how head-over-heels in love he was with Sam."

Though she was shaking inside, Alexa managed to keep her voice even. "When Jackson saw me, he guessed I was running away. He wanted to know why, so I made up excuses. He didn't care for my answers and said he'd put me on the train himself but not before I told him the truth. Then he took my arm and almost dragged me to the hotel restaurant—you know how he can be a force of nature that way. He did his best to make me talk, but I lied. He knew I was lying, but he didn't say so.

"When he escorted me to my room, my bags were there. He must have sent someone from the hotel to get them from the station. Anyway, he told me to hurry and change my clothes so I wouldn't be late for work. Then he patted my arm and said he'd see me later that night. I doubt it occurred to him I might not follow his orders."

Alexa's next words were expressed with a tinge of resentment. "The town gossips made something out of it. I was surprised people believed them. Anyone with half a brain can see Jackson and Sam are perfect for each other. He's a good man, and I'm proud to call him a friend. Every day since then, I've followed his instructions. I get up, dress, and go to work. I do it because I like it here at Gracelyn Palace—and because each day I hope I'll see you."

Alexa searched Morgan's face before adding, "I don't know how many more days I can do it, though." Tears were glistening in her eyes. She stepped close enough to kiss him again—but didn't. "So, I'm asking, Morgan Drake Garner, are you interested in working this out with me or not?"

Morgan caught his breath and held it before reaching out and pulling her into his arms. His mouth closed over hers in a slow, undemanding kiss, content to savor her warmth and response. Alexa's arms encircled his neck as she melted against him. His lips traveled to her neck, her throat, and back to her mouth, where they grew more demanding. Alexa trembled and let her hands roam across the muscles of his back and the breadth of his shoulders. His hands followed the line of her body down to her waist to pull her tighter against him.

Morgan wanted nothing more than to make her his, but he willed himself to think past his desire. It was too soon, and he needed to ask her a favor. He couldn't let her think this was a ploy to entice her to help him. When he finally let her go, they were both breathless. With a queer mixture of emotion and amusement, he murmured, "I believe you can consider this our first merger meeting."

He placed his hands on her upper arms. Emotion was still in his eyes, but the amusement was gone. "Alexa, I'd planned on finding you later because I need to ask a favor. I hope you'll understand that what's just happened between us isn't connected to what I'm going to ask."

Alexa smiled inwardly, marveling at how the confident man she'd kissed a minute ago transformed into an anxious little boy before her very eyes. "Just ask me, Morgan. I'll understand."

Keeping her expression neutral, Alexa listened to Morgan explain someone was trying to kill Sam. Worse, the danger extended to those Sam loved. Her mind racing, Alexa's hand involuntarily clutched Morgan's sleeve. *How could she go to Chicago when she'd promised Sam she'd keep a secret from Morgan?* She yearned to tell him, but she couldn't break her promise to Sam because she didn't understand why Sam asked her to make the promise. Alexa decided to put her concerns regarding the promise and secret aside. Of course, she'd go. Sam needed her help. Jackson was her friend—and she loved Morgan.

Morgan put his arms around Alexa, giving and receiving comfort. She felt good in his arms. After a few seconds of quiet, she stirred against him. Morgan kissed the tip of her nose before seeking her lips.

Alexa put a restraining hand on his chest and leaned back. "Let me go, Morgan. If we start that again, we'll likely miss the train tomorrow. I need to talk to Miss Jenny and pack." She lovingly let her hand caress the side of his face before crossing the room to open the door and step into the hall. Before latching the door, she called, "I could feel you watching my hips sway. In case I forgot to mention it earlier, I like that, too."

Morgan chuckled.

When he finally remembered to check for the tea, it turned out there wasn't any.

Chapter 18

Sometime during the ride from Prosperity to Laramie, Mac decided to begin his investigation with Price Hardin, the Laramie sheriff. Mac had a long acquaintance with Price from the days they'd been gunmen in San Francisco.

Back then, San Francisco was mainly known for being a way station for picking up supplies on the way to the gold fields. The town was rife with brothels, saloons, dance halls, gambling houses, and opium dens. Vice was easier to find than the law. All men, whether prospector, merchant, gunmen, or drifter, could lose their wealth and life in a game of cards, an assault, or a back-alley robbery—most days there was little difference among the three.

Watching each other's backs, they'd fearlessly waded in, as young men are wont to do, and emerged with enviable reputations. Yup. Mac figured Price Hardin would have most of the answers he needed.

***

Vigilance was Sheriff Price Hardin's business, so he studied the gunman expertly guide his horse up Laramie's main street. He had a dangerous, uncompromising air about him that made some folks nervous—most conceivably, the wicked ones.

When the rider stopped and dismounted in front of his office, Price was downright puzzled. The sheriff wasn't normally the first person a gunman visited when he arrived in a town.

As the gunman drew closer, Price noticed something familiar about the way the man walked, with the elbow of his right arm resting on the butt of his holstered six-gun.

When the gunman stopped in front of him, Price drawled, conversationally, "Well, would ya' look at that? When I got up this mornin', I never imagined an honest-to-God legend would grace my office. I thought you were tamed and settled down around Eden Ridge, Mac. What brings you to Laramie?"

Mac warmly grasped his old friend's extended hand. "I'd like to tell you, Price, that I rode here 'cause I knew you'd consider it a grand favor, but I'd be lyin'."

Price chuckled. "As if you need to make that clear. More likely, you came here lookin' for a troublemaker—or is it the other way around?"

Mac almost smiled, and Price knew it, so he winked at him. Mac did smile then.

"I always warned you winkin' would get you killed, Price. Glad to see it ain't happened yet."

Price laughed. "What you need, Mac? If I got it, you can have it."

Mac's expression turned serious. "Just need some information about a rich rancher named Martin Webster. My girl, Sam, and her beau, Jackson Knight, from the Trinity ranch near Prosperity, did some business with the man about two weeks ago. Webster got more than a little nasty with Sam. She needed to put him in his place, sort of hard like, you might say. Next day, the stagecoach they were on overturned near Prosperity. I expect you know about it. The stationmaster that took over driving the rig after the regular driver got sick was killed."

Price nodded. "And your girl, Mac, how is she?"

"My girl was hurt pretty bad, but she'll recover. There's a problem with her memory, though."

Price rubbed his jaw while he watched Mac's eyes.

Mac continued, "Now, while I am interested in learnin' if Webster paid the driver to make the crash look like an accident, I'm even more interested in finding out if he has future plans for my girl."

Price moved to the stove to pour two cups of coffee. "Sure, I know about it, Mac. I didn't know it was your girl on the stage, though. Truth is, I've been gonna take a ride to Prosperity to speak with Sheriff Cooley."

Price's jaw jutted out and his eyes darkened with anger before he shoved a cup of coffee across his desk toward Mac. Some sloshed over the side of the cup. "The first driver's health got worse. His illness blossomed into lead poisoning. 'Course the bullet didn't have much chance to poison him because it went through his heart. Happened two days after the crash. My deputy, Josh Gilbert, has been up north seeing to his ailing mother and won't be back until tomorrow. I was planning to visit Sheriff Cooley day after next."

"You think the killer went south to Prosperity?" Mac asked.

Price shook his head. "Don't know who the killer is, Mac. He might be *from* Prosperity as far as I know."

"Are you insinuating Sam or Jackson might have done the shootin'? That's preposterous! Sam hasn't been well enough to cross a room on her own, and the only time Jackson's been away from Trinity was to start for Cheyenne on business. Sam took a turn, though, and Parker went after him to bring him right back." Mac challenged his friend. "Did you think to look into Webster?"

"Didn't know there might be a connection until now, Mac. Martin Webster is a pisser. Thinks he's so rich and powerful nobody can tell him what to do. If anyone crosses him, he gets even. If your girl messed with him, he won't rest until he makes her pay for it. Thinks he's above the law. Trouble is, we don't have proof."

"Jackson says Webster's foreman, Jake Allen, was part of the scheme to get Sam alone. When Jackson challenged him, he backed off, saying his job wasn't worth his life."

Price Hardin half smiled. "That answers a question I've been ponderin' about why Webster is lookin' for a new foreman. Allen's been with him for almost five years, and I hadn't noticed any bad feelings between them."

"Have you seen Allen around town?"

"Nope, Allen would know the smartest thing he could do was to leave the Territory," Price replied. "By now, I bet he's holed up in Texas or California praying Webster doesn't come after him."

"What about Webster?" Mac questioned. "Would he have killed the driver himself?"

"It's possible, Mac. More likely, he paid one of his men to do the deed. He hires that sort. I can guess what he tried to do to Sam. She's a desirable woman, and he has a reputation for treatin' women like fancy pieces. He's always bought them off in the past. I'm sure he thought he could do the same with Sam. Besides sayin' no, what did she do to him?"

Mac smiled sardonically. "Nothin' the pisser didn't deserve. Way Jackson tells it, when Webster got her alone, he punched her and tried to lift her skirt and take her right there on the desk. Sam kneed him like I taught her and pulled her derringer. After threatening to shoot him in his privates, she made him get in the closet, knocked him cold with a vase from his desk, and wedged a chair under the closet doorknob."

Price slapped his knee. "Of course she did! She's your girl, ain't she? By damn, I would have liked to have seen that! Between Sam and Jackson's testimony, we should be able to put him before a judge to try him for attempted rape. Don't know if we can do anything about the stage crash, though."

"Attempted rape charges won't hold up, Price. Jackson didn't see that part of the fracas. When he got there, Sam was smoothing down her skirt and holding her derringer on Webster."

"But if you put his testimony of what he did see with Sam's, it would be enough, Mac."

Mac shook his head. "It won't, because Sam can't testify. She doesn't remember anything about it. She told Jackson, but then the crash happened. Now, all she remembers is a couple of things from her childhood about her father and Grace—not much of anything else. Doc Baxter says she has amnesia. I told you there are some memory complications."

The worry lines on Price's forehead deepened. "Sam's beau, Jackson—that would be *Providence* Jackson Knight, right?"

Mac nodded. "You know that's who it is, Price."

"No offense, Mac, but he's as good as you. He doesn't take anything from anyone or back down from anything either. You and Jackson gunnin' for Webster?"

"Not necessarily. Jackson mostly stayed out of the whole thing. My girl likes to fight her own battles, and Jackson's soft enough on her to let her have her way. Jackson said he and Sam considered the matter closed—at least that was their thinkin' until they began questioning whether Webster was behind the crash. With Sam not remembering, he figures it's up to us to make sure Webster isn't plannin' anything. Jackson would have come to investigate, but he can't leave Sam just now. I think you know how crazy he is over her."

Price looked sorrowful. "Ain't nothin' ever easy, is it, Mac? I'm right sorry about Sam's memory. Do you figure the place for you and me to start on this is to ride out to the Bar W and pay a social call on Webster?"

Mac hesitated, not wanting to put a target on his friend's back. "I'd welcome the company, Price, but you don't need to get on the wrong side of Webster."

Price grinned. "Who told you I wasn't already on his wrong side?"

***

Martin Webster wasn't at his Bar W ranch and no one, including his son, Holt, knew where he was—not that anyone would admit to anyway. No one would even say the last time he'd seen Webster. Holt explained his father had been in a fury over the deal for the bull, Hercules. Holt had been the one to find his father in the closet a few hours after Sam and Jackson left. Holt swore his father never said why Sam hit his father with the vase and locked him in the closet. Mac noticed the young man didn't look him in the eye when he said it, though. Likely, he was afraid of his father.

When the lawman and the gunman reached the main road after leaving the Bar W, they shook hands solemnly. As Price turned his horse toward Laramie, he called, "I'll watch my winkin', Mac, and you watch your back while you take care of that girl of yours. Tell Jackson too. Webster wouldn't lose no sleep over killin' any of you. When I come to see you in Prosperity, I don't want it to be for a damn funeral."

Mac spurred his horse and turned south to return to Prosperity. He prayed Webster didn't know Sam was on her way to Chicago.

Chapter 19

At the train station, Alexa recognized that the ride into town had been hard on Sam. She was pale and resting against Jackson, who had driven with one arm around her. When Jackson handed her down to Morgan, Sam clung to him until Jackson jumped down and took her back in his arms.

After Morgan glanced uncertainly from Sam to Alexa, she smiled and took charge. "I suggest we leave introductions for later and get settled on the train."

Three heads nodded before Morgan stepped to Alexa's side and helped her mount the stairs to the train car.

Sam noticed and raised an eyebrow in Jackson's direction, as if asking, "What have we here?" Jackson shrugged but seemed pleased.

Last night, Parker had explained that Morgan had asked Alexa to come with them because Mrs. Donovan couldn't go. Later, Jackson mentioned something between Alexa and Morgan early in their relationship had gotten "complicated." A flicker of a smile tugged at the corners of Sam's mouth, her curiosity piqued. She couldn't help wondering what had recently happened to "uncomplicate" things between her brother and Alexa.

***

Reed watched Alexa and Morgan meet Sam and Jackson at the train station and board the private car. Sam appeared very ill.

Briefly, he considered following. After all, he knew Chicago well. It was titillating to imagine stalking her and pretending to brush against her accidentally when she had no idea who he was. Too bad he couldn't do it.

Sam wouldn't know him, but Morgan, Jackson, and Alexa Danforth would.

***

The trip wasn't as bad as Doctor Baxter predicted.

After settling in the private car, Alexa insisted Sam nibble on plain crackers and sip a little water. "Sam, please trust me. You'll feel better. An empty stomach exacerbates motion sickness. You need to eat small, frequent meals. I talked to Doc this morning, and he told me how to help you."

Alexa's care of Sam was a godsend. She saw to Sam the whole way, supervising small meals of white rice and broth procured by special arrangement from the rail dining car, insisting Sam always sit in the direction of the train's travel, and reminding Sam not to look out the windows. From time to time, she instructed Jackson to hold Sam or brace her against his body to absorb and protect her from the worst of the bumps and jolts. Alexa even stayed with Sam during the nights.

Because of Alexa's care, Sam was withstanding the trip more comfortably than Jackson imagined possible, and he was grateful to her. To control his worry and not upset Sam or make it more difficult for Alexa to help Sam, he followed Alexa's orders without question. When he sensed he was making things more difficult for her, he excused himself to pace distractedly from one car of the train to another.

At such times, Morgan watched Jackson uneasily, equating his behavior with that of a caged panther. Only once during the trip did Morgan take Jackson aside and threaten to put him on another train. Jackson growled back that he'd like to see the day when Morgan could do it. Alexa watched the two men nervously from the corner of her eye during the altercation and was noticeably relieved when Jackson relaxed his shoulders and made an apologetic nod in her direction before excusing himself to visit the gentlemen's smoking car. Alexa also noticed how Morgan exhaled in relief when Jackson left peaceably.

Morgan wouldn't have acted on his threat. His intent in making it had been to calm Jackson down. Since the threat accomplished what Morgan had intended, he wouldn't dwell on it. Jackson *was* trying to be conscientious about staying out of the way. It had been brilliant of Alexa to explain to Jackson how it made Sam worry about him.

Upon arriving at Sam's townhouse, Alexa and Jackson put Sam to bed. Jackson wanted Madison Hadley, the housekeeper's husband, to go for Doctor Friedman, but Morgan and Alexa convinced him that Sam needed rest and quiet more than the sedative the doctor would undoubtedly give her.

After settling Sam and dimming the lamp, Alexa motioned Jackson to the hallway. "You might as well go downstairs. She won't sleep with you hovering over her. Haven't you noticed how fretfully her eyes follow you?" She patted Jackson's arm before adding, "I promise she'll be much better tomorrow."

***

Standing in the townhouse library in front of the bourbon decanter, Jackson grumbled, "That sister of yours is making me old before my time."

"Well, you won't get sympathy from me," Morgan retorted. "Neither of you make me feel younger!"

Jackson threw back the bourbon in his glass and managed to look apologetic. "I'm sorry, Morgan. Alexa's been very good for Sam. I'm grateful to you for asking her to help us."

Morgan's good humor returned and he half grinned while he refilled their glasses. "Well, Doc warned me you'd be a handful, and Alexa does have a way about her. Sam is comfortable with her too."

"Something in Sam trusts and responds to Alexa. The human mind is a strange curiosity," mused Jackson. "Well, we're here. What's our next step?"

"I'll go around and see Thomas Miles, Sam's lawyer, tomorrow. He may be able to tell us about Sam's last visit. If he insists on her presence, I'll ask him to call on us the day after tomorrow. I expect that's as long as Sam will be patient."

Madison Hadley interrupted Morgan and Jackson in the library. "Excuse me, Mr. Garner, but the telegram on the table over there came for you and Mr. Knight shortly before you arrived. What with Miss Samantha being under the weather from traveling, I forgot it until just now. I thought I should mention it in case it's important."

Morgan glanced at the table. "Thank you, Madison. And thank you and Mrs. Hadley for getting the house ready on such short notice. Would you care to join us for a drink?"

"Perhaps some other time. It's kind of you to offer, but Mrs. Hadley needs me to tend to a few things in the kitchen while she helps Miss Alexa with Miss Samantha. Since we were expecting Miss Samantha next week, your telegram saying she was arriving earlier with you and Mr. Knight made little difference in our preparations."

After Mr. Hadley excused himself and left the room, Jackson said, "I didn't know Sam had plans to come to Chicago next week. Did you know about it?"

Morgan shook his head and reached for the telegram. "No, I didn't. It isn't like her not to tell us—of course, I was in New York—but you haven't been away. You went to Laramie with her—so why didn't she say something to you?"

"It doesn't make sense," Jackson replied. "Will you hurry and open that telegram? What does it say?"

Morgan looked up from the message after reading it twice. "It's from Parker, but I don't understand what the hell it means."

Impatience getting the best of him, Jackson snatched the paper from Morgan's hand and read the message aloud. "'Withhold merged assets from HQ Lee stock sale.'"

"We don't own any HQ Lee stock do we, Morgan?"

Morgan shook his head. "I've never even heard of HQ Lee stock. Parker must have used this wording to make the message sound benign."

Jackson repeated the name of the stock several times in his mind. *HQ Lee—HQ Lee—HQ Lee.* It began to sound familiar. "Morgan, could Parker mean *Hercules,* as in selling the prize bull, Hercules, to Martin Webster? I think Parker is warning us Martin Webster is in Chicago."

"He's saying more than that. 'Withhold' means protect. 'Merged assets' translates to you and Sam. Mac must have found out Webster was behind the stage crash and is planning something."

"But how could Webster be responsible for the tea, Morgan? I don't get it."

"It's simple. Someone else has it out for Sam, too. Webster is only one of our problems—and who knows what else is going on—don't forget about Sam not telling us about Chicago."

Jackson plowed his hand through his hair. "I wonder what Thomas Miles knows about that? I hope he doesn't make us wait until he can talk to Sam personally. Make sure he understands about Sam's memory and about the danger she's facing."

"Jackson, you need to stay here with Sam and Alexa tomorrow. Hadley's a good man, but I don't think he could hold off Webster or anyone Webster might hire to do his dirty work, not after what you told me about him. Besides, Webster's after you, too. He'll have a harder time getting to you in the house."

"Morgan, we need to tell the Hadleys about this. It's not fair to put them in danger. Alexa needs to know, too. I'll tell Sam tomorrow after you leave for Thomas's office."

"That could make her worse. I told you Doc said she was close to the edge."

"I know, Morgan, but her anxiety level seems better. You know your sister has a sixth sense. I swear one of her ancestors must have been a clairvoyant. Besides, even ill, she can shoot the wings off a fly. Her guns provide some protection, but they can't help if she doesn't have them with her and is ignorant of the reason for using them."

"When you go up to Sam, would you ask Alexa to come see me, Jackson? I'll tell her about Parker's telegram and Webster. If she wants to return to Prosperity, I'll drop her off at the station before I see Thomas."

Jackson eyed Morgan, curious about how the situation between him and Alexa had progressed so quickly, but he didn't ask. In Jackson's opinion, it should have happened when she first came to Gracelyn Palace. When he stopped Alexa from leaving on the train, he never anticipated it would take a year for Morgan to succumb to Alexa's charms. "She won't want to leave, Morgan, but she does need to understand the situation. Give her Sam's derringer—she knows how to fire it—Sam's been teaching her. I'll leave it to you to make sure she understands why she might need to use it."

Looking up from his empty glass, Jackson inquired, "Will you look at Sam's family estate after you talk to Miles tomorrow? I understand it's about nine miles north of the city. I don't expect you'll find much of anything there except a closed-up house."

"Yes, I'll go if there's time," Morgan replied. "When you're part of Sam's world, you quickly learn to expect the unexpected—we both know that."

Jackson nodded in agreement. "You'll get no argument from me."

Chapter 20

By the time Alexa learned of her true parentage, Aaron Stone was dying, slowly and painfully. The man had earned a place in hell, and the devil would be the one to administer his punishments.

Alexa hated secrets because her mother had kept the secret of Aaron Stone from her. It wasn't until her mother's passing that Oliver Danforth, her stepfather, told her the truth. Oliver married Alexa's mother a few weeks after Alexa's birth. To him, Alexa was his cherished daughter in every way. Oliver provided the love, strength, and position to enable her mother to rise above the abuses of Aaron Stone and to protect Alexa.

Because Alexa was curious about Aaron and wondered whether she had other family, Oliver made inquiries. Alexa learned about Chase Stone and his daughter, Sam Hilliard Stone, who was, by all accounts, rich and beautiful.

Alexa was fascinated by her cousin and perhaps a tad envious, so when she learned Sam and Morgan were building Gracelyn Palace, she decided to apply for a job. She saw it as an opportunity to meet Sam without divulging their relationship.

Alexa never envisioned Gracelyn Palace would become her home, nor Sam her friend. Now that she was finding her way with Morgan, almost everything was perfect—except for having made that damned promise not to tell anyone about Sam being her second cousin.

Alexa looked at the clock. Jackson and Morgan would be finishing supper soon.

"What's wrong, Alexa? You've been worried about something since we left Prosperity." Alexa was so startled by Sam's question, she didn't answer.

"Is it Morgan?" Sam gently prodded. "It's easy to see you and Morgan are in love. Is that what worries you?"

Alexa nodded. "Yes. Morgan is part of it. I haven't wanted to burden you, but now I'm concerned not telling you might inadvertently hurt him. Before your memory loss, you asked me to keep a secret from Morgan, but I don't know why you didn't want him to know."

Sam tried to ignore the knot forming in her stomach. *Lord, I wouldn't do anything to hurt Morgan, would I?* "Do you think I told Jackson, Alexa?"

"Maybe."

"We'd better find out. Tell him I've overturned the water pitcher and you need his help while you change the bed and help me into a dry gown. Something like that will take a little while, but it won't make Morgan suspicious. I'm sorry to ask you to fib, but under the circumstances, I think it might be best."

***

Jackson's eyes swept the room. The pitcher was upright on the nightstand. Alexa and Sam were sitting on the edge of the bed. Keeping his tone light, he teased, "Imagine, two beautiful women working in cahoots to get me alone in a bedroom. Should I be flattered—or afraid?" Ignoring their serious expressions, he added, "You didn't need to trick me. I would've come willingly."

Sam fought the pull of a smile and pretended to be stern. "Jackson, stop teasing. It seems I asked Alexa to keep a secret shortly before we traveled to Laramie. Now, of course, I don't know why—and neither does she. Do I always cause so much trouble?" Sam asked, sounding more vexed than concerned.

Although Jackson would have enjoyed offering a long and passionately phrased answer to that question, he knew now wasn't the time. In true male fashion, he answered her question with a noncommittal shrug.

It entertained Jackson to see Sam raise her eyebrows and give him a tolerant smile. It was her way of saying she wasn't fooled but would let him get away with it—*this time.*

Alexa was in no mood for teasing or witticisms. With a ramrod straight back, she moved to the door to ensure it was latched before she sat in the bedside chair.

Watching her, Jackson said, "I apologize, Alexa, I didn't realize the situation was serious."

Frowning, Alexa replied, "I just want to get it out in the open. Sam's great-uncle, Aaron Stone, was my father, though I never met him. I learned about it a few months before I came to Gracelyn Palace. I wanted to meet Sam because I was curious and perhaps a little envious. I didn't expect to like the job, care for Sam, or fall in love with Morgan, but all those things happened. I felt so guilty about my feelings and my deception, I decided the best thing I could do was leave. You already know about that, Jackson. I'll always be grateful to you for intervening, because I've been happy at Gracelyn Palace, except for not being sure about Morgan—until recently. Anyway, a few weeks ago, Sam confronted me about being her cousin. I was relieved to admit it but surprised when she asked me to keep it a secret—especially from Morgan."

Alexa sighed. "I don't like secrets, but I promised because Sam said I wouldn't need to keep quiet for long. Then, of course, Sam lost her memory, and I didn't know what to do."

Alexa's blue eyes were shadowed, and both women were looking at Jackson expectantly. He noticed Sam rubbing the scar on her hand and gently laid his hand over hers. Sam's eyes reflected an array of emotions.

"Did I tell you about any of this, Jackson?"

Jackson shook his head. "No, Sam, you didn't." Then he turned to smile reassuringly at Alexa. "Now that I know, I can see a family resemblance. You're tall like Sam, and your hair color is the same."

Noticing the faint worry lines on Sam's forehead, he said, "Don't look so concerned, darlin'. Morgan and I knew you had something up your sleeve. We know you were planning to visit Chicago next week. We think it was to see Thomas Miles, your lawyer. I'd wager he knows what you have planned. Because of confidentiality, he may not be able to tell Morgan. But you're his client, so he'll be able to talk freely with you. Soon, we'll get some answers. You wouldn't knowingly do anything to hurt any of us, so don't worry about it."

Alexa's face was hopeful. Sam's was incredulous and doubting.

"Can you know me that well, Jackson?" Sam asked.

Grateful for Jackson's sane interpretation of the situation, Alexa started to chuckle. Seeing Sam's baffled expression, Alexa rushed to explain. "I'm sorry, Sam. It's just that I'm relieved, and your question is ludicrously naive. I think you may have lost some of your common sense along with your memory."

"Are you intentionally trying to insult me, Alexa?"

"No. I'm trying to tell you not to doubt how well Jackson knows you. Your caring about the people you love is why he fell in love with you. At least, it's one of the reasons—not the only one." She winked at Jackson and added, "Do you know he thinks your hair is prettier than mine?" She put a hand over her mouth to smother a giggle.

Looking a tad bemused and embarrassed, Jackson muttered, "I almost forgot; Morgan asked me to tell you he's in the study waiting for you."

"Jackson, should I tell Morgan?" Alexa asked.

Jackson looked pensively at Sam before answering. "I trust Sam's judgment. I doubt Morgan will learn much from Thomas. I think you should wait until after Sam talks to Thomas and we know for sure what's going on."

Alexa looked uncertain. "When will that be?"

Sam interrupted. "We'll talk to him tomorrow afternoon. Jackson can take me."

Jackson started to protest but remembered Morgan planned to visit the estate Sam inherited from her father after visiting Thomas. He looked at Sam as if measuring her strength before nodding his consent. Hell, if he didn't agree, she'd sneak out on her own. "We need to discuss another aspect later, but, if you think you're up to it, we'll see Thomas tomorrow afternoon."

Alexa sighed. "I trust Sam, too. I don't like keeping things from Morgan, but one more day won't matter."

"Alexa, why not go with Morgan tomorrow?" Jackson suggested. "You haven't had any time alone since we left Prosperity. This would be an opportunity for you to have an outing, and you could help Sam and me by ensuring Morgan leaves Thomas's office before we arrive. Besides, you shouldn't stay here alone—Morgan will explain why."

***

"So, what's the other aspect we need to discuss, Jackson?" Sam asked suspiciously.

Jackson sighed. *I'll have to tell her about Webster now instead of waiting until morning.* "It's connected to why you weren't sitting next to me on the stage before the crash. You assumed I did something to make you angry. The truth is you sat opposite me because you wanted to work through something that happened between you and Martin Webster, the rancher who bought one of Trinity's bulls, Hercules."

Sam recognized Jackson was trying to ease into the explanation. His voice was gentle and his expression compassionate, much like when he explained about her mother and father being dead. "I can see this is difficult for you, Jackson. I want to tell you something first."

Please let him understand I love him. "My having no memory is like being told my house was robbed when I didn't know I owned a house. I've no idea what it contained. Without that knowledge, I have no way to place a value on the missing items—but *not knowing* helps me understand what you've lost. *You know the value of each memory* because your memory is intact, but you have no one with whom to share your memories. I wish I could take that hurt from you." Tears she hadn't realized she'd been holding back began to flow over her cheeks. She was surprised she had no desire to hide them from him.

Jackson wiped at the tears. Her words weren't as important as the tenderness in her voice and the love shining in her eyes. She'd always had the power to put him under her spell. At this moment, it was her magic drawing him in and making this memory potent. He didn't give a goddamn about what she thought he lost. *She was telling him she was still his.* For a certainty, he knew she loved him, and that's all he cared about.

He told her then about what happened with Webster and how Mac must have discovered he was trying to hurt them because Parker sent a telegram to warn them. He also told her he and Morgan thought someone else had drugged the tea.

"Morgan was afraid telling you would push you over the edge. Doc warned us to be careful. I told Morgan you had a sixth sense and would worry more if I kept it from you." Unsure of Sam's reaction to his admission, he asked, "Was I right to tell you?"

Sam nodded. "You know me as well as Alexa said you do. Not knowing what to guard against is what makes me afraid."

"I want you to keep your Colt near you all the time—no excuses." He sounded stern and gave her a gentle shake. "I mean it, Sam. Please promise me."

"I promise."

"Morgan is explaining about Webster to Alexa and the Hadleys and giving Alexa your derringer." Trying to lighten things, he added, "Morgan said he'd take Alexa to the station tomorrow morning if she wants to return to Prosperity. Can you believe he still doesn't understand how much she loves him?"

Sam raised a questioning brow. "Did you tell me about how you prevented Alexa from leaving on the train?"

Instead of answering, Jackson nibbled the column of her neck.

"Jackson, you've tried that trick one too many times. I know you do it to distract me when you don't want to answer."

Jackson mumbled, "It normally works better than this."

Sam smiled before leaning away. "Why didn't you tell me?"

"Because the town gossips made something out of it that wasn't true—and because I knew you guessed how Alexa and Morgan felt about each other. I think you confronted Alexa about it when you asked her to make that promise. It wouldn't surprise me to find out you told Alexa to force the issue with Morgan. In fact, I'd be willing to bet a fifty percent share in my hotel that *you did meddle* in it."

"If I take the bet, what do you win if you're right?"

Jackson raised her hand and kissed the lightning bolt scar. The green flecks in his eyes darkened and an oddly sad, yet roguish smile flickered at the corners of his lips. "If I'm right, you'll marry me."

The air in Sam's lungs vanished and she jerked her hand away. Her heart began to slog against her ribs. It had been foolhardy of her to take the bait. "Don't look so damned proud of yourself," she snapped, extinguishing the green flecks in Jackson's eyes. *How many times have I crushed his hope? I won't do it again. I can't bear to do it again.*

She stared into Jackson's eyes while slowly extending her hand. "All right, Jackson, I'll take the wager, but with one stipulation—we agree not to settle the bet until after this thing with Webster, the mystery behind the promise Alexa made to me, and the person who's behind the drugged tea is settled—agreed?"

Jackson stared at her hand for what seemed like an endless moment before he grasped it, and they shook. Hardly believing he wasn't dreaming the whole thing, he murmured, "Agreed."

Chapter 21

"Why, Morgan, what a surprise!" exclaimed Thomas Miles as he rounded his desk and reached to grasp Morgan's hand.

Morgan clapped Thomas on the back and shook his hand warmly. Thomas and Morgan had gone to school together. Because Morgan was so far from Eden Ridge when he was at the university with Thomas, he'd been a frequent guest on weekends and holidays at Thomas's parents' home. He had also been the best man at Thomas and Greta's wedding.

Morgan drew Alexa forward. "Thomas, I'd like to present Miss Alexa Danforth. Alexa, this is Thomas Miles, Sam's attorney and our good friend."

"It's a pleasure to meet you, Miss Danforth. I hope you're enjoying your visit."

"I grew up in Chicago, Mr. Miles. I accompanied Morgan and Sam on this trip as I frequently act in the capacity of Sam's personal assistant."

"Of course, I imagine you're a great help to Sam—and Morgan."

Morgan was amused by Thomas's clumsy fishing attempt, so he interrupted. "Yes, Alexa is invaluable." A little shocked by his boldness, he commented, "She recently negotiated a particularly difficult merger with a resistant party."

Alexa felt as if Morgan had tugged an invisible cord strung between them. *The cool devil!* For an instant she allowed herself to recall the surge of desire that she'd felt when he'd run his hand down the length of her body while in Sam's suite. She looked up at Morgan through her lashes. "Well, of course, there's still the matter of assessing and surrendering assets, but I don't anticipate either party will put up any resistance."

Morgan's polished composure crumbled, and an arc of heat shot through him as an image of Alexa's unclad body formed in his imagination. When he could eradicate the fantasy and tear his eyes from Alexa's, he noticed Thomas glancing toward the door as if expecting another guest. "Do you have an appointment with another client, Thomas?"

Thomas brought his eyes back to Morgan. "Why no, Morgan. I was expecting to greet Sam. She scheduled an appointment for next week, so, naturally, I assumed she changed her original plan and decided to visit today. Did she stop to speak with Greta? Sam enjoys hearing about our daughters. Perhaps Miss Danforth would like to join them."

"I think it best Alexa sit in on our conversation, Thomas," Morgan replied.

Thomas nodded and absently shuffled a few papers on his desk. "I'm afraid the papers Sam asked me to draw up aren't ready, but I can hurry them along. I could have them ready for signature by the day after tomorrow. Do you think that would suit?" Thomas's voice trailed off when he glanced up and realized Morgan's normally affable and good-tempered countenance was absent.

Thomas's eyes darted to the door before moving back to his friend's face. "Morgan, is something wrong? Is Sam all right?"

"Sam was in an accident, Thomas. Nothing broken, but she did suffer a head injury that caused amnesia. Jackson's with her at her townhouse."

Morgan went on to explain about Sam's condition, Webster, and the drugged tea. "We came to Chicago because Sam suspects what's happening may be linked to her great-uncle who died recently, Aaron Stone."

"Morgan, I simply can't tell you Sam's plans. This is my first experience working with a client who doesn't remember her instructions. Frankly, I intend to look up a precedent or two for this situation.

"I must consider legal capacity in this situation. As you know, the legal standard for the capacity to contract depends on whether the person in question possesses sufficient mental capacity to understand the nature and effect of the contract. The more complicated the contract, the higher the level of understanding needed to have the legal capacity to make the contract." Thomas paused. "Given Sam's injury, I suppose I could ask for an evaluation by a doctor to ensure Sam has the capacity to enter the particular transactions she asked me to handle for her."

"Damn it, Thomas. I didn't say she's an imbecile! Her personality, intellect, and procedural memory are intact. Doctor Baxter says it is her episodic memory that's gone. She can't remember people or experiences. You'll see when you talk to her. She won't recognize your face, but once you introduce yourself and explain you are her attorney, she'll be able to review contracts and make decisions."

Thomas looked doubtful. "Well, if not, I suppose another way to handle things would be to make the transactions she requested contingent on a court guardianship or conservatorship. If we take that approach, the court would grant authority to a third party to act on Sam's behalf. She gave you that power, Morgan. As her court-appointed conservator, you have the authority to sign on her behalf. However, for one of these transactions, I'm hesitant to allow it, because Sam issued explicit direction you not know about it."

Sam's always trusted me—what the hell is going on? "Thomas, has she done anything like this before—I mean, ask you to keep something from me?"

"No, Morgan. I assure you nothing like this has happened before, not even when my father was her attorney."

Morgan, usually so unflappable, was chagrined, and that was putting it mildly.

"Look, Morgan, Sam intimated she planned to discuss these transactions with you before signing. She mentioned she needed to tie up one loose end first. You know Sam depends on you. She entrusts you with all her business affairs."

Morgan's jaw was clenched. "That's not true, Thomas; otherwise, I'd know about this." Morgan was aware Thomas was doing his best to placate him, but he didn't have a prayer in hell of succeeding.

"As Sam's attorney, I can't say more, but, as your friend, I'll advise you to reserve your judgment and trust Sam. You'll either listen to my advice, or you won't."

"It doesn't matter whether I listen to your advice. It's Sam's game and she holds all the cards. You're her shill, and, for some reason, I'm the intended mark."

Since Thomas could say no more, he sighed and extended his hand to his friend. "Morgan, I'll call on Sam tomorrow as you suggested, and we'll see where we are on all this then."

Morgan shook Thomas's hand. He couldn't fault his friend for loyally executing his sister's instructions. But, damn, he found it aggravating—and hurtful.

***

Morgan's head was spinning as he assisted Alexa into the carriage and gave the driver the address to Sam's family estate. *Goddamn it and sonofabitch! What was going on here?* He couldn't believe Sam would go behind his back like this. *Why didn't she trust him?* His gut told him it had to be tied to that depraved great-uncle of hers. Turning to Alexa, he asked, "How are we going to get to the bottom of this?"

"Morgan, you aren't looking at this with your usual pragmatic coolness. You're hurt because you think Sam doesn't trust you. You need to step back from your emotions. Once you can do that, you'll accept your sister undoubtedly has a good reason for keeping you out of whatever she's planning. I'm sorry to say this so bluntly, darling, but this isn't about you. Let it go. After Thomas talks with Sam, she'll explain, and you'll see what I'm saying is true."

Looking into Alexa's earnest blue eyes, Morgan's feelings of hurt and betrayal faded. Alexa was right. Besides, her calling him "darling" turned his thoughts back to "assessments and surrendering assets." He nudged her chin up with his finger. The first brush of his lips against hers sent a jolt arcing through him, and he felt her tremble. Knowing he affected her as much as she did him stirred a tenderness in him.

Alexa sighed into his mouth and slid her arms around his neck. Her lips moved hungrily with his and her breathing was becoming heavy with need, even while a part of her brain warned they were in a hired carriage and would regret letting things get out of hand here. It took every ounce of her willpower to pull away from him.

Though he was unwilling to release her completely, Morgan understood. He gently drew Alexa back to rest against his side and put one of his hands over one of hers. He settled back into the cushions of the carriage, determined to enjoy the pleasure of her nearness.

Chapter 22

Emerging from Thomas's office into the waning light of the day, Sam fingered the Colt hidden in a specially designed pocket of her shawl. It was against the law to carry a gun in Chicago. In Sam's opinion, some laws were made to be broken. Not carrying a gun could get her killed, so piss on the law.

Sam glanced over her shoulder as if enjoying the scenery on the street. "Jackson, we've got company. Stall so we can pinpoint where they are and give Mr. Hadley time to position the carriage."

"Can you see who it is?" Jackson murmured as he leaned down to kiss Sam's cheek.

Sam bestowed a soft, adoring look on him while pretending to straighten the lapel of his jacket. "No. But I don't recognize anyone. One is across the street behind the hedge in front of the red brick townhouse."

Gazing into Sam's eyes, Jackson tucked a curl behind her ear and kissed her. Against her lips, he said, "One? Does that mean two?" Sam put her arms around his neck in response to his kiss and imperceptibly moved her head up and down.

Jackson broke the kiss. "They'll arrest us if we keep this up."

Sam laughed. "This town is much too civilized for my taste. Is there a law against public affection?"

Chuckling, Jackson put his hand on her waist and turned her toward a garden sculpture two houses down from where they were standing.

Sam pretended she'd never seen anything lovelier while inquiring, "The second one is just past that house, right?"

"Why, yes, darlin'," he answered, nodding. "Are they the same ones we spotted when we arrived?"

"I think so. Webster's men?" she murmured.

"Probably," Jackson replied. "If they approach, I'll take the one across the street, and you deal with this one. If it comes to that, stumble to the right to get out of my man's line of fire."

"I know the move, Jackson. It's not as though I'll wait to be picked off by a bullet. They could be carrying knives rather than guns." Amazingly, she said it with an affectionate expression on her face.

"Just make sure you do it," Jackson growled. He should have his head examined for agreeing to bring her to see Thomas.

"Mac insisted Morgan and I learn that move when I was ten for Christ's sake," Sam snapped. Shocked at the memory, she momentarily let down her guard and locked eyes with Jackson. *How did I know that?*

Jackson's eyes flicked to the man approaching her. He was only thirty feet away and holding a newspaper with something concealed inside. He also noticed that Hadley must have recognized the danger the approaching strangers presented, because he was moving the carriage forward.

The man who'd been standing behind the hedges in front of the red brick townhouse was halfway across the street.

To Sam's horror, two young women emerged from the house next to Thomas's and stepped into the path of Sam's man. In the dusk, Sam saw the man smile politely and slow his steps to allow the women to merge in front of him onto the walk. The innocent females offered her attacker cover. Sam swore under her breath because their presence gave him the advantage—and the bastard knew it.

As Jackson's man advanced, he became aware of Sam's predicament and realized he was in the same situation. Any shots his attacker fired could easily reach the two women—and Sam, because she no longer had a place to duck out of the way. If both attackers had knives, they might have a slim chance. He had no way of knowing, however, and couldn't risk starting a hail of flying bullets. The fading light was also a disadvantage that made them more vulnerable. It meant there was little chance anyone would notice what was happening and come to their assistance.

Jackson stepped back and took Sam's elbow, forcing her onto Thomas's walkway. His man was stepping off the street. Sam's man was two or three paces behind the women who were about to pass in front of them.

Sam's man took several quick steps to position himself behind Sam and jerk her back against him. He held a knife to her throat. In the last of the early evening light, she could see the long steel blade. The man's breath, a mixture of tobacco and whiskey, smelled stale and repugnant, making her want to gag, but she stood perfectly still, refusing to move or cry out, partially because of pride, but mostly because she didn't want to startle either man into doing something unintended.

Holding a four-chamber derringer pointing at his heart, Jackson's attacker had planted himself, feet spread apart, directly in front of Jackson.

Sam's attacker cupped one of her breasts and ran his tongue up the side of her neck. "Did you see her panting over her beau? She couldn't keep her hands off him.

Webster's gonna be happy to pay us for snatching this bitch. I wonder if he'd mind if I did the deed myself. I'd use her up first, to be sure." His hand moved to Sam's other breast and viciously twisted its peak.

Sensing the man was already half-aroused, Sam pressed her bottom against the front of his trousers and made a small sound of pleasure. She wanted his attention focused on something other than the Colt pointing at his foot. The hammer was cocked to fire. She prayed to the devil that she could draw the second attacker's attention to focus on her body instead of Jackson.

Her man's hand slid to her other breast and kneaded it until its peak hardened and he could pull it taut. Sam provocatively moistened her lips with her tongue and dropped her eyelids as if wanton desire were taking her over. She moved her buttocks in a circular motion against the bulge of his arousal and moaned softly.

From beneath her lashes, Sam couldn't clearly see the features of Jackson's attacker, but she could distinguish when his hungry eyes turned to her lips, then moved down to her chest. She readied her arm to push the hand holding the knife away from her body. *Please, God, let Jackson capture the derringer in time to fire into the ground.* With the prayer uttered silently, Sam squeezed the Colt's trigger and pushed with all her might.

The arms pinioning her dropped, and the man fell to the ground howling in pain. The derringer had fired, but Sam had no idea in what direction. She aimed her Colt at Jackson's man but didn't squeeze the trigger.

With his left arm restraining the arm holding the derringer, Jackson slammed an iron-hard fist into his attacker's jaw. As the man staggered back from the force of the blow, Jackson's fist opened to close over the derringer and pluck it from his assailant's loosened grip.

Sam turned her attention back to her assailant who was holding his foot with one hand and clawing with his other to reach the knife behind Jackson. When he realized the barrel of Sam's revolver was leveled at his head, he froze and raised his hands.

Jackson pulled his Colt from his jacket and backed up to lean against the doorframe of Thomas's house to put both men in his sights. On his way there, he deliberately stomped on the injured foot of the man who'd touched Sam. He half hoped the pervert would give him a reason to kill him.

The door opened behind Jackson, and Thomas stepped out. He reached to take the Colt from Jackson's hand. He nodded toward Mr. Hadley, signaling him to do the same with Sam, who hadn't noticed he was standing next to her because her eyes had moved from the blade of the knife to the blood dripping from Jackson's left arm onto Thomas's walkway.

"Can you handle things with the police, Thomas?" Jackson asked. "Our guns will be a problem."

Thomas nodded.

Sam was moving up the walkway toward Jackson, apparently unhurt. At least he thought so until the light from the window reflected in her eyes. They were wide and unblinking, staring at the dark splotches on the walkway. The pain in his arm merged with his anger over her pulling that trick. *What if he hadn't caught on to her plan? Christ, they'd both be dead.* He wanted to kiss her and turn her over his knee at the same time but found he could do neither with her just standing there as if she were in a trance.

Two policemen arrived just then. One cuffed the men while the other collected the guns from Thomas and Hadley. Thomas pulled the senior officer aside and spoke to him in a low voice. A few minutes later, he instructed Hadley to help Jackson and Sam into the carriage and drive them home. The police would call on them tomorrow. Thomas would be there to handle them.

Favoring his arm, Jackson put his other arm around Sam's waist and led her to the carriage. Thomas lifted her, and Hadley took her from him. Then Thomas helped Jackson pull himself up next to Sam. Jackson's jaw was clenched tightly.

Sam hadn't said a word. With his good arm, Jackson pressed her close to his side.

When the carriage started forward, Sam saw Jackson wince. She closed her eyes as a welcome, numbing blackness descended over her.

Chapter 23

S nuggled against Jackson's side in the hour before dawn, it was easy for Sam to ignore the disturbing remnants of a nightmare in which two of Webster's men had tried to abduct her when she and Jackson left Thomas Miles's office. How much nicer it was to concentrate on the warmth of Jackson's body, the solidness of his shoulder supporting her head, and the breadth of his chest beneath her hand.

Christ, sometimes it felt like the air evaporated from the room when she was with him. She let her splayed fingers and palm rove over his chest and around to his side. Jackson tensed when her hand found and explored the uneven welts of a scar that began where his rib cage ended and rounded his side.

Something blazed in Sam's head, stirring fragments of memory to search for their rightful place in a picture puzzle. She shook her head gently to impose order. When that failed, she closed her eyes, peering inward. Suddenly, each piece snapped into its proper place, and the picture came alive.

***

Sam saw herself standing in a shallow pool of icy water that lapped at her hips. A curtain of cascading water fell behind her, filling the pool before pushing the overflow ten yards beyond her to a straight-edged ledge to plunge to the second tier of its journey to the lake at the base of the hill.

The pool was hidden from view unless an observer were to climb to the top of the hillside above it or wander accidentally into the secluded clearing next to it, which was exactly how Sam had discovered it. The sun was hot on Sam's skin, and the water too tempting. She promised herself she'd stay vigilant and keep her back to the wall of water so she'd spot visitors before they spotted her. What she hadn't considered was that the roar of the falling water would obscure the sound of anyone approaching.

Her plain white cotton shirt and navy-blue riding skirt were neatly folded and piled on a large boulder next to the pool with her belt and boots. She'd carefully positioned her Colt on top of the clothes so she could get to it if someone happened by.

Her flesh-pink undergarment wasn't conventional swimming attire, but it covered her well enough from her shoulders to her knees. The button-front camisole-like bodice and fitted drawers skimmed over the curves of her body in soft nainsook muslin. She preferred it to other undergarments because it was easy to wear under split riding skirts and trousers. She hadn't realized the material would become practically transparent when wet.

Suddenly, an arm snaked around her from behind and pinned her against a bare muscular chest with such speed she couldn't elbow her attacker's midsection. Nor could she scream because the man clamped a hand over her mouth. She started to struggle but stopped when the iron band of muscle imprisoning her pressed the barrel of a Colt into the plump underside of her left breast. She froze.

The man moved his lips to her ear. "Sam, be quiet. It's Jackson."

Jackson! She relaxed—then stiffened with anger. How dare he play such a trick—and why the gun? Jackson's arm tightened, and the gun poked her again.

"Trouble's coming. Three rustlers I've been trailing for two days will be here in a minute. Play along or you'll get us both killed. Understand?" His lips brushed her neck beneath her ear as the hand covering her mouth loosened experimentally.

When Sam nodded her acknowledgment of the situation, his hand lifted. Then Jackson turned her in his arms to face him. She could see the falls but not the rock where her clothes and Colt lay. The rustlers would see more of her back and derriere than anything else.

While keeping the falls in his peripheral vision, Jackson had a clear view of the rock and clearing where the rustlers would arrive. Wrapping his arms around Sam in a strong embrace, he drew her against his chest. His dungarees were open at the waist causing them to ride low on his hips. One of his hands dropped to Sam's backside and pressed her hips into his. Bringing his head near her ear, he said, "If you feel my hand push you toward the falls, dash through and get the Colt I left for you on the ledge."

Sam nodded.

Jackson stared down at her breasts. "Unbutton your bodice. I need to hide my gun."

Sam hesitated for a half second before her fingers rushed to unfasten the buttons. Jackson slid the gun inside, his finger resting lightly on the trigger. The side of his hand and arm rested against the softness of her bare breasts—to onlookers, it would appear as if he were fondling her. His other hand cupped her bottom, aligning her hips with his maleness. Embarrassed, she started to retreat, but he easily held her in place.

"Steady, darlin'," Jackson murmured. "Let me hold you tight against me." His hand on her bottom massaged her flesh, urging her to comply. In her ear he instructed, "Put your arms around me, Sam—kiss me for Christ's sake—at least pretend you like me—Hell, I've seen you bluff at poker. You have nerves of steel. Trust me."

His lips left her ear and traveled to her mouth. She put one arm around his neck and the other around his waist. When he deepened the kiss, she opened her mouth and he thrust his tongue inside to explore hers with a slow sensuality. The muscles in his neck and shoulders were tight. His hand holding the gun flexed against her breast. She began to tremble. She wondered if it was his kiss or fear making every nerve in her body tingle.

Sam didn't hear the riders arrive in the clearing, but she knew they were there because Jackson's hand gave her bottom a slight squeeze. Then she heard one of the riders whoop and yell, "He's got the bitch from Gracelyn Palace panting like a common whore."

Sam admired Jackson's deliberate nonchalance. He took his time breaking their kiss, and, when he focused on the riders, he appeared only mildly annoyed at being interrupted in the middle of pleasuring a lady. Without releasing her, he turned his body to clear her path to the falls—should she need it. She slid her arm from his neck to let it wrap loosely around his waist, so it wouldn't encumber his being able to pull the gun out of her bodice. She felt him reposition his grip on the Colt. The barrel's front sight bit into the tender skin near the nipple of her right breast.

As Jackson's eyes roved idly over the three horsemen, they remained quiet. She was wondering whether his lazy unconcern intimidated them when one of them spoke. The words were so coarse, Sam was afraid to look at Jackson's face.

"I'll hump the bitch next, Knight. She's too much for one man."

Recognizing the lust in the man's voice, Sam felt sick. Vomit rising in her throat, she instinctively pressed closer to Jackson, angry with herself for betraying her fear.

At least one of the rustlers must have drawn his gun because Sam felt the Colt scrape her skin as Jackson pulled it from its hiding place. Turning full front to face the three men, he pushed her with his other hand. She heard a gunshot—then another. The second shot was from Jackson's Colt. She didn't know if he was hit because she was plunging through the curtain of water, her eyes searching the ledge for the Colt, her hand poised to heft and cock it the moment her eyes found it.

"That bitch is going to spread her legs for us, Knight, and you ain't gonna be around to stop it."

"You and your brother aren't touching her, Bodner. I'm giving you fair warning. I'll let you leave if you back out now."

Certain Jackson was stalling to give her time to find the gun, she snatched it up and spun toward the clearing. Though the water dragged at her body, slowing the speed of her turn, she gamely slogged the few steps to the open end of the tunnel-like space. Her eyes and the barrel of the gun found her target at the same moment.

Jackson called his final warning, "You're dead men if you don't leave now."

For a brief second, Sam thought they might back off. The man in her direct line of fire backed his horse a step.

It was a ruse. Both men reached for their guns. Each cleared leather, but neither could raise the barrel to get off a shot. Acting on pure reflex, Sam's eyes narrowed as if seeing a bullseye plastered over the heart of her target. She squeezed the trigger. The man pitched backward, dead before he hit the ground. Jackson's bullet caught his man between the eyes. It wasn't until then that Sam saw Jackson's earlier bullet bored through the chest of the first shooter. The man was lying arms outstretched, his face buried in the mud at the edge of the water.

Sam and Jackson took a step forward at the same time and stopped. Their eyes locked, then broke to return to the dead men. Sam screwed her eyes shut, attempting to wipe the grisly scene from her mind. Then she frowned, suddenly recalling the roar of the first *two* shots. *Was Jackson hurt?*

When her eyes found him, she saw a muscle in his jaw contract. Fighting a sickening dread gathering in her stomach, she willed herself to remain calm while she methodically inspected his shoulders, chest, rib cage, and waist. A bullet had plowed a six-inch furrow in Jackson's side. It would have gone through his side if he hadn't been turning toward the men to shield her while shoving her toward the wall of water.

Transfixed, the drag of the water slowing her progress, Sam went to Jackson, her gaze on the flowing blood and torn flesh. Jackson lifted his hand to cover the wound, but Sam grabbed his wrist, holding it back. Her eyes lifted to his.

He shook his head and leaned to her ear, "It's only a scratch, Sam."

She cupped his head and turned her face to position her lips to his ear. "Damn you, Jackson Knight, how am I supposed to trust you when you tell me bald-faced lies?" She swung around to put her arm around his waist and urged him toward the clearing where the three dead men lay.

He'd risked his life and killed for her. He'd taken a bullet for her.

As they stepped from the water, some of his weight shifted on her. It took all her strength not to buckle. She helped lower him to sit with his back braced against the rock where her clothes were piled. She grabbed her shirt and tore it into strips. Fashioning a pad to press against the gash, she hoped the pressure would stop the bleeding.

Jackson's face was pale. He tried to brush her hands away. Failing, he grabbed her wrists and pulled her close.

"Sonofabitch, Sam—even shot up, all I think about is how much I love you and ache for you to love me."

Sam's eyes filled with tears as she gently wriggled her wrists from his grasp. It wasn't difficult. She could see shock setting in. "Jackson," she whispered tenderly.

Jackson's eyes found hers. Sam saw a mixture of wonder and puzzlement reflected in his gaze. "What is it?" she asked.

"When you say my name like that, I go a little crazy. How do you do that?"

***

The memory vanished. Sam shut her eyes and choked back a sob, overwhelmed by emotion. Then her eyes flew open, and she flung herself across Jackson's chest to run her hand up his left arm. When she touched the bandage halfway between his elbow and shoulder, she pulled her hand back as if she'd touched fire. First, the memory of the waterfall, and now proof that yesterday's nightmare in front of Thomas's house had been real.

Jackson's right hand tangled in her hair, urging her to turn toward him. Endeavoring to hide her emotions, she refused to meet his eyes. *She'd almost gotten him killed.*

"Look at me, Sam."

Sam refused, gently shaking her head.

"Look me in the eyes, Sam." His voice was stern.

She tried to bolt from the bed, but Jackson was too quick. His hand left her hair to grip her arm. He was too strong. "Let me go, Jackson. How many times have you been hurt because of me?"

Jackson's voice was sharp. "What do you mean, *how many times*? Goddamn it, did you remember something when you touched my side?"

She didn't answer.

He sat up, and she saw him wince from the pain in his arm. His voice turned gentle and pleading, "Please, Sam, tell me."

She touched the bandage on his wounded arm. "How bad is it? I don't remember anything after we got in the carriage."

"I know, darlin'. I guess you just couldn't take any more by then. You haven't recovered your strength from the injuries you sustained in the stage crash, so going through what you did with Webster's henchmen was too much for you. Morgan carried you in, and Alexa put you to bed. After the doctor saw to my arm, he checked you over. My arm will heal just fine and work just as good as it did before."

"It was the knife, wasn't it? My man stabbed you when I pushed his arm away from me."

Jackson's eyes and jaw hardened. "I reckon that's how it happened, but, Sam, if you hadn't pulled that trick, they would've murdered us. They'd have put me out of my misery fast, but what they intended for—"

Jackson couldn't say it. Still holding her, he said instead, "You didn't answer my question. You remembered something when you touched the scar on my side, didn't you?"

"Yes, I—I remembered how you saved me at the pool by the waterfall." She felt him draw in a sharp breath.

Her arms wrapped around his chest, and she hugged him as close as she could get him. "I love you, Jackson, and now I *know* why."

"Darlin', when your memory returns, you'll know neither of us can exist without the other. It's just the way it is."

Chapter 24

"Thomas, why are you upset?" Sam asked later that same day after the two policemen who'd visited to investigate yesterday's altercation left her townhouse.

Teeming with disapproval and choosing not to answer, Thomas sat behind the desk in Sam's library with his arms crossed.

Uncomfortable with the silence, Sam decided to remind him of just how well things had gone. "You heard everything Jackson and I told them. We followed your advice to the letter. Jackson was charmingly apologetic and presented just the right amount of regret in his portrayal of the 'but-what's-a-man-to-do-when-the-woman-he-loves-is-in-terrible-danger' role. And I must say, as distasteful as it was for me to have to resort to it, I thought I was particularly convincing acting the part of the helpless, frightened, and victimized damsel who broke the law only because 'the villains tried to ravage me so what was a poor girl to do?' I practically had them patting my head and saying, 'There, there, my dear child!' And you and Hadley corroborated our statements."

Thomas rolled his eyes, but Sam pretended not to notice. "Besides, the two henchmen admitted they were guilty and that Webster hired them, which means we won't have to testify. It's unfortunate that Webster got away, though. At least we know he's no longer in Chicago. Morgan has already sent a telegram to Parker and Mac to warn them

Webster may be coming their way. It says, 'Buyer of HQ Lee stock looking for another possible acquisition.'"

Thomas's expression was stern.

Sam tried harder to defuse his anger. Maybe a little flattery would work. "Thomas, you handled everything perfectly. I couldn't believe it when you convinced them to return our guns—so, all in all, it seems to me everything is working out well."

Thomas had heard enough. "Knock it off, Sam. We all know how serious the situation was and how lucky you and Jackson were to come out of it as well as you did. Since I know you don't remember how well I know you, I'll tell you. I'm as clever as you are. You don't need to pretend with me, and you don't need to manipulate me. I trust you, and you trust me because I'm good at what I do, and I care about you and Morgan. Do we understand each other?"

Sam knew he deserved her respect. "Yes, Thomas, we do. I apologize. Thank you for being frank. I can only offer the excuse that things have been so stressful of late that I don't always take the time to think before I act—or speak. Perhaps in this instance, I did get a little overconfident because of my success with the policemen."

"Sam, you're shameless. You just tried it again." Thomas pretended to look at some papers he was holding to hide the twitch of amusement threatening his lips.

"Ah, but I saw it almost made you smile, so I know you forgive me."

Thomas lifted Sam's hand to cover it with his. "I do, Sam. Greta and I will see you tomorrow for your supper party. Earlier this morning, I sent the invitations to your cousin, Tanner, and his fiancée, Miss Gray. You should receive an answer later this afternoon."

Sam was pleased. "It will only be us four couples, Thomas, but I'd like it to be special. That's why I'm requesting everyone dress grandly. Have I given you enough time to finish the paperwork?"

"Yes, Sam, by tomorrow the papers will be ready, and, as part of the festivities, you'll be able to sign over the estate to Tanner. Have you explained things to Morgan yet?"

"No, I intend to take care of that next."

"He'll come around, Sam. Just explain everything except the one thing you aren't ready to tell him, and he'll fall under your spell."

"Why, Thomas, you almost make it sound as if I'm capable of witchcraft."

"That's because you are."

***

"Morgan, would you please just listen to me?" Sam implored. Her brother had come to the library to talk to her soon after Thomas had left. "I know someone is living on the estate. My second cousin, Tanner Roberts, lives there. Thomas told me all about it yesterday." Sam was trying her best to be understanding, but Morgan was more upset than she expected.

"Don't even get me started on yesterday, Sam. I'm the one that carried you in from the carriage last night. For a minute, I thought Webster succeeded in murdering you. Jackson told me about that brazen trick you pulled. Christ, you'll put me in an early grave. Even thinking about it makes my heart stutter."

Feeling guilty, Sam realized Morgan had been more than upset. Hoping to absolve herself and move on, she apologized before playfully taunting him. "I'm truly sorry I gave you a scare, Brother. Besides, what would you do for excitement without me? Kiss Alexa more often?"

"You shameless witch! And don't start with that Brother stuff to get around me. *Cousins?* For Christ's sake, you don't have any cousins, Sam."

"Morgan, for a man normally in control, you're ricocheting between subjects like a bullet in a narrow canyon. I had no idea I had cousins, but I've discovered I have two. When I went to settle the estate, I found my cousin Tanner living there, and he showed me the secret compartment in Uncle Aaron's study containing all sorts of papers. That's how we learned we have another cousin."

"You mean both cousins are illegitimate?"

"Morgan, Aaron fathered them. You know the kind of man he was. Besides killing my father's parents, he took in young girls as wards under the pretense of offering them his protection so he could use them to satisfy his perverse sexual needs. They didn't choose him, nor did their children choose him as a father."

Sam saw Morgan was still resistant. "Aaron didn't publicly acknowledge Tanner. However, because his mother, Celia, threatened to expose Aaron, he did finance Tanner's education. Tanner is nine years older than I am and, as it turns out, a fine man. When Aaron's health began to decline, Aaron begged Tanner to come and live with him. Tanner knew Aaron's ulterior motive was to turn him against me, but Tanner saw it as an opportunity. Although Aaron treated him as little more than a servant, he stayed with my uncle and managed his care until his death." Sam paused to take a breath.

"During that time, Aaron tried to twist Tanner's mind, telling him my father and I cheated him out of what should have been his rightful place. He said if my father hadn't tied his hands, he would've been able to claim Tanner as his son. Aaron tried everything he could to make Tanner resent and hate me, including repeatedly calling him a bastard. He wanted Tanner to believe his life could have taken a different course if not for me. Aaron wanted Tanner to become as vile and evil as he was."

Sam watched Morgan's face. She trusted Tanner and was doing her damnedest to persuade Morgan to keep an open mind. "Tanner didn't turn against me. He had access to everything in the house and soon discovered the agreement my father made with Uncle Aaron. He found the papers hidden in the downstairs study. Everything was there, evidence of all Aaron's crimes. We even found tools he used to satisfy his sexual fetishes."

"But, Sam, these *cousins* may be trying to cash in on their relationship with you."

Sam couldn't fault Morgan's logic. "You know I'm not fool enough to let someone take advantage of me that way— and even if I were, Thomas would never allow it. He would've gone straight to you and told you just enough not to break confidentiality so you could convince me to talk to you."

"Then why isn't he doing that now for what you're keeping from me?"

"Morgan, if you don't stop lifting that questioning eyebrow of yours, I swear I'll shave it off the next time I find you sleeping. It's infuriating! Thomas showed me the report from the Pinkerton agent I hired to investigate the situation. It proved the cousins weren't trying anything underhanded. Before I returned to Trinity, I instructed Thomas to draw up papers transferring the family estate to Tanner, along with a percentage of the profits from some of the investments to allow him to live there comfortably. He's engaged to be married. Perhaps a loving family will be able to remove the taint of Aaron Stone."

Morgan felt as if a big weight had been lifted from his chest. "Why the hell would you try to keep *that* from me? Thomas treated it as if it were a dark secret, for Christ's sake. I thought you were going behind my back because you didn't trust me—or that you were being blackmailed—or, sonofabitch, Sam, I was imagining all kinds of things."

"Well, don't be so relieved yet, because I *am going behind your back* about something."

"What did you say?"

"I asked Thomas to draw up papers for something else I'm not ready to tell you about—yet—*so I'm going behind your back for just a little while longer*. I promise, Morgan, I'll tell you all about it before I sign the papers, and, if you don't agree to my plan, I won't do it. I'll even let you tear up the papers."

"What in the hell does that mean? I don't know the last time I heard that much drivel from any one person!"

"Morgan, it isn't drivel, I swear. I'm simply asking you to trust me. I need to make sure of one detail before I can explain what I'm doing. I truly believe you'll approve. But if you don't, I'll honor your wishes. Even without my memory, I know what we are to each other. Will you trust me?"

"You really aren't in any trouble I should be worried about?"

"No, and, what's more important, I want you to know I never meant to hurt your feelings or make you worry, Brother. I'm very sorry and can only ask you to forgive me."

"All right, Sam, I'll trust you, and I'll forgive you." He almost dropped the subject before recalling a couple of other points to cover. "Why do you still look guilty about something, Sam?"

"Because I need to tell you about the other cousin—you remember, I mentioned that I discovered I have *two* cousins?"

"Trust me, Sis, I didn't forget. I was trying to muster the fortitude to address it."

Sam swallowed hard before speaking, "Yes, well, the other cousin is a woman we're very fond of."

Morgan didn't respond. He knew she'd get to it quicker if he waited her out.

Sam tried to deflect the anger she expected her surprise to provoke by asking, "Would you please promise to take a few seconds to work through it before you react? I think if you do, you'll be as pleased as I am about her."

Morgan gave no indication he heard. He simply sat with his arms crossed and waited.

"Alexa is my cousin."

Morgan stared at Sam. Surely, he'd misheard. "Did you say Alexa Danforth is your cousin?"

Sam studied his face. *What was he thinking?* With trepidation in her voice, she replied, "Yes, Alexa is my cousin. She wanted to tell you herself, but I asked her to keep it a secret. She only promised not to say anything because I swore it wouldn't hurt you."

Astonishment didn't begin to describe Morgan's surprise. Thunderstruck was the better word. In his mind, he remembered the first time he saw Alexa. The resemblance was undeniably there. Now that he knew, he was shocked he hadn't seen it before this.

Sam didn't think it should matter, but she understood why it might temporarily rattle him. *Please don't let this change how he feels about Alexa.* Anxiously, Sam inquired, "Now that you know, will you love her even more?"

Instead of answering Sam's question, Morgan asked one of his own. "Do you think I should love her more, Sis?"

Something in Morgan's voice made Sam think it would be all right. "Jackson said we thought she was the one for you the first day you met. That's why he didn't let her get on the train and run away. Alexa told you about that, didn't she?"

Morgan nodded. "Yes. She also mentioned you advised her to work it out with me. Did you tell her that, Sam?" Morgan saw an odd expression pass over his sister's face.

"I don't remember, Morgan, but, if Alexa said I did, it must be true."

"Why do you look so pale, Sis? Are you feeling unwell?"

"I'm fine. I remembered a little bet I made with Jackson, that's all. I'll tell you about it another time. Would you promise not to mention it to him, though?"

"I don't understand. What is it you don't want me to tell Jackson?"

"Don't tell Jackson I advised Alexa to work it out with you—I prefer to tell him myself. Of course, if he were to ask you straight out, it's all right to tell him the truth. I'm just asking you not to volunteer it."

"Sam, this is very odd."

"I know. It's because we can't settle the bet yet, and I want time to think about it."

"Shouldn't you have thought about it before you accepted it?" Morgan asked, curious.

"I did think about it—now I want some time to get used to the idea—ignore me, Morgan. I know I'm talking in circles. By now, you must realize love can do that to you."

Morgan let it go. He didn't want to make a problem for Jackson. The man had his hands full, and he didn't intend to stir the proverbial pot.

Sam returned to her question about Morgan loving Alexa. He hadn't answered her. "Morgan, does it matter that Alexa is my cousin? Are you angry we didn't tell you?"

"Hell, Sis, I don't care if Alexa is related to Jesse James. I'd love her even if she were the devil's mistress."

Chapter 25

Alexa stepped into Sam's room. She looked regal in a red satin, silver-bead-trimmed evening gown that followed the contours of her figure past her knees before flaring out dramatically.

"That dress looks as if it were custom-made for your shape," Sam remarked. "Morgan won't be able to take his eyes off you. The off-the-shoulder neckline is breathtaking."

Alexa critically inspected herself in the mirror. "Breathtaking may be an aptly dangerous description, Sam. I'm afraid if I take a deep breath, the whole thing will fall away."

"Nonsense, my dress is the one to worry about," Sam assured her.

Alexa reported on the status of the guests. "Morgan and Jackson are downstairs already. Tanner and Miss Gray are here. I heard Thomas and Greta arrive when I passed the top of the stairs. Are you ready, Sam?"

"Yes, but I'm nervous."

"Understandable," Alexa commented before adding, "Remember, you need to make an entrance, so don't start down the stairs until I reach the bottom and take Morgan's arm. The whole evening will be spoiled for me if I miss Jackson's reaction to seeing you in that dress. The man's heart is likely to stop at the sight of you."

After allowing Alexa time to descend the staircase, Sam moved to the landing and paused. Having selected a dress designed solely for igniting men's passion, she hoped it would fulfill its function—seduction. She stood motionless while waiting for Jackson's eyes to search up. When the moment came, she watched his eyes slowly devour her, traveling over every curve showcased in the clinging silk.

Jackson was as entranced as he was stunned. Christ almighty, the sight of her could reduce a man to ashes. The last time he'd seen that dress, it was pooled on the floor at the foot of their bed. His mind began replaying all the intricacies of removing it.

Sam's eyes didn't waver from Jackson as she descended the stairs. Her feet fairly floated above the treads and the hem of the emerald green silk gown she wore in her first remembrance of Jackson flowed behind her in soft rustling whispers.

Morgan's eyes widened. He couldn't remember ever seeing Sam in such a daring dress. "Sis, you look devastating."

Thomas Miles looked knowingly at his wife, Greta, and she squeezed his arm, acknowledging discreetly she concurred with his opinion.

Tanner Roberts, Sam's cousin and guest of honor, watched Jackson's reaction to Sam's entrance and caught on quickly. When he noticed his fiancée's shocked expression, he pressed his lips to her temple and whispered a few words near her ear. A benign smile replaced her shock, and her eyes sparkled, anticipating the evening's events.

Sam turned her full attention to Jackson and almost stopped breathing when she recognized the fire smoldering in his eyes. She raised an inquiring eyebrow and pasted on what she hoped was a demure smile. "I remembered wearing this dress once before," she commented. Then, lowering her tone, she added, "As I recall, you remarked it set off my—attributes—admirably."

Already reeling, Jackson was stunned to hear her use the words "remembered" and "recall." *What does she mean she remembers?* Moving his gaze to the creamy mounds of flesh overflowing Sam's dress, Jackson let a mildly puzzled expression settle on his face before replying in a puzzled tone, "I'm surprised I didn't inquire whether you feared suffering a chill in the night air." Then, shrugging as if it made no difference, he added, "For this occasion, I wonder if your gown might not be a little too—grand."

Sam smiled innocently, but her reply was intentionally provocative. "I believe it's the *perfect* gown for the evening I've planned."

Jackson almost lost his mind. Christ, did she know how that sounded to a man, especially one who wanted her as much as he did? It took almost a full two seconds for him to catch on. He blamed his slow comprehension on the fact his blood was rushing from his brain to another place in his body. *Of course, the witch knew exactly how her words sounded. She's casting another of her spells.*

Thomas and Morgan exchanged glances, recognizing the invitation and challenge in Sam's tone. Thomas thought Jackson looked as if he wanted to throw Sam over his shoulder, carry her upstairs, and change her dress for her. Morgan suspected Sam was trying to provoke Jackson into taking exactly that sort of action. Morgan's eyes wandered speculatively to Alexa only to find her gaze waiting for his.

***

Sam tossed Jackson one last sultry look before turning to her cousin. "Tanner and Miss Gray—Helen, if I may, Thomas explained we spent some time together on my last visit, but my amnesia prevents me from recollecting the details. I'm so pleased you could join us tonight. We have a surprise planned for you."

Tanner reminded Sam of her father. His hair was slightly darker than her father's had been, but he had the same honey-tinged highlights. His blue eyes were more sky blue than the darker, slate blue that shadowed her and Alexa's eyes. Not as tall as Jackson, Tanner's height would have matched her father's, which put him a little past the six-foot mark. Sam smiled fondly, recalling the brief memory of her tall, handsome father bending to kiss Grace.

"Helen and I are sorry about your memory, Sam," Tanner replied, his voice warm and sincere. "Jackson and Morgan told us you've remembered a few things, though, so perhaps you'll recover soon."

Sam thought the timbre of Tanner's voice was faintly familiar. Perhaps it also reminded her of her father. "It's of no consequence, Tanner. I'm among family and friends and that's all that matters. Jackson has been devoted, as have Morgan and Alexa. Memory or no, I'm a very lucky woman."

Smoothly, Sam continued, "Tanner, you were with me when we discovered you have a sister and I have a cousin." Motioning to Alexa, she said, "This is Miss Alexa Danforth." Then turning to Tanner, she completed the introduction, "Alexa, this is Tanner Benjamin Roberts and his fiancée, Miss Helen Gray."

Alexa stepped forward. "I'm very pleased to meet you both." Directing her gaze to Tanner's, she added, "I was delighted to learn from Sam that I have a brother. I'm truly sorry the circumstances of our births didn't allow us the opportunity to know one another before this."

"As am I, Alexa. But now that we've found each other, I hope, in time, we'll be able to establish the closeness we were denied through no fault of our own."

"I'm looking forward to it, Tanner."

"Shall we get acquainted over dinner?" Sam suggested. Jackson offered his arm to escort her to the dining room. As she took it, Sam whispered, "You look extraordinarily handsome, Jackson. I thank my stars no other women are here to steal your attention."

Surprised at her remark, Jackson murmured, "You're the only woman I notice, darlin'." He felt her hand on his arm tighten and saw her eyes sweep over him tenderly. He felt as if she'd physically caressed him. His heart turned over with one big thump.

While Jackson held Sam's chair, she let her fingers linger on his arm before tilting her head so he could see deep into the cleavage of her siren dress. A surge of desire slammed through his body with such intensity it forced him to slide into the chair next to hers and drop his napkin in his lap. Willing his mind to focus on anything but Sam, he considered knocking his water glass into his lap to cool his ardor. Unfortunately, the thought of Sam helping to sop it up inflated his condition. Damn, the blood in his veins was raging as if he were an inexperienced youth with no self-control.

Finally, after dessert was served, Sam turned the conversation to the purpose of the gathering, while Thomas removed papers from his inside coat pocket and passed them to Tanner.

"You may examine these papers at your leisure," Sam said, addressing her cousin. "Stone Bluffs Manor is now yours. I'm gifting you our family home and a percentage of profits from several enterprises so you may live there comfortably until the day you choose to bequeath it to your children, should you and Helen be so blessed. Thomas will record the deed after you sign in the necessary places."

Tanner was stunned and started to say so, but Sam laid a hand over his and said quietly, "Just say thank you, Tanner, and let it go. We have many years to get to know one another and to share our lives. It is my pleasure to do this."

Humbled, Tanner covered her hand and did as she asked. "Thank you, Sam. Helen and I thank you and look forward to the future years you just mentioned."

***

For Jackson, the night was one long agony. *Was Sam baiting him or making a promise?* He told himself she may not have made up her mind; although, he'd believed she'd passed that hurdle the previous morning when she admitted she remembered the waterfall.

He was uncertain, so he told himself to be prepared for disappointment—but the truth was, his patience was wearing thin. He'd never wanted her more. The desire she stirred in him was painful. Hell, much more and he'd have no recourse except to excuse himself. He couldn't take his eyes off her breasts straining against the décolleté of that dress nor could he stop imagining what she'd look like when the dress fell from her. Would she welcome him?

Eventually, Sam moved close to whisper in his ear. "Jackson, I've wanted to ask you all evening if you know when I first remembered about this gown."

The teasing witch. *If she's not careful, she'll have me crushing her under me where everyone can see us.* She leaned closer, and her breasts brushed his arm. He swore under his breath and forced his eyes up. In a low, warning voice, he said, "Sam, you're playing with fire. You can't expect a man to be patient when you wear something like that and tease him for three hours. I'll humor you, though. Did you remember the gown when you saw it in your wardrobe?"

204

The corners of Sam's mouth turned up playfully, and she shook her head. "Oh, no, Jackson." She lowered her eyes as if shy. "Come, I'll show you."

"But your guests."

"Alexa is already ushering them into the library to admire a portrait of my father's parents that Tanner and I found in a storage room of the estate. She'll tell them we've retired because my head's aching and your arm is bothering you."

She took Jackson's hand and drew him toward the stairs. As she took the first step, she said, "I remembered about the dress much sooner than when I saw it in the wardrobe." She took three more steps. "Remember that day after the crash when I panicked after you teased me about carrying me down the stairs to the study?"

Caught in the spell she was weaving, Jackson nodded and let her draw him up the rest of the stairs and down the hall to their bedroom door. She turned and let her eyes travel boldly up the length of his body until she once again was staring into his eyes. He couldn't look away.

"Parker watched from the downstairs hallway. I think he knew I remembered something, just not what. I didn't tell him—or anyone else for that matter—not even you."

Sam grasped the doorknob behind her and turned it. Gently tugging Jackson's hand, she backed into the room. "At first, the memory was too intimate and confusing. It frightened me—I wasn't afraid of you, mind, but of whoever was watching us ascend those stairs in that strange house." She dipped her shoulder forward, allowing him to see deeper into the valley between her breasts. Then she leaned against his chest to reach around him to push the door shut.

"Sam, this isn't fair—I've warned you."

"I was wearing this dress, almost falling out of it just as I am now. You were in a black formal coat. Very handsome, I might add. Just looking at you made me want you. I was vaguely aware of something being wrong with my right leg, but I don't know what. I assume that's the reason you were carrying me."

She moved closer to him. "Do I need to remind you of—the liberties you took with me? I was afraid to encourage you, though, because someone was watching us—I was afraid for you and afraid for myself."

Sam's voice lowered as if inviting him to step into a vortex of temptation. "Do I need to tell you what you said to me and how you touched me? I wanted to respond, you know, but I held back because of my fear for you. Instead, I persuaded you to take me to my room."

Jackson's desire was almost molten, but he willed himself to speak in a normal voice. "No, you don't need to tell me. I believe I could describe every caress, every kiss, and every moment of the time we were together there." Then he let his lips follow the line of her neck.

Sam inhaled a sharp breath. She hadn't expected him to admit it. Nor had she expected her knees to feel weak so quickly.

Jackson spoke again, this time with amazement. "You already knew we had feelings for each other and were lovers?"

Nodding with her eyes lowered, Sam spoke in a sad, loving tone. "I felt it, but I didn't understand. The memory was brief. I recognized the passion and desire flowing between us—What I *felt* was more a revelation. I *felt* I loved you. The love was what made the passion possible for me. But I wondered what you felt for me and whether any of the things I sensed were real. Feelings aren't facts. I trusted you, though I had no understanding of why. I was sick, dependent, afraid, and, as it turned out, drugged and having nightmares. I questioned my feelings and I worried about that watcher. I almost went out of my mind worrying about how much danger I was putting you in. On the day you carried me to the study, even as dizzy and sick as I was, all I could think about were your hands on my body and how it felt when you kissed me. I remembered the lake and the falls because I tried to distract myself by thinking about a cool bath." Sam stopped speaking—giving time for the meaning to sink in.

Her voice turned suggestive again. "Tell me Jackson, what did we do by that lake? I have a feeling it moved me— deeply." She pressed against him. "Did I encourage you to touch me? Did you grasp my waist and pull me against you so I could feel how much you wanted me—as I feel you now?"

She reached for the back of his head to bring his lips to hers. "How could it be that I was unsure? When I can make you feel like this—and you can make me do this?" She kissed him then and placed one of his hands on her breast. She wanted everything at once. Her lips parted, and her tongue began a sensual exploration.

Jackson ran his hands down the sides of her body and around to her backside, pushing her hips firmly against him.

She broke the kiss and whispered, "I tortured you and myself. Even that night when I tried to pretend to Morgan that you weren't important to me, I knew different. I was ashamed of what I said before the words left my lips. If you'd stayed, you would've heard me admit it. There's no one else in this world for me. Am I the only woman for you?"

Jackson gripped her upper arms and kissed her as if he'd never be satiated.

Breathless, but needing him to understand, she drew her mouth away from his only far enough to ask, "Can you feel my bones melt? Whenever you come near me, I feel like this. Would you like me to show you how much I love you?"

Jackson half groaned, tightened his arms to pull her back, and bent his head to capture her mouth again. Then he swung her into his arms to put her on the bed.

"Wait, Jackson."

"I can't anymore, Sam."

"You can, Jackson," Sam pleaded. "Help me take off this god-awful dress."

Jackson took a calming breath. Had she changed her mind? "Are you afraid, Sam? Do you want to stop?"

"No, Jackson, I want this. I *planned* this—but I don't want to disappoint you, so I'm a little anxious." Her slate blue eyes had an unmistakable sheen.

"There's no reason to feel anxious. Everything you do pleases me. You'll see."

Sam smiled. "And if I don't see, you'll show me."

"More likely, you'll show me, you witch." He kissed her and turned her around to make quick work of unfastening the dress. As it slid to the floor, he began kissing and caressing his way through the buttons and bows of each remaining garment.

Somewhere between removing her clothes and touching her until she was crazy with need, he managed to shrug off his jacket and shirt. The feel of his bare skin on her skin sent bursts of heat racing through her. When he kissed her again, it was a hungry, aching kiss that replaced her anxiety with a desire so deep it felt as though it touched her soul.

Without breaking the kiss, Jackson swept her up in his arms. He laid her gently on the bed, shed the rest of his clothes, and joined her. They coupled with an urgency that shook them both. When she went over the edge, he followed her.

Still joined, Sam whispered against his mouth, "Was it always like this, Jackson?"

Jackson nodded.

Sam's lips curved in a smile, and she laughed softly, lovingly. "It's inconceivable I could have forgotten that. Perhaps we should repeat it just to make sure I never forget it again."

Jackson laughed and kissed her languorously. "Let's see if I can remember all the steps, darlin'."

"Before you do, tell me you'll take me home tomorrow or the day after. We're done with Chicago, aren't we? I want to go home to Prosperity and be with you."

Jackson held her against him, never wanting to let her go. "Yes, Sam, we'll go home."

Chapter 26

A day and a half out of Chicago on the train back to Prosperity, Jackson slouched against the arm of the settee in Sam's private rail car watching the scenery stream by. Feeling warm and sleepy, Sam was curled up next to him with her head nestled on his chest.

Impulsively, Sam raised her head to place a feather-light kiss on Jackson's throat before tucking her arms beneath his jacket and snuggling close. His arm tightened protectively around her as he dropped a kiss to the top of her head.

Alexa and Morgan would follow in two days. Morgan had said something peculiar about a recent merger for which he still needed to assess and negotiate the surrender of assets. He'd suggested Alexa stay to help because she was responsible for bringing the interested parties together. Morgan indicated her presence was essential.

Looking mildly flustered, Alexa had readily agreed to Morgan's suggestion if he promised they could pay a visit to her father, Oliver Danforth, before returning to Prosperity.

Jackson had been inordinately amused by the whole conversation. Whenever Sam had tried to interject a comment or ask a question, he'd squeezed her arm to warn her to stay quiet or had interrupted so she couldn't finish. Sam understood what was going on. Although it was none of her business, she thought it silly of them to fabricate an excuse for wanting to be alone. It wasn't until later it occurred to her to wonder if Morgan would ask Oliver Danforth for permission to marry his daughter.

"Jackson?"

"Hmm?"

"It's amazing how much better I feel. The motion of the train doesn't bother me much." She felt his lips brush her temple. "It's nice to be alone with you." His lips moved to the soft curve of her cheek. Aware he couldn't reach her mouth, she tilted her head up. He was waiting for her and covered her mouth with a gentle kiss. When he leaned back against the settee, she said, "You say I'm a witch, but it appears you have a few spells of your own."

Jackson's voice sounded content and amused when he replied, "You've taught me an incantation or two. Now let me rest so you can teach me another one later."

***

When Sam woke, she had no idea how long they'd slept. She drew back from Jackson to peer out the windows. It was dark, and, obviously, deep enough into the night for the moon and stars to have come out. Jackson didn't wake as he typically did when she moved away. Instead, he pulled her back against him and murmured something about being cold. His breathing sounded labored, and she felt him shiver.

Sam touched his forehead. His skin was abnormally warm—hot. She remembered he hadn't eaten much. He'd pushed his food around on his plate while encouraging her to eat. She started to ease from his side when his voice stopped her.

"Sam, I'm cold. Before you go, would you kiss me?" His voice sounded weak and hoarse. His eyes remained closed.

"Darling, you read my mind. Let's go into the bedroom where we can stretch out under the blankets. It will be nice and warm, and I'll give you all the kisses you want." He didn't stir.

Sam cupped his face while letting her lips linger on his. Then, inching away, she prayed he would follow. "Jackson, darling, I need you in bed if I'm to teach you a new incantation."

When he struggled to stand, she moved close, wrapping an arm around his waist to support him. He was unsteady but still strong enough to walk. She guided him into the bedroom, where he pulled her down with him to sit on the bed.

"Sam?"

"Yes, Jackson."

"I was worried you wouldn't love me. Without your love, I doubted I could soldier on like my father taught me."

The strong surge of love Sam felt made it difficult to speak. "If I lost my memory a hundred times, I would never lose my love for you, Jackson."

"Kiss me, Sam."

She kissed him while her hands sought the buttons on his shirt. "Let me take off your clothes, Jackson. Wouldn't you like me to undress you?"

"Kiss me again."

As she placed her parted lips on his, Sam slipped one arm around his neck and the other on his shoulder. Then, deepening her kiss, she slid her hand gently from the top of his shoulder down onto his injured arm. He winced.

Resting her hand back on his shoulder, she leaned back to study his face. "Jackson, your eyes are glassy, and you feel overly warm."

"I could get much warmer if you stayed close, darlin'," he murmured. The man was a marvel. Had she not been so worried, she would have laughed. Instead, she held his jacket, while he slipped his right arm from the sleeve. When he didn't attempt to move his injured arm, Sam carefully inched his jacket off. Then she started on his shirt. He cooperated for the first arm but left the second to her. Once she worked the cloth past his bandage, she pulled it over his wrist and hand.

After sweeping his jacket and shirt to the floor, she fluffed two pillows and gently pressed her upper body against Jackson's bare torso, persuading him to turn and lean back. Then, she lifted one leg at a time onto the bed and tugged off his boots. Instead of removing his trousers, she settled for unfastening them at the waist.

"Jackson, your arm has been bleeding, and there's some seepage. I think it's infected," Sam pronounced after inspecting his bandage.

As if he hadn't heard her, Jackson said, "I'm still cold, Sam. Lie down with me." His voice was weaker, breathy, as if he didn't have enough air to say more than a few words at a time.

Sam moved to the other side of the bed and slid in next to him. While pulling the bedcovers up around his shoulders, she said, "I'll stay with you, but you must close your eyes and rest." He didn't protest.

When he was asleep, Sam strapped on her Colt and went in search of a doctor.

***

While the doctor was tending Jackson, Sam hurried to the mail car to send a telegraph to Parker and Mac.

Major asset damaged. Pulling back position. Will know outcome by Weds latest. Standby.

Sam had struggled to compose a message Parker and Mac would understand. The "major asset damaged" meant Jackson was hurt. The words "pulling back position" meant they were returning to Prosperity. By adding "will know outcome by Weds latest," she was telling them she and Jackson would be arriving on the last train on Wednesday. "Standby" was the word meant to convey she wanted them to meet the train.

Sam threw down the money to pay for the wire and hurried away before the operator could count the words and make change. Striding back to their private car, her gun hand hovered over her Colt. Webster had supposedly left Chicago, but she knew he might have hired replacements for the men who had failed outside Thomas's office. She wasn't taking any chances.

Advancing through the door, Sam saw the doctor was still working on Jackson's arm. That wasn't a good sign. Blood soaked the layers of towels supporting his arm, and the basin of hot water she'd placed near the doctor before she left was bright red. Jackson's eyes were closed, his jaw was clenched, and his head thrashed from side to side, pushing deep into the pillow in response to the various instruments the doctor used to clean the suppuration out of the wound. Sam's stomach lurched. When he stifled a groan and called her name, she bolted to the side of the bed, fell on her knees, and scooped up his right hand to hold it against her chest. She placed her other hand on his bare shoulder. Jackson quieted at her touch, and the doctor gave her an approving nod.

"Just a little more, son. I'm almost done. Hold on to the little lady."

Jackson's eyes flicked open before he passed out. Sam was relieved he didn't regain consciousness. After bandaging his arm, the doctor fashioned a sling to immobilize it.

"Don't let him take his arm out of the sling over the next three days. I want you to check the wound and change the bandage every six hours. Use your strength to move his arm. Don't let him do it." Then he demonstrated the motions to use and explained how to care for the wound and replace the bandage.

"As you saw, I opened the wound and cleaned out the infection. I'm afraid it looks worse now, but it had to be done. It will be painful. I gave him some laudanum and measured out his next dose. Give him a dose each time you change the dressing—you say the wound is almost four days old?"

Sam nodded.

"We caught it early enough. He's strong and healthy. It will heal, and he'll have full use of the arm if he follows orders," the doctor reported before giving Sam instructions on dosing Jackson with medicine to clear his lungs. "A colleague of mine, Roy Baxter, is the doctor in Prosperity. When you get there, see that Roy treats him right away. We don't want that congestion to turn into pneumonia. Until then, take care of the arm, dosing him with the laudanum, and keep him quiet. His fever will get worse before it gets better, but I'm betting it will break by tomorrow morning."

The doctor ran his eyes over the young woman, sizing her up. She looked capable of shooting the fancy Colt she wore strapped over the skirt of her dress, but she was too damn frail and wan by far to wrestle the tall, powerfully muscled cowboy if he went out of his head with fever. "Are you sure you're up to this? I could inquire in the passenger cars to find a woman willing to help you."

Sam locked eyes with the doctor. "I can handle it."

The doctor noticed the set of her jaw and the determination in her eyes. "Humph, well, eat something. Then get some rest yourself. It won't hurt him. It might even help keep him quiet. The less he tries to move that arm, the better. I'll be back to check on him around the time you need to change the bandage. I get off the train soon after. You'll be on your own then."

Sam followed the doctor to the door and locked it behind him. Then she moved to the side table, poured a glass of brandy, tossed it back in two gulps, and swiped her mouth with the back of her hand. She remembered lecturing Jackson about sipping it the night he cut the buttons off her nightdress. Aloud she said, "Words have a way of coming back to haunt you."

Ignoring the doctor's order to eat, Sam went back to the bedroom. Jackson's breathing was raspy. Quietly, she spoke to him. "The things you suffer because of me, Providence Jackson Knight." She unstrapped her gun belt and placed her Colt next to her pillow. After removing her shoes, she slipped out of her dress and laid her robe on the end of the bed so she could shrug it on later when the doctor returned.

After easing under the covers next to Jackson, she brushed a few strands of his black hair off his forehead and murmured, "We'll be home soon. By tomorrow, around suppertime, the train will pull into Prosperity. Parker and Mac will be there, and I'll go and get Doc right away. Doc will make you well. If Webster tries anything between now and then, I promise I'll shoot him so full of holes the devil won't recognize him when he plummets into hell."

***

While Jackson's fever raged, Sam's attempts to restrain him physically failed. Even in his weakened state, her strength was no match for his. Her forearms and wrists were bruised. She couldn't imagine the bruises she'd have if he'd been able to use both arms. He responded best when she applied a firm and gentle touch.

While Sam kept to the schedule of redressing his wound, dosing him with the laudanum, and applying cold compresses to cool his body, Jackson faded in and out of lucidity. Each time he woke, she forced water to his lips, and he drank. She couldn't get him to do the same with food. He wouldn't even take a little broth. As she tended him, she tried not to notice how deathly pale he looked.

Fever caused Jackson to ramble through bits and pieces of memories, and Sam learned just how much the name Providence had contributed to the development of his quick reflexes and well-toned physique. It sounded as if he'd grown up having to fight some boy or other twice a day.

In his delirium, he sometimes became so disoriented he acted out events. Once, he threw himself in her arms and pleaded, "Please forgive me, Mother, I swear I tried to save him, but I couldn't reach him in time." Sam felt his wet tears fall on her breast. The remorse in his voice was heartbreaking. After a few seconds, he pushed her away and began shouting, vowing to kill two men. Sam guessed the men had murdered his father.

Though Sam didn't remember what she'd known of Jackson's past, she did her best to reassure him. "It's all right, darling. You couldn't have saved him." She gently urged him to lie back and tucked the blankets close to his body. Then she laid her arm comfortingly on his chest. Slowly, the tension drained from him, and he closed his eyes. His sallow complexion and the ragged sound of his breathing worried her.

Sam wondered how many of the events Jackson relived in those fevered hours she'd known about and lost because of the crash. Once he called out for Parker. She also heard her name woven in and out of some of his disjointed ramblings.

***

Soon they'd be home. Jackson was resting a little easier. Sam was bone weary. When she felt herself dozing off, she jerked her head up to find Jackson looking at her. Sam searched his face for recognition. *Was he in the present?*

"Do you know where Sam is?" he asked.

Sam touched his shoulder and replied, "I'm not sure where she is, Jackson. With my memories gone, I can't find her." Then wistfully, as if she'd forgotten his presence, she whispered, "I wish I could remember. I'm grateful for the few bits of memory that have come back, but they torture me almost as much as they comfort me. I feel as if I'm wandering in the desert, dying of thirst, when I find a few precious drops of water. It's enough to keep me alive but too little to quench my thirst and bring me all the way back to life." As her whispered words died away, she turned to Jackson and found he was looking at her expectantly.

"Would you find Sam for me?" he asked.

Sam sighed. "I'll try, Jackson. If you promise to rest, I'll try to find her for you."

By the time the train pulled into Prosperity, Jackson's fever had burned itself out, and his breathing was less strained.

Sam peered anxiously through the window, searching the platform for Parker and Mac. She was surprised at the surge of emotion she felt when she saw their faces. They were her family, her comfort, and her joy. She loved them.

She thought of Jackson's suffering, the worried expressions on Parker and Mac's faces, and her empty feeling of loss. Her anger kindled and flamed at what Webster was doing to them. Aloud she swore, "When I know Jackson is well, I'm going after that rabid polecat. I should have taken him out of the world the day he touched me. When an animal is infected, it needs to be put down. I'm gonna rectify that mistake right soon."

***

It hadn't taken much effort for Reed Ferguson to learn about Martin Webster's vendetta. He hoped the telegram Parker and Mac sent to Chicago effectively warned Morgan and Jackson of Webster's plans so Sam would be protected.

Relief flooded through him when he saw her anxiously supervising Jackson's removal from the train. Noticing it took Parker and Mac to support Jackson, Reed wondered how severely the man was hurt.

He was pleased to observe Sam's health was much improved. After all, it was important she be healthy when he killed her.

He chuckled to himself, delighting in the irony of his reasoning.

Chapter 27

Doc and Grace waited in Sam's suite at Gracelyn Palace for Mac and Parker to bring Jackson and Sam from the train. When the door opened and the group entered, Doc's and Grace's eyes raked over Sam before moving to Jackson. Although Mac had assured them that the "major asset" wording in the telegram applied to Jackson, they hadn't been convinced.

Before tending to Jackson, Doc ordered Sam to bed, but she refused to leave Jackson. He wasn't surprised. He growled at her to find a place to sit. Grace hovered between Jackson and Sam, assisting the doctor.

Doc stayed with Jackson until he was sure he was out of danger. In the early morning hours, he wearily announced he was going home because Jackson was better.

Sam fell into a dead sleep soon after. Grace went for Parker, and he carried Sam to the second bedroom. He patted Grace's hand before he left the room and told her to stay with Sam while he and Mac took turns sitting with Jackson and guarding against Webster.

***

By midafternoon the next day, propped up on pillows, Jackson was already talking about getting out of bed. Although his arm was painful, his breathing was almost back to normal. Sam had been in and out of the room several times checking on him, but each time some of the others were in the room with them, and she seemed preoccupied. When she touched his forehead and smiled at him, he wanted to pull her down on the bed to sit with him but hesitated when he saw the bruises on her wrists and forearms. *Had he done that to her?*

Sam saw his hesitation and thought the pain in his arm had flared up again. "Is it your arm, Jackson? Has the pain gotten worse?" She moved to the other side of the bed and gently shifted the sling and bandage to check for evidence of new injury or infection.

Jackson covered one of Sam's hands with one of his before touching her wrist. Quietly he asked, "Did I do that to you, Sam?" He knew he hadn't been in his right mind part of the time. He vaguely remembered resisting her attempts to get him to lie quiet, but he never meant to hurt her. The thought made him nauseous.

Sam leaned down and kissed his cheek before putting her lips close to his ear. "You thought you were fighting some boys who made fun of your name," she teased. Then after playfully kissing his nose before straightening, she added, "No wonder you have so many muscles."

Jackson was relieved she wasn't mad at him, but still felt remorse. If they'd been alone, he would have held her in his good arm and kissed each bruise to show her how sorry he was. He knew there was no chance of that happening before they went to bed that night—not with Doc Baxter due within the next hour and Mac, Parker, and Grace staying in Prosperity to watch for Webster. Mac's friend, Price Hardin, the Laramie sheriff, had arrived in town yesterday afternoon with the news that Webster and four other men were on their way to Prosperity. Jackson sighed and settled back into his pillows, suddenly certain it would be a long afternoon.

***

Sam was standing near Mac by the window overlooking the front of Gracelyn Palace when she noticed Mac's interest quicken from something he saw on the street. When she leaned nearer, she caught a glimpse of a tall, rangy man stepping off the boardwalk in front of the Fortune Queen Saloon, obviously headed for Gracelyn Palace's entrance. Sam caught Mac's eye and nodded once toward the street. Mac hooked a thumb in his gun belt and edged toward the door. Sam followed.

Jackson noticed Mac and Sam leave the room. He wondered what they'd seen that was so damn interesting, although he was almost certain he knew. He'd bet it had to do with Webster.

Grace pretended she didn't notice Sam and Mac's exit. She tried engaging Jackson in small talk by asking him whether he thought Morgan and Alexa would return to Prosperity tomorrow.

Jackson barely heard Grace's question. Instead of answering her, he asked her to get Parker.

Grace sighed and murmured, "Well, I tried." Then she nodded, rose from her chair, and went in search of Parker. She intended to take her time about it, though.

As soon as the door closed, Jackson swung his legs to the floor and searched for his trousers.

***

Outside the suite, standing at the top of the stairs leading down to the gaming salon, Mac was holding Sam's arm and talking in a low voice.

Sam pulled her arm from Mac's hold. "I'm sorry, Mac. You said Price crossing the street to Gracelyn Palace was the signal that Webster was here. Now that I know, I'm gonna end it. That's all there is to it."

Mac sighed and took her arm again. "Sweetheart, if that's the way you're gonna handle it, Price and I aren't gonna let you do it alone."

Sam kissed Mac's cheek. Together, she and her beloved gunman descended the stairs.

***

Filled with patrons and the sounds of wheels humming, glasses clinking, and cards shuffling, Gracelyn Palace's main gambling salon was alive with activity.

The chill in the eyes of the young man propped against the wall near one of the roulette tables drew Sam's gaze. Dropping her eyes to the table to the man's right, she saw three men straighten in their chairs and swivel their heads in her direction.

Mac's friend, Price Hardin, stood at the bottom of the stairs sizing up the competition. Mac was on Sam's right, still holding her arm. Sam saw a hard look pass between Mac and Price.

When Mac's gaze fell on the young rapscallion leaning against the wall, he dropped Sam's arm and moved away from her. His face wore the expressionless mask he'd perfected when facing adversaries in countless gunfights. He didn't so much as flicker an eyelash.

Sam knew the prudent thing to do was to turn around and go back upstairs to Jackson, Grace, and Parker. But she was tired of being prudent, tired of being careful, and tired of Martin Webster. She wouldn't have minded taking on all four men right then and there, all by herself, except she didn't want Gracelyn Palace's gaming salon riddled with bullets, blood, and dead bodies.

More importantly, she didn't think Webster was one of the four men. From what Mac and Price told her, the young man was Webster's son, Holt. Sam had no idea what

Webster looked like, but it seemed to her none of the others looked prosperous, arrogant, or old enough to be him. In her estimation, two of them were professional gunmen. One was dressed in fancy black clothes and carried a fancy gun. The other had an ivory-carved revolver tucked in a tooled holster. Both were doing their best to appear bored and deadly. She guessed the third was one of Webster's ranch hands—foolish enough and proficient enough with a gun that Webster had let him join the gang.

***

Backing Sam and Mac, Price Hardin watched the four men through narrowed eyes. He hadn't bothered sending a telegram when he'd learned Webster's gang was headed for Prosperity because he was in the mood to witness Webster getting a taste of justice. Once Mac had told him what Webster had tried to do to Sam and Jackson in Chicago, he was doubly glad he'd come to help his friends put Webster out of business. Why, just seeing the whole thing go down would be worth the ride. It made him feel young again. Back in the day, he and Mac had been a force to be reckoned with. In fact, he'd bet they still were.

***

Like a rattlesnake uncoiling, Holt Webster straightened to his full height. He ran his eyes up and down Sam's body, finally resting his eyes on her bust as if he were seeing her naked. He lowered a hand to cup his crotch while running his tongue over his lips. His lewd, lascivious gestures set Sam's teeth on edge. She felt a spurt of loathing that made her want to jerk her knee up into his privates.

Sam walked toward him. It was foolish to bait him, but she couldn't resist. "Where's your father, boy?" She asked it in a tone riddled with disdain, losing no ground to the sexual intimidation he'd tried to inflict on her. She halted a couple of paces away and stared at him with her cool, unblinking, slate blue eyes. "Tell your father not to send a boy to do a man's job."

The quiet that followed her command was almost palpable. Patrons near her and Holt stepped back. The prickling muscles at the base of her neck warned Sam the eyes of the three men at the table were focused on her back.

She took another step forward. Then taking her time, she looked Holt up and down before her gaze stopped at his crotch. "I can see there's nothing I want from you, absolutely—nothing." The slow smile that crept across her mouth came nowhere near touching her eyes. She let the words sink in before turning to walk away, head held high, breasts thrust forward, and hips swaying, sure he'd watch her exit and follow.

Holt was too embarrassed and angry to recognize he should be afraid. In his maddened state, he forgot to take note of his three companions and, more importantly, of what Mac and Price were doing.

Sam heard the three chairs in which Holt's companions sat scrape on the floor as they pushed back from their table and rose in unison. Outside, she stepped from the boardwalk into the street before nonchalantly glancing over her shoulder. She pretended surprise to see Holt standing behind her with his gun in his hand. Behind Holt, she saw the other three men file out the door, step into the street, and spread out.

Sam laughed while sauntering toward Holt. Before addressing him, she let her eyes connect with each of the others. "I think you boys should know I can get him and one of you. What I don't take out, my friends over there will clean up for me." She nodded toward Mac and Price, who had unobtrusively followed her outside and taken positions backing her. Of the four men, only the ranch hand had sense enough to look frightened.

Mac knew his girl, and she was hell-bent on finishing this thing. Mac took a step forward, putting weight to Sam's words. His shoulders were squared and his back straight. He wore his gun with casual indifference. He watched the eyes of the fancy gunman dressed in black. He knew Sam had sent a clear message about her targets. She'd do exactly what she said. She was leaving the two gunmen to him and Price.

Mac saw Price scratch his cheek and jerk his thumb at the gunman with the ivory-handled revolver, indicating his choice of targets. Price stood much like Mac, giving the impression he didn't think his competition was that tough.

Sam's eyes turned to Holt and she taunted him. "Shoot me or get that thing out of my face, sonny." Her smile was as thin as her waning patience.

Holt's eyes darted to something behind Sam before licking his lips nervously. Seeing the ranch hand go for his gun, Sam drew and dodged to her left. She had a smooth, catchless draw, so fast the gun seemed to just appear in her hand. Her Colt barked, and the revolver flew from the ranch hand's grip. Sam's body continued its rotation to bring Holt into her line of fire. Her bullet hit him in the shoulder of his gun arm. He staggered back before dropping to his knees. His gun fell from his hand. Aware someone was behind her, Sam spun and trained her gun on the man to whom Holt's eyes had darted before the shooting started. Behind her, the air exploded with the deadly roar of two gunshots. Then all was quiet.

Mac and Price advanced toward the two fallen gunmen. Only one had been fast enough to clear leather. Price looked at Mac.

"Glad you decided to draw instead of wink," Mac commented, dryly.

A slow smile of satisfaction touched Price's lips. Holstering his gun, he deliberately winked at Mac before turning to take in the sight of Sam holstering her gun while watching Martin Webster kneel next to his wounded son.

Sam didn't recognize Webster. Here was the man who stole her memory, almost killed Jackson, and threatened the lives of the people she loved. He looked more outlaw than wealthy rancher. His eyes sent a little shiver of fear down her spine because they were slanted and piercing, resembling the rabid polecat she'd imagined him to be.

A muscle ticked in Webster's cheek, and he wore an expression of pure fury. The goddamned bitch was taking everything he'd worked for, everything he'd ever wanted. She was a good-for-nothing whore, and he was gonna kill her once and for all.

Webster bared his lips as if showing fangs to sink into his prey. He was incensed. His hand twitched. He palmed his son's gun and sought the trigger while raising the barrel. He wasn't near fast enough.

Sam drew, fired, and holstered her gun before he could fire. Martin Webster died face down in the street in front of Gracelyn Palace.

When Sam looked up from Webster's body, it was to meet Jackson's eyes. He was standing between Parker and Grace with the shirt he hadn't bothered to put on draped over his shoulder.

Mac and Price were moving toward Sam. When Mac stopped in front of her and wrapped his arms around her, Sam's mind flashed to a time when Mac carried her as a little girl from her father's grave. She rested her head on his shoulder and murmured, "You held me like this on the day they buried Papa."

Mac's arms tightened around her. "You're my girl, sweetheart. I'll always take care of you."

Chapter 28

Sam sat alone in a cell of the Prosperity jail. In another cell, one over from hers, Mac and Price sat together. The ranch hand and Holt Webster were with Doc and the sheriff's deputy. Sam cringed when she thought about what Doc would say about this business. Then she shrugged. Nothing she could do about it now.

Sheriff Rem Cooley sat in his office with his boots crossed. Jackson was standing in front of his desk, madder than a wet hen, and bellowing vehemently. "What do you mean they're staying until tomorrow? You know Sam, Rem. You can't mean to keep her in jail all night!"

Sam was worried Jackson wasn't up to the excitement. She hoped he was at least wearing his shirt by now.

Sheriff Cooley pretty much ignored Jackson and looked past him to Parker. "Parker, would you please make Jackson sit down before he falls down?"

Since Jackson falling was exactly what Sam feared, she called out, "Sonofabitch, Jackson, if you fall and hurt that arm again, I swear I'll make you suffer a month of Sundays in bed before I call Doc to come and patch you up."

Jackson grinned, thinking that right about now he could use a month of Sundays in bed, especially if she stayed in it with him.

Parker looked at Jackson's grin and put a hand on his shoulder to steer him to a chair. In Jackson's ear, he said,

"Down, boy. It's a good thing she can't see that look on your face or she'd break out of jail and give you some hurting in a place where you're thinking of pleasure."

The grin slid from Jackson's face, and he leaned toward the sheriff. "Rem, that's the goddamned Sheriff of Laramie in there for Christ's sake! Are you telling me you'll keep him in jail too? He told you the fight was fair all around and that every one of those low-life rat bastards drew first."

Rem nodded. "He told me, Jackson, and I believe him. Problem is, I got witnesses over in Gracelyn that claim Sam started it. They say neither Holt nor his men spoke to her. Sam walked right up to the young whippersnapper and gave him some grief about his father sending in a boy to do a man's job."

"So, what?" Jackson mumbled.

Rem narrowed his eyes. "Well, I'll tell you so what, Jackson. I hear tell she glared at the boy's—equipment, so to speak, and said—well—you get the idea." Rem halted, embarrassed to report the woman Jackson loved acted less than the lady she was.

Sam yelled, "That sonofabitch looked at me as if I were naked and touched his—equipment, as you call it—so let me make it clear—you're damned right, I looked at his crotch and said, 'I can see there's nothing I want from you, absolutely—nothing.'"

Jackson almost fell from his chair. Price Hardin slapped his knee and chuckled. Parker looked through the open doorway to the cellblock and arched an eyebrow at Sam. She shrugged and smiled at him innocently. Rem was beet red and disgusted with the whole lot of 'em.

Mac folded his arms and called out, "My girl didn't start anything, but she damn well finished it. You all need to grow up. That young pervert did just what Sam said. He raked his eyes over her curves so vicious like, it practically left her standing there in nothin' but the skin God gave her. When she said what she said, his eyes were still roaming over her front like he was thinkin' she was cotton candy and he was gonna lick her."

Jackson's chest constricted, and he couldn't breathe. When he finally managed to inhale, it set him to coughing.

Sam admonished Mac, "You shouldn't have said that." Turning her attention to Jackson, she ordered, "For God's sake, Parker, take Jackson to Doc Baxter. He'll go south again. Hell, I killed one man and wounded two others today. I don't need Jackson on my conscience, too."

Rem Cooley jumped to his feet and yelled, "Enough!" He picked up the keys, strode to the back, and unlocked both cells. "Get the hell out of here, and take that hothead Jackson Knight with you. I don't want to see any of you until tomorrow when the circuit court judge convenes the court. Do you understand?"

Two heads nodded silently while easing out of their cells to head for the front door, where Jackson and Parker waited for them.

Sam didn't nod her head, but she left her cell and followed Rem to his desk. Then she stepped right up to him and put her hands on her hips. "I'm not leaving without my gun, Rem. Are you gonna give it to me or am I gonna go back into that cell and talk you to death until the judge comes?"

Rem stared down into Sam's eyes. Sam didn't back off.

A couple of seconds ticked by before Rem raised his hands in defeat. He unlocked a desk drawer containing all their gun belts. Sam's eyes never left Rem's as she reached in and gathered them up.

Sam mumbled, "Much obliged, Sheriff." Then she marched toward the four men waiting for her near the door.

Price Hardin elbowed Mac in the ribs. "Yessiree, Mac, that there sure is your girl." Then he winked.

When the door closed behind Sam, Rem Cooley plopped down on his chair, wiped the sweat from his forehead, and tried not to laugh.

***

Reed assumed Sam didn't start the fight with young Holt Webster inside Gracelyn Palace because she didn't want the bloodshed to taint her beloved gaming salon.

Just before the shooting started, Reed saw Jackson Knight standing between Parker and Grace on the boardwalk. When he noticed Jackson's bandaged arm, he muttered a silent prayer a bullet would go astray and plow through Jackson's heart.

He wasn't surprised when Sam and the four men left the jail. He'd known Rem Cooley wouldn't be able to hold them. The woman had brains and skills.

A disturbing light flared in Reed's eyes. He looked forward to the day he'd demonstrate his skill.

***

While talking with Sam in her Gracelyn Palace suite, Morgan nudged out the chair near Sam's desk with the shiny toe of his boot so it directly faced his sister before he settled himself comfortably in it. "I heard Sheriff Cooley decided you, Mac, and Price Hardin didn't have to stand before the circuit court judge. How come?"

A shallow furrow dipped between Sam's brows. "Poor Rem. He threw us out of the jail."

Morgan tried to look stern but couldn't. Amused, he said, "Price Hardin told me the whole story. When he got to the part about you demanding your guns back, I thought he would bust a gut. He said even 'back in the day' he and Mac would never have had the balls to do that. Sorry, Sam, I forgot my manners. I meant to say 'guts.'"

Sam laughed. "No need to apologize, Brother. I love it when you treat me like one of the boys. It's a good thing Grace wasn't around to hear you, though."

Morgan paled at the thought of Grace hearing vulgarity come from his mouth.

Sam laughed again. "You almost look sick. What do you think Grace would do? Spank you?"

Morgan looked affronted by the suggestion before letting the corners of his mouth turn up mischievously. "Sam, you know Grace never once spanked either of us— guilt has always been her weapon of choice."

Sam pressed her hand to the stitch in her side from laughing. "Of course I don't remember, Brother, but thanks for the information. I'll keep it in mind."

Sam leaned against the wall behind her desk and changed her tone. "To answer your question about the judge, Holt Webster and the ranch hand confessed to Sheriff Cooley about how the fight started and about how his father treated me at their ranch. He even told how his father bragged about causing the stage wreck. Holt was under his father's thumb, forced to follow orders or suffer his father's wrath and abuse. The ranch hand was in the same position."

Sam paused to glance toward the bedroom door, where Jackson was sleeping before continuing, "I told Rem I didn't want to press charges and asked him to petition the judge to release them into Price Hardin's custody. Price offered to keep an eye on them for the next year to see they stay out of trouble."

Morgan noticed Sam's eyes move to her bedroom door for a second time. He wondered what was bothering her. "Why do you look so regretful about it?"

Sam sighed and brushed her hand across her forehead. "It's not that. Jackson is mad at me. When we got back to Gracelyn after Rem released us from jail, he passed out and we called Doc. Be glad you missed that lecture. Doc nearly chewed me up and spit me out. I'm surprised I have any skin left on my bones."

Morgan knew about Jackson's relapse. Doc Baxter had told him Jackson would recover in a couple of days if Sam could stay out of trouble that long. Morgan tried to paste a sympathetic expression on his face for Sam's benefit but failed when he imagined what Doc must have said about his sister's behavior.

Sam saw her brother's smile and stamped her foot. "It's not funny, Morgan. Jackson wasn't well enough to be out of bed. He was so sick on the train, I was afraid I would lose him. In a way, I don't blame him for being mad. If the situation had been reversed, I would've been as mad as hell." Wanting him to understand, she explained, "Webster was coming for me, and he didn't care who else he hurt. I had to go after him—besides, I didn't do it alone. Mac and Price backed me up. I wasn't as foolish as Jackson and Doc tell it."

Morgan rose from the chair and went to Sam to place an arm around her shoulders. "Jackson will come around, Sis. You know he's crazy about you."

"Well, he didn't even kiss me good night," she pouted.

"Now you're just trying to transfer blame."

Sam kicked at the desk leg. "Why do you always have to be so reasonable?"

"Because if we both had your temperament," Morgan said dryly, "we'd be in trouble all the time."

Sam had to smile at that, and her mood lifted. Switching subjects, she asked, "Did Thomas send any papers with you?"

So now we get down to it Morgan thought. "Yes, Sam. Are you going to tell me what's in them?"

"Maybe," Sam replied.

Morgan was annoyed. "What kind of an answer is that?"

"It means I might tell you if you answer a question or two for me."

"Sam, my patience is wearing thin," Morgan warned.

Sam tried to look contrite. "I want to tell you—but first, tell me if you asked Oliver Danforth for permission to marry Alexa."

Morgan sucked in his breath. "Are you a clairvoyant, Sis? How did you know I'd ask him that?"

Sam couldn't hide her smile. "Morgan, you love Alexa, and you're the kind of man who'd insist on doing things properly. That's how I knew. Have you asked her yet?"

"Not yet," Morgan admitted. "Her birthday is next week, and I thought I'd propose then."

Sam threw her arms around Morgan and hugged him. "I'm happy for you, Brother."

Morgan held her away from him. "Maybe one of these days, you'll have good news for me. You need to marry Jackson. It's time."

Sam sighed. "I know. Remember the bet I mentioned to you? The one I made with Jackson? It's about that."

Morgan looked puzzled. "I don't understand."

"Well, Jackson bet that I told Alexa to confront you about how you felt about each other. He said he'd give me fifty percent of his hotel if he were wrong."

"Alexa told me you advised her to work it out with me. When I asked you about it, you said you didn't remember—that if Alexa said you did, you must have done it. Then you asked me not to tell Jackson. Are you trying to back out of the bet?"

"No, I intend to honor the bet. I asked you not to tell Jackson because I want to be the one to tell him he's won. There's no hurry, though, because we agreed not to settle the bet until we resolved the situation with Webster, learned the reason I asked Alexa to keep our relationship secret, and identified the person and motive for drugging the tea."

"What does Jackson win?" Morgan asked, despite believing he knew the answer. He wanted to hear Sam say it.

"If Jackson's right, I promised to marry him."

Morgan's eyes narrowed, studying his sister's expression. "You were pretty sure you'd lose the bet when you made it, weren't you, Sis?"

Sam lifted her chin and looked him in the eye. "Yes, I was. I know I love him, and I know *why* I love him. I also know not marrying him isn't protecting him from my enemies. I want him to be mine, and I want him to know I'm his."

Morgan held out his arms and Sam moved into them. "So why don't you look happy?"

Sam put her head on Morgan's chest and mumbled, "Because I've been insufferable to him and because I should have let him make me the luckiest woman in the world, except for Alexa, of course, long before this. I shouldn't have let my stubborn willfulness hurt him."

Morgan saw Sam smooth suspicious dampness from her cheeks before she took a deep breath and stepped back. He would have commented except for her asking, "Do you want me to answer your question about the papers, Morgan?"

"I figured you'd get around to it if I gave you enough rope."

Sam flashed him a smile. "Well, I'll answer now that I know things are settled between you and Alexa. If you approve, I'm giving Alexa twenty-five percent of my share of Gracelyn Palace. I want her to be a partner in our business—but only if you agree. If you don't approve, I'll tear the papers up and we'll never speak of it again."

Morgan was flabbergasted. "I should have known. It's incredibly generous of you, but it leaves you only forty percent."

Sam shrugged, "What difference does that make? Are you afraid Alexa and I will join forces to oppose you?"

"Well, maybe—but I'll get over it."

"So, you do approve?"

"Yes, Sis, I approve. I'm sorry I doubted you."

Chapter 29

Though Sam had scared the bejesus out of him yesterday confronting Webster's gang in that gunfight, Jackson knew he shouldn't be acting like a sullen five-year-old over it. But his stomach still felt as if he'd swallowed lead every time he thought about it.

When Sam joined him in bed, coolly pulling the covers up and turning her back to him, Jackson was unable to feign indifference. He wanted her to snuggle up to him so he could forgive her. Then, suddenly, it hit him. She didn't think she'd done anything that required forgiveness—*and that was the goddamned problem—his problem, not hers.* She expected him to understand she'd only done what she thought she needed to do.

Reaching for her, he asked, "Would you come over here and give me a kiss?"

She didn't turn to him when she answered. "It depends on whether you'll kiss me back or continue acting like a little boy."

"I *want* to kiss you. It's just that you scared the hell out of me." He offered the words by way of apology.

Sam turned and plastered herself to his side. "I'd say I'm sorry, except that polecat Webster had to go. Mac and Price backed me up."

"I know," Jackson conceded, "but I can't talk about it. Would you kiss me?"

Sam started dropping hot little kisses along his neck, moving up to his mouth, where she lingered. Then she kissed him with a heart-stopping boldness. When she broke the kiss, she murmured, "That was just to show you I could never love anyone like I love you." Then she snuggled down against his side and patted his chest. "Now go to sleep."

"You expect me to go to sleep after you kiss me like that?"

"You expected me to go to sleep last night without *any* kiss, so my answer is *yes, darlin'*."

Sam felt Jackson take a steadying breath and let it out slowly. She was amused he was trying to stay calm. Goading him, she asked, "Would you like me to tell you something to take your mind off it?"

Jackson grumbled, "It's not my mind that needs distracting."

Pretending not to understand, Sam explained, "I'm giving Alexa twenty-five percent of my share of Gracelyn Palace. That's why I asked Alexa to make me that promise. I wanted to know things between her and Morgan were settled before I made the gift. I told Morgan today, and he approved."

"I thought it might be because of something like that. How do you know things are settled between them?" Jackson asked.

"Because Morgan told me he asked Oliver Danforth for permission to marry Alexa. He intends to propose to her next week on her birthday."

"I'm not surprised. If I win our bet, I'll legitimately be able to call you my fiancée—then my wife. Maybe we can have a double ceremony."

Jackson's words echoed in Sam's head as if he were speaking from a great distance. She heard herself ask, "What did you say?"

Detecting an odd, hesitant quality in Sam's tone, as if her mind didn't recognize her words, Jackson peered into her face. Her eyes were unfocused, staring past him at the wall—as if her body was in the present while her mind wandered to some other place.

*****

"You want me to pretend to be your fiancée so Melinda Kensington will understand why you aren't in love with her? Are you so bored with my charms, Jackson, that you've been wooing another woman? Maybe I should return the affections of other men?" Sam's left hand was on Jackson's right shoulder while she poked him in his chest with the index finger of her right hand, feigning anger. She felt a little satisfaction when she saw the scowl and jealous shadow that darkened his eyes at her suggestion.

"You're a vixen, Sam. You know I can't stand the thought of anyone else touching you."

"Why should I pretend to be your fiancée when I'm not?"

"You are, Sam, and you know it. You're more than that. If you married me instead of living with me, we'd be husband and wife. Saying we're promised isn't a lie. It's just a matter of semantics. Melinda is only seventeen and imagines herself in love with me. She doesn't think an eleven-year age gap is a deterrent. She didn't believe me when I told her I'm promised to you. She thinks I made you up to discourage her. I don't want to hurt her feelings. I thought if she saw us together, it would help her understand."

Sam wondered why she bothered to tease Jackson about pretending to be his fiancée when all she wanted to do was kiss him. He was so damned handsome. She saw his eyes linger on her mouth. She knew he wanted her. It flared in his eyes. Biting at her lip, she tried to control her rising passion and excitement at being with him.

She wanted Jackson to catch her wrists and draw them to his shoulders so he could kiss her until she arched against him, warm and willing. Instead, he entwined his hand into the mass of curls draped in front of her shoulder and let the backs of his fingers follow the line of her neck before wandering to where her cleavage disappeared into the modest neckline of her water blue silk traveling dress.

Shivering, she pretended to admonish him. "Jackson, stop that. You're trying to distract me. You know when you do that I can barely think."

Jackson smiled a dangerous, predatory smile and pushed her hair away from her cheekbone to the back of her shoulder. Then he let his lips follow the same path he'd traced with his fingers.

Sam arched to expose more of her neck, and Jackson caught her waist and lowered her as if dipping her in a waltz. His other hand unfastened the row of buttons that began at the place where his mouth stopped.

"I do believe I remember you telling me something about that, darlin'," he murmured. "Is that why I feel you trembling?"

Sam continued to play the game. "Jackson, I hate it when you do this when I'm trying to have a serious conversation with you."

With the buttons undone and Jackson's hand in her bodice, Sam moaned.

Jackson chuckled. "Sorry, darlin', could you say that again? I thought you said you hate it when I do this?" Jackson's hand drew back the blue silk of her dress and her chemise so his mouth could replace his hand.

Sam gasped and wrapped her arms around his shoulders. "Jackson—"

"Hmm?"

"Could we at least continue this on the bed?"

"Did you think I would take you on the floor?"

Sam laughed. "It's been a week. I'm surprised we made it to the room."

Jackson lifted her into his arms and put her on the bed. He started to remove his shirt, but Sam got on her knees and crooked her finger for him to come nearer. "Come here, cowboy, I feel like unwrapping you myself." She tilted her head so Jackson could kiss her while she opened his shirt, button by button, and trailed her hand down his chest to the fastenings at his waist.

Jackson made a low sound of pleasure.

"Did you say something, cowboy?" Sam asked.

"Only that you're a witch and I love you—and please hurry."

"Didn't you teach me that some things shouldn't be rushed?" Sam responded.

Jackson groaned as Sam's hand disappeared inside his trousers. He shrugged off his shirt and pressed against her, urging her to lean back until he could place both hands on the bed, one to her right and the other to her left. Then he raised his knee to the edge of the bed and slowly lowered himself above her until she was lying on the bed beneath him.

"Revenge is sweet, Sam. Now it's my turn to finish unwrapping you."

"Jackson, I'm not sure I can wait to be unwrapped. Do you think we could enjoy the main course now to take the edge off our hunger and save the unwrapping for dessert?"

Jackson's voice was ragged with need as his hands followed the shape of her legs up to her thighs. "Just what I had in mind, darlin'."

Sam laughed to see Jackson's stunned reaction when he realized no undergarments were barring his path. "I anticipated our conversation would be a short one, cowboy."

Her laughter was replaced by raw desire as Jackson touched her. "Jackson, please don't make me wait—"

He entered her and began moving in slow deliberate thrusts, building in intensity until there was only heat, pleasure, and the mingling of their molten crescendo.

"I missed you, Jackson."

"Is that your way of saying, 'I love you, Jackson?'"

Sam's eyes searched his face. Then the devil leaped in her eyes. "I might say I love you, cowboy, if you show me what you're offering for dessert."

"I might give you dessert if you agree to pretend to be my fiancée."

"You'd give me dessert even if I refused. It's one of the reasons I love you so much."

***

Jackson gently shook Sam's shoulder. When her eyelids fluttered, he brushed his lips against hers. "Sam, are you all right? Did you remember something?" His voice sounded anxious even to his ears.

Sam nodded while trying desperately to comprehend the meaning of what she'd experienced. She was positive it denoted something far more significant than the depth of their love or the passion in their lovemaking. The craving and pleasure aspect of the memory pleased her—hell, to be honest, it *aroused* her—but there was something ominous beneath the pleasure—something threatening—something she didn't understand. She knew she wouldn't be able to explain it. It was just there—like a wild, half-starved wolf waiting in the shadows to attack if she came too close. It didn't make sense. There was no hidden voyeur, no hint of anything amiss, no reason to be afraid. *So why did this memory feel as if it were connected to the first memory?*

Jackson was studying her face, trying to interpret her expression. "Sam, why aren't you saying anything? Was it something bad?"

Sam put her head on Jackson's shoulder, clinging to the solidness and strength of him. His arms wrapped protectively around her and pulled her closer. Sam could feel his heart beating. She drew a deep, quivering breath. Now that she was in his arms, her fear and uncertainty dissipated, becoming nothing more than a natural reaction to losing her place in time.

The heat of Jackson's body stirred her senses. The truth of her memory was Jackson, her need for him, her love for him, and his love for her. She raised her head, and his mouth covered hers. His kiss became more demanding. He withdrew from her mouth only to enter it again, probing deeper in long languishing thrusts. His hands moved over her body, caressing, teasing, and cupping. When he settled her back against the bed, she uncurled her legs so he could press the full length of his lean, hard body against hers.

Sam answered Jackson's question. "It wasn't bad." Then she kissed him while pushing against his shoulders, urging him to lie back against his pillow. Her body rolled with his so she could position herself on top of him. In a low, sultry voice she said, "It was about a tall, handsome cowboy I met in Cheyenne who served me supper and dessert in my room—dessert was particularly satisfying."

Jackson's hand came to the back of her head to guide her mouth to his. "You are a witch, Sam. Is this another one of your spells?"

Sam shook her head and pushed his hand away. Instead of allowing him to pull her forward, she bent her knees and leaned away. Crossing her arms, she caught the hem of her nightdress and drew it over her head, wriggling her bottom to free the folds of material separating her from Jackson. She gazed into his eyes before bending to kiss one corner of his mouth, then the other. "No, Jackson. This is a spell you taught me."

Chapter 30

Alone in their suite, Jackson sat in the chair opposite Sam's desk flexing his injured arm. Satisfied with its progress, Doc encouraged him to begin exercising it, although he warned him to use common sense so he didn't overtax it.

Sam had gone to see Alexa after Doc Baxter left. Grace was downstairs in the gaming salon. Jackson had no idea where Mac, Parker, and Price were.

Before she'd left, Jackson had watched Sam at three different times thumb her Colt's hammer to half cock and rotate the cylinder, checking it—a clear indication she was particularly uneasy about something. He'd also noticed she absently reached inside her jacket for her derringer before remembering she'd lent it to Alexa. When Sam realized he was watching her, she'd shrugged and mumbled, "Force of habit, I guess."

Hearing the faint click of the door latch releasing, Jackson slid to the edge of his chair and poised his gun hand over the butt of his Colt. Briefly, he conceded he might be overreacting, but whoever had drugged the tea was still unknown. Better safe than sorry. In his experience, things tended to happen when a person let his guard down.

The door swung inward and Morgan stepped inside. He observed Jackson relax his gun hand. With a hint of mockery, he said, "I can see you're feeling better. Where's Sam?"

"She went to give Alexa the partnership papers. She wanted it to be a private thing. She said she'd explain things to Miss Jenny after that."

"Good. I wanted to talk to you while she wasn't around. Thomas hired a Pinkerton detective to investigate Reed Ferguson as we requested. I expect by now, he's received a preliminary report. Did Parker or Mac talk to Sheriff Cooley so he won't be surprised when the report comes to him?"

Jackson nodded. "Parker took care of it. Rem knows to keep Sam out of it for now. I won't tell her unless she asks. With Webster out of the way, I thought she'd relax some, but she hasn't. I think her sixth sense is working overtime. She's on edge. She checked her Colt several times before she left this morning. She only does that when she expects serious trouble."

Morgan took Sam's sixth sense almost as seriously as Jackson did. Worry lines appeared on his forehead. "You figure we should leave Ferguson alone until we get the Pinkerton report?"

Jackson nodded again. "I'd say watching him is the most we should do for now, if we can do it without him noticing. We don't want to alert him we're any more curious about him being involved than we indicated when he walked in on Parker questioning Hank Bainbridge about the tea paperwork. I expect Rem will receive something from Thomas within the next few days. Rem said he'd keep an eye on Ferguson, too—when he can."

Curious, Morgan asked, "Did you decide to forgive Sam for the gunfight and kiss her good night?"

Jackson pinned Morgan with a dark glower. "How the hell did you know about that?"

"When I admitted I was going to propose to Alexa, it came up. I could tell Sam was worried about something so I wormed it out of her."

"I'm sure there is more to it than that, but I'll let it go. To answer your question, let's just say, we kissed and made up."

"I wish you'd learn to say things like that without that satisfied smile on your face," Morgan admonished. "There are some things mothers and brothers should never know, and that smile of yours says way too much."

Jackson had the good sense to look apologetic and mumble, "Sorry." After a short pause, he asked, "Have you noticed how she presses her hand to her temple?"

"Yes, but I think she's doing it less than when she was in Chicago. Do you have a different opinion?" Morgan asked.

"She's struggling. On the train, when I was out of my head with fever, I think she said something about feeling as if she were wandering in the desert. I told Grace about it."

"What did Grace say?"

"She told me to be patient. She said Sam would find her way."

Morgan nodded his agreement. "Grace knows. I think she's right, Jackson. Sam's not only finding her way back, she's finding her way forward." He was tempted to tell Jackson that Sam was planning to marry him—and would've made the decision even if they hadn't made that ridiculous bet—but he couldn't betray Sam's trust.

"Your mother used almost the same words," Jackson remarked. "It's odd how pieces of memory come to Sam. Sometimes she says things so matter of fact; it's as if she hasn't forgotten anything. At other times, it's like her spirit leaves her body while her mind travels to the past."

"I haven't been around when that's happened, Jackson. As long as the memories return, does it matter?"

Jackson's gaze rose to meet Morgan's. He wasn't sure of the answer. "I don't know. I've seen it happen three times, although the first time I didn't realize it was happening. She had a memory about wearing that scandalous green dress—the one she wore to Tanner's party. She recalled I was carrying her upstairs to her room in an unfamiliar house while someone watched us. She didn't tell anyone about it at the time because it frightened her."

Morgan frowned, recalling something Sam had said. "When I first came home from New York after the stage crash, Sam admitted she was afraid. I thought she might have remembered something, but she was evasive and denied it. She compared her fear to that of a child afraid to get out of bed because a monster was lurking nearby. I didn't press her because I saw it upset her and because I can understand a person with no memory could experience that kind of anxiety. Tell me about the second time, Jackson."

"The second time was the morning after she pulled that trick to save us from Webster's men in Chicago. She remembered the three rustlers at the waterfall pool. I think her subconscious associated my being stabbed with catching the bullet in my side protecting her that day. She didn't want to admit she'd remembered something—even tried to leave so I couldn't see how upset she was. She thinks it's her fault when I'm hurt and worries I'll get killed because of her."

Jackson pressed Morgan for confirmation. "You know what I'm talking about, Morgan. I know you've seen her look at us as if she were calculating odds, ascertaining whether her going away would protect us. Sometimes, I wonder if she'll leave me because of it. She believes marrying me would put me in even more danger."

Morgan knew what Jackson meant. He remembered how worried Sam was when Becky was almost late for dinner while Parker was away finding Jackson to bring him back to Trinity. "Sam takes on responsibility for things she shouldn't."

"The third time it happened was last night. One minute she was telling me about how you'll propose to Alexa and the next, it was like she disappeared from the room and left a life-size, porcelain doll in her place. Last night's memory was about the time she met me in Cheyenne when I was buying the pure-bred horses from the Kensington stables."

Despite feeling embarrassment from recalling details of Sam's memory, Jackson remarked, "Now that I think about it, she wore that green dress to taunt me one night while we were in Cheyenne during the same visit."

Morgan grinned. "Jackson, we both know that dress was designed for the sole purpose of seduction—in its purest form. You understate its power when you use the word 'taunt.' Why did Sam *taunt* you?"

Remembering Morgan's earlier admonition about telling mothers and brothers certain things, Jackson chose his words carefully. "Tease is a better word. She wore that dress to tease me during the evening because I'd asked her to pretend to be my fiancée while we were in Cheyenne. Melinda Kensington had developed a crush on me. When I explained to Melinda that I was promised to Sam, I used the word affianced to describe our relationship. It wouldn't have been proper for me to tell a young girl that Sam and I live together. I would've preferred to tell her we were married, but since Sam won't stand in front of a preacher or justice of the peace with me, I couldn't say that. In my heart, we're married. I've felt that way since the first time Sam let me love her."

"Wasn't there some trouble in Cheyenne when you went to buy those horses?" Morgan asked.

Up until that moment, Jackson thought Sam's two memories of Cheyenne were connected because they were about his and Sam's passion—nothing else. But now that Morgan asked the question, Jackson began to wonder. Sam hadn't said anything last night about being frightened, but was she? A tiny sprout of suspicion took root. If something about the memory frightened her, why hadn't she told him?

"Sam was uncomfortable with the situation in Cheyenne. She understood about Melinda and was kind to the girl; but Melinda's mother, Ruth, worried her. She swore Ruth was up to no good. After Sam took a tumble into a corral full of wild mustangs and hurt her leg, I began to think Sam was right. Sam wasn't seriously hurt in the fall. She was lucky it was only a sprain and a muscle pull, but it could have been very serious. As soon as Sam could travel, we left."

"Maybe we should find out what Melinda and Ruth are up to these days, Jackson."

***

Sitting behind the desk in her office, facing Sam and Grace, Miss Jenny smiled. Gracelyn Palace's manager was a beautiful, raven-haired woman with pale, creamy skin and startling blue eyes. She exuded the competent demeanor of a no-nonsense businesswoman and had a gift for making people feel comfortable and welcome.

"Imagine Alexa working here all this time and none of us guessing about her being your cousin," Jenny exclaimed. "With her becoming a partner, she'd be the perfect person to take over the daily operation when Ryder and I marry. Is that your plan, Sam?"

Sam glanced uncertainly at Grace before turning back to Jenny. "I hadn't thought about it," she admitted. "I expect you're right. Thank you, for suggesting it."

Sam looked down at her hands, wondering why it was difficult for her to explain about her memory. Each person she met was a new puzzle, and she doubted she'd ever be able to collect enough pieces to answer the thousands of questions that popped up higgledy-piggledy in her head.

Miss Jenny darted Grace a questioning look.

"Sam, Jenny knows about your memory," Grace interjected, encouraging her daughter not to let her discomfiture with her amnesia hold her back.

Sam looked up. "I know, Grace." Directing her gaze to Jenny, she said, "I'm sorry, Jenny. I feel strange not remembering people, especially when I've been told how important they are to me. You speak with such warmth, it makes me ashamed I can't remember about your wedding."

Jenny felt a surge of sympathy for her friend and employer. "Sam, your memory loss isn't your fault. You've been a good friend to Ryder and me, and your memory doesn't diminish our friendship. We'll marry the first day of the new year. Ryder owns land just north of Trinity, and he built a house for us, so we'll be your neighbor. In time, you'll get so tired of hearing our stories that you'll curse the day you asked your first question."

Sam laughed, appreciating Jenny's humor.

In a practical tone, Jenny continued, "Your memory may or may not come back, Sam. Who's to know? My da used to say, 'Steer your ship to the horizon and you *might* find your way home.' There are no guarantees. In the long run, it won't matter. You have many friends and time to make new memories."

With effort, Sam found her voice, "Thank you for the kind words."

Jenny rose from her desk and moved around it to put a hand on Sam's shoulder. "Would now be a good time to tell you you'll have an opportunity to get reacquainted with your friends a week from Saturday night at Alexa's birthday celebration?"

"Oh, Jenny, no. Tell me you're joking."

Jenny laughed. "If your eyes were any bigger, Sam, people would mistake you for an owl. You asked me to plan her party more than a month ago."

Sam rubbed her temple. "Sorry, I'm afraid my first reaction is dread. The thought of greeting a room full of people I don't remember is daunting."

Seeing Sam's anxiety, Grace patted her daughter's arm while catching Jenny's eye. "A party will allow you to greet people without having to explain your memory problem to each person. After seeing you at the party, their curiosity will be satisfied, and there will be less need for further explanation."

Catching on, Jenny chimed in, "Grace is right. Alexa will be the center of attention, so people won't pay much attention to your memory issues."

Sam sighed. There was nothing she could do about it, so she listened with a resigned smile as Jenny went on to describe the arrangements. She'd invited half the town, ordered cases of champagne, and hired an orchestra from Cheyenne. Jenny also mentioned Sam had ordered a new dress in a lovely shade of sapphire blue and that she'd asked one of the hostesses to hang it in Sam's armoire.

Because Sam's enthusiasm for the event remained lackluster, Grace took command. With a nod to Jenny, she stood and grasped Sam's elbow urging her to her feet as she politely expressed how it all sounded enchanting and how grateful she and Sam were for all the planning and preparation Jenny had put into the party. Sam rallied, managing to swallow her aversion, and echoed her mother's gracious words.

Jenny chuckled. "Alexa will appreciate the party, Sam, even if you don't."

***

"You don't need to look as if someone is planning your lynching, Daughter," Grace said, as Sam pulled Jenny's office door shut. "You'll survive."

"Humph," Sam muttered. "Easy for you to say. You won't be the one looking into unfamiliar faces and wondering whether they're friend or enemy."

"Why, Daughter, how naive of you to say such a thing," Grace replied, shrewdly. "That's something each of us does every day of our lives. Well, whatever you do, please don't express that sentiment to Mac, or he'll be inclined to drag you home to Highbreeze to begin training you again on how to protect yourself." With that advisement, Grace dropped Sam's arm and started across the room to join Mac, Price, and Parker.

Sam scowled as she followed her mother. She preferred to believe the celebration would be a tedious, agonizing ordeal. When she and Grace arrived at the men's table, they politely rose to their feet. Mac held a chair for Grace, while Parker did the same for Sam.

Sam smiled at all three men fondly. Despite a deck of cards and a "half-full" bottle of bourbon sitting in the center of the table, they looked bored. No wonder. Waiting wasn't in their nature. These were men of action and purpose.

Price would return to Laramie in a day or two—as soon as Holt Webster could ride. Until then, Sheriff Cooley was giving the two prisoners "room and board" at the jail, which suited Sam just fine. Though she doubted they'd make any more trouble, it was nice knowing she didn't need to worry about it. Mac and Grace intended to stick close to her until the drugged tea mystery was solved, but nothing else had happened.

Sam felt especially sorry for Parker because Becky had been relegated to her aunt's care until things returned to normal. Sam knew he missed his daughter and would rather be at Trinity than wait for something to happen in Prosperity.

Making conversation, Sam teased the men. "Don't you boys look like sorry cases? You don't appear to have the energy to drain a bottle."

Price sat up straighter in his chair. Flashing Sam a devilish smile, he drawled, "We figured if we waited long enough, Sam, you'd get around to stirring something up to take our minds off our troubles. Ain't there something else we can help you with? If nothin' is happenin' in Prosperity, maybe you, Mac, and I could take a ride to flush out some train robbers or murderers. I hear tell the James and Younger brothers hooked up. These days they're taking down banks and stagecoaches wherever they go, getting rich and too bold by far. We could amuse ourselves takin' out some of those boys."

Pretending to be serious, Price stared at Sam with hopeful eyes. Mac pushed his hat forward to hide his eyes. Parker leaned back in his chair, stretched out his legs, and crossed his boots. Grace watched her daughter, interested in how Sam would choose to play the game with Price.

Sam adjusted her expression, appearing almost as willing, eager, and hopeful as Price. Batting her lashes, she spoke in her best imitation of Price's exaggerated drawl. "You sure know how to tempt a filly. For a man like you, I might even throw over Jackson. When do you figure we should leave? The James and Younger brothers shouldn't take the three of us more than a couple of hours to handle once we find 'em. If Parker and Morgan come along, we'd get every last one of 'em." She said the last sentence with confidence.

Delighted Sam was going along with his joke, Price watched her expectantly, wondering how she'd extricate herself from participating in the ridiculous proposition without revealing she knew it was a ruse suggested solely to idle away time.

Sam glanced over her shoulder at the stairs as if expecting to see someone standing there. When she turned to Price, she looked anxious. Shifting in her chair, she dropped her eyes to the table.

"Somethin' wrong, Sam?" Price inquired. "You ain't scared of those varmints are ya'?"

Sam's right hand moved to her side to rest on her Colt while her slate blue eyes darted up to lock with Price's eyes. In a cold voice, she challenged him. "Are you calling me a coward, Price?"

Price forgot he and Sam were joshing and shivered involuntarily, recognizing the ice in her tone and the murderous calm in her unblinking stare. He wondered how many men had backed down when she'd pinned them with that dark, angel-of-death glower. It was enough to turn a man's balls into shriveled walnuts.

Mac thought Price would fold when Sam fixed him with her deadly stare, but his old friend surprised him.

Price pretended innocent surprise and replied, "Why no, Sam. I never meant to imply such a thing." Darting a sideways glance at Mac, he defended himself. "Are you forgettin' I backed you in that shootout with Webster?"

Coldly, Sam replied, "I ain't been hit in the head since the gunfight, so I remember just fine, Price."

Mac's hand moved to cover the twitch of a smile he couldn't control upon hearing Sam's reply. He watched as Price swallowed hard.

Price recovered and tried a diverting tactic. Clapping Mac on the back, he exclaimed admiringly, "You're Mac's girl, all right! There ain't no question he raised a female hellcat. Then Grace here polished off the edges to make you into a lady—I'd say that's a deadly combination. Why, a woman like you, Sam, wouldn't even know how to spell the word coward."

Sam narrowed her eyes as if questioning Price's sincerity. Then she relaxed her shoulders and raised her right hand to rest on the table. Leaning forward, she glanced first at Mac, then Parker. When her eyes returned to Price, her tone was conspiratorial as she asked, "Do you reckon we'd be back before Jackson takes it in his head to come after us?" Sam sat back in her chair and waited for Price to work through how pissed Jackson would be and what he might do to Price for involving her in such a hare-brained scheme.

As Sam intended, Price could easily imagine how short his life would be in such a circumstance. He swallowed around a lump in his throat before reaching for the bottle in the center of the table to fill his glass and gulp some liquid courage. The liquor appeared to restore him because he produced a smile as bright as the sun before shrugging his shoulders and conceding, "You got me on that one, Sam. We might enjoy takin' out those boys, but Jackson would make quick work of us."

Nodding in agreement, she declared, "He'd be mad as a wild Mustang backed into a stall, but he'd not harm me or Mac. It's you that's worrying me, Price. Jackson has a right bad temper when I go off and do things like this, and he always makes someone pay when he's riled."

Price took another swig of his drink. "On second thought, Sam, I believe we'll just sit tight—unless you're willing to outdraw Jackson. I'd bet you're a touch faster, but

I can't help wondering if you'd do it. Something tells me you aren't done with that man yet—however, if you say different, I'm your suitor. Otherwise, I think I'll just sit here and get better acquainted with this bottle, ma'am."

Though she hated bourbon, Sam poured herself a drink while Price spoke. As she took a sip, he finished running his lines. She could barely swallow past the chuckle bubbling up into her throat. Flashing Price a grin, she said, "Remind me never to play poker with you, Price."

Price opened his eyes wide before replying innocently, "Whatever do you mean, Sam, by sayin' somethin' like that?"

Sam shoved back her chair. "I can't go another round, Price. I'm not as good as you are. I'm on my way to the mercantile." Parker and Mac stood. Sam directed an apologetic gaze to Parker. "I don't know where it is."

"We'll go with you, Sam. On the way there, we'll stop at Mr. Branson's."

Sam looked puzzled.

Parker leaned close to Sam's ear and explained, "He's the gunsmith. His gun shop is next to the mercantile. He told me yesterday you ordered Alexa a derringer and a Colt for her birthday. They came in two weeks ago. He heard about you being ill and was unsure whether he should say anything to you about it. I thanked him for his kindness and told him we'd be along to pick up the guns."

Reaching for Parker's arm, Sam gave him a grateful nod. "Alexa needs her own guns. I loaned her my derringer when we were in Chicago."

Parker covered Sam's hand with one of his and took a step toward the door. Mac offered his arm to Grace. As Price fell in behind his friends, he tipped his hat goodbye to the unfinished bottle of bourbon.

Chapter 31

After visiting Branson's to pick up Alexa's guns, Sam and Grace went to Harper's mercantile. Saying he'd be back in time to help carry packages, Parker went to the freight office to talk to Hank Bainbridge. Price split off to catch up with Sheriff Cooley. Mac took up a leaning position against a post in front of the mercantile to survey the street as if expecting trouble at any second.

Inside the store, Grace sorted through tissue paper and ribbons to select something suitable for wrapping Alexa's presents, while Sam examined a table full of hats. Earlier that morning, convinced there must be a hat somewhere in the suite, she'd searched every drawer and shelf. She'd found a pair of soft woolen pants, a couple of plain shirts and riding skirts, a black leather vest with deep pockets, a few bandannas, and two pairs of boots, but no hat. To go riding or shooting with Alexa, she'd need a hat.

Sam had to tip up her head to see the face of the clerk who approached her. The man was tall, an inch or so taller than Jackson. He was also very good-looking, with nicely spaced, light-brown eyes, a rugged jawline, and a generous mouth that smiled at her in welcome. He looked to be about thirty-five.

Sam recalled Wade Harper's name from Becky mentioning it when she and Parker served her the tea that turned out to be drugged a few days after the crash. Jackson's body had gone rigid when Becky let slip Wade

Harper's name and mentioned Ryder thought Wade was "sweet" on her.

Assuming this was Wade, Sam could understand why Jackson would be jealous. She noticed the width of his impressive shoulders and the muscles flexing in his forearm when he negligently brushed a lock of sandy hair off his forehead while his eyes roved over her. His gaze lingered on her mouth for a fraction of a second too long.

Nodding in greeting, he said, "We've met before, but I understand because of your injury, you may not remember. I'm Wade Harper, and this is my business."

Sam's hand was swallowed up in Wade's warm, strong handshake. "Becky and Ryder said you made certain a tin of tea was delivered to the ranch for me. It was kind of you to go to the trouble, Mr. Harper."

Wade looked pleased she was aware of the gesture and assured her he was only doing his job. He said it in such a way as to imply nothing he did for her would be too much trouble. Sam heard Grace gently clear her throat.

Wade brought Sam's attention back to him by asking, "Are you interested in a hat?"

"Yes, I am. I was thinking of going riding with Miss Danforth and discovered I don't have a suitable hat."

"You typically wear a black, Texas-style hat, Sam. Is that what you had in mind?"

Sam was surprised he used her first name and knew her preference in hats. "Why yes, Mr. Harper, that's exactly what I was hoping to find. Is there one in my size?"

Wade took the opportunity to study her face and hair, pretending he was judging her hat size. "Please call me Wade. You permitted me to call you Sam shortly after you came to Prosperity."

"Very well, Wade."

Wade shuffled through the hats until he found one he thought appropriate. Eyeing it critically, he stepped closer to settle it on her head. He placed one hand on her shoulder while allowing the back of his index finger to graze her cheek.

Surprised by the intimacy, Sam started at his touch, brushed his hand angrily from her shoulder, and took a step back. Instead of pretending innocence, Wade raised one of his eyebrows as if daring her to reprimand him for the impropriety. Though she didn't approve, Sam begrudgingly conceded he must possess a modicum of character since he'd been honest enough not to hide he'd done it deliberately. Or was he arrogant enough to believe she'd forgive him for being an unrepentant scoundrel?

Coolly, Wade reached for a mirror and held it for her. In the reflection, Sam saw Parker standing at the store entrance. Jackson was next to him, leaning stiffly against the doorframe with his arms crossed over his chest. The grim line of his mouth and the rigid set of his jaw told her he was livid. A disturbing light flared in his eyes. He looked as dangerous as a loaded gun with a hair trigger.

Sam's eyes darted back to Wade, who was now intently studying Jackson to gauge how deeply he'd riled him.

Sam snatched the hat off her head and tossed it on the table. Damn if the unconscionable bushwhacker hadn't played her and Jackson for his own purpose. Behind her, she heard Jackson's boots scrape on the floor before echoing on the boardwalk while marching away.

"It wasn't proper to use me to dry-gulch Jackson, Wade." Sam's face was expressionless and her voice cold. "That trick was lower than a sidewinder striking from the bottom of a barrel. In the future, when you're looking to lock horns with Jackson, leave me out of it. With me havin' no memories pullin' at my conscience, I could take pleasure in ensuring you don't age another day."

Not intimidated by Sam's words, Wade shrugged. "I'm not a slow-witted lunk, Sam. I understand your point. I concede it was bad manners to put a lady in the middle of my grievance with Jackson, even if said lady is part of the grievance." Wade punctuated the last remark with an insincere smile.

Sam bit back the stream of curses that surged to the tip of her tongue. *Why, the varmint thinks this is amusing and doesn't care who knows! Sonofabitch, he should be stammering a red-faced apology instead of facing her down.*

Casually Sam picked up the hat and ran her hand around the brim. In an offhand tone she warned, "If you're not careful, Wade, I'll give you the opportunity to show me you know how to die standing up."

The grin slid from Wade's face.

Turning her back, Sam announced, "I'm leaving because I have an itch in my gun hand I'm bound to scratch if I don't get you out of my sight." As she approached the door, she added dismissively, "Put the hat on my bill, shopkeeper."

Chuckling, Parker took the hat from Sam's hand, pinched a crease in the crown, and dropped it on her head. "You've been spending too much time with Price, Sam. Damn if that's not the first time I've ever heard of a sidewinder striking from the bottom of a barrel."

"Well, now," Sam drawled, "the bottom of a barrel is low, Parker, but I heard there was one snake that crawled so low, he was trapped in purgatory and named the devil."

Glancing at Wade, Parker laughed appreciatively and took Sam's elbow to steer her outside. He was eager to leave because he didn't want her to notice the woman standing in the shadows at the back of the store. From the fine cut of her dress to the regal set of her shoulders and neck, everything about the woman spoke of privilege. One would expect to see such a woman in couturiers' shops, drawing rooms, and ballrooms, not a mercantile in Prosperity. The woman was so obviously out of place that Sam would have undoubtedly asked questions that Parker preferred not to answer.

***

Wades' brazen advances had sparked a surge of jealousy in Jackson so strong it felt as if his insides were being squeezed in a vise. It had been a long time since he'd experienced that kind of jealousy. Hell, if anyone had bothered to ask, he'd have said he was accustomed to male heads turning Sam's way and men making overtures and advances. Perhaps her memory loss had undermined his confidence. Sam had never given him a reason to doubt her. His jealousy was his weakness, and he cursed it.

He tried to convince himself his reaction was because he'd spotted Ruth Kensington in the back corner of the store staring at Sam with hate-filled eyes. *What the hell was Ruth doing in Prosperity?* He fervently hoped Melinda, Ruth's daughter, wasn't with her, especially if she still believed she was in love with him.

After recognizing Ruth, Jackson caught Parker's eye, nodded toward the place Ruth stood, and crooked his thumb at Sam. Parker's eyes darted to the back of the store before nodding his understanding. Jackson backed over the threshold and stomped his way down the boardwalk, hoping Sam would believe jealousy was the reason for his hasty exit. He intended to trail Ruth when she left the store.

A sick sensation washed over him when he considered how his angry retreat might have hurt Sam. She'd think he didn't love her enough to trust her. In her place, he'd think the same. Unfortunately, he couldn't wait around to explain things because he'd lose the opportunity to spy on Ruth.

Though Jackson couldn't deny a twinge of jealousy, his feelings hadn't sprung from it or anything Sam had done. He was man enough to admit self-doubt was the cause—he was questioning whether he was the right man for her. Wade had known how to goad him, and Jackson had given Wade the satisfaction of letting him see he'd hit his mark dead center.

The fact Parker had been at the mercantile to discover Ruth's presence in Prosperity was the one positive in the whole incident. Because Parker recognized Ruth and knew what she'd done to Sam in Cheyenne, Jackson could count on him to distract and protect Sam.

Jackson cut through Branson's gun shop to circle back to the alley between the gunsmith and the mercantile to watch for Ruth. When she exited the mercantile, she turned in the opposite direction and unexpectedly entered the alley at the end of the walk. Fearing he'd lose her, he ran alongside the building, then behind it.

Arriving at the opposite end of the alley in which Ruth disappeared, he risked a peek around the corner and was surprised to see a covered buggy. Ducking behind a stack of wooden crates, Jackson waited for the buggy to pass by. He'd expected the conveyance to return to the hotel, but it turned onto Doc's street. *Where was Ruth going?*

Striding quickly down the same street, Jackson cradled his left arm. It gave him an excuse to see Doc. Since Reed Ferguson's house was across the street from Doc's, Jackson hoped to confirm his suspicion Ruth was visiting Ferguson. He wondered how Ruth and Ferguson knew each other.

***

"You're wasting your time, Jackson. I've seen that buggy come and go several times over the last few days. If you saw Ruth Kensington get in it, then it's for sure she's in cahoots with Ferguson, so why are you watching the house?" Doc asked.

From Doc's parlor window, Jackson had a clear view of Ferguson's house. "I wonder what the connection is between Ruth Kensington and Reed Ferguson. Who'd know that, Doc?"

Doc shrugged. "Maybe Thornton McKinley at the bank. His daughter went to the same private school as Melinda Kensington. I've heard him brag about it on several occasions. Parker could talk to McKinley."

"We need to do some digging," Jackson replied, nodding his agreement. "Doc, I need to ask something else."

"Well, while you're asking, let me look at that arm. I notice you hold it against you when you move around."

"That's because I used it as an excuse to visit you. My arm is fine."

"You've been favoring it the whole time you've been here, Jackson. Does it hurt?"

"Not so much it really bothers me."

"Well, let me change the bandage and look at it. Maybe I was too quick to tell you to start using it."

Jackson took off his shirt, and Doc removed the bandage. "It looks all right, except the infection has made it slow to heal and easy to open. I've changed my mind about your exercising it. I want you to rest it for a few more days. I'll fashion you a new sling."

"Don't bother, Doc. Another day or two and I'll hardly notice it."

"Suffering doesn't make you more of a man. If you had as many brains as you do muscles, you'd recognize a new bandage and sling could help you bypass Sam's temper. Didn't you tell me not more than half an hour ago how Wade made that play for her and you let it turn you green with jealousy before you saw Ruth in the back of the store and high-tailed it out of there? If Sam believes your arm is bothering you enough to come to see me, she'll likely forget all about your jealousy and not trusting her."

"You wily reprobate! You're usually on Sam's side. Why are you helping me?"

"Let's just say, I don't feel like being summoned over to Gracelyn tonight to patch you up after Sam takes a hunk out of your hide. Besides, she doesn't need the aggravation. She's fragile in case you haven't noticed."

"I've noticed," Jackson barked, worry lines creasing his forehead. "She told Morgan she wanted to ride her stallion. I don't think she's well enough. You said yourself she's bound to be having headaches and bouts of dizziness. She isn't eating or sleeping well. In Chicago, she—she came to me, so I thought the nightmares would stop, but they haven't. If anything, I think they're worse and more frequent."

"She'll do what she wants, no matter what I say, Jackson. You know that."

"Normally, I'd agree with you, but it's like you said, Doc. She's not a hundred percent, and she's questioning her instincts. She trusts you. I think she'll listen to you because she doesn't trust herself."

"I'll talk to her, Jackson, but if we're overprotective, she'll defy us for sure. I'll broach it with her in terms of using common sense. I'll advise her to start with a nice gentle mare. Hooker is too much horse for her to handle right now. She can't risk taking another fall."

Chapter 32

Instead of going to supper, Sam dealt twenty-one at Gracelyn Palace. When she played cards, she thought of little else, and Jackson was what she didn't want to think about. He was being insufferable.

Near midnight, Sam's eyes were drawn to the aisle near her table to find Jackson watching her. When her eyes fell on him, he turned and scanned the room. Seeing Morgan, Parker, and Mac sitting together, he approached their table to say something to them. All three men rose from the table and followed Jackson through the arch into the hotel lobby.

Sam sucked in a breath. Why was his arm back in a sling? Had he been so angry with her and Wade, he'd picked a fight and hurt it again?

Damn him for being jealous. She hadn't done anything to encourage Wade. It wasn't fair for Jackson to punish her. If he weren't careful, he'd be looking for another bed to sleep in tonight. As soon as the thought entered her head, she wished she could forget it, because a man like Jackson wouldn't have to sleep alone. To clear that unsettling thought, she questioned why Jackson left Gracelyn with her brother, Parker, and Mac. Coming up blank, she shrugged. She needed to stop thinking and concentrate on dealing cards.

A short while later, Sam noticed Morgan and Parker return. Morgan joined Alexa, while Parker went to pull up a chair next to Thornton McKinley, the bank president. She knew he was the banker because she'd asked one of the players. Assuming Mac was still with Jackson or had gone up to Grace, Sam kept dealing, focusing on bets and payoffs.

***

Sam was tired and had a throbbing headache. She signaled for a replacement, and when one of the other dealers arrived, she stepped back from the table and announced, "Miss Angie will be your new dealer, gentlemen. I bid you good night and good luck."

Moving quickly, she passed under the arch to the hotel lobby, nodded at the night clerk, and glanced up the staircase before exiting onto the boardwalk. Needing fresh air but not wanting to draw the attention of patrons, she stood in the shelter of the shadows at the periphery of light shining through the hotel's decorative picture window.

"It's not safe for you to be out here by yourself, Sam. You never know who you'll find hiding in the shadows," a familiar voice said.

"What do you want, Wade?" Sam replied, her tone unwelcoming.

"Your forgiveness."

"I can't forgive meanness."

"I know, Sam. You never could. I shouldn't have taken advantage of the situation today. When I started it, I didn't intend to take it so far."

"Why did you do it, Wade? Have I been unkind to you?"

"Not in the sense you're suggesting. When you first came to Prosperity, you accepted a few of my invitations."

"Are you saying I allowed you to court me?"

"Yes, but only superficially. You accepted a few supper invitations and let me escort you to a couple of socials. I think you used me to make a point to Jackson that you had options."

"So, today you used me to provoke Jackson?"

"Partly," Wade admitted.

"It's been a long day and an even longer night, Wade. Could you make your point?" Sam rubbed her forehead. "I have no memory of our relationship. Believe me, I wish I did."

"I didn't mean to distress you, Sam. It must be difficult for you. I'm only trying to say I was, and still am, interested in you; but you've always been honest about your feelings for me, saying you enjoyed my company and friendship, nothing more. I kissed you once, and you asked me not to do it again."

Sam looked uninterested but didn't turn away, so Wade offered more of an explanation. "Jackson and I have been rivals over several things, including you. Jackson has always won, fair and square. Most days I'm a big enough man to admit it. However, a crazy hope got the better of me today because I wondered if your amnesia would give me a second chance with you. I didn't expect Jackson to show up. When he did, I exercised poor judgment and used the opportunity to goad him. I realize by doing that, I only made myself look small. I'm truly sorry. I'll make it a point to apologize to Jackson, too."

"I think I understand, Wade, perhaps enough to forget and forgive."

"You mean you're not going to make me die standing up?" Wade teased.

"Don't press your luck," Sam warned. "You've redeemed yourself with your apology and charm tonight. It could go bad for you if I need to rethink my decision."

Wade offered his arm. "Would I be putting my life in danger if I offered to escort you back inside Gracelyn?"

Sam smiled and took his arm. "You're safe tonight. I'm too tired to explain shooting you to Sheriff Cooley."

Wade chuckled. "I do envy Jackson, Sam. If you ever decide to throw him over, I'd appreciate another chance to convince you I could be more than a friend."

Sam didn't comment; instead, she switched topics. "Have you heard the name Melinda Kensington?"

"Ruth Kensington's daughter? Why would you ask about her?"

"Because I had a memory of going to Cheyenne to meet Jackson, and her name was part of the memory."

"She's in Prosperity, Sam."

"Melinda Kensington is in Prosperity? How do you know?"

"I don't know if *Melinda* Kensington is in town, Sam. I meant her mother, Ruth, is here. I saw her today. She was in the store when you were there, but with everything else going on, you didn't notice her."

Having strolled back into the gaming salon, Sam paused at a table. "Have you a few minutes for a drink, Wade? I'd like to hear more about Ruth Kensington."

"Sure, Sam," Wade acceded, while holding a chair for her before seating himself. "I don't know her other than by reputation. We don't travel in the same social circles. I've been successful in my endeavors, but Ruth Kensington is a rich and powerful woman. Parker and Jackson can tell you about her. I know Trinity purchased horses from the Kensington stables."

While listening to Wade, Sam caught Miss Jenny's eye and nodded.

"Noah, Ruth's husband, was originally a New York native. He was educated in Europe and practiced architecture when he returned—this is public record, Sam."

Sam shrugged. "It's all new to me."

Wade momentarily looked confused. "Sorry, Sam, I forgot about your amnesia. The Kensingtons are equestrians and famous breeders, known in the eastern and southern horse world. Their stallions often take the stallion prize. Noah brought the breeding venture to Wyoming and attained fame for his purebred Morgan horses. Some say the Kensington ranch is the most impressive and richest in the Territory. I've never seen it, but I've been present when Parker and several other ranchers described how it has separate quarters for mares and studs, as well as a covered training school constructed from native rock and cedar shingles. In the last few years, they've branched out to develop wild mustangs, too." Wade paused before continuing.

"Some of the ladies talk about how the ranch house resembles a New England country farm. It has formal gardens and an elaborate carriage house. Noah also designed a townhouse in Cheyenne and several other homes and businesses."

Miss Jenny approached with two brandies. "Good evening, Wade, it's nice to see you."

Wade stood. "Good evening, Miss Jenny. How's that handsome fiancé of yours? It appears Trinity men have a monopoly on the beautiful women of Gracelyn Palace."

Jenny laughed. "Do you say that because of Jackson and Ryder, Wade?"

Wade glanced over at Alexa and Morgan. "It appears Miss Danforth is also taken."

"You're observant, Wade."

"Not really. It was just a matter of time before Morgan capitulated. It took longer than I would have predicted."

Sam laughed. "My thinking exactly, Wade."

Jenny started to leave, but Sam stopped her. "Miss Jenny, before you go, would you tell me the name of the man playing roulette near the table where I was dealing twenty-one? He's wearing a black suit and a decorative silver vest. With that rusty orange hair, I would guess he's Irish."

Jenny didn't need to look at the man. She knew him from Sam's description. "That's Reed Ferguson from the freight office. He's Hank Bainbridge's partner."

Wade kept his eyes on Jenny's face so he didn't betray to Ferguson that Sam was asking about him. In Wade's opinion, Reed Ferguson was condescending and secretive. He especially didn't like the way Reed looked at women, particularly Sam.

"He's been here most of the evening and has spent an inordinate amount of time watching me while trying to appear he's not. Have I done something to him?" Sam asked.

Jenny smiled and shook her head. "I know your memory is damaged, but surely it isn't a surprise that men watch you. Although I grant you, Ferguson does it with a disconcerting intensity. He's always polite, but I've noticed you stay clear of him."

Sam pressed two fingers to her temple. Her headache wasn't any better. Something about Ferguson made her uncomfortable. Maybe it was how he'd stared at Jackson earlier. His eyes had narrowed and darkened when Jackson passed by him. He'd looked as if he would enjoy plunging a knife into Jackson's back. Sam shrugged. "Thanks, Jenny. With no memory, it's hard for me to know with whom I'm dealing."

Jenny nodded and excused herself. Sam turned to Wade. "I hope I didn't make you uncomfortable asking about Ferguson. I didn't consider he might be your friend."

Wade studied Sam's face before replying, "Don't apologize, Sam. He's an acquaintance, not a friend. My guess is most people in Prosperity would say that about him. He mostly keeps to himself. I've never seen him do anything objectionable, but something about him sets my teeth on edge. I'm not surprised you asked about him."

Sam was sure Wade was being tactful. In fact, she was certain he'd wanted to add a warning to what he'd volunteered—maybe something like, "I'd advise you to stay away from him. I think he's dangerous."

Sam let it go. "I'll steer clear of him for now. I'm sorry I interrupted. Is Noah Kensington still alive?"

"He was ill for a long time and died about three years ago. Gossips say Ruth poisoned him. There was no formal investigation, though, and she runs the whole empire. I don't know anything about her life before she married Noah."

"Do you know why Ruth is visiting Prosperity? Is she staying at the hotel?"

"I don't know the answer to either of those questions, Sam. Why are you so interested?"

"Since the crash, I've remembered a few things. One of them was about meeting Jackson in Cheyenne where he mentioned the name of Melinda Kensington. It made me curious."

Wade grinned. "Jealous, Sam?"

Sam's brow furrowed, and she answered without thinking, "No, not jealous, but something about that memory makes me apprehensive. I have no idea why, but I don't like the feeling."

***

After Wade departed, Sam looked up to find Jackson glaring at her. She glared back.

Jackson didn't let Sam's angry eyes keep him from striding to her table. "Are you as surprised to see me tonight as you were at Wade Harper's store, Sam?"

"I'm tired, Jackson. Amuse yourself with some other lady." She couldn't help but notice that Jackson looked every inch the gentleman in a tailored black broad coat and trousers. He drew the openly interested smiles of several women. His eyes, dark and questioning, held Sam's eyes. She felt her pulse quicken. *God, don't let him see anything but my anger.*

"But I see you aren't too tired to spend time with Wade," Jackson accused.

It hurt knowing he didn't trust her. Sam stood and walked away. The gamblers parted to let her pass. She could feel their eyes rest on her bust and hips. When she reached the far end of the bar, she cupped her hand as if holding a brandy snifter. A few moments later, a glass of topaz nectar was deposited next to her. She lifted the glass and swirled the liquid appreciatively before taking a sip.

Regret stabbing her heart, she remembered the night she and Jackson shared brandy after he coerced her into drinking laudanum and bared her back to massage the soothing liniment over her painful bruises. Had she known, even then, how much she loved him? She must have because she'd craved his touch. She took two deep sips of the brandy and felt it warm her blood. *Not half as well as Jackson's hands did, though.* The thought popped, uninvited, into her head. She took another healthy swallow.

She felt Jackson's warm breath and the feather-light caress of his mouth near her ear. "You're supposed to sip it, darlin'," he whispered. She'd said close to the same thing to him on the night she'd just been remembering. *Was she that transparent?*

Sam lifted her chin, raised the glass, and tipped the remaining liquid into her mouth to swallow it in a single gulp, welcoming the fire of it within her. She signaled for a refill and downed a second glass. In the gilded mirror, she saw Jackson's eyebrows arch up and his hand reach to remove the glass from her hand.

"Careful, Jackson. I don't remember, but I'd guess men have lost their lives over less," she purred.

"You wouldn't hurt me, Sam."

Her eyes sparked with outrage. "Too bad you don't have the same boundaries. You thought nothing of how it would hurt me when you left the mercantile—or earlier tonight when you walked away to disappear into the hotel."

The hurt in her voice caught at Jackson's heart. "I didn't do those things to hurt you, Sam. I left the store because I needed to take care of some business and see Doc."

Sam's eyes slid to the sling she'd noticed earlier in the evening.

"I *was* jealous," Jackson admitted. "I would have sworn I was past feeling rage like that—but, obviously, I'm not. It hit me so hard that I felt as if I'd been kicked in the gut by a mule. Nor did I like seeing you with Wade tonight."

Jackson's arm encircled her waist and spun her around. He pressed against her, holding her between him and the bar. Slate blue eyes clashed with green-flecked brown eyes, the sparks flying like embers from a campfire on a windy night.

With a forced smile and through clenched teeth, Sam hissed, "You don't have the right to manhandle me." He was too damned close and had too much power over her. The brandy was affecting her. She shouldn't have drunk it on an empty stomach. It was becoming difficult to keep her wits about her. She couldn't ignore the pressure of his body pressed against hers. She wanted to lean closer. She made a feeble attempt to twist away.

Jackson gentled his hold. "Don't go, Sam."

"Why shouldn't I?" she challenged.

"Because I'm sorry, and I don't want to fight with you," he said. "I'd rather love you." Jackson let the words sink in before adding, "Please forgive me, Sam, and let's go upstairs."

Sam wondered if he meant it. Her fingers curled into the narrow lapels of his jacket. His body crowded closer. She uncurled her fingers and splayed them flat on his chest, weakly pushing him away. "It's tempting, Jackson," she admitted. Her heart was racing.

His eyes were imploring her to see his remorse, surrender her anger, and forgive him. Sam felt a hot flush suffuse her body as his gaze moved to her mouth before traveling slowly to the bare flesh across her bosom. It reminded her of how good it felt when he held her and loved her in the most elemental way. A bit of her resolve crumbled. It was futile to pretend she could do anything other than love him.

"Sam, if you won't forgive me, will you at least let me escort you upstairs? I'm worried about you. I can see your head is aching and the brandy hasn't helped. I'll sleep at the hotel, and we can talk tomorrow if you prefer. Just, please, come with me now." He waited for her to speak, to give him some sign.

She searched his eyes before leaning against him. He led her up the stairs. She stumbled on the top step. He caught her, pulling her into an embrace. She clung to him, her breasts rising and falling against his chest. "Jackson, I don't want you to go to the hotel."

"Good, because I wouldn't have gone beyond the floor outside the bedroom and would have hated facing Mac in the morning."

No, loving Jackson wasn't something Sam could get over—nor did she want to.

***

Several times during the evening, Reed Ferguson thought of how helpless the drugged tea would have made Sam. It was a pity he wouldn't be able to use it to his advantage.

He fantasized about her teasing him as she'd teased Wade Harper and Jackson Knight. She made men pay a million times over—not in money but in lust and lowly groveling.

He watched Jackson and Sam go up the stairs together. It angered him that Jackson would once again be the one to bed her.

Soon she'd understand she'd been wasting her time with Jackson. Before she died, she'd experience the ecstasy of his flesh joining with hers.

Chapter 33

The torment of Sam's nightmare roused Jackson from deep sleep. Christ, he wished he could shield her from the horror of its assault instead of vanquishing it after it tortured her. She'd never had the dreams with this frequency. Hell, this was three nights in a row.

"No, please no!" she screamed. "Mac—Oh God, Mac, help me!" The desperation and pain in her voice became a wild keening and she struggled like a hellcat.

"Sam, it's a nightmare. He can't hurt you. I'm here." Jackson caught her flailing arms and trapped her thrashing body against his. He began rocking her gently, whispering endearments in a low soothing voice, reassuring her. One of her arms broke free and struck his bad arm. Biting back the pain, he caught it and brought it back into the circle of his embrace. He continued to rock her, repeating, "It's a nightmare, Sam. I'm here to chase it away." Gradually, her body relaxed, and Jackson loosened his hold to cradle her gently.

Her eyes closed, not fully awake, Sam whispered, "The boy wouldn't help me—he ran away when I killed the man." Her voice trailed off.

She killed him? What boy? This was the first time Jackson heard her mention a boy. Grace and Mac said the man died the day he raped Sam. Was she confusing dreams or was this a repressed memory coming to the surface because of the anxiety and stress she'd been under since the crash?

When he felt the even rise and fall of her breathing against his chest, he lowered her to rest in the warm shelter of his body. If he had magical powers, he'd cast a spell to annihilate this ugly memory and restore all the pleasant memories she'd lost.

***

Sam was still sleeping when Jackson replaced his shoulder with his pillow beneath her head and arranged the covers around her. Quietly, he dressed before rounding the bed to pick up his boots. She emitted a deep sigh, and he stood for a moment looking down at her honey-gold hair spread across the pillow, her long lashes dusting her pale cheeks, and the tempting curve of her mouth. For a brief second, he considered returning to the bed.

When he held Sam in his arms, he held happiness. Before Trinity and Sam came into his life, he thought happiness was a fairy tale. Now that he'd experienced it, he was afraid it could disappear. What if Sam's mind became unglued from reliving the nightmare? He knew she was strong, but Christ, how much could a person stand?

In the last few weeks, her whole world had turned upside down. Her memories were gone. Every person was a stranger. She struggled to recover from her physical injuries, battled Webster's assassins, nursed him on the train, killed Webster in a gunfight, guarded against an unknown person trying to hurt her, and repeatedly suffered nightmares revealing repressed details of the brutal rape she'd endured as a young girl.

Jackson slipped quietly from the room to find Grace and Mac in the sitting room drinking coffee. He sat next to Mac, and Grace passed him a cup. "She had the nightmare again, Grace—for the third time in as many nights. She said something I don't understand. She wasn't fully awake when she said it. It was something about a boy who wouldn't help her—she said the boy ran away when she killed the man."

Mac's eyes trained on Jackson. Talking about that day always upset him. He should have protected her. "I know those nightmares are bad, Son," he said, keeping his tone level. "She must have confused the usual one with something else because the man lived alone. He died when he fell out of the loft in his barn and broke his neck."

"Jackson, has she mentioned a boy before?" Grace asked.

"No—never. Are you and Mac sure the man died like you say? Is it a possibility Sam had anything to do with it?"

"That day is the biggest regret of my life, Jackson," Mac replied. "I taught her to defend herself and to shoot straight. Sam wore her gun wherever she went. I didn't know the damned schoolmarm took it from her when she got to school and locked it in a drawer until school let out. On the day it happened, the teacher was called away, and Sam had to come home without her gun. The man was a neighbor. We had no idea he wanted to harm her. Sam didn't remember much about what happened, but she knew for sure who hurt her and where it happened."

A cold stillness settled over Mac's features. "I intended to—to kill him, Jackson. I'm not gonna lie and say different. If that low life hadn't already been dead, I would have— well, I won't say it in front of Grace. But I'd barely started toward his place when I saw smoke. By the time I got there, the barn was fully engulfed. I couldn't find him anywhere on the property so I prayed he was in there, burning in hell's fire. Later, they did find him in the barn. The doctor said his neck was broken and he likely died before the fire started. The sheriff figured he knocked the oil lantern over when he fell from the loft and broke his neck."

There was a moment of silence before Mac continued. "His wife had left him years before, and she took their son with her. I don't see how a boy could be there or how Sam could have killed the man. She was still a slip of a girl, hadn't grown to her full height—or done much more than show a few signs of starting to—fill out, so to speak."

Jackson clutched the coffee cup. The hot liquid sloshed over the edge. "Christ, dyin' was too good for that pervert."

From the bedroom door, a tremulous voice said, "I killed him, Mac."

Jackson and Grace jumped to their feet.

White-faced, with huge, haunted eyes, Sam put out her hand and shook her head to keep them from coming to her. "No, wait—please listen. He was lying on top of me after— he hurt me—and I shoved him with all my might. I don't know where I got the strength. He rolled off me, over the edge, and hit the floor with a terrible sound."

Sam sank to her knees in the doorway. She felt the bile in her throat rise and leaned her forehead on the doorframe. Grace knelt beside her, stroking her hair. "I'm going to be sick, Mother."

"No, you aren't, Sam. He's dead. He can't hurt you anymore. You survived. He didn't."

Sam looked into Grace's eyes and found the strength to swallow without retching, although her gut roiled from remembering the violation she'd suffered. "Why does surviving mean that sick bastard can torture me in my dreams? Why can't I remember the good things and forget that horror?"

Gripping the doorframe for support, Sam rose unsteadily to her feet, half expecting to slide back down. Jackson stepped near and she reached for his arm. "I promise I won't be sick. I just need a little help getting to the chair. I'll be fine then."

After seating Sam, Jackson pulled a chair close and draped his arm on the back of hers, wordlessly reassuring her.

"Jackson, your arm is bleeding again," Sam said, noticing the spot of blood on his shirtsleeve.

Jackson lied. "I bumped it against the bed table this morning, Sam. I'll stop by Doc's and let him look at it again."

Sam nodded woodenly. "I'll dress in a few minutes. May I walk with you to Doc's? I need some fresh air."

Jackson darted a quick, uncertain glance toward Grace. "Sure, darlin'. Do you want Grace to help you dress?"

"I can do it myself."

Jackson didn't think she could. "Doc will chew me out if I don't wear the new sling he gave me yesterday. It's in the bedroom. Will you help me with it?"

She nodded and placed a hand on Jackson's shoulder to pull herself up. He let her lead but stayed close as they crossed to the bedroom. Sam's shoulders were straight, but her steps were hesitant. While Jackson pulled the door shut behind them, she moved to the washbasin.

"Jackson?"

"Yes, darlin'."

"I'm going to be sick now."

Jackson gathered her hair and circled her waist to support her as she leaned over the basin. "It's all right," he crooned sympathetically. "You'll feel better. You should have done it before."

***

From the window, Grace watched her son and Jackson cross the street to the boardwalk opposite Gracelyn. They were on their way to see Sheriff Cooley. Her thoughts shifted to Sam and what she'd remembered in her nightmare about pushing her attacker to his death. After all these years, the repressed details of that terrible day were returning. Grace knew her daughter was strong. However, with everything else Sam was dealing with, could she handle this too?

Grace's gaze returned to the street. She loved Sam. Fondly, she recalled the memory of Sam's chubby little arms wrapped around her neck. Sam had always been kind and loving—as good inside as she was beautiful on the outside. Whenever Jackson spoke of Sam's sixth sense or teased about Sam being a witch, Grace smiled. She knew Sam's ability had nothing to do with witchcraft, magic, or clairvoyance. Sam's talents were manifestations of her goodness, free spirit, intellect, and powers of observation.

Behind her, Grace heard Mac's steps. When his hand settled on her shoulder, she leaned back against him. "More will come out of this, Mac. You know how Sam's mind works. She'll need us."

Mac kissed Grace's cheek. "Sam's our girl. She'll work it out, and when she does, we'll be here for her." He slid his arms around Grace's midriff and spoke into the soft curve of her neck. "I won't fail her again. I couldn't live with it."

"I know, Mac," Grace murmured.

***

At the Prosperity jailhouse, Rem Cooley held out an envelope to Morgan. "A letter from your lawyer friend came. If you hadn't stopped in, I would have brought it to you."

Jackson plopped down in a chair while Rem poured coffee. After carefully setting three steaming tin cups on the desk, Rem bent to open a bottom drawer and came up with a bottle of Monongahela. After pouring a generous amount of whiskey into each cup, he picked his up and went to lean against the doorframe to study the street. Behind him, he heard the envelope rip. He hoped the report contained helpful information. He didn't like to think about anyone trying to hurt Sam. He'd not argue with anyone who said she was feisty, headstrong, and argumentative, but he'd defend to his dying breath that she was also caring, kind, and generous.

Jackson watched Morgan's eyes travel over the words on the two pages of the report. Part of him wanted to snatch the pages from Morgan's hands. Another part of him was afraid to read them because they might not contain anything useful.

Jackson dropped his eyes to his coffee and wrapped his hands around his cup. He had an impulse to throw it at the wall to vent some of his frustration, but he reined in the notion. Sam would have been amused at his control. She'd reminded him of a cracked piece of china this morning, still able to function but in danger of breaking apart if made to bear too much weight. He'd persuaded her to rest after getting sick, saying he, Morgan, and Parker needed to take care of some ranch business, and he'd call for her after dinner so they could go to Doc Baxter's together. She'd started to protest he shouldn't wait to see Doc but gave up the argument all too easily. Jackson took a deep breath and rubbed his eyes.

Across the desk, Morgan put down the papers and slid them toward Jackson.

Other than being rich, Reed Ferguson's privileged life had been unremarkable. His widowed mother was from an affluent Chicago family, and he'd lived with her and his grandparents in Chicago until he was ten, at which time his mother remarried and moved to Cheyenne.

His new stepfather was a rich man, not as rich as Noah Kensington, but rich enough to belong to the same social circle and for Reed to be considered a possible future husband for Melinda, Kensington's daughter.

Ferguson's grandmother died when he was twenty-one and left him a modest income. Less than a year later, he inherited everything when his grandfather passed away. Given his wealth, social status, and good looks, he was a better choice for marriage to the young heiress, Melinda Kensington, than Jackson. Ferguson began courting Melinda when she turned seventeen, and it appeared they would marry.

Reed Ferguson had moved to Prosperity approximately seven months ago. Jackson didn't recall anyone mentioning Ferguson's name during his and Sam's visit to Cheyenne. He wondered if Reed and Melinda were engaged by now. Briefly, Jackson considered how awkward it would be for him and Sam if Melinda moved to Prosperity. *Was that the reason Ruth was here?*

***

After leaving the sheriff's office, Jackson and Morgan joined Parker in the dining room at the hotel. Parker had learned several things from Thornton McKinley the preceding night. "Melinda Kensington isn't with Ruth, Jackson, nor is she going to marry Ferguson."

Surprised, Jackson asked, "Are you sure Parker? The report Thomas sent said he was courting Melinda."

"I'm sure, Jackson," Parker replied, looking uncomfortable. "Thornton McKinley told me Melinda Kensington is dead. She drowned shortly after you and Sam left Cheyenne."

Jackson was stunned. "How is it we didn't hear about it? Wouldn't it have been in the papers?"

"It may have been, Jackson, but Ruth has a business interest in almost everything that happens in Cheyenne. She likely put a lid on it."

"Did Thornton say how it happened? How about his daughter, Ashley? Does she know anything?"

"Ashley told Thornton and his wife that the girls at her school say it was suicide, but Ruth Kensington passed the whole thing off as an accidental drowning. The Kensington housekeeper was hired by the mother of Ashley's best friend after Melinda's death. The housekeeper claims to have found a suicide note from Melinda. Ruth kept the note from the officials. According to the housekeeper, the note said Melinda didn't want to marry her fiancé and knew her mother would force her. It also said she didn't want to live if she couldn't marry the man she really loved."

Christ, Jackson had never dreamed the girl felt that deeply about him. He'd believed she'd get over him and find someone else. He could barely take it in. "How could I have been so wrong? How could a one-sided infatuation drive her to suicide? There must be more to it."

Parker glanced at Morgan before replying, "Ashley told her parents Melinda was a beautiful, intelligent, and spoiled girl. She didn't have many friends, and the ones she did have were because of her being rich, not well liked. Melinda's behavior was erratic. She could be cruel, doling out punishment for imagined slights. At times she'd barely say a word and would avoid people. Then surprisingly, she'd transform into a social whirlwind, strangely enthusiastic and over-animated. People were wary of her—on guard—as they couldn't predict which Melinda they'd encounter."

"Did Thornton say anything about Ruth?" Jackson asked.

"Only that no one seems to know much about Ruth's background before she married her husband. Thornton intimated he heard a rumor there is a history of madness in her family. He even went so far as to say gossips believe she killed her husband."

"For once, the gossip might be right," Jackson commented. "Sam and I saw evidence of Ruth's unnatural preoccupation to fulfill her daughter's smallest wish. She watched us constantly and baited Sam whenever she got the chance. Ruth engineered Sam's accidental fall into the corral. If the stable manager hadn't pulled her out, Sam would have been trampled to death. We didn't stay long enough after that for Ruth to try anything else."

Chapter 34

Deep in thought, Jackson didn't see Wade Harper move from the bar in Gracelyn Palace to block his path. Looking Wade coldly in the eye, Jackson noticed the merchant held his body stiffly as if expecting him to throw a punch. The thought did cross his mind.

Wade cleared his throat. "I know after my behavior yesterday, you'd just as soon shoot me as look at me, Jackson, and I don't blame you."

Jackson made no comment.

"I'm here to say I'm sorry. I can offer no excuse for my behavior. I was an ass. I apologized to Sam last night for putting her in the middle of what, up until yesterday, had been a good-natured rivalry between us. I went too far, and I know better. You've always played fair with me, and it shames me to say I didn't."

Jackson still made no comment, but Wade noticed his shoulders relax before taking a step forward to brush past him. Wade risked putting a hand on his arm to stop him. "Jackson, I need to say something else. Will you please sit for a minute? It's about Reed Ferguson and Sam."

Jackson's eyes narrowed in surprise. Abruptly, he took two strides to the nearest table and jerked back a chair.

Wade followed and sat across from Jackson. "Last night when I was talking to Sam, she asked Miss Jenny about Ferguson. She'd noticed him watching her, and something about him bothered her. I'm telling you because I've never seen Sam look so uncomfortable about someone. If I were telling you about a woman other than Sam, I'd say she was afraid of him."

"Did she say that, Wade?"

"No, it was the way she acted that put me in mind of it. I don't like Ferguson. Contrary to my behavior yesterday, I do like you and Sam. That's why I'm telling you."

"I appreciate it, Wade," Jackson replied, offering his hand. "I'm concerned about Sam. And Reed Ferguson doesn't set well with me either."

Wade grasped Jackson's hand. "One more thing. The reason Sam asked me to have a drink with her last night was to ask questions about Ruth and Melinda Kensington. She mentioned Melinda's name came up in something she'd remembered. I thought you should know about that, too."

Wade stood. "Jackson, I sense trouble brewing. If you need any help, just say the word. I know how to keep my mouth shut, and I'm better than most with my fists. I don't shoot as well as you and Sam, but I'm a fair shot. Sometimes numbers are more important than drawing fast—anyway, the offer stands should you need it."

***

The wind and temperature were brisk as Sam and Jackson rounded the corner onto the street where Doc lived. Releasing Sam's arm, Jackson wrapped his arm around her waist and pulled her close to his side. "Are you cold, darlin'?"

She smiled up at him. "Yes, but the fresh air is good for me, and I have you to keep me warm." Jackson planted a kiss on her temple.

As they neared Doc's house, Jackson glanced at Ferguson's house, recalling his conversation with Wade.

Impulsively, he said, "I saw Wade Harper while I was out this morning. He apologized for his behavior yesterday."

Sam didn't alter her pace and kept her eyes focused straight ahead. Casually, she replied, "Wade mentioned last night he intended to apologize." Curious, she asked, "Did you accept the apology?"

"Yes. We shook hands."

Sam stopped walking.

Jackson laughed. He'd expected she'd be surprised by his answer, but not that surprised. He put his hand under her chin to tip her head up and give her a quick, playful kiss. Then he turned her back toward Doc's house. She matched her steps to his.

As he raised his hand to knock on Doc's door, Jackson said, "Wade told me that you asked him about Reed Ferguson and Ruth and Melinda Kensington. He said you seemed concerned."

"Jackson, you said that as if I were keeping secrets from you. I would have asked you the questions if—well, never mind. I don't want to rehash all that."

Doc opened the door and looked from Sam to Jackson. "Haven't you two made up yet? I mend broken bones, not lovers' quarrels."

Sam laughed and hugged him. "I forgave Jackson for yesterday, Doc. He's scowling because he stuck his foot in his mouth about something else."

"I didn't accuse you of anything, Sam. I only mentioned Wade said you were concerned about Reed Ferguson and the Kensingtons."

Sam disregarded Jackson's protest. "We came to see you, Doc, so you can look at Jackson's arm."

Doc raised an eyebrow. "I looked at it yesterday and decided he should rest it a few more days before he uses it. Did something happen to it?"

Before Sam could say anything, Jackson cut in. "I accidentally banged it on the nightstand, Doc. That's all."

Sam gave Jackson a knowing look and an affectionate pat. "He's lying because he doesn't want me to feel guilty for punching him. I had a nightmare last night."

Jackson was flabbergasted. The witch. How the hell did she know?

"Let me take a look, Jackson." While assessing the damage, he murmured, "You broke open the wound, but not deep."

"I'm sorry, Jackson," Sam mumbled.

"Sam, you have nothing to be sorry for. It's not like you did it intentionally." She was too quick to take on blame. He noticed her stroking the scar on her hand.

"The dream changed last night," Sam said, directing her remark to Doc. "I remembered I pushed the man to his death."

Doc's head jerked up.

Jackson was watching Sam's face. She'd said the words bravely, but he saw they hadn't come easy. He wondered why she was so determined Doc know.

Doc went to stand in front of Sam before asking, "How do you feel about that?"

Sam knew she was in too deep to back out now. If she didn't tell Doc the truth, Jackson would. "It knocked me to my knees, Doc, and I got sick to my stomach. I'm good enough now, though."

"So you say," Doc replied, glancing sideways at Jackson.

"Damn it, Doc, he was hurting me! I can live with it. I'm telling you because I need to know if something other than my memory was damaged in the stage crash. Why am I remembering about the attack?"

Doc shook his head. "These things have a way of coming to the surface over time. I've read a few cases where a person remembers twenty or thirty years after the fact. I doubt your damaged memory has anything to do with your nightmares."

Sam wanted to believe him, but she couldn't accept it. Jackson had told her she hadn't had the nightmares for a long time before the crash. "I want to believe you, Doc. What you say sounds logical, but I can't buy it. I think there's a reason for the dreams, and I have a bad feeling about them."

Jackson was startled. She hadn't voiced that concern before. He wondered whether her sixth sense was the reason for her apprehension, or had something else she hadn't shared with him caused it?

"For some people, remembering a bad thing helps put it to rest," Doc said patiently. "That may be what's happening to you. After all, you're in a good place in your life. You have Jackson, family, friends, and even a couple of cousins. All this coming to the surface may be your way of clearing your mind of it so it won't haunt you anymore."

Sam looked over at Jackson. "I hope you're right, Doc. I'd like nothing better than to leave it behind and get back to normal. The problem is I don't know what that means."

Doc patted her hand. "Nobody knows, Sam, because everyone has a different concept of normal. You need to concentrate on recovering. Poking too hard at the other things will slow you down."

"You sound like Grace. She tells me some things can't be controlled, and I would be happier if I could accept that fact."

Doc smiled. "Grace is as wise as she is beautiful—there's one other thing I want to say."

Sam waited, wondering why he looked anxious.

"I heard you were thinking of riding. If you do, you need to use good judgment."

"Doc, it's not like you to beat around the bush, just say it."

"All right, Sam. I'm saying choose a gentle mare from the livery. Hooker is too much for you to handle right now. Becky hasn't been home to exercise him properly. The truth is you won't walk away from another blow to the head. Do you understand?"

"I do, Doc," Sam replied, her tone uncharacteristically docile. "I'll be careful, and I promise I won't ride Hooker."

***

"Where were we the first time I wore the green silk dress?" Sam asked as she and Jackson walked from Doc's back to Gracelyn Palace. "Did it have anything to do with Melinda Kensington?"

"Why would you think that?" Jackson countered, surprised by her question.

Ignoring the knot in her stomach and the dryness in her throat, Sam explained. "It's something I sense. The memory of meeting you in Cheyenne began with you asking me to pretend to be your fiancée because Melinda Kensington thought she was in love with you. I think the first memory of you carrying me when I was wearing the green dress and the memory of Melinda are connected. Something about those memories frightens me."

Jackson stopped walking and turned to face her. "The memories are connected, Sam. I carried you up the stairs the last night we were at Ruth Kensington's home because earlier in the day you hurt your leg. You were pitched into the corral with a bunch of wild mustangs when the top rail of the fence broke. We couldn't prove it, but we believed Ruth arranged the accident."

Feeling a sudden chill, Sam gripped the lapels of her jacket together to keep the cold air from her neck and shoulders. "Did I wear the dress that night to anger Ruth? I wasn't trying to make Melinda feel bad, was I?"

A fleeting smile touched Jackson's mouth. "No, you didn't wear the dress for either of those reasons. You wore it to tease me because I'd asked you to pretend to be my fiancée. It was your way of telling me you knew I loved you and couldn't resist your charms, so to speak."

Sam searched Jackson's expression for any indication his answer was less than the truth. She wanted to believe him. "It doesn't speak well of my good judgment, does it?"

Jackson's mouth pulled into a grim line. "It's my judgment that should be criticized, Sam. My anger over your being hurt made me arrogant and reckless that night. I knew we were getting the hell out of there the next morning, so I deliberately provoked Ruth by brazenly demonstrating my feelings for you. You recognized my behavior was fanning Ruth's rage and tried to defuse the situation, but I refused to cooperate. I'm sorry for it, Sam. I let my temper get out of control and made a bad situation worse. Ruth Kensington watched me carry you up to your room after supper."

"Jackson, are you saying Ruth wants me dead because her daughter wants to marry you?"

In a weary, resigned voice, Jackson replied, "No, Sam. Melinda committed suicide. Ruth wants revenge for her daughter's death. I think Reed Ferguson and Ruth want to murder you."

***

Mac pushed past Jackson and gathered Sam in his arms. "Sweetheart, I'm here. You're safe now." Sam immediately stopped calling his name and calmed down, but she didn't wake. Mac smoothed her hair and held her until her breathing returned to normal and she slept naturally. When he settled her back against her pillow, she didn't stir.

Jackson and Grace hovered by the door until Mac joined them. When they moved to the sitting room, Jackson left the bedroom door partially open. He wanted to be able to hear if she woke. In a low voice, he said, "Thank God you came, Mac. I couldn't wake her. The nightmare has never been like this."

Grace dropped into a chair with none of her usual poise. "She's recalling the details of what happened to her, Jackson." She turned her eyes on Mac. "I'm right, aren't I, Mac? She was acting out how she came home to you. It's what you told me." Her voice was filled with worry.

Mac looked down at his bare feet. He'd hastily pulled on his pants and shirt before going to Sam. Distracted, he began to button his shirt. "Yes, it was like that, Grace. I'd been waiting by the corral. She was late coming home from school. When I heard her—saw her, I couldn't believe it was my girl—hurt like that." Mac swiped his hand across his eyes as if he were wiping the image from his memory. "She didn't stop saying my name until I lifted her in my arms. Then she told me the man's name. You know the rest."

***

Sam woke before Jackson did and immediately recalled the latest nightmare and that Mac had come to comfort her. The nightmare had been very different from the others and revealed details she'd rather not know. Why was she remembering the cruel torture of being raped when she longed to remember the first time Jackson kissed her?

Wearily Sam put the back of her hand to her forehead. Her head was already aching. She was comforted by the even sound of Jackson's breathing, the warm pressure of his body snuggled up to her backside. With her in his bed, he was lucky to get a couple of uninterrupted hours of sleep at a time.

The nightmare had begun with her hurting and alone in the loft, slowly coming to the realization she needed to get to Mac, which meant she'd have to climb down the ladder, the same way the boy left. She told herself that if he could do it, she could too—maybe, except her legs didn't want to obey her. Everything hurt, especially the place at the top of her legs. She knew she was naked and that there was blood; she could feel it and smell it, along with the odors of the man's sweat and fluids. She convinced herself if she didn't look, the pain and the blood wouldn't be real. She would concentrate only on what would help her get to Mac.

She rolled onto her stomach and pushed herself up on her hands and knees to crawl the few feet to the ladder. Shuddering, she lowered a foot to the first rung. Was the man waiting for her? By sheer will, she inched down. With only four more rungs left, the fear and uncertainty overwhelmed her, and she froze in place. Was she going to Mac or the man?

Suddenly there was a whoosh of air beneath her and the sound of shattering glass. Someone had thrown a lit lantern at the base of the ladder. She didn't see where it came from or who threw it. The flames flared, devouring the splattered splashes of oil. Her only chance for survival was to leap beyond the flames and escape through the open door.

The man was lying face up near the ladder. He didn't move. She looked beyond him, searching for a safe place. Before leaping, she screwed her eyes closed and imagined Mac was standing there to catch her.

She landed face down, her upper torso on the spot she'd aimed for, but one of her feet was on the man's chest. She imagined his hand clawed at her ankle, trying to imprison her. Fear of capture, the smoke, and the scorching heat gave her the strength to scramble to her feet and run. She snatched a horse blanket hanging on a stall as she sprinted for the open door but didn't wrap it around her until she was clear of the barn.

Mac was only a quarter mile away. She put everything else out of her mind—the pain, the blood, her nakedness. She repeated Mac's name as if it were a prayer. When she saw him look up from the corral, relief flooded through her and sapped her remaining strength. *Mac would come to her*. She let the numbness set in because she needed it to block the pain and her memory. Mac loved her and would protect her. When he lifted her in his arms, she knew she was safe and could let go.

***

Sam argued with her brother as they crossed the hotel dining room. "Morgan, you aren't my keeper. I'm riding to the ranch tomorrow morning with Alexa and Parker whether you like it or not. Doc said I can ride if I choose a gentle mare from the livery."

Morgan rolled his eyes and tightened his grip on Sam's elbow. "I'm not that gullible, Sis. You know damn well Doc didn't say you're fit to ride. I'll bet it was more like 'You can try riding in a couple of weeks.'"

Oblivious to the stares of other diners, Sam stopped in the middle of the room, pulled her arm from Morgan's grasp, and stamped her foot. "Are you calling me a liar? I ought to make you eat those words."

Belatedly, Morgan realized he'd gone too far. "Calm down, Sam. I didn't say you lied. I only suggested you left out a few facts."

Sam opened her mouth to reply but closed it when she saw Grace looking at them with sad eyes, a slight frown, and pursed lips. It was the disapproving, long-suffering expression all mothers give to misbehaving children.

Morgan's eyes followed Sam's and his face paled. "We're in for it now. You know how Grace feels about us forgetting manners and causing a scene."

Sam raised an amused brow and started to chuckle. "I know what you told me about it, Morgan. Besides, you started it. I told you the truth. You can ask Jackson." Sam turned her back on her brother and crossed the few remaining steps to the table where Mac, Grace, Parker, Alexa, and Jackson were already seated.

Incensed by Sam's dismissal, Morgan clenched his fists and called after her, "Damn it, Sam, don't turn your back on me. I didn't call you a liar!"

Risking more disapproval from Grace, Sam turned to goad Morgan. "Could you say that louder, Brother? I don't think the guests in the hotel lobby heard you."

Grace's eyes followed Morgan as he traced Sam's steps to the table.

Parker, Mac, and Jackson politely stood for Sam. Jackson reached for the back of her chair but withdrew when he saw her jab Morgan in the ribs with her elbow. When Morgan didn't respond, she whispered, "My chair, you dolt! Do you want to get in more trouble?"

Jackson turned his head so Morgan couldn't see his grin.

Morgan swore under his breath before drawing back Sam's chair, bowing, and waving his hand over it as if seating royalty.

Sam swallowed a chuckle and began to sit, but when she was halfway down, Morgan prematurely shoved the chair in, catching her behind her knees. She fell clumsily back, landing with a loud plop.

Morgan hid his smile of satisfaction and dove for the chair next to Alexa.

Pretending he hadn't noticed, Parker made a production out of repositioning his silverware. Jackson gave up trying to hide his amusement and laughed aloud. Mac looked disapproving and patted Grace's shoulder. Alexa covered her mouth and patted Morgan's leg sympathetically. Grace sighed, smoothed her skirt, and softly murmured, "Children."

Despite Grace's gentle admonition, Mac saw his girl wasn't going to give up the battle. Quietly, he intervened, "That's enough, Sam."

Recognizing Mac's authoritarian tone, Sam began to turn toward him but froze when she saw a woman with clenched hands and a malevolent expression staring at Jackson. In a plain silk mourning gown, the woman resembled a black thundercloud gathering the forces of nature to unleash mayhem on whatever passed beneath. The unbridled fury in her green eyes was so intense Sam half expected to see lightning flash and strike Jackson dead where he sat.

The woman's dark brown hair, tinged with gray at the temples, was pulled back into a smooth chignon. Sam had no doubt the woman was Ruth Kensington. She may have once been beautiful, but now, with thin lips drawn into an ugly sneer and dark circles under her eyes, what little remained of her former beauty was hidden. This was a woman incapable of forgiveness or compassion. Sam imagined a malignant tumor had long ago replaced Ruth Kensington's heart.

Ruth took a step toward the table.

Reacting to the threat, Sam shoved her chair back and rose to confront Ruth, who reluctantly transferred her gaze from Jackson to Sam's face. Locking eyes with Ruth, Sam felt as if she were being sucked into a bottomless pool of quicksand.

Ruth advanced another step.

Stiff-backed and defiant, Sam raked Ruth with cold eyes darkened to the color of blue steel, warning any action toward Jackson would result in severe injury.

Sam might have taken it further except Jackson took her hand in his and began rubbing gentle circles on her inner wrist. "Darlin', if looks could kill, a minister would already be giving the eulogy," he murmured, his tone equal parts amusement and admiration.

Although the corners of Sam's mouth twitched, her body didn't relax. She dragged her eyes from Jackson back to Ruth, whose mottled cheeks were stained with red. "No one looks at the man I love with that kind of hate," Sam pronounced. "You hurt him, I guarantee you won't walk away," she warned, her tone ringing with contempt.

Jackson gently tugged Sam's hand, urging her to sit.

Holding Ruth's gaze, Sam sank onto her chair. Jackson cupped her chin to turn her head toward him. She knew every eye in the room was trained on them, but she didn't care.

Jackson leaned in to kiss her. Sam's breath caught, and he adjusted the slant of his mouth over hers and deepened the kiss. He hadn't intended to take the kiss that far but couldn't resist when she fairly melted against him. When he ended the kiss, she was trembling, but not from anger.

Ruth was gone.

Though her eyes were sparkling, the frown was back on Grace's face. Mac's expression vacillated between pride and fatherly pique. Parker and Morgan hid their grins behind napkins. Becky and Alexa cast their eyes down, pretending they hadn't recognized the passion flaring between the couple.

"That kiss said more than any look or words could have done," Jackson murmured.

"That's why I let you kiss me like that," Sam agreed, sounding out of breath.

Amused, Jackson leaned forward to whisper in her ear, his lips grazing her neck as he spoke. "Ah, but then you forgot all about Ruth. How do you feel about skipping supper and going upstairs? I find I'm hungry for something not on the menu."

"I'm willing," she breathed, her tremulous voice just above a whisper. "But just so you know, I don't intend to *skip anything.*"

They were both so caught up in their feelings, the diverse array of reactions rustling in waves around them barely penetrated their awareness as they murmured their excuses and left the others behind.

Chapter 35

While walking the horses sedately out of town, Sam initially thought the ride to Trinity would be pleasant and all the fuss about her riding had been needless. However, once the horses began to trot, each bounce felt as if a knifepoint at the back of her head threatened to pierce the tautly stretched membrane housing her brain.

Sam pulled on the reins to slow the mare's pace and experienced a sudden memory of riding her fiery stallion. Hooker was two hands higher than this sweet little mare and all sinew and power, with a broad chest and thick neck. She recalled how he loved to toss his head, snort derisively, and prance impatiently, challenging her to bring him under control.

Sam adjusted her handling to find a stride she and the mare could tolerate. She knew Mac and Parker were holding back to accommodate her illness and Alexa's inexperience. Truth was, given her condition, their pace pushed the limits of her present capability.

For Sam, dismounting when they arrived at the practice range involved gripping the saddle horn, sliding to the ground, and clinging to the saddle while she waited for her head to clear and legs to hold her. She was sure her performance didn't go unnoticed by Mac and Parker.

***

Price Hardin hooked his thumbs in his gun belt and arched an eyebrow while watching Mac, Parker, Alexa, and Sam ride out of town. He knew he should be thinking about moseying on back to Laramie, but hanging around Prosperity while Sam stirred up trouble was the most fun he'd had in more than a month of Sundays. Holt Webster was well enough to ride, but Price wasn't about to rush away. He could feel in his bones things were coming to a head.

Price chuckled aloud. Last night in Gracelyn Palace, after Sam and Jackson went upstairs, the whole town talked about the show they'd put on in the hotel dining room for the Kensington woman. Sam was a spitfire and Jackson her match. Half the town was impressed and the other half scandalized. Ladies were fanning themselves just thinking about Jackson's kiss, while their menfolk fantasized about having a woman like Sam in their arms. The gossipmongers were making up stories about what went on in their bedroom later.

Price's head did a swivel when he saw Reed Ferguson go into the livery. Now what was he up to? Only one way to find out. He wouldn't stand by and let anyone take a piece out of Mac's girl.

*****

Sheriff Rem Cooley tapped the newly arrived letter from Thomas Miles against his desk and wondered what trouble would transpire from it. He'd heard several renditions of the goings-on in the hotel dining room last night. They included everything from how "decent folk shouldn't have to see depravities between a man and a woman" to amused, knee-slapping accounts of "it wasn't nothin' but Sam and Jackson making a point to the rich, old biddy."

Rem sighed. Ruth Kensington could make trouble for lots of folks. He didn't want anyone hurt, least of all the folks from Gracelyn and Trinity, so he'd been particularly interested when he'd noticed Ruth's driver carry out her trunks and lash them to her conveyance. For such a huge man, he moved gracefully, and it was evident he was as strong as he was tall because he handled the trunks as if they were packed with air.

After the driver assisted Ruth Kensington into the waiting buggy and drove off, Rem had made it his business to visit the hotel to confirm with the day manager, Jeffrey Howell, that the Kensington woman wouldn't be returning. Rem wouldn't be ashamed to admit to anyone who might be curious that he felt a great sense of relief. Good riddance.

Feeling a sense of urgency about passing the letter to Morgan and Jackson, Rem rose from his desk and clapped his hat on his head. When he dispatched the letter, he'd also be sure to mention he'd seen Reed Ferguson ride out after Sam, with Price Hardin hot on his trail. It would also be his pleasure to report Ruth Kensington had left town.

***

Before beginning Alexa's instruction, Mac pulled his Winchester from his scabbard and handed it to Sam. Then he began to set up bottles on one of two benches for Alexa.

Sam studied the two six-foot wooden silhouettes standing a distance from the benches. Each silhouette had a head fashioned out of straw and had a canvas circle tacked on it with the painted features of a man's face. Someone had taken the trouble to shape the stuffing to resemble human features.

Parker went to one of the gallery benches and withdrew a metal box containing painted targets. He tacked one on two of the silhouettes before pointing to red-painted boulders placed at one-hundred-yard intervals. He explained that she'd engineered that part of the range and taught him and Ryder to estimate distance and accuracy based on the form, features, and light visible between the legs of the targets, depending on the distance.

Looking at the rifle resting in her hands, Sam didn't find it difficult to remember the basics of her training. At one hundred yards, most people with no vision impairment could see a face well enough to recognize features. At two hundred yards, features were obscured, but arms, hands, a firearm, and the space between the legs were visible. At three hundred yards, most people could only recognize a human form because the hands and body parts blended. At four hundred yards, a human being didn't resemble a human anymore because even the head blended with the body, so a marksman looked for the light through the legs. At five hundred yards, the light through the legs disappeared and only a form remained. At six hundred yards, with the naked eye, a person looked like a triangle.

Sam heard Mac's voice, "At six hundred yards, sweetheart, with a familiar rifle, a marksman has at best an eighty percent chance of hitting the target. You're better than most. You can hit it at least ninety-five percent of the time—it might not be a kill shot, but a body won't walk away unharmed."

Sam turned, expecting to find Mac standing nearby. Instead, she found Parker's eyes leveled on her. "Is something wrong, Sam?"

Sam grinned sheepishly. "I'm just a little spooked, Parker. I had a sudden recollection of Mac. His voice was so clear I thought he'd come up behind me."

At that moment, Mac stepped back from Alexa and she squeezed off six shots, hitting five of the six targets Mac had lined up for her. Mac nodded approvingly.

Next, Mac pitched a can into the air from behind a boulder, and before it began its descent, Alexa's bullet caught the rim and sent the tin spinning back up into the sky.

Sam turned and drew her revolver; but, before firing, she wobbled and took a half step to the right. Her bullet hit dead center, causing metal to fly in all directions. Sam's eyes anxiously darted to Mac. The disapproval on his face told her he saw the half step and knew she made the shot because of luck rather than skill.

Disappointed in her performance, Sam joined Parker at the four-hundred-yard marker. While pretending to check the wind, Sam said in a low voice, "Parker, someone is watching us from that clump of trees near the bend in the stream. Did you notice?"

Parker raised an eyebrow in surprise before allowing Sam to step to a safe distance behind him. He took his shot, leaned forward to squint at the target, then turned and crossed the distance to where Sam stood. "Someone is there. Take your shot, then we'll warn Mac and Alexa."

Sam accepted the rifle and stepped to the marker. She took her time aiming before squeezing the trigger. The loud report and forceful recoil sent a sharp, piercing pain from the back of her head to the center of her forehead. She was so affected she barely noticed when Parker took the rifle out of her hand and grasped her elbow.

"Are you all right, Sam?"

She managed to nod.

As they approached their targets, they saw Parker's shot was respectable, only an inch high and to the right. Sam's had found dead center. Given her earlier performance, she was pleased.

Mac joined them to examine the targets. "I think we should go on to the ranch. I noticed we got company."

"We noticed, too, and were just coming to tell you," Parker replied. "Besides, I think Sam has had enough for today." Looking past Sam to Mac, he suggested, "Maybe Sam should spend the night at the ranch."

Sam didn't give Mac a chance to voice an opinion. "It's only seven miles back to town. With any luck, whoever is watching us won't start anything. If I take it easy rest of the day, I can ride back later. Jackson will have our heads if I stay at our place alone, even though Ryder and the hands will be close by in the bunkhouse."

Parker wasn't buying it. "You can stay at the main house with me. There's no reason I need to hurry back. Alexa and Mac can stay too."

"Jackson, Morgan, and Grace will worry," Sam protested.

"Not if we send Ryder to town to tell them. He can take care of a few things here at the ranch and get to town about the time the others would expect us. He won't mind because of seeing Miss Jenny."

Mac nodded. He agreed with Parker but wouldn't stand around jawing about it, especially when a rifle might be trained on them. The sooner they got to Trinity the better.

***

Price was puzzled when he saw Reed Ferguson leave right after Sam took her shot. Why would a man spy for a brief time and leave? Price struggled with himself deciding whether to stick with Reed or warn his friends. Chances were good Mac had noticed his shooting party had an audience; however, Mac was pretty taken up with keeping an eye on Sam, and rightly so. His girl was hurting, though she was doing her best to hide it.

Price reluctantly turned his horse toward the main road to catch up with his friends. He was damned curious about where Reed was going and why, but it was more important to warn Sam and Mac.

***

From the thick grove of trees on the hill overlooking Trinity, Reed Ferguson could see everything on the ranch, including anyone coming or going on the main road. At this time of day, only a few hands would be around. Sam and the others wouldn't arrive for at least a quarter-hour.

Leaving his horse tethered in the underbrush, he made his way down the side of the hill to Sam's house. He felt in his pocket for the tool he'd made months ago for flipping the latch when the bedroom window was locked. It wouldn't take him long to drug Sam's brandy and whiskey. The possible benefits made the gamble he was taking worth the risk. If Sam stayed at her house, the drugged liquor could make her abduction easy. If he caught Jackson in the same snare, so much the better. He'd return tonight with Ruth's driver and buggy to check.

If luck favored him, Deke Conover would do more than drive the buggy. He was a hulk of a man with the strength of three men in his six-foot-seven, muscular frame. Though slow-witted, Deke knew how to keep his mouth shut and obey orders, especially Ruth's orders. Besides, a man who handled Ruth's trunks as if they were hatboxes would have no problem lugging Sam or Jackson up the hill.

Reed was getting tired of dealing with Ruth. Her patience was wearing thin, and she was demanding action. Sam and Jackson's performance in the hotel dining room had been almost more than she could endure. When he left Sam's, he'd meet Ruth at Ryder's house. He chuckled at the irony of Sam's friends providing the accommodations for her demise. Ryder and Miss Jenny weren't marrying for another two months, so the partially furnished house stood empty most of the time. Ryder had even built a barn, convenient for hiding Ruth's buggy and the horses. There was nothing like hiding in plain sight.

Chapter 36

"What brought you and Morgan to Trinity, Jackson?" Parker asked, although he was certain he already knew the answer.

"Sheriff Cooley looked us up soon after you and the others rode out this morning to give us another report from Thomas," Jackson replied. "He mentioned he saw Reed Ferguson follow you and that Price trailed him, presumably to see what he was up to."

Morgan added, "Rem also thought we should know Ruth Kensington and her driver checked out of the hotel."

Nodding at Mac, the only other person with Parker in the dining room, Jackson asked, "Where are Sam and Alexa?"

"Alexa is upstairs, and Sam is at your house," Mac replied. "And before you pin us to the wall, Price Hardin is with her. He came to warn us Reed was spying on us shortly after we left the shooting range."

Jackson relaxed; however, worry lines etched his forehead almost immediately. "If Reed returned to town after he left the range, Morgan and I would've seen him unless he deliberately avoided us. I don't like the idea of him being somewhere nearby."

"We don't like it either, Jackson," Mac assured him. "That's why one of us is always with Alexa and Sam."

Turning to Morgan, Parker said, "Alexa yawned through supper, complaining the fresh air and ride made her almost as weary as Sam. She barely ate anything before excusing herself to go upstairs. She said she'd look through one of Becky's pattern books if she could keep her eyes open."

Morgan frowned. "That doesn't sound like Alexa. She's accustomed to being up most of the night. I'll check on her after we eat."

Mac spoke up. "Assuming you both will be staying here tonight, I'm going back to town. I don't like the idea of Grace being there alone." Turning to Parker, he said, "It might be a good idea to let Price sleep in the study. He wakes at the drop of a hat."

All three men nodded, agreeing it was a good suggestion.

"Why didn't Sam come to supper?" Jackson asked Parker.

"She fell asleep while Alexa was sorting through the armoire looking for some things Sam wants to take to town tomorrow. Alexa said Sam didn't move a muscle when she tried to wake her, so she removed her boots and gun belt before covering her with a quilt."

Mac put his hand on Jackson's shoulder. "The ride to the shooting range exhausted her, Son. Although Parker and I kept it slow and easy, she struggled to keep the pace. When we arrived, her dismount consisted of sliding down and clutching the saddle to stay upright. Parker said the recoil from the Winchester rattled her. Her headache was bad. With all those nightmares she's been having, she needs the rest."

Parker chimed in, "I thought the ride back to town today would be too much for her, so I suggested we stay here tonight. Mac and Alexa backed me. Frankly, I'm glad Rem told you about Reed Ferguson and that you and Morgan are here." Motioning to a basket on the dining table, he said, "Eat before you relieve Price and take that basket with you when you go. JB made sandwiches in case Sam wakes later."

***

After Price left for the main house, Jackson looked in on Sam and was grateful to see she was sleeping peacefully. He noticed an empty brandy glass on the bedside table and imagined her dropping off to sleep after drinking it. He was about to back out of the bedroom when he noticed another glass, about two-thirds full, on the small table near the armoire. Alexa must have been sipping it while looking for the things she and Sam wanted, then forgot about it. He decided he'd better retrieve it now. He didn't want to risk knocking it over when he went to bed. In the dark, it would be too easy to bump the table accidentally. The tip of his boot caught on the edge of the braided rug at the foot of the bed, causing his other boot to come down hard on the wood floor. Cringing, he cut his eyes to Sam, concerned the noise would wake her. She didn't stir.

Leaving the bedroom door ajar after retrieving the brandy glass, Jackson went through the house checking windows and doors. All were secure except for a window in the corner bedroom at the back of the house.

Returning to the study, Jackson sat at the desk and took Thomas's letter from his vest pocket. He and Morgan hadn't taken the time to read it because Rem told them he saw Ferguson follow Sam and the others. He started to reach for the whiskey decanter but decided against it. He needed to be alert in case of trouble.

At first, Jackson thought the report contained little new information. Melinda and Ferguson were engaged at the time of Melinda's death, and she'd been with him the night

310

she died. After she'd left him, she'd walked into the river and let herself be swept away. It took two days to find her body.

The report confirmed Ferguson's mother had been a widow when she remarried, but her first husband hadn't died until Reed was ten. She'd been separated from Reed's father for seven years by that time. She'd moved back to her parents' home in Chicago when Reed was three. It appeared she and Reed had no contact with Reed's father until she needed a divorce to remarry, but the divorce was never finalized because Reed's father, Nathaniel McBride, died in an accident. Stunned, Jackson read the final paragraphs.

Reed's parents had christened him Reed Nathaniel McBride, but Reed's surname changed to Ferguson when his mother's new husband adopted him. Reed had been born on the ranch next to Highbreeze.

Jackson pushed his chair back from the desk and began pacing the room, his mind racing. Nathaniel McBride, Reed's father, was the man that raped Sam. Jackson didn't know how it had come about, but Reed must have been the boy Sam said was there in the barn that day.

Jackson was half-tempted to rush to the main house and shake Morgan awake, but he couldn't leave Sam alone. Even if he did talk to Morgan tonight, they wouldn't be able to formulate a plan until they could talk to Mac. Damn, none of them had suspected a connection to Reed other than his engagement to Melinda.

Did Sam subconsciously suspect? Her wariness of Ferguson and the frequency of her nightmares suggested that on some level she did. Distractedly, Jackson reached for the whiskey decanter, poured generously, and knocked it back in three gulps.

Jackson made a face. Whiskey was supposed to get better with age, but this had a bitter aftertaste. Perhaps something else had been stored in the decanter and it hadn't been cleaned properly before it had been filled. Jackson smiled. Sam would be the first to admit housekeeping was a talent she hadn't bothered to acquire. Hell, she didn't even know how to light the stove to make coffee or heat water to make tea. She'd wait for him to do it. If he weren't obliging, she'd go to the bunkhouse or JB's kitchen.

Thinking about Ferguson being the boy Sam remembered in her nightmare, Jackson wondered if she had any idea what the boy looked like or how the fire started. None of them had thought to ask her. Had those details been in her nightmares? If the fire started when Sam pushed McBride from the loft, she wouldn't have been able to escape. Was it possible for a ten-year-old boy to be an arsonist? Jackson suspected it was, and if Sam hadn't escaped when she did, the boy would have been a murderer.

Suddenly weary, Jackson considered putting his head down on the desk and sleeping. Frowning, he struggled to remember when he'd quit pacing and returned to the desk. It couldn't have been long ago. God, but he was tired. That must be why he couldn't remember. He turned to look at the bedroom door. Hell, why was he thinking about sleeping at the desk? He'd much rather be in bed snuggled up with Sam. So, what was keeping him from her?

Damnation, his head felt as if it were stuffed with spent shells and his body weighted with lead. He pushed clumsily to his feet and felt the room tilt. He grabbed for the edge of the desk but couldn't prevent his legs from buckling beneath him. While clutching the edge of the desk to pull himself up, he remembered Sam desperately clinging to things to keep from falling. With sudden clarity, he realized the whiskey had been drugged. Alexa barely made it through supper after drinking a third of a glass of brandy, and Sam had been in a dead sleep since late afternoon. The son of a bitch had drugged them.

***

Jackson heard someone groan but wasn't aware the sound came from him. That was just before he felt his Colt jerked from his holster. Ferguson was in front of him and a behemoth of a man towered over him from behind. Ferguson was explaining something. Jackson knew it was something he needed to understand.

"If my father hadn't threatened my mother with not signing the divorce papers unless I was allowed to visit, I wouldn't have had the opportunity to learn from him. I was young, but even so, I'd begun having stirrings that enabled me to recognize the truth in his teachings."

A knowing look crept across Reed's face. "You see, my father had been adamant I learn how women like Sam incite lust, and how they rarely ask for what they want. Instead, they tease and petulantly pretend to reject the gift a man offers. Sam behaved just as my father said. She pretended innocence and fear, knowing it would stir my father into a frenzy of need. She begged, saying, 'no, please,' when she meant 'yes, please.' I saw how she took my father into her and moved against him. Her frenetic responses urged him to a fevered climax while throughout his ministrations she screamed and fought. She would not be satisfied."

Reed peered questioningly into Jackson's face. "Would you like me to describe all the ways he bedded her?" Without waiting for an answer, he continued, "No, I don't think I'll tell you. I won't teach you the secrets, but perhaps I'll allow you to watch when I pleasure her. After that, I'll kill you."

Jackson struggled to rise and failed. "You perverted bastard."

Reed chuckled. "Don't be angry because you aren't man enough to satisfy her."

Peering down at the desk, Reed noticed the report Jackson had been reading and picked it up. His eyes skimmed over the words before folding and tucking it into his vest pocket. "I see you've learned how she repaid my father," he commented. Then he paused, his breathing accelerated, undoubtedly aroused from recalling erotic memories. "A boy doesn't have the strength to kill with his bare hands, you know, so I threw the lantern. I wanted her to burn in hell's fire for what she'd done. Much later, of course, I came to understand her escape was my salvation because she'll be the means by which I will achieve sexual mastery."

Disgusted, Jackson couldn't look at Reed. He wanted to crush the life out of the pervert with his bare hands but didn't have the strength because he'd allowed himself to fall victim to Ferguson's incapacitating drug. A quick and painless death would be too good for the twisted monster.

Just then, the goliath behind him thrust a knee into Jackson's back and pried his hands from the desk to twist his arms behind his back. Jackson's head came up as he was forced to curve his spine back while his wrists were being tied. He didn't have the strength to resist; his muscles had dissolved to jelly. He knew he still had a heart, though, because seeing Ferguson carry Sam from the bedroom with her feet and hands bound made it feel as if a cold steel spike were being driven through it. His vision blurred and began to fill with swirling black spots. When he toppled sideways, he didn't feel the floor rise to meet him.

***

Price tried to deny the uneasiness inching up his spine, but his instincts were rarely wrong. A man in his profession who ignored his gut frequently found a home on Boot Hill or caused others to move into that neighborhood. Truth was, Reed Ferguson not returning to town was as clear a message to brace for trouble as a wagon master's call to circle the wagons before fighting off an attack of marauding Indians.

From experience, Price could think of two probable reasons Ferguson hadn't returned to Prosperity. The first was because he needed to set a trap of some sort at Trinity before Sam and the others arrived. The second was because he was meeting his accomplice, Ruth Kensington. Price's ears had pricked up when Jackson reported Ruth had moved out of the hotel but hadn't taken the train to Cheyenne. Why did she have her driver and buggy with her? It was a fair bet she and Ferguson were up to no good.

The more Price thought about it, the more it gnawed at him. Morgan and Sam's playful argument in the hotel dining room the night before had informed the whole town she was going to Trinity the next morning. Yup, Price was convinced Ferguson and Ruth had made a plan. He was as certain of it as he was about recognizing the split second an opponent would go for his gun.

Price stepped out to the porch, his eyes immediately turning to survey the terrain around Sam's house. The hill was the only spot from which a person could approach the house without being seen. Whatever Reed's plan was, it would be easier to do it here at the ranch. There were just too many people and too much risk of being discovered in town. Yessiree, Price sure as hell was gonna check the hill, and he wasn't about to wait for daylight to do it.

Quietly entering the house, Price headed to the study to gather his hat, rifle, and saddlebags. He hesitated at the bottom of the stairs, questioning whether he should bring Morgan and Parker into it. Only one of them would be able to go with him because the other needed to stay with Alexa and keep an eye on Sam's place should Jackson need backup. Just then, as if Price had conjured him, Morgan padded down the stairs with hat, boots, and gun belt in hand.

Morgan took Price's elbow and steered him out the door onto the porch. In a low voice, he said, "I woke Parker and told him to stay with Alexa and stand watch while you and I check the hill. That's the only place Ferguson could approach from without being seen. I can't shake the feeling something's going to happen tonight. Ferguson must have had a good reason for leaving the shooting range before we did. And I'm suspicious Alexa's been drugged, which means Sam has too."

Price put up his hand. "You read my mind. I was just coming to tell you the same thing. Put on those boots, son, and let's get a move on."

Glancing up from buckling his gun belt, Morgan said, "Maybe we should tell Jackson and stop in at the bunkhouse to talk to Ryder."

Price shook his head, disagreeing, "We want to make as little disturbance as possible leavin' here. No sense warnin' Ferguson that we're on to him."

***

When the door of Sam and Jackson's Gracelyn Palace suite swung inward, Wade Harper found himself staring into the barrel of a six-gun. The eyes of the man holding the gun narrowed, fixing a hard, unwelcoming stare on Wade's face. Wade took a step back from the door and slowly raised his hands.

Clearing his throat, Wade tried to keep his tone friendly, "Perhaps you remember me from the mercantile? I'm Wade Harper. I was hoping to speak with Jackson." Wade, like most of the folks in Prosperity, knew Mac's reputation and had no illusions about his skill. Sam sure as hell didn't learn to handle guns from an ordinary cowpoke.

Mac said nothing but motioned Wade inside. As the door clicked shut behind him, Wade began to lower his hands. Mac moved the barrel of the gun sharply up, silently commanding Wade to keep them aloft. While obeying the unspoken order, Wade spied Grace standing behind Mac, near the sitting room divan.

Watching for Mac's reaction, Wade dared to inch his right hand to touch the brim of his hat. "Ma'am, my apologies for calling on you unannounced."

Grace nodded but said nothing.

After clearing his throat again, Wade ventured, "It appears Jackson isn't around. Could you get word to him that I saw Ruth Kensington at Ryder's place? I have reason to believe he'd want to know about it."

Grace's eyes widened and darted to Mac, who was leaning toward Wade, listening to every word.

Wade wasn't sure what to do.

"Go on, son," Mac encouraged. "It appears you touched on a topic I find interestin'."

Wade exhaled slowly before speaking. "I was out that way on business late this afternoon and thought my eyes were playing tricks on me. The Kensington woman was standing in front of the house watching Reed Ferguson and her driver guide her buggy out of Ryder's barn. I made sure they didn't see me. My guess is they were headed for Trinity."

Wade paused, expecting Mac to ask questions. When he didn't, Wade plowed on, explaining how Sam had questioned him about Ruth Kensington and appeared afraid of Ferguson. Her behavior was so out of character that Wade had made it a point to tell Jackson. Then he recounted how Jackson said he was suspicious of Ferguson and worried about Sam. Wade ended his explanation with how he'd hate anything to happen to Sam, so he'd rushed back to town to tell Jackson.

Mac motioned Wade to lower his hands and holstered his gun. Pointing to the table, he said, "Have a seat, son. Jackson and Morgan are at Trinity. They know the Kensington woman left town and that Reed Ferguson followed Sam." Pausing to turn toward Grace, he said, "We'll be going to the ranch, Grace. Would you put a few things in a bag while Mr. Harper and I make a plan?"

Mac wouldn't fail his girl a second time.

Chapter 37

Feigning unconsciousness, hands and feet tied, Sam sat on the barn floor, bound to one of the eight-by-eight rectangular support posts set in place to transfer the load from the main roof beams to the foundation. Surveilling her surroundings, she was careful not to move her lids more than needed to get her bearings and ascertain whether she was alone.

She had no idea where the barn was located or how she'd gotten there. A lantern, with its wick turned back to preserve oil, hung from the back of the post above her. Measuring the length and depth of the shadows, it must be dark outside. The sounds around her came from the structure settling and rodents scurrying around. She was alone.

Feeling weak, nauseous, and dizzy, Sam recognized the symptoms were the same as those she'd experienced from the drug in the tainted tea. Someone must have put it in the brandy she drank while she was with Alexa in her bedroom. Reminded of Alexa and Price, she was concerned they may have been harmed, but then reason told her they were probably safe. The fact her kidnapper drugged her was strong evidence he preferred her disappearance be accomplished surreptitiously with little to no resistance so others wouldn't notice or interfere.

Relaxing a little, she comforted herself with the knowledge it wouldn't take long for someone to discover she was gone. When that happened, they'd send word to

Jackson and Morgan and turn over every rock in Wyoming Territory to find her. Meanwhile, she needed to keep calm—and look for an opportunity to help herself. Sweet mother of God! At this moment, she doubted she could spell the word calm.

***

Price and Morgan dismounted and tethered their horses near the road just inside the tree line at the top of the hill.

"Price, I see a path running down the side of the hill. The bushes hide it so you wouldn't notice it from the ranch house."

"I figure that's about the only way to get to Sam's house and not be seen," Price replied. "Ferguson was here earlier today. I can see where he tied up his horse. When I was followin' him, I noticed the shoe on his horse's left foreleg had a wedge missin' from the outer edge."

After examining the bushes at the top of the path, Morgan reported, "Some of these branches are bent and broken. The breaks aren't dried out yet, so they came through here less than an hour ago. Sonofabitch! Come look at these prints, Price. There are two sets, and judging by the size, one of the men must be a giant."

Peering around Morgan's side, Price commented, "Mac taught you to read sign real good, son." Nodding toward a spot near the road, he added, "I see where a buggy was waitin' over there, and it was heavier when it left. Damned if those varmints didn't kidnap Sam and Jackson right out from under our noses." Pushing the brim of his hat back, Price stared in the direction the buggy had taken. "When you ponder it, it's as plain as the nose on your face. There had to be two men, a big one to lug Jackson up that hill and another one to carry Sam."

Morgan's voice was raw with anger and frustration. "The only way they could have done it without making a ruckus was if Sam and Jackson had been drugged. Damn me for being so slow-witted. Which way was the buggy headed when it left here, Price?"

Thumbing the air, Price replied, "See for yourself, son. Do you know what's in that direction?"

Morgan's eyes followed Price's thumb and the corners of his mouth relaxed. "Yeah, I know. Ryder's ranch is in that direction. Ryder built a good-sized barn and a nice house for Miss Jenny. The place is empty most of the time because they aren't hitched yet. Ryder is training his replacement, so he still bunks at Trinity. His livestock and herd are at Trinity, too."

Recognizing the sounds of an approaching buggy and a rider, both men drew their guns and bent at the waist. Price pointed to his left to indicate Morgan should circle in that direction. Then Price faded into the shadows and moved to the right.

Catching a glimpse of his mother's pale hair in the moonlight and Mac's familiar silhouette astride the horse, Morgan relaxed. His attention then focused on the man driving the buggy, looking for any indication he posed a threat. Seeing none, Morgan whistled softly.

"Show yourself, Son," Mac responded. "Is Price with you?"

An amused voice answered from the buggy's far side, near the right, rear wheel. "You must be gettin' old, Mac, or you'd already have your gun trained on me."

Morgan smiled at the gibe because the iridescent pearl stock of Mac's six-gun glowed in the moonlight, and the barrel *was* trained on Price.

Wryly Mac, drawled, "If I'm so old, how is that my pea-shooter has had your forehead in its sights for the last thirty seconds?" Chuckling, Mac quipped, "Hell, I knew you were there before I heard Morgan whistle." After pausing for effect, he added quietly, "I knew because I could hear you winkin'." With a satisfied grunt, Mac returned the six-gun to its holster.

***

Sam heard approaching footsteps just before she caught a faint whiff of cigar smoke. She felt the air stir as a man crouched next to her. He roughly palmed her right breast through her thin blouse—no doubt watching for her reaction.

No reaction would have given her away, so Sam rolled her head from one shoulder to the other, muttered an unintelligible word, then pulled her shoulders back against the post to which she was bound as if trying to evade the man's groping hand. With her head lolling to the side, she gradually allowed her shoulders to relax and droop forward, consciously controlling her breathing to mimic that of a woman pulled back into a restless, drugged sleep.

She'd hoped her performance would fool the man into moving away from her, but it didn't. She could feel his eyes studying her. When she risked a quick peek from beneath her lashes, she saw Reed Ferguson's eyes devouring her with a lust that almost shocked her into giving away her pretense.

Something nagged at the edge of her memory, something about him. Because of the drug, she still felt disoriented and disconnected, making her wonder if she was dreaming. *Dreaming! Was that it?* In her dreams, the man who'd hurt her was sprawled naked on the barn floor, face up, eyes wide open, and neck twisted at an odd angle. His dull, copper-tinged green eyes, though sightless, had appeared to follow her descent on the ladder. His ruddy cheeks stood out against his lifeless gray skin as if they'd been painted a garish color to clash with his rusty-orange hair. Ferguson's eyes and hair were the same as the man who had hurt her.

Reed Ferguson was a younger version of the man she'd pushed from the loft. It didn't take much after that realization to strip away the years and see him as he appeared when he was ten watching her brutal rape. He was the boy who had thrown the lantern starting the fire. Now, a full-grown man, his lips were but a breath from her ear.

***

Raking his eyes over Sam's body, Ferguson felt a surge of lust ignite an ache in his groin. Sam was no longer the pubescent girl that had stirred his father to take her so many years ago. Now, she was a fully ripened, sensual woman with passion and needs so wild and deep, she'd be the death of most men. She was nothing like Melinda Kensington.

Melinda. The silly girl had arrived at his home with a letter saying she didn't want to marry him. She thought he'd gone out for the night and that she could simply leave the letter without having to face him. She'd been surprised when he greeted her at the door. He'd taken one look at her face, seen the letter clutched in her hand, and deduced the purpose of her unexpected visit. He knew all about her infatuation with Jackson Knight.

He'd pretended that he was flattered and pleased by her unexpected visit before dismissing the hired carriage she'd arranged to wait for her. She'd reluctantly followed him to his study. The misguided little whore believed breaking their engagement would leave him broken-hearted.

After Melinda tearfully read her letter explaining she wanted to marry a man she truly loved rather than someone her mother chose for her, she asked him to forgive her. He'd pretended he not only forgave her but loved her so much her happiness was more important to him than his own. He was proud of his performance, especially because he'd wanted to laugh while enacting it.

He hadn't desired the erratic spoiled bitch. He'd lost all interest in her when he'd learned that Sam Hilliard Stone had taken Providence Jackson Knight as her lover. The scene he'd enacted for Melinda was simply an amusement. It made him feel as if he were a panther playing with its prey before the kill.

***

Jackson regained consciousness in stages, aware first he was lying face down on a cold wood floor, then discovering his hands and feet were bound. The walls of the room rippled in waves, giving him reason to fear spilling the contents of his stomach. When his head cleared enough for him to orient himself to his surroundings, the soft rustle of silk drew his attention before the pointed toe of a woman's shoe jabbed him in the ribs.

"Ah, finally, he's awake," the woman commented. Fingers snapped near his ear and the feminine voice issued a command. "Put him in that chair, Deke."

The muscled giant that had taken Jackson's Colt and trussed him up lifted him effortlessly by the back of his leather belt and slung him, ass first, into a winged chair. The rough treatment re-triggered the dizziness and nausea he'd forced back earlier. Now he understood how Sam had suffered.

Lowering his head to quell the dizziness, Jackson squirmed awkwardly to anchor himself in the chair. When he could look up, it was into the cold, green fury of Ruth Kensington's gaze. Now able to see the whole room, his gaze dropped from Ruth's to search for Sam.

"Where are Sam and Reed Ferguson?" he asked. He needed to see Sam, to know she was alive and unharmed.

"Always so worried about Sam, Jackson," Ruth taunted. "If you had shown even a tenth of that concern for my daughter, she'd still be alive."

Jackson bit back an angry growl. *Patience.* He needed to exercise patience. He didn't know where Sam was. One misstep or wrong word could get her killed, but, God, it froze the marrow in his bones to think of her being alone with Ferguson and what he might do to her.

Ruth leaned forward and pointed a long, slim finger at him. "My daughter killed herself because you spurned her love—because you wanted Sam. I hold you responsible for Melinda's death."

Staring into Ruth's eyes, Jackson saw past Ruth's accusation and fury to the raw grief of a mother who had loved her child above all else. He felt a pang of sympathy for her. In other circumstances, he'd have treated her with gentleness and compassion, but her need for revenge wouldn't allow it.

He watched as she put aside her grief and began hissing ugly words at him with a rancor befitting a serpent escaped from hell. "Sam will die, and I intend to make you watch. You'll be responsible for her death." Ruth paused to pull Jackson's gun from her dress pocket and check to make sure it was loaded. "Reed and Deke will drown Sam. Then I'll use your gun to put a bullet through your head. People will think you killed her before killing yourself. It won't bring my daughter back, but exacting vengeance will provide some comfort on sleepless nights."

Jackson turned away as if blocking her vile words. He told himself reasoning with a woman who had lost all ability to reason made him as crazy as she was; nevertheless, he had to try. "Ruth, I never courted Melinda. I never even kissed her. I'm sorry about her death. I truly am, but I'm not responsible." Continuing before she could rebut his words, he asked, "What do you really know about Reed Ferguson? Do you know his birth father was a rapist?"

Ruth's head jerked up.

Now that he'd captured her attention, Jackson revealed the shocking facts. "It's true. Reed's father brutally raped Sam when she was thirteen years' old while Reed watched. Then Reed tried to murder Sam by setting the barn on fire. He admitted it."

"You'll say anything to save her."

"That's true," Jackson admitted. "But I don't need to lie about this. Ask Sam. She'll tell you she has cruel nightmares about it. She shoved Reed's father off her and he fell from the loft to his death. Reed saw everything but wouldn't help her. If you won't believe me or question Sam, ask Reed to give you the Pinkerton report he stole from our house when he kidnapped us. He put it in his vest pocket. Read it for yourself. It confirms Reed was with Melinda the night she drowned. Did you know that? Did you ask him what he said and did to Melinda that night? If a boy of ten is willing to commit murder, why would he be different when fully grown, especially if his father turned him into a sexual deviant?"

When Jackson stopped speaking, there was only silence.

Barely able to tear her gaze from Jackson, Ruth angled her head toward Deke. "Did Reed do as he said?"

Deke nodded like a shaggy dog eager to please its master. "He talked about some of those things and took papers."

"Untie his feet," Ruth commanded. "We're going to the barn."

***

After sending Wade and Grace on to Trinity to inform the others about what was happening, Mac, Morgan, and Price rode the three miles to Ryder's ranch in silence and tethered their horses well out of sight. They approached the ranch buildings cautiously. Nothing moved anywhere in the yard or near the structures. If Ruth had men guarding the house or barn, they saw no evidence of them. The barn and the house were dimly lit. Blankets had been draped over windows to prevent light from spilling into the darkness and attracting attention. They wouldn't be able to find Sam and Jackson by simply peeking through windows.

If Ruth hired no outside talent, they'd face three opponents: Ruth, Reed, and Ruth's driver. Considering the location, Mac, Price, and Morgan reasoned Ruth wouldn't recruit additional manpower because it would increase the chance of her plan being discovered and thwarted before she could execute it. Though probability was on the rescuers' side, they knew it would be foolhardy to disregard the possibility. Since none of them were foolish, they would exercise caution.

After a few whispers and gestures to issue instructions, the trio of rescuers split up, their first goal being to determine where Sam and Jackson were being held captive. Price and Morgan vanished in the deep shadows alongside the barn, while Mac faded into the dark gloom cast by the eaves of the house.

Having rounded the corner of the house, Mac heard the distinct click of a door latch and the sound of wood scraping against wood. The sounds were followed by a wedge of light pouring from the open front door. He hastily changed direction to disappear into the thick blackness edging the side of the house. At the barn, one man on each side of the entrance, Morgan and Price did likewise.

From their hiding places, they watched as Jackson, hands tied behind his back, unsteadily emerged from the house. Ruth's driver forcefully shoved him toward the barn. Ruth walked next to the driver with a six-gun aimed at the center of Jackson's back.

***

Reed Ferguson had removed the rope binding Sam to the post before freeing her ankles. Her hands remained tied in front of her. She averted her head and gazed at the empty stalls, preventing Reed from watching her eyes. His hands wrapped around her calves and traveled beneath the folds of her split riding skirt to circle the back of her knees and caress her outer thighs. Unable to go farther, he followed the inseam of her skirt to stroke the sensitive skin of her inner thigh.

It was becoming increasingly difficult for Sam to ignore the waves of panic washing through her. *He wants me to fight and to beg—I won't give him what he wants.* Shutting her eyes, she concentrated on rallying her internal defenses, telling herself his invasive caresses were simply something to be endured. *She'd survived once. She could do it again.* He couldn't hurt her worse than his father had—but, even as she thought it, she knew it was a lie. He'd set fire to the barn. Not only would Reed be more brutal than his father, when he was finished with her, he'd kill her.

She wouldn't give in. She had power over her mind and could channel her thoughts to block Reed. She'd think of Jackson so Reed couldn't take her sanity.

Willfully, she withdrew to shelter in the sanctuary of her feelings for Jackson. *He is the only man whose touch has meaning—the only man with the ability to awaken every part, portion, and particle of my being to experience passion; the only man whose caresses and tenderness can fill my heart with love and my body with pleasure.*

In her reflections, Sam admired Jackson's handsome face, felt his gentle touch, and heard his loving words. She made him promises about how she'd pretend he was there with her, protecting her until he could come for her. She swore she wouldn't let herself be lost.

Her thoughts shielded her until Reed breached them by sharply nipping her ear lobe, drawing blood. Then, when he captured her lower lip between his teeth, a soft, involuntary gasp of surprise escaped. She clamped her jaw tight to prevent more sounds from following and willed her mind to go back to her thoughts of Jackson, but Reed wouldn't allow it.

He released her lip and scraped his teeth along her jawline. When his breath blew hot on her neck, he shifted his weight against her to wedge one of his knees between her legs. She withheld the gasps and whimpers of pain and fear she knew he wanted to hear. He gathered a fist full of her hair at the back of her head and savagely jerked it. Her eyes watered, but she didn't cry out. *Damn the bastard to a pit of vipers. I swear I'll bite through my jaw before I give him the satisfaction of hearing my torment.*

In a low, intimate voice, Reed taunted her. "Trying to pretend you don't want me, Sam? I know the games you play. I've seen you. I can feel your pulse racing with your desire." Gathering her tied hands in one of his, he forced them to the front of his trousers and moved them over the hard ridge of his arousal. "Feel how you stir me with your teasing? If I were a lesser man, I'd give you what you demand now. You'll find I'm not weak."

The madness in Reed's voice chilled Sam's bones, but she wouldn't allow her body to tremble.

"I know how long you've waited for a man like me. I've seen you there in your house. I know you sensed my presence because you used your tricks to stir me. Each time your tongue touched your lips, one of your arms brushed your breasts, or your hand smoothed the fabric of your skirt over your hips, you heated my blood and hardened my manhood until I was almost mad with need. You teased and tantalized me unmercifully. Then you gave yourself to Jackson."

In her house? Sam was so stunned she could barely make out his words for the buzzing in her head. The calm she'd gained earlier thinking about Jackson deserted her. *Please, God, don't let me give him the satisfaction of hearing me scream. If I start, I won't be able to stop.* She dug her nails into the palms of her hands, but even that distraction couldn't prevent her involuntary recoil when he cupped her chin and tilted her head to force her to look at him.

"Ruth has a different plan from the one I've arranged for you. But don't worry. After I kill her and that dolt, Deke, who serves her, I'll give you everything you crave and more. I'm only giving you a small taste now so when I take you, your blood will already pulsate with your need and you'll be aware of exactly what man you're with and what I'm doing to you. Jackson will watch. You'll like that, won't you, Sam? It will be your revenge for his inability to satisfy you."

Desperate to block out his words and to push down her panic and nausea, Sam jerked her chin out of his grasp. His hand circled her throat. The pressure of his palm and fingers slowly increased, cutting off her air. His other hand cupped her right breast, testing its weight, kneading its softness, seeking its peak.

Sam's heart, slogging painfully against her ribs, slowed as the pressure on her throat increased. Unable to save herself, she struggled weakly. Darkness gathered at the edge of her vision, quickly overwhelming her consciousness.

Unexpectedly, Reed loosened his grip on her throat, and blessed air flooded into her lungs, triggering a fit of convulsive wheezing and coughing. Reed watched her efforts to recover through half-lowered lids, while his index finger erotically circled and stroked the drawn tip of her breast.

Pleased with his efforts, he arrogantly boasted, "I'm getting good at this. When I killed Melinda, I couldn't control the pressure half as well as I can now." He was silent for a moment, remembering how he'd enjoyed Melinda's struggle. Strangulation added a dimension to the pleasure of sex. The power to decide when to take life made him feel as omnipresent and all-prevailing as God.

"Melinda was a spoiled, demanding bitch, undeserving of my prowess. It amused me to spread her legs. I didn't try to please her as I will please you because she couldn't give back as you will. I took her because I could and because I needed some release. Her wild flailing and struggle for air stirred me to experience a deeper level of eroticism. I couldn't resist repeating it. My release was so forceful I failed to notice I was crushing her windpipe. Sadly, a third release wasn't possible—pleasurable experiences rarely last. It won't be that way with you, though, Sam, because now I know the secret of how to ensure you give as much as you take."

Reed's hand, still resting on her throat, gradually began reapplying pressure. His other hand worked to unfasten the row of buttons on her blouse before delving inside to fondle the bare flesh of her breasts. So intent was he in his ministrations, he didn't notice Ruth, Jackson, and Deke had entered the barn and were standing motionless, stunned by what they heard and witnessed.

Chapter 38

Jackson's fear for Sam was already a lump of sickness churning in his stomach, so when his eyes adjusted to the barn's dim lighting and he saw Reed's hand gripping Sam's neck and the other inside her blouse groping her breasts, he was enraged. All thoughts of his precarious situation were wiped from his mind. *Sam*—the deranged bastard was hurting Sam. A harsh, feral sound came from his throat before he lunged, tackling Ferguson, knocking him off and away from Sam.

Ferguson's head collided forcefully with the massive support post from which he'd released Sam earlier. Jackson landed face down several feet away. Desperate to put himself between Sam and Ferguson, but hampered by his tied hands, he struggled to his knees.

"Don't move!" Ruth ordered, her voice strident and cold as the ice in her green eyes.

Jackson froze.

Gesturing with Jackson's Colt, Ruth barked at Ferguson to raise his hands. Warily eyeing his "partner," he touched a hand to the lump on his head before wisely following her order.

Relieved to see Ferguson's hands raise, Jackson's gaze turned to Sam. Her mind didn't appear to be tracking events around her. Her gaze was puzzled when she lifted it to rest briefly on Ruth before moving on to the driver. When she dropped it to him, her forehead wrinkled in confusion. She leaned forward to peer at him more closely, as if unable to comprehend she was really seeing him.

Sam closed her eyes and took a deep, calming breath, willing her breathing to slow and her chest to rise and fall evenly. Slowly, the haze in her brain began to clear. *Did she dare believe Jackson was here?* She opened her eyes. *Jackson was here*—but so was Ruth Kensington, with a gun and a slack-jawed giant by her side.

Jackson watched the muscles in Sam's face relax, then immediately tense as her mind associated his presence with the likelihood he'd be killed. Believing she was responsible for placing him in danger, Jackson knew she'd do whatever it took to hide her emotions from him so nothing she did would propel him to do more than he already had.

Attempting to convey hope to Sam, Jackson forced a reassuring smile. He needed her to work with him. Together, they could buy time for Mac and the others to find and free them. Besides rescue, there was a decent chance Ruth's anger could be redirected to Reed Ferguson. Ruth was beginning to believe Reed had done something to cause Melinda's death. Sam didn't know Reed's actions here in the barn supported what Jackson had told Ruth.

Ruth's voice cut into Jackson's thoughts.

"Deke, check Reed's vest and bring me the Pinkerton report if it's there."

Careful not to come between Ruth and the gun she held on the captives, Deke warily advanced on Reed, stepping around him to approach him from behind. He screwed Reed's right arm behind his back before he fished the papers out of his pocket.

Reed didn't resist. Outwardly, he appeared unconcerned by Ruth's behavior and Deke's harsh treatment. When Deke released his arm, Reed circled his shoulder to work out the stitch in it before raising his arm back in the air.

Deke handed the papers to Ruth like a faithful dog that had retrieved a stick for its master in a game of fetch.

Sam's eyes hadn't left Jackson's. Her head tilted and one of her eyebrows arched in a silent question. Jackson nodded toward Ruth to answer before turning to watch Ruth's reaction to what she'd read.

Ruth's eyes scanned the first page of the report. When she reached the bottom, her eyes flicked up to rest on Reed. She let the page fall to the barn floor. While her eyes moved over the second page, the line of her mouth tightened and the gun in her hand trembled. By the time the second page was resting next to the first, Ruth's gaze was pinned on Reed. "You never mentioned anything about being with Melinda the night she died." Her voice was accusing.

"Of course, I didn't, Ruth," Reed replied, with just the right amount of sincerity and hurt in his tone. "You had grief enough without me adding to it." He'd prepared a plausible lie. It even contained a few elements of the truth.

"Melinda thought I wasn't home and came to leave a letter explaining she was breaking our engagement because she wanted to marry a man she really loved—not a man you chose for her. She asked for my forgiveness, which, of course, I gave her. I only wanted her happiness. You know that. I told her I understood, but I begged her to go home and think about it before she ruined her chance of finding happiness with me. She promised she would. I never dreamed she'd go to the river and do what she did. I swear I loved her. I wouldn't have let her leave if I'd known she was planning to take her life."

"He's lying, Ruth," Sam interjected. Her throat ached, and her voice cracked. "You saw what he was doing when you came into the barn. He's sick. He told me that after he kills you, he'll do to me what he did to Melinda. He strangled her, while—" Her voice caught. She lowered her head and bent forward, feeling she might retch. Swallowing with difficulty, she managed to raise her head. Her eyes were shining with compassionate tears. Her hands, still bound, pressed against her stomach. "He told me—he strangled her—while violating her," Sam stammered. "He said it gave him more—more pleasure—a stronger—release when she—struggled for air." Sam turned her head, no longer able to look at Ruth.

Reed remained calm. "She'll say anything to save herself, Ruth. She doesn't care how her words hurt you. You know she's a whore. Even as a young girl, she was a whore. She teased my father into a crazed lust, and when he gave her what she asked for, it wasn't enough. She rewarded him by shoving him from the loft to his death. She teased and tortured me too. I was only giving her what she asked from me."

"Yes, I know, Reed," Ruth replied soothingly, recognizing his madness. "I understand. Did Melinda do that to you, too, or was she just an inconvenience because you were obsessed with Sam?"

***

Mac, Morgan, and Price had decided to employ a divide and conquer strategy. With all the players already assembled in the barn, they didn't have much choice.

Morgan inched open the horizontal sliding door to the loft just enough to accommodate his shoulders. He reminded himself to remember to thank Ryder for keeping the track clean and the rollers in good repair. The door slid smoothly with no tell-tale grating noises. At the base of the ladder, Price leaned his weight to counterbalance Morgan's, preventing it from scraping against the barn when he pushed off from the rung next to the loft before thrusting his upper body through the door and pulling his legs after him.

At the back of the barn, Mac waited for Price to ram the log pulled from the woodpile against the barn to signal Morgan was in the loft and the coast was clear for Mac to enter through the back door. Once inside, he'd use what little cover the stalls provided to get a drop on the kidnappers while Morgan covered him from the loft. He hoped Price's diversionary signal would lure one of the abductors outside to investigate.

***

All eyes turned to the barn entrance as the unmistakable thump of wood striking wood reverberated through the structure. Unevenly spaced, the sound repeated three times, first provoking curiosity, then arousing fear, and finally inspiring visions of death personified, as if after knocking, death hunkered down, just out of sight, patiently waiting to claim the soul of any person foolish enough to answer the call.

As if drawn by the power of a magnet, Sam's gaze fastened on Jackson's face. When she saw his lips move silently to form Mac's one-syllable name, she nodded imperceptibly to acknowledge she understood.

***

When the pounding began, Morgan shifted from the loft window to a position where he could see over the edge but remain out of sight. Ruth Kensington, with the stalls at her back, was visible. Sam was kneeling six feet in front of Ruth, facing Morgan, but looking at someone or something beneath the loft, out of Morgan's field of vision. He couldn't see anyone else. Ruth's head had turned from the barn entrance back to focus on Sam and whoever else was there—presumably Jackson, Ferguson, and her driver.

Morgan was relieved to see Mac stretched flat on his belly along the bottom rail of the stall at the back of the barn. From Mac's vantage point, he'd be able to see all the players.

Outside, Price waited, hidden behind a nearby woodpile, praying the loud thumps he'd sent echoing through the barn would flush out at least one of the varmints.

***

When the pounding stopped, Ruth ordered Deke outside to investigate.

Sweat filmed Deke's forehead, but he drew his gun. He took several steps toward the front of the barn before Ruth's voice stopped him.

"Use the livestock door. There's more cover that way."

***

Price heard movement near the water trough in the corral. A grim smile settled on his face. It seemed God was in the mood to answer his prayers today. By the lack of stealth, Price guessed the giant had snuck out through the livestock door and was attempting to hide behind the trough, which wasn't near large enough to conceal a man that big. *Big was rarely fast. Wonder what kind of aim he has?* Price knew he needed to eliminate any threat posed by the driver before Mac and Morgan engaged Ruth and Ferguson. The driver returning to the barn unexpectedly could ruin their plan.

***

After Deke left the barn, Ruth turned her attention back to Reed Ferguson. "Did you forge the suicide note? Was it as simple as tracing words from the letter Melinda brought you that night?" Her stiff posture belied the casualness of her tone.

Sam wasn't fooled. She could feel the leashed wrath lying beneath the timbre and modulation of Ruth's questions.

It was clear Reed didn't take Ruth seriously. His tone carried a hint of disdain when he replied. "Yes, I traced her words. It was easy and even easier the next day to plant the note in your house. I was amazed no one questioned why it hadn't been found the night before, but people wanted to believe it was suicide. Even you believed it, Ruth. That's why you kept the note from the newspapers and the authorities."

Cold prickles of warning were raising goosebumps on Sam's skin. She watched Reed speak, gesturing with his arms to punctuate his statements. Ruth didn't seem to notice they were no longer above his head or that Reed was watching Ruth for signs of weakness and inattention.

***

Price hefted a rock, testing its weight. It was about the size of an axe head and covered in white paint, so he reckoned it would be visible even in the dark. He'd snatched it up earlier from a border of stones defining the edges of what would be flowerbeds on either side of the front steps in the spring. Price sent the rock sailing in a high arc through the night sky over the corral fence to land to the left of the trough. A decent marksman, even in the dark, should have been able to spot it, track its path, and plow a bullet into it within a fraction of a second of it hitting the ground. An expert marksman like Sam could hit it as many times as she wished. The driver proved he was neither a good nor an expert marksman when he made no attempt to fire his gun.

Relying on his assessment that Ruth's driver was no gunman, Price stayed low and darted from the woodpile to the well. Under his left arm, he carried a two-foot-long log. He held his Colt in his right hand. The moonlight was dim and the shadows deep. Taking advantage of the inky black cover cast by first a shade tree, then a bush, Price silently worked his way to the corral fence that ran parallel to the barn.

Flat on his belly, facing the fence, Price positioned the log in the space beneath the bottom rail. Price's Colt was cocked and ready to fire. With his left arm, Price shoved the log, forcing it to roll noisily about eight feet into the corral. The driver was paying attention. A gunshot cracked out of the darkness. The bullet fell short of the log.

Price fired directly into the muzzle flame from the driver's gun, then immediately to the right of the flame, and a third time to the left. He heard a grunt, followed by a thud. Price had no trouble believing the giant had collapsed face first into the hard-packed dirt.

When no movement or sounds followed, Price cautiously approached and kicked the man's gun out of reach before applying the toe of his boot to the man's hip. Nothing. Then, putting considerable strain on his muscles, he flipped the giant onto his back. There were three holes, one for each bullet Price had fired—and two of the three were kill shots.

***

Inside the barn, as one shot, followed in quick succession by three others, rang out from the corral, Reed Ferguson swept his hand across the front of his chest. It disappeared inside his jacket and came out holding a Marston three-shot derringer.

With the gun leveled at Ruth, Reed Ferguson edged behind Sam and stooped to imprison her neck and pull her to her feet. Her throat already tender and bruised from his earlier assault, Sam gasped for air. In her peripheral vision, she saw Jackson struggling to his feet, intending to sacrifice himself by tackling Ferguson again. But with his attention on Ruth, Reed didn't notice Jackson.

Reed fired the derringer at Ruth. Her body jerked from the impact of the bullet, but she didn't fall or drop her gun. Reed advanced a step, keeping his gun steady, intending to fire again.

Ruth fired before he did, though, and caught Reed in the shoulder, sending his arm up. His finger jerked the trigger so his second shot went wild up into the loft.

No longer able to stand, Ruth crumpled to the floor. Her eyes connected with Sam's. Though blood trickled from the corner of her mouth, her voice still sounded forceful as she issued her final command. "Finish it—for Melinda." She sent Jackson's Colt skidding across the floor to Sam. The light in Ruth's eyes died about the same time her head came to rest on the floor.

Though Reed still had one bullet left, Sam tore herself from his grasp and dove for the Colt. She came up on her knees with the gun firmly grasped in her hands. Despite her tied wrists, the revolver was already cocked and pointed at Reed's head, except he'd turned to face an opponent who stood, feet spread, gun drawn, in the gray shadow next to the stalls. Sam reflexively adjusted her aim to target Reed's temple, deciding he posed a greater threat than the unknown opponent did. She pulled the trigger. The shooter by the stalls fired a fraction of a second before she did.

Sam spun after firing at Reed to face the other shooter, so she didn't see her bullet harmlessly pass by Reed's face because his head jerked back, then forward from the other shooter's bullet entering and exiting his head.

Sam heard Reed's body crash to the floor, but she didn't let it distract her from the gunman she now faced. *The gunman was Mac.* Sam was barely able to relax her finger on the trigger in time. Smoke curled from the barrel of

Mac's revolver. He holstered his gun and covered the distance to her before Sam could finish lowering her gun.

"Mac." She wasn't sure she said his name aloud.

Dropping to one knee, Mac wrapped a protective arm around Sam, cupping her chin, turning her head from side to side, looking for signs of injury before hugging her to his chest. Then he sliced through the rope binding her hands.

In a low gravelly voice, Sam tried to reassure him. "I'm not hurt, Mac." Her eyes were filled with gratitude and love. Seeing the bruises on her throat, Mac wanted to prop the bastard up and unload his gun into him.

Controlling his anger, Mac shouted up to the loft, "Morgan, are you all right?"

Morgan's head popped over the edge. "The bastard grazed the top of my shoulder with that wild shot, but it barely broke the skin. It spoiled my aim, though. It's a good thing you got him, Mac. I wouldn't have been able to shoot him before he got Sam."

"Sam," Jackson called, anguish in his voice. "For God's sake, will someone untie me?"

Morgan scrambled down the loft ladder in a matter of seconds. He hauled Jackson to his feet and sliced through the ropes binding his hands. Then he rubbed Jackson's wrists and arms to restore circulation.

After Mac's strong arms helped Sam to her feet, he supported her while guiding her to Jackson.

Looking into Sam's upturned face, Jackson murmured, "My heart about stopped when you dove for Ruth's gun. What the hell did you think you were doing?"

A sob caught in Sam's throat. With the swelling in her throat, it was difficult to talk. "Ruth gave us a chance, and I took it." She lifted her chin and explained, "I'm an expert marksman. Reed wasn't. Even if he hit me, odds were it wouldn't kill me. But if he did, I would have been able to take him with me." Sam's voice trailed off, her throat too raw to continue.

All three men drew in a sharp breath. Hearing it from her lips was like living it again.

Jackson stopped rubbing his arms. Damn it, they worked well enough by now. He managed to wrap them around Sam, and she clung to him, her cheek against his shoulder. "Finish what you didn't say, Sam." Jackson's voice was gentle now that she was safe in his arms.

She couldn't say it.

Jackson spoke the words for her. "Taking him with you would have saved me, right, darlin'?"

Sam spoke her answer against his shoulder. "Keeping you in my mind kept me sane when he—I mean, he couldn't hurt me because I would only let myself think about you." When she finally did look up, she completely disarmed him by adding, "I'm done with that nightmare. I love you, you know."

Jackson's mouth came down over hers, gently at first, then with longing. When he pulled back, he teased, "That's good because when I have nightmares about the crazy stunts you pull, you'll have to chase them away."

She threw her arms around his neck and raised her mouth for another kiss.

***

Looking away from Sam and Jackson, Morgan and Mac let their eyes wander around the barn. Practically in unison, they said, "Where's Price?"

"Here," Price answered. He was leaning nonchalantly against the livestock doorjamb with his arms crossed and the toe end of one boot hooked over the back heel of his other boot.

"Ruth's driver?" Morgan questioned.

Price glanced over his shoulder to the corral. "I showed him a shortcut to hell. Reckon he was on hand to introduce that crazy sonofabitch Ferguson to the devil."

Mac lowered the brim of his hat to hide the amusement in his eyes while he helped Morgan steer his girl and Jackson out of the barn. Both were weaving, and Sam was clutching Jackson's arm as if she believed he'd disappear if she let go.

Mac called to Price, "Reckon you could hitch up Ruth's buggy? Sam and Jackson aren't in any shape to sit a horse, even if we had extra. When we get back to Trinity, we'll send Wilson or one of the other hands into town to get the sheriff so we can clean up this mess later."

"I reckon I can do that, Mac," Price drawled, "if you and Morgan are willing to stand with me when Rem sees this. He won't be tryin' to take Sam with us this time, so I ain't too certain what our chances would be gettin' sprung if he decides to throw us in jail."

Pausing, he rubbed his jaw while studying Morgan. "Though, I ain't discountin' Morgan's Alexa, now that I think on it. I bet she could step in and handle Rem just fine. I saw how well Sam schooled her on shootin' and watched her handle a few ornery varmints in Gracelyn. That's a good thing for you, Morgan, or your chances of her sayin' yes when you propose with the ring your daddy gave Grace would be pretty slim."

Morgan's jaw dropped open in surprise. Jackson and Mac's eyes met over the top of Sam's head. Mac clapped a hand down on Morgan's shoulder. "If you don't close your mouth, you're bound to catch a fly or two instead of that pretty woman waitin' for you back at the ranch."

Chapter 39

Price Hardin stood in front of Gracelyn Palace holding the reins of his horse. He was returning to Laramie with Holt Webster and the other Bar W ranch hand. As he, Mac, and Sam companionably watched the street, young Holt Webster stepped up to them, removed his hat, and apologized for all the trouble. He added he hoped Sam would recover her memory. After saying his piece, he kicked at the dirt in embarrassment before heading for his horse, hat still in hand. Price figured he meant what he said because no one had urged him to do it.

When Price shook hands with Mac and Sam, he told them to send a wire anytime they needed him. Then he pushed his hat further back on his head and readjusted his gun in his holster. Price always parted with a joke and a wink. This time was no different. He dove into his vest pocket and pulled out a thick square of folded papers, which he handed to Sam. "When you get a chance, go through these, Sam. I know you're a rich woman and don't need the reward money. But if you were lookin' for some excitement sometime when Jackson is out of town, you might consider fixatin' on one or two *hombres* so, just for fun you understand, we could team up and do this here Territory a favor cleanin' out the riffraff. We'd ask Mac along, of course."

From the visible printing, Sam saw they were wanted posters—old ones judging by the yellowing color. He'd undoubtedly "borrowed" them from Sheriff Cooley's office. Sam blinked before stepping close to hug him and plant a kiss on the side of his turned-up mouth. "Sure thing, Price—you're my suitor."

Price looked as pleased as a satisfied customer leaving a brothel. After adjusting his gun again, he mounted his horse. Then he winked and doffed his hat before turning toward Laramie.

Mac stood in the street with his arm around his girl's shoulders and watched his old friend, a former gunman, now the Sheriff of Laramie, ride out of town with his "parolees." He and Price had been through some tough times together. A man couldn't have a better friend.

***

The guests were enjoying themselves, partaking of the lavish buffet and dancing to the music of the orchestra Miss Jenny had hired from Cheyenne for Alexa's birthday celebration. While enjoying various libations, friends chatted enthusiastically with friends. All were dazzled by Alexa's beauty and poise. Her hair was arranged in loose ringlets cascading past her shoulders. In a dusty pink, voile gown, which bared her white shoulders and clung to her curves, she looked as beautiful as a French courtier attending a ball held by royalty. Her radiant smile reflected her happiness. When she and Morgan danced, a heart-shaped red ruby ring encircled with diamonds sparkled in the lamplight. Morgan had given her the ring his father, Drake, had given his mother.

Though it was Alexa and Morgan's night, Sam found herself the center of far too much attention. A stream of well-meaning guests made it a point to introduce themselves. Many approached her expectantly, as if they believed their face or words would be the key to unlocking her memory. She knew she disappointed them all. With each failure, her anxiety mounted. It was easier to bear when Jackson or one of the others offered small tidbits of information and facts to smooth over the awkwardness, but, too often, she was alone.

As the evening wore on, Jackson observed the polite smile on Sam's lips become stiff and the friendly warmth in her eyes dim. From time to time, she touched her temple and let her eyes move longingly to the entrance of the ballroom.

Jackson edged closer to her side, placed his hand on the small of her back, and wrapped his other hand around one of hers. "I know it's difficult, Sam. Most of them mean well. They aren't judging you, although it must feel that way to you. Think about how happy Alexa and Morgan are and how nice the party is. It will soon be over."

He knew her so well. Sam squeezed Jackson's hand and relaxed the tightness of her mouth. "I feel like the main attraction in a traveling medicine show. Perhaps my choosing to flout convention makes people more curious about me than they normally would be." She sighed. "I expect I'll live through it. It *is* a very nice party, and I'm happy for Alexa and Morgan." She brushed her lips against his cheek and murmured, "And I'm the luckiest woman in the room because I have you."

Feeling the soft brush of Sam's lips and hearing the emotion in her words, Jackson returned her gaze, the green flecks in his brown eyes warming with his love. For her and that tender caress in her voice that righted every wrong that had ever touched his life, he'd do almost anything. He wondered for the thousandth time how it was she could be so perfectly made for him.

***

When Thornton McKinley, founder and President of McKinley Trust and Savings Bank, invited Jackson to join him, the Prosperity Mayor, and a group of prominent businessmen for a drink, Sam murmured that she needed to attend to some arrangements for Miss Jenny. Then smiling to herself for having adroitly avoided more awkward introductions, she sought out Becky, who was standing near a group of her friends, surreptitiously watching her father talking with a young man.

Sam leaned close to Becky's ear, aware the question she wanted to ask would embarrass her if overheard. "Becky, are you going to introduce me to John Monroe? Didn't you tell me you danced with him and Morgan at the last social?"

Becky's eyes darted from Sam to the corner of the room. "I want to, but Daddy is talking to him. I'm not sure Daddy likes John dancing with me."

Sam waved her hand dismissively. "I fear fathers are like that. But he can't keep all the boys occupied. Since I see at least three other young men trying to get your attention, I can understand why your father might be a little anxious. By the way, who's that tall, handsome cowboy leaning against the wall near the front entrance? He reminds me of Jackson."

"That's Cal Ennis. He's good-looking, but he's almost six years older than I am. All the girls swoon over him. He thinks he's quite the catch."

"Hmm. If he liked older women, I might be tempted myself."

"Sam, you don't mean that. You know you only have eyes for Jackson."

"True. I'm a fortunate woman, and I know it."

"You have a dreamy look on your face, Sam."

"Do I, Becky?"

Becky laughed. "Where's Jackson? I'm surprised he left your side. I bet if Cal danced with you, Jackson would show up in two seconds flat."

Sam only wanted to dance with Jackson. "I think Cal wants to ask you to dance, Becky. He hasn't looked at another girl since he got here. Since Morgan's spoken for, you'll need to cast your lasso wider," she teased.

"Oh, Sam," Becky mumbled, before blushing and turning to watch Morgan and Alexa dance. "When I was younger, I did think Morgan was the most attractive, fascinating man I ever met. Now, of course, I realize he's much too old for me. Alexa's very lucky to have won him."

Sam hugged Becky. "Cal's coming this way. I'll go and talk to your father while you dance."

***

Sam threaded her way through the guests to reach Parker's side just as Becky accepted Cal Ennis's invitation to dance. Evidently, John Monroe had made his escape, because Parker was alone, watching his daughter and Cal join the other dancers. The expression on his face was not approving.

Sam caught Parker's eye and nodded toward Becky and Cal before commenting, "She's a beautiful girl—in every way." Then she laid her hand on Parker's arm and placed a kiss on his cheek. "Thank you for sharing her with us and for sending her to your sister to keep her safe. I know it was difficult for you."

Parker squeezed Sam's hand. "I wanted to send *you* away with her, Sam. I was concerned about you."

"After the crash," Sam replied, "when I was so anxious and afraid because I couldn't remember, you explained how I was part of your family and that you and Becky were grateful. It meant so much to me, Parker. I doubt I can ever repay you."

"Becky and I came to Trinity because we needed a new start, Sam. I wasn't sure how to go on after I lost my wife.

It's still hard, but Becky is my center. She and Trinity breathed life into me—then drew the rest of you to us. We're rich with love and caring."

"You're our anchor, Parker. I hope we're not too much for you."

Parker's eyes left Sam's to watch his daughter whirl by with Cal. "I'll tell you what's too much for me. All those young bucks who are interested in my little girl. And Cal Ennis worries me the most. Whenever she's not looking, he stares at her as if he's worshiping at the door to heaven. He's too old for her."

"Becky knows that, Parker. She told me earlier. Would you like me to dance with him and find out his intentions?"

"Hell, yes, but no—Becky would guess what you were doing. I rather expect she'll come to you if he gives her trouble or she begins to have feelings for him. Will you watch over her and let me know if I need to worry?"

"You can count on me, Parker. She has a good head on her shoulders, though. She'll be all right."

"You and Jackson will be all right too, won't you, Sam?" Parker asked.

"I plan to get that settled a little later tonight."

***

From the opposite side of the room, Sam watched Jackson purposely stride toward Morgan.

Doc glanced over his shoulder to see what had captured Sam's attention. "I told you the day the pig died that you have a way of turning his heart near inside-out. Are you finally going to marry him?"

"Maybe I should give you an evasive answer, Doc."

"Go ahead, but it won't do any good. I can see the truth."

Sam pretended annoyance. "You old curmudgeon, I'll repeat what I told you before. I don't *know* anything." She crossed her arms in a defiant gesture, but the expression on her face was soft and filled with tender affection.

Doc Baxter simply waited.

"I may never remember the past, Doc, but remembering isn't what matters. I love him. I love you, too. How would I have found my way without you? We need and depend on one another, and each of us has a special gift to offer. We're very lucky. It would be nice to remember, but the more important thing is to feel the rightness of things and embrace the future. Hell, maybe it's the most important thing of all."

Approving, Doc patted Sam's arm. "If I'd had a daughter, she'd be just like you."

Sam kissed his cheek. "That thing you say about my having a way of turning Jackson's heart inside out. I think you have it turned around. *You* have a way of turning *my* heart near inside-out."

***

Having separated Morgan from Alexa for a private moment, Jackson asked, "I'm curious. How did you and Alexa get together?"

"Sam told Alexa to confront me about how I felt about her."

"I see. So, Sam meddled in your business?"

"Yes. I guess you could put it that way," Morgan admitted. "Sam advised Alexa to force the issue with me." Then he casually volunteered, "Sam told me not to tell you unless you asked."

Jackson's eyes searched Morgan's. *What was Morgan implying?* "Do you know why Sam asked you not to tell me?"

Morgan shrugged. "She said she wanted time to think about it." Jackson didn't react, so Morgan prodded. "You look disappointed, Jackson."

Distracted, Jackson mumbled, "I thought she was past that point."

Morgan suppressed a smile and almost told Jackson that Sam *was* past thinking and *had* decided. Instead, he asked, "Are you going to tell me the reason you're asking about this?"

Jackson hesitated, confident it was one of those things brothers and mothers shouldn't be told. *What would Morgan think about Sam marrying him because she lost a bet?*

Quietly, Morgan said, "I know about the bet, Jackson. In fact, I asked Sam if she was trying to figure a way to back out of it."

"What did she say?"

"She said she intended to honor the bet but couldn't settle it yet."

Morgan studied Jackson's reaction. He saw relief, but it was mixed with something else. *Disappointment?* "Are you happy she's not backing out?"

"I want Sam to marry me because she loves me, not because we made a bet."

"Maybe you should tell her. Sam has a few thoughts of her own about that."

***

Jackson was across the room, near the doors leading to the balcony, talking with Morgan. It seemed as if the party would go on forever, and Sam felt she'd been separated from him for far too long.

As if sensing her gaze, Jackson looked up and gave Sam a slow, sinfully roguish smile that made her pulse quicken. Her eyes locked with his, beckoning him to come to her.

***

Jackson crossed the room as if spellbound. Sam's sapphire blue taffeta dress was overlaid with jet beading that augmented the fullness of her breasts, smallness of her waist, and curve of her thighs. How was it she could appear to be an innocent, temptress, and witch all at the same time? Her honey-gold hair flowed over her shoulders and down her back in loose curls. Light reflected off the sapphire-encrusted combs holding the soft waves framing her face. The color deepened the irises of her slate blue eyes. A wide, black velvet ribbon adorned with sapphire ovals hid the bruises on her neck.

Jackson was caught up in her magic and the smoldering intimacy he saw deep in her eyes. "Dance with me, Sam."

"All right, but please don't spin me. I'll lose my balance and make a spectacle falling."

"If you get dizzy, I'll catch you."

She knew he would.

Grasping her hand while placing his other hand on the curve of her waist, he swept her onto the dance floor. Catching a wisp of her fragrance, he buried his face in her hair, inhaling deeply, her scent filling him with emotion. Lifting his head, he looked into her eyes again and felt as if he were a drowning man. "Have you any idea how much I love you?" he murmured.

"Darling, there are times I doubt I even knew how to breathe before you loved me."

His hand tightened on her waist and drew her closer. "No woman can bewitch a man as you can, darlin'. When you look at me like that, I go mad with the need to touch you."

"That's part of my spell, darling. You can touch me all you want."

"Are you offering me your body but not your heart?"

"You have my heart, Jackson, and my body—there just isn't a ring on my finger."

"I intend to change that, you know."

Sam smiled. *And I intend to let you.*

***

Watching Jackson and Sam dance, Grace took Mac's hand and leaned near. "Our girl is going to marry Jackson, Mac."

"It's more than time she did." After a few seconds passed, he leaned close to Grace's ear and murmured, "Do you think you might make an honest man out of me, too, Grace? Chase would understand, you know."

"I know. He'd be happy for us, Mac. Sometimes I wonder if he knew he wouldn't be with me long. I know he knew you were exactly what Sam, Morgan, and I needed if he couldn't be with us. I love him for that, just as I know you do."

"So, is that your way of saying you'll marry me after all these years?"

"In my heart, I've been married to you all this time, but yes, like Sam and Jackson and Morgan and Alexa, it's time we all made it legal and proper. It won't make me love you more, Mac. It will only mean no one can say different about us. I'm your girl just as much as Sam is."

Turning her to face him so he could look into her serene eyes, Mac said, "You're my life, Grace. We've grown together, you and me, had our heartaches and raised those children. I love you."

"I know, Mac," Grace whispered. "I love you, too."

***

Moving off the dance floor and steering Sam out into the night air, Jackson said, "Let's talk about settling our bet."

"What bet are you talking about, Jackson?" she asked, crinkling her forehead and tilting her head as if she forgot.

Jackson called her bluff. "Darlin', that's not funny. I know you remember the bet you made with me in Chicago about meddling in Alexa and Morgan's business. Morgan told me you meddled, so I know I won."

"Oh, *that* bet—"

"Sam, are you trying to back out?"

"No, not exactly. It's just that—"

Jackson cut her off, muttering, "Like hell!" Holding up his hand, he said, "Never mind, Sam. We shouldn't have made the bet. Forget the whole thing."

"Jackson, why are you angry?"

His gaze held steady on her. "I can't believe you're asking me that. I'm not going to beg you, or trick you, or force you into marriage, Sam. Like I said, forget it."

"Jackson, I wish we never made that bet. I wish—"

Jackson interrupted. "I don't want to talk about it anymore, Sam. As a matter of fact, I don't want to talk about it ever again."

"But, Jackson, I was sure I'd lose the bet when I made it."

Jackson was flabbergasted. "Is that the truth?"

Disappointed that he doubted her, Sam had no one to blame but herself. She sighed. "It's true, Jackson. When we were in Chicago, you told me when my memory returns, I'd know neither of us can exist without the other. Well, I'm telling you, I can't wait for my memory to come back.

Everything I've remembered and experienced since the crash is all I need to know."

He gave her a half-perplexed look. "What does that mean, Sam?"

"It means I don't want to settle the bet, Jackson. It means I want you to ask me to marry you because you love me, not because we made a bet."

"Sam—" Jackson's voice caught.

She reached out and caught his sleeve.

"Let me finish, Jackson—I know you asked me to marry you before because you told me you did, but I don't remember—and I don't remember what I answered." Her voice broke. "I only know what you told me I said." She slid her hand from his sleeve up to his cheek. "Could you pretend you didn't ask, and I didn't answer? If you could, then, in a way, it would be the first time for both of us. The other memories may never come back, you know."

Sam's slate blue eyes shone between tear-spiked lashes as she stared up at him. Jackson closed his eyes and pressed his lips to her temple. "You could conjure the moon from the sky, Sam."

Sam sighed. Though spoken with tenderness, those words weren't the ones she longed to hear. "But I don't want the moon, Jackson. I want you. If it's in your heart to ask, I'll give you the answer I denied you in the past."

His arms pulled her hard against him, but he still didn't say the words. If he didn't say something soon, she'd have to leave.

Jackson ignored how his heart skipped a beat. He'd always been under her spell. "*Sam Hilliard Stone*, will you marry me?"

"Yes, *Providence Jackson Knight*, I will marry you." Then the devil leaped in Sam's eyes and she said, "I'll give you my body *with a ring on my finger*." As she melted against him and raised her lips to his, she added, "I gave you my heart that day at the waterfall and you've had it ever since."

"You really are a witch, Sam."

"Of course, I am. But my spells only work with you."

Epilogue

Jackson was dreaming, but it wasn't a nightmare. Sam's lips ignited a trail of fire as they traveled past his waist and inched down over his flat belly. Her silken curls shrouded his arousal.

"Jackson?"

"Hmm."

"Are you going to wake up and love me?"

"I'm awake—and up—but it appears you're the one doing the loving, darlin'." He took pleasure from feeling the gold band on her ring finger gently abrade his skin as she caressed the fine hairs on his chest. When she reversed the direction of her lips to find and circle each of his nipples with her tongue, the heat of her breasts scorched his skin everywhere they pressed against his body.

Before replying, Sam lifted her head and lazily stretched against him to reach his lips. "I am, but it'd be more satisfying if you did some of the same to me." Then she covered his mouth in a lingering kiss as she tunneled her arms under him and rolled to her side, urging him to follow and take control.

Lord, help him, this woman could turn an angel into a sinner. Jackson's lips moved to Sam's neck, sipping her skin, knowing it would leave a faint mark but send a flame of desire straight to her core. She arched against him, sucked in a breath, and made room for him against the juncture where she needed him most. She drew up her knees while her hands on his buttocks pressed him forward. He glided into her warmth.

With a soft gasp of pleasure, she teased him. "I told you it would be more fun if you reciprocated."

"Those weren't your exact words, *Sam Hilliard Knight*." He flexed his hips, sinking deeper until he'd buried himself completely. "Is this what you meant?" The huskiness of his voice intensified her desire.

In answer, she rocked her hips, beginning the rhythm of their climb to the pinnacle of carnal gratification until there was only unrestrained passion and the need to satiate craving.

They were made for each other. It was just the way it was.

Memory be damned.

Excerpt From

BOOK 2—PROSPERITY SERIES

EVERYTHING IN PROSPERITY

Prologue

Occasionally, after accepting Sam Hilliard Stone Knight had been christened with a man's name, a new acquaintance would ask how it felt not having memories. Sam didn't mind the question as much as she minded not knowing the complete answer.

Ordinarily, she offered the same short response, comparing it to being born fully grown, already immersed in a life in which she was cognizant of only the present. She didn't bother explaining the doubts and uncertainty of wondering what her place in life was—or the anxiety she suffered from worrying about past events influencing the future.

In the first weeks after the stage wreck that caused her amnesia, the question had concerned her more than it did now. But as she adjusted to her condition, she came to understand not remembering wasn't such a bad thing— especially when she acknowledged the future was all any person could count on—for however long a person's future might last. When she thought of memory in that context, its importance diminished—its significance reduced to the simple ability to trace the path a person traveled to get to the next moment in life. She found a modicum of solace in that concept.

She also garnered comfort from people in the present sharing their memories with her. And, when God allowed her a glimpse of her past—the bad and the good—the people who loved her helped her bear the pain or celebrate the joy.

But during the times when the confusion and isolation of having no memory threatened to overwhelm her, she forced herself to think of the twenty-six years of her life in terms of before and after. Before was the life she couldn't remember because of being catapulted from a sabotaged stagecoach and hitting her head on a granite ledge suspended over a fifty-foot drop to a boulder-strewn ravine. After were the seven months since the crash in which she'd learned to live without the memories from the before.

And Jackson Knight, the man she'd loved before she forgot how she came to be the woman she was, was the man who still loved her after she lost that awareness. In the before, hampered by her past, she'd held a piece of herself from him, believing she was unworthy to be his wife because her body was unable to carry a child.

But in the after, she'd discovered a different truth. She saw it in Jackson's eyes when he looked at her—felt it in his lips when he kissed her—sensed it in his touch when he loved her. His body made promises each time they joined; and in return, she gave him everything she had to give.

Together, they had everything that mattered.

And when they'd married, she'd vowed they would find their way forward—because he was everything—the present and the future.

Not once did she consider the possibility everything could disappear.

Chapter 1

March 1876, Wyoming Territory

Struck by a sudden longing to remain home—near his wife—Jackson Knight paused on his front porch while pressing the flat of his hand against his belly as if it could calm the unease pooling there since rising at dawn.

Until the discomfort began plaguing him, he'd been looking forward to accompanying some of the ranch's cowhands and his foreman, Davis Wilson, to Trinity's south range to check on how the cattle were wintering. Though only early March, a stretch of mild weather, unusual for a Wyoming winter, was providing a welcome opportunity to see the chore done ahead of schedule.

Behind him, clad in a thin wrapper, her feet bare, his wife launched herself out the door he'd purposely left open and stepped into him, raising her arms to twine them behind his neck. Bending to cover her lips with his, he savored her kisses while wrapping his arms around her and pulling her closer to feel her breasts against his chest.

"Hmm, but you're tempting," she purred, parting her lips, inviting his tongue to sweep past her teeth in a tantalizing glide to tangle with hers. A growl, low in her husband's throat, sparked a flame of sexual heat in her core. He tightened the embrace and lifted her against him so her toes barely touched the boards beneath her feet. She was tall, but he was more than half a head taller than she. He slanted his mouth over hers to take the kiss deeper. Their lips clung, and their tongues swirled and enticed.

Hot, supple skin burned Jackson through the silk of Sam's wrapper. She tasted of sweet tea and sultry seduction. They both were breathing fast. He wanted to carry her into the house, part the sides of her wrapper, run his hands over her bare skin, keep her safe… Wait. Keep her safe? The unexpectedness of the thought had him wrenching his mouth from Sam's to search her eyes. But nothing in her return gaze explained his sudden need to protect her.

"Jackson?" Sam questioned, tilting her head, and raising delicate eyebrows. With her swollen breasts and tight nipples pressed against his hard-packed chest, the man had her body craving his. Why had he withdrawn from her so unexpectedly?

Realizing he'd been staring; Jackson brushed a honey-gold curl from Sam's cheek. But the warmth of her skin beneath his fingertips supplanted his protective concern—persuading him to focus on his senses—to taste the rich nectar of her soft lips, rub his chest against her pebbled peaks, press his arousal into the cradle of her thighs. His eyes moved back to her lips, where a corner of her mouth lifted.

"Are you thinking of telling Wilson something has come up that needs your attention?" she asked, laughter in her voice, and beneath that—seduction.

The muscles of his abdomen clenched, stirring his already hard cock. "Something has come up, darlin'. Should I tell him to go without me?"

Yes. "No," Sam murmured, resisting the sexual need tempting her to say otherwise. "But you can expect I'll do whatever it takes to make sure it comes up again when you return."

"I like when you plan my work for me, darlin'."

"And I like it better when you do the work. However, I warn you, I may not be satisfied with it coming up only once."

"Jesus, Sam. Are you trying to kill me?"

"Think of it as an incentive to hurry home." Wilson and the other cowpokes were mounted and waiting. One of the men's horses stamped impatiently. She had to let him go.

When Sam stepped back, Jackson didn't turn away. The desire flaring between them had him hard and aching, not a condition compatible with beginning a two-hour ride—in a saddle, that is. Wilson could wait a little longer.

"Christ, I need a minute, Sam," he murmured, huskiness raw in his voice. He shifted his gaze to the door standing open behind her. "I should have kissed you while we were on the other side of the door where it wouldn't have mattered if things got out of hand."

She was smiling when his eyes came back to her. "We've provided enough entertainment for the morning. Tonight's performance will be private. You'd better go."

But he still hesitated. The unease in his gut hadn't lessened. "Sam, is everything all right? I have this feeling—" Her fingers came up to rest lightly on his lips, stopping his words.

"I'll miss you. That's all," she admitted, wishing he wasn't looking at her as if trying to see into her soul. "Truly," she added in a soft murmur, lowering her hand.

Holding her gaze, he pushed down his doubt and reluctantly turned to descend the porch steps. Striding to his mount, he concentrated on regaining control over his body and his apprehension. After swinging up onto his saddle, he picked up the reins and nudged the sides of his horse. The sooner he left, the sooner he'd return.

When he reined in next to his foreman, Davis Wilson shot him a knowing look before abruptly turning to follow the other riders who'd begun climbing the hill overlooking the ranch. The trail to the south range began at its base on the other side.

Halfway up the hill, Jackson looked back. Sam hadn't moved from the porch. He suppressed a wild urge to race back and haul her up onto the saddle with him.

At the top of the hill, he twisted in his saddle again, his gaze tunneling past the main house, where his partner, Parker Evans, lived with his daughter, Becky. Sam's white wrapper was visible in the heavy shadow cast by the porch roof. Why didn't she go inside? She must be freezing. Hell, she hadn't bothered with shoes or a shawl when she'd followed him for that goodbye kiss.

Sonofabitch.

Something didn't feel right, and he couldn't help but worry.

"What's the matter, Jackson?" Wilson teased after noticing his boss had turned for a second time to peer behind him. "Afraid Sam will get into trouble while you're gone?"

Damn, if that wasn't exactly what he was thinking. Jackson pinned Wilson with a scowl that would make most men leap from their saddle and run for cover. Unfortunately, it was wasted on the cowman. Wilson knew him too well to be intimidated.

Chuckling softly, pleased his guess had been spot on, Wilson raised a leather-gloved hand to the crown of his hat to shove it forward, effectively concealing the amusement twinkling in his eyes. Knowing from experience it wouldn't be wise to take another poke at the man when he was worried about his wife, he made a clucking noise to urge his mount to pick up its pace. "If you're not going to be any friendlier than the look you singed me with, Jackson, I'll leave you in the company of your horse. Maybe he won't mind you acting like a riled polecat."

While riding to catch up with the other cowpokes, Wilson's thoughts stayed with his boss. Though few knew it, Jackson's first name was Providence. But any man bold enough to have used it to his face was living the remainder of his life wishing he'd been born mute. Personally, Wilson thought the exalted moniker fit. After all, Divine Providence hadn't only blessed Jackson with good looks, intelligence, confidence, and a cool head, but also with opportunities to use those gifts to amass a fortune and win the heart of a remarkable woman.

While Jackson's wife might be considered unconventional, willful, and impulsive by a few no-account, pious hypocrites, her goodness and fair nature won over most folks. It was true she had a temper, but she usually had a good reason for displaying it. It was also true she wasn't good at doing traditional wifely things, like cleaning house, mending, or cooking an edible meal. But to make up for those deficits, she could ride like the wind, shoot faster and truer than a body could believe, deal cards like a dream, and nearly blind a man if he forgot himself and stared at her for more than ten seconds at a time. Yessiree, Sam Hilliard Stone Knight was an extraordinary woman. And Jackson lived and breathed for her.

Having crested the hill, the ranch no longer visible, Jackson kept his eyes glued to Wilson's back while struggling to review the day's chores instead of wallowing in the dread gnawing his insides. Two hours later, his mount again alongside Wilson's, it was all he could do to pay attention to his foreman giving out assignments to the men. Then it was his turn to point out the hills and gullies in which the beeves were most likely sheltering. After that, each man turned his mount and headed to his designated area.

While canvassing a grove of cottonwoods and losing count for the second time, Jackson gave a frustrated growl, admitting defeat. He could no longer ignore his gut. His intuition was rarely wrong, and it was telling him Sam needed him. His men could do this job without him.

When Wilson noticed Jackson signaling from the edge of the cottonwood grove that he was returning to Trinity, he wasn't surprised. Raising an arm in acknowledgment, he muttered a prayer under his breath asking Divine Providence to continue to ride at his boss's side. With Sam's gift for trouble, Providence Jackson Knight would need all the help he could get.

*****

With the warmth of Jackson's goodbye kiss fading from her lips, the fear Sam had been repressing since she'd first awakened began testing her strength, a little push here and a little prod there, so by the time Jackson mounted his horse, she could think of little else. Arms wrapped across her chest for warmth, she stood as if frozen, watching the distance grow between them. When he disappeared, her fear doubled in strength.

To keep emotion from overwhelming her, Sam reminded herself Jackson would return by sunset. And though his presence wouldn't force the fear into hiding, it would lessen its power. But suddenly, the fear took on an unexpected sharpness—an edge she hadn't experienced before. Was it getting stronger or was she sensing some other danger?

Having tiptoed across the cold floorboards of the porch to the door, Sam stepped over the threshold and eased the door shut. Resting her back and shoulders against its heavy planks, she considered barring it. A tremor moved through her, not a chill from the outside air, but rather an inner one, whispering the depraved sexual taunts of the stalker who'd once hidden within the house watching her and imagining a dark and erotic purpose for her every gesture. His twisted mind had likened her movements to a siren's call performed to arouse his lust. He'd interpreted even so innocent a thing as smoothing a wrinkle in her skirt as a silent invitation— no, that wasn't right—as a silent command—demanding he come to her to satisfy unnatural, wanton needs. Though her stalker was dead, whenever she was alone in the house, she felt his presence. Remnants of his depraved lust reverberated from wall to wall, filling each room, seeking to capture and violate.

With Jackson away, Sam invented a plausible reason to flee the house. No one would suspect she fabricated the excuse to conceal her cowardice. Only she knew the truth.

***

Dressed for riding and headed to the barn, Sam wasn't especially surprised when Cal Ennis, the young owner of the Double Bar ranch, arrived with a telegram he'd picked up while doing errands in Prosperity. Though she greeted him warmly, she suspected whatever the missive contained wouldn't be welcome.

Because Sam Knight was uncommonly tall for a woman, Cal barely needed to lean from his saddle to press the telegram into the open palm of her outstretched hand. After straightening, he sat quietly, reins held loosely in one gloved hand, studying her face as she scanned the paper. When she looked up, her gaze shot to the top of the hill as if expecting to see someone approaching. When she brought it back to him, it was to ask a favor.

"Jackson is on the south range with Wilson. It's a two-hour ride, but I'd be beholden to you if you took him this telegram and a note from me."

Though Sam hadn't said it, the worry in her slate blue eyes communicated her concern well enough to convince

Cal to nod his willingness to do the favor without asking questions. He had his own ranch to run but deemed Sam's errand more important.

Grateful not to be asked for an explanation, Sam disappeared inside to pen a quick note. Back outside, Cal reached from his saddle to take the envelope she offered. "I'll ride as fast as I can, Sam," he promised. But his words didn't lift the tiny furrow he'd noticed between her perfectly arched brows.

"I know you will, Cal. Thank you—and please tell Jackson I said not to worry."

Cal flashed a grin. "I'll tell him, but you know I might as well tell a coyote to stop howling at the moon. Jackson will worry."

Sam's answering smile was so slight it made Cal wonder how sadness could be more powerful than mirth. Pulling the reins to turn his horse south, he touched the edge of his hat in farewell, determined to reach Jackson as quickly as possible.

Rather than watch Cal, Sam strode purposefully toward her house and, once inside, paused to rub the annoying ache pulsing in her temple. The telegram that summoned her and Jackson to an unexpected meeting had been delayed because a storm northwest of Prosperity had taken down wires. The meeting place was to be the Webster ranch, now owned by Holt Webster.

Martin Webster, Holt's father, became their enemy after Sam rejected his sexual advances. In retaliation, Webster sabotaged their stage, sure they'd die in the crash. When that failed, he'd hired assassins in Chicago to murder them in what was to resemble an attempted robbery. Webster's bid for revenge ended when he snatched up the gun Sam had shot from his son's hand in a gunfight and turned it on Sam. Her bullet killed Webster before he could pull the trigger.

Because Webster's son, Holt, had been a victim of his father's bullying and abuse, he was sentenced to serve one year probation under Sheriff Price Hardin's supervision for his participation in his father's crimes. Remorseful and grateful, Holt pledged his friendship and buckled down to the business of running the prosperous ranch he'd inherited.

The meeting Price communicated in the telegram was tonight, and Sam knew no matter how fast Cal rode, it would take two hours to reach Jackson, then another two for Jackson to return home, assuming Cal had no difficulty finding him. She couldn't wait for Jackson's return if she were to arrive anywhere near the meeting time specified.

After changing her clothes and gathering her bedroll and other supplies, Sam searched for Old Charlie, the hand who'd know about the bull, Hercules, that she and Jackson delivered to Martin Webster's ranch last fall. Under the pretense Jackson had a potential buyer for another of Trinity's bulls, Sam questioned Charlie about the arrangements for transporting Hercules. From Charlie's rambling answers, Sam managed to extract sketchy directions to the Webster ranch. Lord knew, because of her amnesia, she didn't *remember* how to get there.

Having mounted her black stallion, Hooker, Sam huffed a frustrated oath while skillfully controlling Hooker's playful prancing. Jackson would soon follow—but he'd be angry—because of his worry. And Sam couldn't help feeling sorry about that.

With miles to Laramie stretching ahead of her, Sam's thoughts returned to the message. When she'd first examined the telegram's remittance and saw it was from the Chairman of the HQ Lee Stock Corporation, she'd expected it to be from her stepfather, Mac. But seeing "bylaws" precede the word "meeting" had shifted her thinking, leaving no doubt in her mind Price Hardin, the sheriff of

Laramie, was the sender. Price wasn't a man who casually called in favors.

***

Three quarters of an hour from home, Jackson was surprised to see Cal Ennis making a beeline for him. Cal was a frequent visitor at Trinity because he was courting Becky Evans, his partner's daughter. Well, maybe courting was too strong a word since Becky wasn't yet sixteen. Though only twenty-one, Cal was mature beyond his years and patient enough to wait for Becky to finish growing up. He was also confident about his feelings and what he wanted. When he declared his intentions to Becky's father, he'd told Parker Evans he'd delay making a formal proposal for the year or two he needed to ensure the financial success of his ranch.

Certain only a matter of urgency would send Cal racing in his direction, the dread burgeoning in Jackson suddenly felt as if it were a shovel full of cow dung hitting him dead center in the chest. Reining in and snatching the envelope Cal held out to him, Jackson barely heard Cal tell him Sam said not to worry. He read the telegram first.

IMPORTANT SAM AND JACKSON ATTEND BYLAWS MEETING FOR HQ LEE STOCK AT HOME OFFICE 7 PM MARCH 13 STOP

It was obvious something delayed the wire. No amount of hard riding would enable him or Sam to arrive on time for the meeting. But Jackson would've bet the percentage of profit he earned from the mining of his South Pass gold claims that Sam would disregard the dangers of traveling alone and leave without him.

Skimming Sam's note, he saw it offered her interpretation of the telegram and confirmed she'd leave for the rendezvous before he returned. She also wrote their friend, Price Hardin, had sent the wire, but Jackson had already figured that out. The "Home Office" was Holt Webster's ranch, near Laramie, easily recognizable because "HQ Lee" was the code name they'd used in the past for Hercules, the prize bull they'd sold to Martin Webster. The fact Price used code warned of danger and the need for secrecy.

Without a word of explanation to Cal, Jackson shoved the papers in his shirt pocket and spurred his horse to race the remaining distance to the ranch. He couldn't waste a second if he were to have a prayer in hell of catching Sam.

Sonofabitch.

***

Having visited JB, Trinity's cook at the main house, to pick up grub, Jackson strode to his and Sam's partner's office. Parker Evans was a man he and Sam respected and trusted.

Years ago, after Jackson's mother died from pneumonia in South Pass a few short weeks after his father was murdered, Jackson began a relentless hunt for the two brothers who'd left his father's broken body wedged between two rocks in the stream running through his family's claims. After three months of following leads and sightings, bribing disloyal outlaws, and scouring hideouts and gold fields through the Colorado and Wyoming territories, Jackson traveled full circle back to South Pass, where his quarry, Jeremy and Colter Brogan, ambushed him from the protection of a played-out mining tunnel.

Fortunately, the brothers didn't check to make sure Jackson was dead from the bullet they drilled into his back because he'd had enough life in him to crawl to the mine entrance, jam a fuse into a dynamite keg, light it, and use his legs to roll it into the tunnel. He didn't stay conscious long enough after that to hear the explosion.

When he woke the next day, he was surprised to learn his nurse was the wife of one of the men who shot him. Jessa Nolan Brogan, also a victim of the brothers, grateful to Jackson for making her a widow, had done everything in her power to keep him alive.

After Jackson recovered, he drifted here and there, even traveling to New York and Chicago to experience the sights and investigate investment opportunities. He was rich, but money couldn't make him forget—couldn't provide a true purpose. Restless and missing the openness of the land and country he loved, he returned to Wyoming Territory and began taking temporary jobs as a cowhand, not for the money but because he enjoyed the work, and it kept him from thinking about what he'd lost.

Like other ranches he'd worked, Jackson hadn't planned to stay at Trinity more than a few months, but Parker and his young daughter, restarting their lives after Parker's wife died, needed him as much as he needed them. So, when Parker offered him a partnership in the ranch, he couldn't turn it down, believing it was a chance to start over. Until Trinity, none of Jackson's business concerns had appealed to him enough to entice him to put down roots—or let people he could care for into his life. Later, when Sam came to Prosperity, Parker and Becky warmly absorbed her into their family, just as they had Jackson.

Before his father had uprooted him and his mother to search for gold in South Pass, Jackson had dreamed of owning a spread of his own. His experience with ranching and horse breeding exceeded Parker's, so Jackson becoming a partner was a natural fit. At Parker's side, Jackson could fulfill his dream of ranching, yet have the freedom to pursue other enterprises, such as the hotel he'd built in Prosperity next to Sam's gambling parlor.

Shrewdly recognizing surface gold would run out long before a big investment, equipment, and mining experience would be needed to extract it, Jackson had had the foresight to sell his two claims to a large mining corporation. Rather than sell outright, he'd opted to accept a modest share of the profits, which he wisely poured into other investments.

Worried about Sam and anxious to be on his way, Jackson handed Parker a sealed envelope containing the wire and Sam's note. "Sam and I are running an errand. If anyone asks, say we're in Eden Ridge with Mac and Grace." Jackson knew their visiting Sam's stepparents wouldn't seem out-of-the-ordinary to anyone curious enough to inquire.

"If you don't hear from one of us in the next forty-eight hours, read this, then wire Mac where to start looking for us." Should they need help, Jackson had confidence Sam's stepfather would be able to find them. Mac and Price Hardin had been partners in their younger days.

"You'll know what to tell Mac after you read the contents. Then find Morgan and come after us." Sam's stepbrother was six years older than Sam. Guided by his mother, Grace, proprietress of the Golden Crown gambling salon, and Sam's stepfather, Morgan had grown into an intelligent, level-headed man, as capable of chairing a big city boardroom as he was of trail bossing beeves to railheads. He could track, rope, and shoot as proficiently as he negotiated contracts. And he'd do anything for Sam.

"Give Sheriff Cooley a heads up about what's transpired if you need to come after us, but don't tell anyone else, at least not until you've investigated enough to know how deep in trouble Price Hardin has sunk us."

The faint creases in Parker's forehead deepened as he listened to Jackson's instructions. "But, Jackson, I saw Sam ride out two hours ago."

"I know, Parker," Jackson replied. "I can't explain more right now. I've got to catch up with her."

"Well, get going then. You can trust me to follow your instructions. Sam's amnesia makes it too dangerous for her to be out there alone. Too many people from her past, not to mention yours and Mac's, could catch her unaware."

Jackson agreed. "If this is one of Price Hardin's jokes and one hair on Sam's head is harmed because of it, friend, or no friend, I swear it'll be the last prank he plays."

Sonofabitch.

About the Author

Even before reading Owen Wister's, *The Virginian: A Horseman of the Plains*, in tenth grade, Judy Hannigan loved historical westerns.

In the Old West, where a good man and a good woman can prevail—together—the heroes and heroines in Judy's romance adventure novels persevere to find enduring love. They do what's right, instead of what they're told—and justice triumphs. And her supporting characters demonstrate blood isn't the primary factor that binds people to one another.

Raised in Southwest Michigan's "fruit belt" country near the shores of Lake Michigan, she earned a BA in Secondary Education (English and American History) and an MA in Reading at the Secondary Level from Western Michigan University.

She taught high school for more than six years before deciding technical editing was a better fit. Presently, she writes full-time and resides in Southern Maryland with her husband and the best neighbors in the world.

Judy loves to hear from her readers. Visit her website and sign up for her newsletter:

www.Judyhannigan.com

Write to her at:

judy@judyhannigan.com